A three-time Golden Heart® finalist, **Tina Beckett** is the product of a Navy upbringing. Fortunately, she found someone who enjoys travelling just as much as she does and married him! Having lived in Brazil for many years, Tina is fluent in Portuguese and loves to use that beautiful country as a backdrop for many of her stories. When not writing, or visiting far-flung places, Tina enjoys riding horses, hiking with her family and hanging out on Facebook and Twitter.

There's never been a day when there haven't been stories in **Amalie Berlin**'s head. When she was a child they were called daydreams. Now when someone interrupts her daydreams she delights in saying, 'I'm working!'

Amalie lives in Southern Ohio with her family and a passel of critters. When *not* working, she reads, watches movies, geeks out over documentar~~ies~~ decides to learn antiquate~~d~~ apocalypse, she'll still ha~~ve~~ granulated sugar, and alwa~~ys something~~ new to read.

After trying out everything from acting in musicals, singing opera, travelling and writing for a business newspaper, **Lucy Ryder** finally settled down to have a family and teach at a local community college, where she currently teaches English and Communication. However, she insists that writing is her first love. She currently lives in South Africa, with her crazy dogs and two beautiful teenage daughters. When she's not driving her daughters around to their afternoon activities, cooking those endless meals or officiating at swim mee~~ts~~ ~~d~~, wea~~~~ ~~~~s.

The Hot Docs on Call

COLLECTION

July 2019

August 2019

September 2019

October 2019

November 2019

December 2019

Hot Docs on Call: New York City Nights

TINA BECKETT

AMALIE BERLIN

LUCY RYDER

MILLS & BOON

First Published in Great Britain 2019
By Mills & Boon, an imprint of HarperCollins *Publishers*
1 London Bridge Street, London, SE1 9GF

HOT DOCS ON CALL: NEW YORK CITY NIGHTS
© 2019 Harlequin Books S.A.

Hot Doc from Her Past © Tina Beckett 2015
Surgeons, Rivals...Lovers © Amalie Berlin 2015
Falling at the Surgeon's Feet © Bev Riley 2015

ISBN: 978-0-263-27662-6

0719

MIX
Paper from
responsible sources
FSC™ C007454
www.fsc.org

Printed and bound in Spain
by CPI, Barcelona

HOT DOC FROM HER PAST

TINA BECKETT

To those who hold two countries in their hearts.

CHAPTER ONE

Twelve years earlier

THERÉSIA CAMARA SAT cross-legged on her bedroom floor surrounded by clothes. Someone else's clothes. Two huge garbage bags full, to be exact. She glanced down at the brand-new sundress she'd worked ten hours to buy and felt sick. What had seemed like an extravagant purchase two days ago—one that had made her feel grown-up and independent—looked cheap when compared with the designer labels on what she'd just been given.

And how could she not wear them? Worse, how could she not be utterly grateful that her best friend had thought of her when sorting through her closet? There were more clothes in those two sacks than she'd ever owned.

What it made her feel, though, was poor.

She swallowed. It was okay. She'd make good use of them, including the plum-colored prom dress tucked inside a boutique garment bag that now hung on the back of her closet door. No one would remember that Abby had worn it last year, right?

Tessa's parents—who'd worked hard ever since moving from Brazil to the United States—were just getting their painting and remodeling business off the ground.

In fact, they'd recently secured a huge contract with a Manhattan firm, redoing a group of office buildings, a project that would keep them busy for the next few years, if the owner was happy with the first batch. But there were materials and supplies to buy in preparation for the work. They certainly didn't have the money to buy her a fancy party dress she would wear only once. Or clothes in preparation for her senior year in high school, which started in two short weeks.

She straightened her back and picked up a pair of dark-wash skinny jeans that were almost new. Luckily she and her friend were the same size. This was a godsend really, and she would see it for what it was. It would take a load off her parents—which was also the reason she'd sought a job stocking the shelves at a local supermarket to help ease their burden. There would be enough expenses as it was, with graduation and applying for scholarships for college. And then medical school. She crossed her fingers and kissed them in the hope that this particular dream came true.

And someday… She brought the jeans to her chest and squeezed them tight, her heart filling with hope. Someday *she* would be the one helping others. She was going to work harder than she ever thought possible to make sure her grades stayed as high as they were now. Then she would see that her parents were taken care of—even if their new contract went bust. It was what they'd done for her by moving to a new country. And she did have everything she needed, even if those things didn't come from exclusive stores.

Tessa didn't need labels. Or a ton of money. She just needed to succeed, no matter what sacrifices she had to make. As of now, she was making a pact with herself. She was going to get through school on her own. Without any help.

From anyone.

CHAPTER TWO

"*Domingo, Segunda-feira, Terça-feira, Quarta-feira...*"
Reciting the days of the week in Portuguese had always helped center her before. But as Tessa continued to enunciate each syllable of each word, the bubble of horror that was trapped in her throat refused to burst. Instead, it grew larger with every breath.

She stared at the huge cardboard placard propped on an easel in the lobby of West Manhattan Saints, the one welcoming the hospital's newest orthopedic surgeon.

People swerved to avoid her as they made their way into the medical facility, and one man bumped her shoulder with a muttered apology about being late as he passed her. Tessa was running late, too, but at the moment she was powerless to do anything except stand there.

Clayton Matthews, a blast from the past—*her* past—sported the same lazy half smile she knew so well. The one that tipped up one corner of his mouth and made everything inside her liquefy. And he seemed to be aiming that smile squarely at her, and in turn at everyone who might stop to gaze upon him.

Ha! *Gaze upon him.* That made him sound like a god or something.

He had been godlike to her at one time. Before she'd realized exactly who had provided her "scholarship" to medical school. The one that had paid for almost her entire education.

Not him. But his parents. She had no idea why they had, other than the fact that her parents and Clay's had become fast friends as her mom and dad worked on a huge block of Clay's dad's buildings. Her dad was still in partnership with them, as a matter of fact.

That partnership was how she'd met Clay in the first place. And the placard brought that last terrible scene on graduation night rushing back.

She swallowed. *God.* She did not want to face him. Especially now. Not with the second anniversary of her mother's death weighing on her mind.

So she wouldn't. This final part of her residency was in cutaneous oncology—another reminder of her mom's courageous battle—while Clay was an orthopedic surgeon. They would be on different floors, even. How likely was it that they would really run into each other in the huge hospital?

Taking a deep breath, she let herself relax slightly.

"Wow, Tessa, you look like you've just seen a ghost." Holly Buchanan, one of the housemates at the Brooklyn brownstone where she lived, stopped beside her. Long brown locks shifted to the left as the other woman tilted her head and looked at the poster. "Ooh, although he's not a bad-looking ghost. Is that the newest member of our happy family?"

Tessa's mouth twisted in a wry grimace. Happy? With the grueling hours they were putting in on the final year of their residency, no one had much time to notice the general atmosphere around the teaching hospital. Harried and exhausted described most of the people Tessa knew. That included her female housemates, Holly and Caren, and her one male housemate, Sam, who lived in the other three units at the brownstone. The friends saw each other more at the hospital than they did at the house.

"I guess he is." She did her best to stifle the bitter edge to her voice, but something must have come across.

"Do you know him?" Holly's shoulder nudged hers.

"No." Because it was true. The man she had thought she'd known had been nothing like the man he'd turned out to be. "No, I don't know him. At all."

It had been how long? A little over four years. Besides, he was married now, at least that's what she'd heard.

A warm scent tickled her nose, just as a warning tingle lifted the fine hairs on her neck.

"I think 'at all' might be stretching the truth, don't you think, Tess?" That voice. Mellow. Matching the half smile on the poster to a T. "Because I *definitely* know you."

She wrenched her body around to face the newest threat, just as he held out his hand to Holly. "Clayton Matthews, Orthopedics, nice to meet you."

Holly's eyes widened as they flicked to meet hers, and then she accepted Clay's proffered hand and murmured her own name and specialty. Tessa sent out a desperate plea to her housemate that was summarily ignored.

"Well, I need to get back to work," her friend said, "before Langley takes me down. Again."

The head of surgical residents, Gareth Langley didn't suffer fools lightly, and somehow he and Holly had gotten off to a rocky start. Tessa steered clear of the man whenever possible.

Her housemate then slipped from between them and hurried down the hallway, blinking out of sight as she rounded the corner to the elevators. That left her alone with Clay. And his poster.

"Tessa, good to see you again. How are you?"

Really? That was the best he could do, after everything that had gone on between them? "Fine. You?"

"Surprised." A flash of teeth accompanied that word. "I had no idea you were doing your residency at West Manhattan Saints."

Didn't he? Since West Manhattan was one of the biggest teaching hospitals in the city, how could he not realize this was where she'd wind up?

Unless he really had known and had come here to torment her.

Delusional, Tess. That's what you are. He did not follow you to this hospital.

She decided to ignore his comment, nodding at the placard instead. "Nice likeness."

The impulse to start counting days again winked through her head...this time in English. She fought the urge. And the picture *was* nice. It showed off his thick black hair, strong chin, those deep blue eyes that could slide over you and make you think you were the only person in the world.

Even when you weren't.

At least it was only a head shot, because from the chest down he was no less mouthwatering than he'd been four years ago—something she was doing her damnedest not to dwell on.

He glanced at the picture. "You do what you have to. You should know that better than anyone."

Yes, she did. Like continue working your heart out when you discovered your so-called free ride hadn't actually been free at all. And that the man standing in front of her had known where things stood the whole time they'd shared classes...when they'd become an item. When he'd laid her down on the bed in his dorm room and become her very first lover.

Then had come the gifts. Small at first. Then more expensive, despite her protests.

It had all blown apart at her graduation ceremony when he'd handed her a flat jeweler's box with a kiss and murmured congratulations. A half hour later she'd learned over a loudspeaker that the Wilma Grandon Memorial Scholarship had actually been named after Clay's maternal grandmother and that Tessa had been its one and only recipient.

A thousand eyes had swiveled in her direction.

At that moment, she'd been transported back to her childhood bedroom and those sacks of used clothes. Only this was much, much worse. Once again, she was the poor immigrant girl from Brazil who had nothing. Waves of humiliation washed up her face and flooded her body. How could he do that to her?

The embarrassment ignited, turning into something else that scorched across her soul. Only this time the passion she'd inherited from her homeland turned everything inside her to a barren wasteland.

Tessa sent his parents a warm thank-you letter, expressing her gratitude. She sent Clay a completely different kind of letter—returning his graduation present and telling him it was over. That she needed to concentrate on her residency. She repeated that refrain when he showed up at her dorm room—not letting him see how gutted she was that he'd kept such a huge piece of information from her. He evidently bought the excuse, because it was the last time she'd seen him.

Until now. But at least she could be cordial to him. Maybe he would take the hint, and they would settle on polite indifference in any future encounters.

She held out her hand, as he'd done to Holly moments

earlier. "Well, it's good to see you again, Clay. I hope you like it here."

There was a moment's hesitation, and then he took her hand, his palm skimming across hers in a heart-stopping combination of warmth and friction as his fingers closed around hers.

Heat poured into her belly and rushed up her face.

Too late she realized her mistake. Because this was no squeeze-and-release grip. This was intimate—a connection that went far beyond the physical realm—and her body reacted to the promise it brought along with it.

A shiver ran over her as he drew her a step closer. "I think I already do."

She blinked for a second before realizing his words were in response to hers…that she hoped he'd like it here.

How bad would it be if she turned tail and ran right back out of the hospital, abandoning everything she'd worked so hard for?

Very bad. She was here for a specific reason. To treat those with skin diseases that were sometimes benign—and sometimes deadly.

She wasn't going to run. Not from anyone. Time to nip whatever this was in the bud. She tossed her head as the perfect solution came to mind.

"I heard you got married. How's your wife?" She allowed a little acid to color her voice as she gave her hand a slight tug, hoping he'd take the hint.

He did. But not before his thumb skimmed over the back of her wrist in a way she recognized. Her temper died as her heart cracked in two. How could he do this?

"She's not my wife anymore." His throat moved as if he suddenly needed to swallow. When he spoke again, there was a rough edge to his voice. "We're divorced."

Divorced. Oh, God. How was she going to survive if she ran into him every day?

"I'm sorry to hear that. But I'm running late…"

Maybe he heard the frantic words that were echoing in her brain, because he took a step back, his expression cooling. "I'll let you go, then. I'm sure we'll see each other around the hospital."

Whether it was a threat or a promise, she had no idea, but she saw her opportunity and grasped it with both hands, throwing him a quick, empty smile and walking away from him as fast as her legs could carry her.

And yet he watched her go. She could feel his gaze on her back, and from the heating of her hindquarters she wondered if those blue eyes had skimmed over that part of her, as well.

Divorced. Oh, how much easier it would have been if he was happily married with a van full of squawking progeny.

What had happened between him and his wife? He hadn't sounded all that happy that his marriage was over.

It's none of your business, Tessa. She quickened her steps, switching into what she called waddle mode— when her pace became too fast for her legs to handle and the wiggle of her hips shifted into overdrive.

But, waddle or not, she had to get away from him. And stay away. At least until the end of her current residency cycle. Maybe she should rethink her plans of applying for that Mohs micrographic surgery fellowship here at West Manhattan. She could always move to another teaching facility.

But she loved it here. Loved the hospital. Loved living in the brownstone with Sam, Caren and Holly. Was she really going to let Clay drive her out?

She turned the corner, but she didn't slow down until

she was on the elevator and heading toward the third floor. Then she sagged against the wall.

Clayton Matthews. Here in her hospital.

Her lips tightened. No. She was here to stay. She'd been toying with getting her own place and possibly even starting a family once her residency was done—a huge decision, but one she'd been thinking about for a while. She wasn't going to drastically alter her course, no matter how much he made her insides melt. He'd lost none of his sizzle factor, she'd give him that.

So she was going to continue doing the things she loved as if she'd never seen him—although she had no idea how that was possible. She'd just have to come up with some kind of strategy for future sightings.

The doors to the elevator swished back open, and she stepped out onto the busy floor of the world she knew and loved.

Strategy.

She mulled that word over for a second or two before discarding it. Right now, she would practice *preventative* medicine. If it worked in health care, it could surely work in her love life—not that she had one. Since Clay, she'd dated two men. Neither had lasted more than a couple of months. She could never seem to relinquish enough control to make a steady relationship work.

Okay. So *prevention* was the word of the day—the word for avoiding negative consequences. Starting now, Tessa would practice prevention when it came to Clay.

Which meant avoiding him. At all costs.

"Traditional Capoeira of Brazil."

The familiar name on the list of businesses supporting the hospital's annual summer Health Can Be Fun festival caught Clay's eye. At the bottom of the page were hundreds of lines—many already filled in with the names of volunteers. Hospital staff had been encouraged to find a place to serve ahead of the July 19 event. Most of the easier tasks—like raffle drawings, the ticket booth and kiddie face painting—were taken. He shook his head. He'd have to look at it again when he was a little calmer.

Seeing Tessa this morning had thrown him for a loop. Maybe he would have handled it better had she not been standing in front of that ridiculous poster the hospital had insisted on putting up. But there she'd been, talking with one of her friends. His gut had tightened when he heard the other woman laugh at something Tessa said. Because there'd been nothing funny about what had happened between the two of them.

And when Tessa denied knowing him…

Well, that had been the last straw. Any thought of sliding by the pair unnoticed had fled in a rush of anger.

Except he'd seen something flit through Tessa's eyes when she turned and saw him standing there. Dismay? Horror? Guilt? He couldn't place what it had been exactly, but he refused to believe what had come to mind when he'd first seen that look: pain.

There'd been no pain in the tight lips and steady gaze on the day he'd shown up on her doorstep, only to have her confirm they were through. If anyone should have felt pain back then, it had been him. Things had been tense between them for the last six months of their relationship, but he'd never dreamed she'd been that unhappy. Unless it had been about the money all along. Except she'd returned his bracelet.

His teeth clenched until his jaw ached. He'd been over and over this years ago and had come up empty.

Someone else came into the lounge and cleared her throat, making him realize a woman was waiting, pen in hand, to sign up for something. He took a couple of steps back and let her take his place.

His gaze cut back to the name of the local *capoeira* studio. Did Tessa still train there? When they'd been together, she'd sent him a handwritten invitation, asking him to come and learn a little more about her Brazilian heritage. He'd accepted without hesitation. And it had been worth it. Watching her work out inside the circle they called a *roda* had been beyond sexy—the intricate, flowing moves had highlighted the lean lines of her body and made *capoeira* look more like a dance than a true martial art.

He'd soon learned differently. It was just as passionate and fiery as Tessa was—and just as proud.

He shook himself back to the present as the attractive brunette finished writing her name and turned toward him with a smile, her dark eyes skipping over him. "Thanks. Better get in there and choose something. Pickings are getting mighty slim."

"So it would seem." He managed to return her smile, although the last thing he wanted to do was engage in small talk with a member of the opposite sex. He'd been burned twice now. Maybe he should have become a priest, like his cousin.

Except he did like women. He just didn't have the knack for long-term relationships, evidently. That was one gene his parents—married for thirty-five years now—hadn't passed down to him.

"See ya," the brunette said with yet another smile, although she didn't try to introduce herself, as Tessa's friend had. He was just as glad.

"Yep. Good luck with that." He nodded toward the board.

"You, too. Maybe we'll wind up volunteering for the same thing."

That was probably meant as a hint, but since Clay hadn't even noticed what she'd signed up for, she was out of luck. "Maybe."

She exited the room, leaving Clay to stare at the sheet again and wonder about Tessa and the studio. Especially when he looked closer and noticed that she hadn't signed up for anything, either, although the list of businesses didn't have slots for sign-ups. They must be using their own people in the rented booths.

It didn't matter. How hard could an hour or two of volunteer work be? He could always sign up for the cleanup crew, which still had several time periods available. That way he wouldn't have to interact with anyone.

But right now all he wanted to do was get to work and forget about his encounter with a certain redhead.

Except that a few parts of Clay were still smoldering from seeing her again. Time to remedy that. The sooner he could locate his mental fire extinguisher and douse those areas with a mixture of foam and water, the better it would be. For both of them.

CHAPTER THREE

Clay sat in the hospital cafeteria with Molly and listened to his daughter chatter on about all she'd done with Grandma and Grandpa yesterday evening. He couldn't hold back a sigh as she bounced in her chair and scooped up a bite of fruit from her plate.

His parents had been stoic all during his divorce, although they must have been disappointed in him for not working harder to make things work. He'd tried. Hell, he'd never expected his marriage to end in divorce any more than they had. But nothing he'd tried had worked. He'd compromised on where he'd practiced medicine to be closer to the house. He'd taken on the bulk of Molly's care when she'd been a baby. He'd even gone to marriage counseling.

And yet here he sat.

His biggest failures in life, it seemed, had to do with women.

One thing his mom and dad *had* been overjoyed about had been getting the chance to be deeply involved in their granddaughter's life. And it seemed yesterday had been no exception—with the trio heading out to Central Park for a walk with their Dalmatian, Jack.

He glanced at his watch, his impatience growing.

Lizza was almost a half hour late, and he was supposed to be at work in a few more minutes. He'd been hoping to have a little time to get to know the ropes before jumping right into his morning rounds. But it looked as if that wasn't going to happen.

Out of the corner of his eye he spied a familiar figure at the checkout counter. Only it wasn't Lizza. He groaned out loud.

"What is it, Daddy?"

He pulled his attention back to his daughter's blue eyes. "Nothing. I was just thinking about work."

"Oh. Okay. Do I *have* to go to Mommy's?"

The same question had been repeated for the past two visits. Clay didn't know what to do about it. Lizza traveled for weeks at a time, visiting European fashion houses in search of ideas for new designs. Molly hadn't spent more than a handful of weekends with her mom in the past year. And Lizza didn't help by being so fastidious about her house and furniture. Molly wasn't even three and a half yet. She needed to be a kid. But he'd learned to keep his mouth shut, as long as his ex didn't do anything to damage their daughter's self-esteem.

So he settled for a response that he hoped was conciliatory. "Mommy would be sad if you didn't."

"I know." Said with a sigh that made his gut clench.

If someone had told him four years ago that after his breakup with Tessa he'd have rebound sex that would result in a pregnancy and marriage, he'd have said that person was out of their gourd. And yet here he was. Only he was crazy about his daughter. So were his parents. It made all the crap he'd put up with from Lizza bearable.

He looked back toward the checkout area just as Tessa turned around, scanning the place for a spot to sit. It was breakfast time and the place was packed with medical personnel, all scarfing down a quick bite before facing a new day.

Her glance skidded past his and then stopped for a long second, her green eyes closing for a brief instant before reopening and sliding back his way again. She gave him a quick nod and then kept looking for someplace to sit.

Only there wasn't any.

Come on, Lizza. Hurry up.

In the meantime, he couldn't leave Tessa standing there, so he motioned her over. He could have sworn her mouth gave a pained grimace before she moved in their direction. He had no doubt if there had been any other person in the place that she knew, she would have gone to sit with them instead.

He was her last choice.

Well, some things never changed.

She set her tray next to Molly's, her brows coming together slightly, although she didn't ask the question he knew had to be swirling around her head.

His daughter had no such inhibitions. "I'm Molly. Who are you?"

Tessa blinked. "I'm Dr. Camara. How are you?"

"I'm waiting on my mommy."

His stomach tightened again. Left with no other choice, he made the introductions. "Tessa, this is my daughter."

"Is she your friend?" Molly asked.

"An old friend, yes." He looked at Tessa and dared her to correct him. She didn't, dropping into the chair across from him instead.

"That's right. Your dad and I knew each other a long time ago when we were both in school."

"Oh. Did you know Mommy, too?"

Tessa's teeth came down on her lower lip for a minute. "No. I didn't. Is your mom a doctor?"

"No, she makes pretty dresses and fancy clothes."

Tessa's body language changed, fingers clenching on her tray for a second before finally letting go and picking up her glass of juice. "How lucky for you. You must have all kinds of wonderful outfits."

Only she didn't make it sound as if Molly was lucky at all. There was an edge of sadness that made him look at her a little bit closer. He didn't voice the question in his head, however. "You look like you're in a hurry."

"I have a Mohs procedure to assist with today."

Interesting.

"Mohs? Are you specializing in plastic surgery?" The famed technique, named after its inventor, was used on skin lesions. Lesions that were normally cancerous.

She took a sip of her drink and then shook her head. "Dermatologic surgery. But I hope to do a fellowship in Mohs."

He'd thought her plans had been to go into craniofacial surgery. "That's quite a jump, isn't it?"

"Things change."

"They absolutely do." He couldn't hold back the sardonic note to his voice.

He and Tessa stared across the table at each other for several seconds as the atmosphere around them began to crackle with tension.

No. It wasn't tension. It was the distinctive clickety-clack of a pair of high heels moving quickly across the space.

"Mommy's coming." His daughter's whispered words had a fatalistic sound to them.

He swiveled around in his chair to find that Lizza was indeed headed their way, her perfectly made-up face a huge contrast to Tessa's unadorned freckles and simple style. Tessa wasn't the only one who'd made a huge leap from one specialty to another. The difference between his two exes could give a psychologist enough material to fill a volume or two.

Lizza stopped beside their table, brows lifting slightly in question, while Tessa looked as if she wanted to drop off the face of the earth.

Join the club, honey.

"Hello, Clayton."

She'd always used his full name, rather than the shortened version. He'd liked it at first, because it had been yet another thing that had unlinked him from Tessa, but after a while her formality had worn thin. As had those stupid air-kisses she insisted on giving to everyone. Even as he thought it, she bent down and made a popping sound beside Molly's cheek that never made contact. Neither did his ex attempt to embrace her daughter.

His molars ground together.

No wonder Molly had such a difficult time bonding with her. His parents were all about hugs and real, down-to-earth kisses.

When he stood, though, Lizza made no effort to lean into his cheek as she normally did. Probably because she was now looking at Tessa.

He wasn't going to get out of introducing them, evidently. Perfect. He glanced at his watch. And now he was five minutes late for his shift. "Lizza, this is an old friend from medical school, Tessa."

Tessa murmured that she was happy to meet her, while his ex did nothing but reach for Molly's hand. "Are you ready to go, sweetie? Mommy has some important phone calls to make."

His hands curled at his sides, although he tried to rein

in his temper. "Are you sure you have time for her this weekend? I could always drop her back off at Mom and Dad's place."

"It's my weekend." Said as if Molly were simply one more appointment on an already busy calendar.

His chest ached. Molly didn't even have a suitcase, since his ex had a second wardrobe and toys for their daughter at her house. She would launder Molly's current clothes and return her to him in them. Lizza insisted on keeping their households entirely separate. Shades of Tessa and her unwillingness to accept anything from him.

Maybe the women were more alike than he'd thought.

Clay squatted in front of Molly. "I'll see you Monday morning, chipmunk."

One of Lizza's heels clicked in that way she did when she was annoyed at something. Too damn bad.

His daughter threw her arms around his neck. "Love you, Daddy. Be good."

"Aren't I always?" He tweaked one of her braids.

A second later, Lizza and his daughter were headed toward the hospital entrance. A couple of masculine heads turned toward his ex-wife. She was beautiful, he acknowledged, with long blond hair and a delicate bone structure, although he now saw it as a brittle kind of grace that didn't stand up to pressure.

When he examined his feelings about other men ogling her, he found he didn't care. He'd stopped caring when she'd accidentally forwarded texts to his phone from another man. Someone in Italy that she evidently met up with whenever she was there, despite having a young daughter at home. All that money on counseling for nothing.

The only thing he was grateful to her for was that she'd signed over primary custody of Molly to him without batting an eyelid, saying that with her schedule it was probably for the best.

He couldn't agree more.

Dropping back in his seat, he noticed that Tessa was studying her bowl of oatmeal as if it were fascinating.

He blew out a breath. "And how has *your* morning been?"

The smile he expected didn't come. Instead, she swirled her spoon through the mixture in her bowl.

"It must be embarrassing to have her meet me."

"It was a little different than introducing two colleagues at a medical conference, I'll give you that."

This time her head came up, eyes flashing, color seeping into her face. "You could have pretended not to know me."

"Why would I do…?" He frowned. "You think I'm embarrassed by you?"

He glanced at his watch for a third time and found that five minutes late had morphed into fifteen. He didn't have time to hash this out with her right now. Not that it even mattered.

Tessa had always had a chip on her shoulder about money or anything associated with it—that probably extended to Lizza's display of expensive clothing.

It wasn't as if she was poor, her parents did well enough for themselves, even if his grandmother's memorial fund had helped pay for her education. Their parents were good friends—they'd worked together for years. When Tessa's parents had realized they weren't going to be able to help her achieve her dreams, his mom and dad had quietly stepped in to help. They were generous people—it was what they did.

In the past, Clay would have tried to smooth things

over with her. Right now, however, he was out of both time and patience.

Standing to his feet, he looked down at her. "I think you've got it backward, sweetheart. You always acted like *you* were the one embarrassed, not me."

"I don't understand."

"I don't suppose you do." Time to leave. But first there was a little itch he just had to scratch. "Before I forget, I saw the *capoeira* studio on the list of businesses involved with the festival."

She nodded. "They're putting on an exhibition to garner interest."

"Are you participating in it?" Why he'd asked that, he had no idea.

This time her answer came even slower. "I am."

"You always were good. I'll have to stop by the studio sometime."

He tried to stop the memory of Tessa's long, lithe movements as she trained in *capoeira* from crowding his head, but it was too late—the memories were too vivid...and too raw.

A tightening sensation in his gut—as well as her less-than-enthusiastic response—told him it was time to get out while the getting was good.

So he cut the conversation short with a quick wave and a "Have a nice day" thrown in for good measure.

As it was, Tessa was the only one with the slightest chance of that happening. Because, between his first ex and his second, his day was well and truly shot.

The foot connected with her cheek with a sharp smack.

Down Tessa went in a tangle of arms and legs.

Marcos was immediately kneeling beside her. "That wasn't supposed to happen. Where is your head, *moça*?"

Her head was where it had been for the past two days. On Clay and the thought of him showing up at the studio unannounced, maybe even with his daughter in tow. Or, worse, with his gorgeous-enough-to-be-a-model ex-wife. The one who fashioned clothes like the ones she'd been given all those years ago. That would be the worst. She'd felt like a field mouse next to an exotic cat as she'd sat there in the hospital cafeteria. Surely Clay had compared them as well and wondered why the hell he hadn't stuck with his wife. Or wondered what he'd seen in Tessa in the first place.

She shook the thoughts away, angry with herself. She was supposed to be training for the hospital festival. And this was geared to be a demonstration that showed off *capoeira*'s romantic side, from its circle of constantly switching partners to the cartwheels, spins and beating drums that made the martial art both beautiful and different. It was more about skill than combat nowadays, but it still clung to some of its former roots. As she'd found out on several occasions. Today being one of them.

One wrong move—or right move, depending on your perspective—and you could take an opponent down. Just as she'd done when she and Clay had been dating, and she'd sent that invitation asking him to come to the studio.

He'd soon been hooked. In fact, she'd done the *batismo* ceremony on him—a match where a more advanced *capoeirista* took down an inexperienced student, formally inducting him into the studio. She'd even presented him with his white cord—the ranking system used by the sport—helping him tie it around his waist. Memories of sweeping his legs out from under him still haunted her dreams on occasion. As did the memory of leaning over him in victory once he'd been flat on his back. His response had made her shiver. With a single raised brow he'd promised retribution later that night.

And he'd kept that promise. Sweet, sweet retribution that had had her begging for more.

"Tessa?"

She blinked back to the present. "Sorry. I just lost my concentration for a second or two."

"A second or two?" Several Portuguese swearwords accompanied the question as the owner of the studio stared down at her. "It's been more like the entire match." He touched a finger to her still-stinging cheek. "I don't want you bruised up before the festival. It defeats the purpose of emphasizing the workout benefits of *capoeira*. *Intende?*"

"Yes, I understand. Let's try again."

Marcos helped her up and then motioned for the next person in the circle to join her. "Begin."

The percussion instruments set the rhythm once again as Tessa concentrated on the ebb and flow that accompanied her current partner, the feinting and parrying looking almost choreographed. Two minutes later, she was standing back in the ring of participants as someone else danced in to take her place. When it was once again her turn she slid forward, only to find herself on the wrong side of a foot for the third or fourth time. Mortified, she crashed to the mat, wondering if Marcos was going to take away her purple and green *cordão* and demote her to a lower level.

He knelt beside her once again. "I think that is enough for today, Tessita."

She grimaced. Marcos only resorted to calling her "little Tessa" when he was upset with her. And he had every right to be. She'd trained with him for years and years. He knew exactly what she was capable of. "I don't know what's wrong with me."

"I do not, either, but when you come back next week, try to make our *capoeira* look a little less…brutal."

Everyone laughed, including Tessa, and the tension eased as he helped her to her feet. She sighed. "Point taken. I'll work on it."

"Good. The festival will be here before we know it."

She grabbed her towel from on top of her bag and blotted the sweat from her face and neck. "Four weeks. I know. Maybe I'll find a few extra hours this week and come in for a private session."

"I think that would be good, Tessita."

Ugh. Still upset. Well, Marcos wasn't the only one. She was upset at herself. Ever since her encounter with Clay in the cafeteria she'd been on edge. Something about the way his ex had looked at her, the acid in her gaze making Tessa feel like a criminal of some sort, even though she'd done nothing wrong.

Well, it was time to put Clay and his ex—and most especially his cute little daughter—from her mind. Once and for all.

How she was going to do that, though, remained to be seen.

CHAPTER FOUR

HE WAS WATCHING HER.

Tessa had caught a glimpse of movement out of the corner of her eye as she continued to section the diseased skin tissue, teasing it away from healthy cells. The Mohs surgery had been put off for three days due to a cold her patient had developed.

How had Clay found out when she would be operating? Maybe Brian Perry, her attending cutaneous oncologist, had clued him in. But why would he have done that? Clay was an orthopedic surgeon, a whole different realm than cutaneous surgery.

She had already marked the surgical site before proceeding and when she lifted the thin layer of tissue and placed it onto a glass slide, she made sure to match the marks so they would know where to continue cutting if the margins weren't completely clear. Brian glanced down at the site and nodded to the lab assistant. "Once you're ready, let us know."

They would section the tissue sample and stain it, looking for areas that still contained cancer cells. Either Tessa or Brian would then remove more tissue just at the specific location. That way they conserved as much healthy tissue as possible.

"How are you doing, Mandy?" Her patient was lying

on her stomach with her head to one side, but was wide-awake. Mohs surgery was generally done under a local anesthetic. The only hard part was that there was quite a bit of waiting involved if the tumor had roots that went deeper than expected.

"I'm okay. How's it coming?"

"We'll know in a few minutes."

The buzzer at her waistband went off, as did Brian's. The lab was ready for them to view the slide.

Tessa was glad to get out from beneath Clay's stare. She still had no idea why he was there.

The results under the microscope showed that there was still one area that contained tumor cells. Brian marked the graph they'd been charting to match what they saw on the slide.

After shaving off two more layers of skin in that area, they finally got the results they were looking for: clear margins. This wasn't melanoma but a squamous cell tumor on the patient's lower left back. While not as dangerous as the type of cancer that had killed Tessa's mom, it could still grow out of control, dividing and penetrating to other organ systems if not caught in time. Fortunately this patient had a known history of skin cancer and had screened herself on a regular basis.

Sucking down a breath, she peered again at her patient as they got ready to close the surgical site. In a calm voice she explained what they'd done and what to expect, thankful they wouldn't need to do a skin graft. Even as she hoped Clay had gotten bored and left, he probably hadn't. She was still stumped as to his presence. Didn't he have his own patients to attend to?

Maybe he wanted to discuss something with her. Lord, she hoped not. The last thing she needed after the day she'd had was to do a dissection of a different kind.

Especially if it involved their shared past. It had been over four years. There was nothing left to dissect.

"Looks good, Tessa. I think you got everything. Congratulations."

"Thanks." The praise should have elated her but she was still on edge over Clay's appearance.

As if hearing her thoughts, Brian glanced up at the window, evidently noticing what she had a half hour earlier. "Looks like you had an audience."

What did she say to that? I know? Or act as if she had no idea who it was.

She chose a different route. "Wonder why."

"Not sure. If you feel up to finishing on your own, I'll go see if I can help him with something. Maybe he has a surgery in here afterward and is scoping out the room. He's new." He paused. "I think you're well on your way to a fellowship in Mohs, if that's what you're looking for."

Just beneath the hum of excitement that went through her at the other man's words lurked a trill of annoyance. This should have been a moment of triumph for her. She was so close to finishing up her residency. And now a dark specter of the past had to sweep in and ruin it.

Forget it. You did the surgery. Without any assistance or input, for the very first time. That should be all she was thinking about right now.

But it wasn't. And as Brian headed out the door she bit her lip.

She wasn't thrilled about her attending going up to chitchat with her ex, but it wasn't as if she could say anything in a roomful of other medical staff. So she just gritted her teeth and hoped she'd be able to get through the final part of the surgery.

And she should be proud. Clay had seen she *could* do this on her own. Just as she'd promised herself. She refrained from glancing up and making sure he actually *had* seen her finish. But just barely.

She asked for the suture material, and the surgical nurse handed her the pre-threaded needle. Closing the deeper layers first, she worked her way back up to the surface tissue, stopping from time to time to make sure her patient was doing okay. Fifteen minutes later she was done. Brian hadn't come back, and she couldn't bring herself to sneak a peek at the observation room. Instead, she settled for putting the final piece of tape on the gauze and talking to her patient, giving her care instructions and telling her to come back and see Dr. Perry in a week to have her stitches removed. Then she squeezed her shoulder and said her goodbyes.

Pulling off her surgical loupes and then stripping off her gown and gloves, she dropped everything into the appropriate bins. As if pulled on a string, her head went up, eyes seeking the space above her. It was empty. Clay wasn't there, and neither was Brian. Disappointment sloshed through her, followed by relief. The relief was what she chose to focus on. Maybe Clay really did need to see her attending for something. Which meant he hadn't been there because of her. None of that mattered. What mattered was that she could relax.

She pushed through the door to leave the operating room and pulled the clip from her hair so she could redo it. Except the person who'd been in the suite above her was now just outside the door. Quickly finger-combing her hair and cramming the mass back into the clip, she tried to look nonchalant, although her heart was thumping out a nonsensical rhythm in her chest.

"Where's Brian?"

Stupid question. But it was the only thing she could think of to say at the moment.

"He said he had another patient and left me here to wait for you."

Why would he be waiting for her instead of her attending?

"Any specific reason?"

He turned to face her, propping his shoulder against the wall. His face bore no trace of the sardonic amusement she'd come to expect from him. Instead, it was deadly serious. "I talked to my mom last night."

At that, Tessa tensed. She and Clay's parents had maintained a cordial relationship over the years—and despite how uncomfortable it made her feel that they'd shelled out so much money for her education, she was grateful to them. Even after she and Clay had broken up, she'd still had some contact with them. That was until her mom died. She'd barely been able to hold herself together during that time, much less carry on a coherent conversation with anyone outside work. "Oh?"

His eyes searched her face. "I didn't know your mother passed away, Tessa."

Oh, no. Don't do this. Not right now. Not here. Especially since the anniversary of her death had just barely passed.

A sudden rush of moisture coated her lower lids, forcing her to blink several times to hold the flow at bay. "Yes, she did." Licking her lips, she tried to get away. "I have a couple more patients to see, so if you'll excuse me…"

Before she could move past him, though, he reached out and encircled her wrist, his fingers warm and solid against her icy skin. "I'm sorry, Tess. I had no idea. Is that why you changed your specialty?" He nodded toward the double doors of the operating room.

She decided to cut past all the chatter. "Is it why I went

into dermatologic surgery? Yes. I suppose your mom also told you what she died of."

"She did." He let go of her hand and cupped her cheek, stroking his thumb beneath her left eyelid. The compassion in his gaze was so different from the blasé attitude he'd shown in front of his poster in the lobby. Then he'd been all cocky with his confident swagger and veiled references to their past.

Tessa felt a telling hint of moisture beneath his fingertip and gave an inward curse. She hadn't quite banished the tears after all.

Taking a step back, she attempted to break free of his touch. "I decided that the best way to serve her memory was to try to help others like her." She stiffened her spine just a bit. "Is that why you were watching me? Because of your mom?"

"You noticed me." One brow went up.

The swagger was back.

Her lips curved despite herself. There was something about this man that did a number on her even after all these years. Did he really think she would miss seeing him there? "It was kind of hard to avoid seeing you, since you were almost directly in front of me."

Well, not quite. He'd been off to the side, but she'd gotten used to scanning that observation room, which was used quite a bit by both senior doctors and residents in different stages of their work. So, yeah. She'd spotted him almost right away.

"It seemed the best place to find you. You float around this hospital like a ghost."

A ghost? That was one way of putting it. A ghost on a mission was more like it. She'd caught sight of Clay twice on her floor yesterday and had ducked into a patient's room to avoid being seen by him.

Really mature, Tessa.

"Hospitals keep their residents pretty busy. I'm sure you know that from experience." The doors opened and her patient was wheeled out by one of the male nurses. That old wheeling-patients-out-of-the-hospital-instead-of-letting-them-walk-out-on-their-own-two-feet rule was still alive and well. This was the perfect opportunity to escape. "I need to go."

"I'll walk with you. Wouldn't want you disappearing on me again."

What?

"Was there something else you wanted to discuss?" Other than her personal life, that was. She didn't say it, though, since she wasn't anxious for anyone to know that she and Clay knew each other in any way other than as a pair of colleagues…casual acquaintances. She let the wheelchair move a few more yards ahead before turning to follow it.

Clay fell into step beside her. "Yes. Actually, there is."

Clay wasn't sure why he'd gone to the observation room. Maybe out of a sense of nostalgia or morbid curiosity. Or it could be that after his mother told him about Gloria's death from melanoma, something inside him had needed to tell her he was sorry. Despite all of the ugly stuff that had happened between them at the end of their relationship, he'd never wanted anything bad to happen to her or her family.

Why hadn't his mom said anything earlier? Probably because he'd cut her off anytime she'd mentioned Tessa's name. His parents had never known how angry he'd been that she'd thrown his graduation gift back in his face—because he'd never told them. Still, they'd quickly learned she was a touchy subject, one best avoided altogether. The only reason they'd found out that Tessa was at West Manhattan Saints was because of Molly—who'd mentioned the pretty lady that had sat with them at breakfast.

They'd been all ears, probably thinking he was dating again.

Hardly. He was done with marriage, with dating… with women in general.

Then Tessa's name had come up. And the news of Gloria's death had been the first thing out of his mother's mouth.

Regret for all he'd said and done streamed through him. It had grown until the weight of needing to offer his condolences had gotten too heavy. Which was why he was here.

Except as soon as he'd gotten the words out of his mouth he'd felt the need to counter them with a flip comeback seconds later. Why? And why was it only Tessa who brought out that side of him? He didn't do the back-and-forth banter stuff with Lizza—he never had. In fact, he avoided speaking with her as much as possible nowadays.

Tessa was waiting for him to tell her what that other subject he wanted to discuss was. "Remember I asked you about the studio?"

"Studio?" The way she said it, with studied indifference, told him she knew exactly what he was talking about.

"Your *capoeira* studio. I've been thinking about it, and I think Molly might really like to watch one of the training sessions. And if they're practicing for an exhibition, it's the perfect opportunity."

She turned to glance at him, her puzzlement obvious. "You know where it is. It hasn't moved. So why ask me?"

"I wanted to see if you knew when they were practicing. Marcos—if he's still there—probably wouldn't even remember me."

And that was the only reason you wanted to see her, right?

"He'll remember you."

Something about the way she said it made him slow down just a bit. Tessa, probably not even realizing she was doing it, slowed her pace, as well.

It had been over four years. Surely the studio had had lots of people come and go in that period of time.

"How do you know he will?"

Her glance skittered away. "He may have mentioned you once or twice."

Ah, yes. Clay could see how that might have been awkward for her: explaining why they'd broken off their relationship and why he would no longer be training at the studio.

He could have kept going—he liked the sport. But he'd been so angry at Tessa back then, he hadn't wanted any reminders. Besides, he'd been intent on making a clean break. Seeing her every week at the studio wasn't exactly the best way to do that.

"And I'm sure you gave him nothing but glowing reports."

This time, Tessa stopped completely, an odd look coming over her face. "I never said anything bad about you, Clay." She seemed to hesitate, then continued. "Why don't you let me call him, and I'll get back in touch about a time."

Okay, so she'd just gone from basically telling him to get in contact with them himself to offering to do it for him. What gives?

He decided to press a little harder. "Any particular reason you want to do it?"

She shrugged. "I speak the language. It might be easier for me to explain things."

Somehow he doubted that was it at all. She just wanted to be in control of how much information the school's owner had. It certainly wasn't because of Marcos's English skills, since he spoke it perfectly, although he still had a Brazilian accent. As did Tessa. Just a smidgen… when she got angry or emotional. Clay could still remember some pretty heady times as they'd made love. In the heat of the moment, when she'd been squirming with need, she'd gritted out something in Portuguese. And, man, had it done a number on his control, breaking it into tiny pieces.

The accent had also been there when she'd cut things off between them, the anger and pain in her eyes unmistakable, although he still had no idea what he'd done that had been so terrible. It had only been a bracelet. Lizza would have taken it and run. Except that had all changed after their divorce.

Women.

But now wasn't the time to go into any of that. And going to the studio was probably a bad idea. A really bad idea judging from Tessa's wary expression. But he admired the athleticism of *capoeira* and wanted Molly to experience what he had the first time he'd seen it. Especially since she was going through a phase where she was giving karate chops to everything in sight, including him. He wanted her to see what a real martial art looked like. And to understand that it wasn't about "chopping" people or breaking boards, but about discipline and self-control.

Maybe his daughter could even take lessons, although he had no idea what ages they accepted.

And maybe Clay could even start training again himself. He could use something to help him stay in shape.

He could go when Tessa wasn't there. They could still keep their lives completely separate—he'd learned a thing or two from Lizza's insistence on maintaining a his and hers division of households.

His and Tessa's circles never needed to intersect.

Okay, then. He'd done what he'd come to do. Offer his condolences. Now it was time to get the hell out.

He took his wallet from his back pocket and pulled out a business card. "Give me a call when you know something."

Tessa hesitated, and for a moment Clay wondered if she was going to refuse to take it. Then she reached out and plucked it from his fingers, careful not to touch him. At least that's the way Clay perceived it. So he did something about it. He caught her hand, the card trapped between them. He felt her muscles jerk and then relax. "Give my best to your dad, okay?"

"I will. Thanks." Then she tugged free and spun away from him, striding after her patient, who was now long gone. Leaving Clay wondering what the hell he'd been thinking for going after her…for touching her. Because she wasn't the only one who'd reacted. His hand had wanted to linger, his fingers itching to stroke over her palm the way he used to when they were together.

He knew far too well why he'd done it. It had irked him to see her attending standing so close to her while she'd been doing that surgery. And how, when the man had touched her sleeve, she hadn't flinched away from him, as she did with *him*.

He hadn't liked the way it made him feel. Had felt the need to see if she still responded to his touch the way he remembered. She'd responded, all right. He just couldn't tell if she'd been repelled by the warm slide of flesh against flesh or if she'd been bothered in a completely different way.

He could only hope her reaction had been no less disturbing than his had been—a kind of knee-jerk muscle memory that happened without conscious thought. He'd been stunned the first time it happened. And the second.

He needed to somehow erase that memory and everything that went with it. Because if he couldn't, he was in big, big trouble.

The first thing to do was make sure he didn't touch her again.

No matter what.

Tessa plopped onto one of the dark dining room chairs in the brownstone house where she lived and put her head down on her arms. Caren Riggs was already home, standing in the kitchen rolling and cutting what looked to be square noodles on the marble island in the center of the space. Right now, though, Tessa was too wrung out to care, even though whatever Caren was cooking smelled divine.

Interacting with Clay was turning out to be even harder than she'd expected. Because when he touched her she quaked. And felt wistful about long-gone days.

She didn't want to yearn for him. That was a million times worse, in her opinion, than simply lusting after that scrumptious bod. Because lust she could explain away—after all, Clay was a hunk of the first order, a vital man who dominated whatever space he happened to stroll past. Even Brian, who was a little older than Clay and just as attractive, with a touch of gray in his sandy-brown hair, didn't make her insides squirm and twist the way her ex did.

And that was bad. Very bad. Because she didn't want

to have any kind of reaction at all to him. She was afraid she'd learn something she didn't want to know. That she'd never quite gotten over him.

Sure you did. You broke up with him.

No. She'd broken it off because she'd known they weren't going to be good for each other and had gotten out while the getting was good. That didn't mean it hadn't been painful or that it hadn't ripped her heart from her chest to contemplate never seeing him again.

A few minutes passed as she sat there, and then the table beneath her cheek shifted a bit. Caren had evidently come over and set something down.

"Hey," the other woman said. "You look tired."

"Am." The mumbled word was all she could manage.

"Then eat something. I made chicken and dumplings—classic comfort food. Besides, I have something I need to talk to you about."

Oh, no. This was the second time today someone had used those words.

Tessa looked up to find her friend sitting across from her, and, yes, there was now a shallow, wide-rimmed bowl sitting in front of her. A second bowl sat in front of Caren. The concoction smelled even more heavenly this close to her nose. "What's the occasion?"

"Not really an occasion. I may just not get any Southern cooking for a while, so I thought I'd make some now while I still can."

Caren wasn't from New York, and Tessa found her slow drawl soothing somehow. Even now it seemed to drift through her soul, pushing back the tide of confusion and grief that had gripped her ever since her surprise encounter with Clay in the hospital lobby.

She tilted her head, accepting the spoon the other woman handed across to her. The brownstone, owned

by Holly and her family, was decorated in classic dark
woods and rich upholstery. It reminded her of what she
might find in Clay's parents' home. Wealthy, understated.
But for some reason this place didn't make her cringe the
way it might have had she not been paying her own way.

"Why wouldn't you get Southern cooking for a while?"
She stirred the mixture in her bowl to help cool it.

"That's the thing. I was going to talk to you, Holly and
Sam after you all got home. But when you came in first,
I thought I'd sound you out about it." Caren paused and
eyed her for a second. "Is everything okay?"

"Peachy." She cut into one of the dumplings and blew
on it for a second before sliding it into her mouth. Her
tastebuds perked right up, a low groan sounding from
her throat. She'd never tried honest-to-goodness Southern cuisine before meeting Caren, but she was rapidly
becoming addicted. Swallowing it, she smiled. "This
stuff is awesome."

"Told you you'd like it. Aren't you glad I forced you to
try homemade dumplings after you moved in?"

"I hate to admit it but yes. I've only had the fluffy
biscuit kind. These are so good." She waited until Caren
had eaten a couple of bites before continuing. "So what's
going on?"

Setting her spoon down in her bowl, her friend
propped her elbows on the table. "I'm thinking of going
on a medical mission."

"What?" Caren had never mentioned leaving the hospital or the brownstone. "Where to?"

"Africa. Cameroon, actually. I just got the go-ahead
to start packing."

"Wow, that was fast. What about your fellowship, are
you just going to let it go? And what about your unit?"

The house had been divided into four separate units

with a shared kitchen, living room and dining room. Over the course of their residency the four roomies had become fast friends. Maybe because they were all young and single, but it was probably also because they shared a common goal of becoming doctors.

She'd just assumed things would stay the way they were for a while. To think of Caren no longer being here…

"That's the thing. I have a cousin who is thinking of coming to West Manhattan Saints and applying for a fellowship." Caren scooped up another bite of dumpling and waved it around for a minute. "She could sublet my unit. All my furniture would stay put. There would just be a new face to go along with it."

A key scraped in the lock just before the front door was pushed open. Sam Napier appeared, carrying a couple of bags, which he switched to the other hand before closing the door again. He glanced at them. "Hi. Am I interrupting something?"

With his longish hair, lean build and the slightest hint of a Scottish accent, Sam could only be described as superhot, but he was also something of an enigma, quiet and intense, rarely sharing anything personal about himself. Maybe it was just a guy trait, but Tessa had a feeling there was more to it than that. Whatever it was, he was definitely the quietest of the housemates.

She shrugged. "You're not. Caren was just…" She glanced at the other woman, wondering if she wanted the medical mission thing kept a secret.

"I was just telling Tessa that I might be leaving for a while. My cousin Kimberlyn—who's also on her way to becoming a doctor—would be able to move in and take over my share of the expenses, if that's okay. I wanted to check with everyone first before giving her a definite answer."

Sam came over to stand by the table. "I don't have a problem with it. I guess it's really up to Holly, though, since she and her folks own the place."

"You're probably right. I'll ask her tonight."

"Is Kimberlyn still in med school?" Sam asked.

"She's a resident, like us. She's just getting ready to apply for a fellowship."

Sam slung a bag over his shoulder. "Sounds like the perfect solution, then."

"I think so, too," Caren said with a smile. "I'm so relieved. I was worried you guys might be upset with me for bailing on you so close to the end of our residency."

Tessa smiled back. "Of course not. I'm excited for you. Besides, you'll be back. And you'll have to send loads of pictures of Cameroon."

"I will." She popped two more spoonfuls into her mouth and then stood. "I'm on call tonight, so I need to jump in the shower really quick. And I'll start packing for the trip."

"Go," Tessa said. "I'll clean this up."

Caren squinched her nose. "It's a mess out there— there's flour everywhere. Are you sure you want to tackle it?"

"Definitely." Besides, it would give her something to think about other than Clay.

"Well, I've got an early surgery in the morning, so I'm going to turn in." With a wave, Sam went up the stairs toward his unit.

"Thanks again. I think you're all really going to love Kimber."

Tessa stood and stacked their bowls. "If she's anything like you, I'm sure we will."

CHAPTER FIVE

"Dr. Matthews? You're needed down in Emergency," one of the nurses at the central station called over to him, phone still to her ear.

Six hours into his shift, Clay had performed two surgeries and done a phone consultation with a doctor from one of the other local hospitals. It had been hectic enough that there'd been whole blocks of time in which he hadn't thought about Tessa once.

Until now.

"What have you got?"

"Looks like they have an elderly gentleman who fell down his front porch steps and broke a leg. Or maybe a hip."

"Tell them I'm on my way." Clay pushed the button on the elevator. The funny thing about fractures in the elderly was that cause and effect were rarely quite as simple as the nurse made it seem. Whether the break caused the fall or the fall caused the break was often up in the air. He'd seen enough spontaneous fractures in his time that he knew brittle bones could suddenly give way under the stress of years' worth of use and abuse.

By the time he got down to the first floor his thoughts were all on his patient, already planning for various scenarios and how he'd deal with each.

One of the attendings stopped him just as he stepped into the hallway where the exam rooms were. "Are you the new orthopedist?"

"Yes, Clay Matthews."

"Anthony Stark. Good to meet you. Your patient is in exam room four. I called in one of the residents as well, once we got a good look at him."

That was odd, since the only orthopedic resident Clay knew of was at dinner. Maybe he'd come back early. "Okay, thanks. Has he been up to Radiology yet?"

"Yes. He just came back. It looks like a displaced break."

Perfect. Displaced meant the two ends of the bone weren't aligned—a more complicated situation to address. Compassion tickled the back of his throat. Another tricky piece of news. He knew of at least one patient in the past month whose heart hadn't been strong enough to do the surgery needed to repair a broken pelvis. He could only hope that was not the case with the current patient.

The sound of someone bellowing came from the exam room where he was headed.

The ER doc gave him a half smile. "All I can say is good luck. Let me know if you need some help in there."

Clay frowned and headed toward the curtained-off area where the sound of voices was growing louder. One female and one male...who sounded none too happy.

Noting that there was no chart in the holder, he swished open enough of the curtain to get through. He stopped in his tracks. Even though her back was turned, the female arguing with his patient wasn't a nurse. It was Tessa. And she was trying her damnedest to pull back the sheet covering the patient, while he held on to the fabric with all his might. Her Brazilian accent was there in all its blazing glory.

Not that it was doing her any good.

"No one is seeing my privates except my doctor!"

"I *am* a doctor, Mr. Phillips. I'm here to look at your leg."

What the hell? Why was Tessa trying to look at his patient's leg? Dr. Stark had said he'd called in another resident, but Clay had assumed it was an orthopedic resident.

If it wasn't for the seriousness of the man's injury, he might have been tempted to just stand back and see how things played out between the two of them, because the Tessa he knew didn't give up once she got going. For anything.

That probably wasn't in the best interest of his patient, though.

He stepped closer. "Anything I can do to help?"

Two heads craned around to look at him. Surprisingly, Tessa's normal irritation at seeing him was nowhere to be seen. Instead, she looked almost relieved.

The patient—Mr. Phillips—yanked harder on the sheet. "This little lady is trying to get a look at my equipment."

He wasn't sure whether he was more shocked by the "little lady" description or by the fact that a patient was basically calling Tessa a Peeping Tom.

"I'm trying to see his mole."

Ouch.

Wait. Maybe she really did mean mole as in…

"I thought this was my patient. Broken left femur?"

Tessa nodded. "And a suspicious skin lesion on his other leg. Which is why Dr. Stark called me in."

Damn. Of all the rotten luck. So much for the idea that keeping busy could keep him from thinking about her. Because right now his job included the very person he was trying to block out of his mind.

Even more pressing, though, was the need to keep the patient calm. Which meant he just might have to ruffle a few of Tessa's feathers.

Stepping to the other side of the bed, he ignored her for a moment. "How about if I ask Dr. Camara to step back while I take a look? Would that be better?"

"But—"

He stopped her words with a look. Surprisingly, instead of the dark anger he expected to see on her face she simply nodded, let go of the sheet and took ten steps back until she was against the curtain on the far side of the space.

Glancing at the patient's face and seeing it crumple in relief, he noted a dark bruise where the man had evidently fallen already apparent on his right cheek. As was the pain he'd been holding back. Clay touched the top edge of the sheet. "May I?"

Mr. Phillips released the covering and allowed Clay to pull it down. He edged the gown up as far as he could without totally exposing the man. The area just above his left knee was obviously broken, the frail-looking limb bent at a five-degree angle. And at the top of his other thigh was a dark mark about the size of a quarter.

Irregular edges. Mottled coloring that looked like the boiling up of a tar pit.

Tessa was the expert when it came to skin conditions, but Clay knew enough to bet this was exactly what she thought it might be. Melanoma. The deadliest form of skin cancer. And the most likely to have spread. Whether it had metastasized to his bones and caused the femur to break was something they wouldn't be able to determine without more tests. Regardless, both conditions needed immediate treatment. The break was the most urgent, but the size of the growth on his other leg was also worrisome.

He glanced up at her and gave a nod. "He does have a lesion." He added a quick description, leaving out the actual word.

"I need to see it to be sure."

Mr. Phillips started to reach for the sheet again, but Clay stopped him with a hand to the shoulder. He glanced back up at Tessa. "Could you leave us alone for a moment?"

Even with her red hair pulled back in a clip and twin smudges of exhaustion beneath her deep green eyes, Tessa was beautiful. Probably even more so now than she'd been back in medical school. There was an iron determination that hadn't been there when they'd been together. Or maybe it had been and he'd simply been too busy—and too entranced by her porcelain skin and vibrant personality—to notice.

But he saw it now, and so he added, "Please? Trust me on this."

Without another word, she ducked beneath the fabric of the privacy screen rather than pulling it to the side.

He turned back to his patient. "Mr. Phillips, Dr. Camara is a professional."

"Still. My wife has been the only woman to see me naked in all these years."

"You've never had a female doctor?"

The man shook his head. The pain had to be excruciating, but evidently the thought of having Tessa see him was even more uncomfortable than his injuries. Clay could always call in another dermatologist—a male one—and risk bringing Tessa's wrath down on his head. But that wasn't fair, either. Tessa was a doctor, and to send her away just because she was a woman made something stick in the lower regions of his gut. So he came up with another solution instead.

"How about if we do this? We'll keep your hospital gown where it is, and I'll cover you with the sheet like this." Clay arranged the folds so that it draped over his waist and created a little "U" of exposed skin. Only the skin lesion was visible. Nothing else. They'd have to examine the rest of him to see if there were any other suspicious areas but they could do that while he was under anesthesia for his leg, if tests showed he was strong enough to even have the operation.

The head of the bed had been cranked up so that Mr. Phillips could see what Clay was doing, and the man visibly relaxed. "I guess that would be okay. But don't let her pull it any farther."

Clay gave him a grave nod. "You have my word."

"Well, okay, then."

"Tessa? Could you step back in here?"

The man turned his head sharply. "I have a daughter named Tessa."

"Well, see there? That must be a sign."

Tessa came over to stand by the bed. "Did I hear you right? You have a Tessa at home?"

"Well, not at home. She'll be forty-nine next week. Lives in Montana with her husband and three horses."

"Do you have any other family members you want us to call?"

Even as she spoke, her eyes were already on the skin lesion, and Clay could see her mentally sizing it up in her head.

"My wife's been gone for ten years and my two kids—Tessa and Jeremy—live a long way away."

Clay's gut tightened. Maybe Mr. Phillips should think about moving closer to them. But that wasn't up to him.

It was up to his family. "Did you give the front desk a way to reach either of them?"

"Yes."

Tessa rounded the exam table until she stood across from Clay, although she didn't look directly at him. Instead, she kept her gaze on their patient. "Thank you for letting me see the spot. We'll need to take that off, maybe even while Dr. Matthews fixes your leg. Would that be all right?"

"I s'pose so. As long as you keep your eyes where they're supposed to be, young lady."

Tessa smiled. "Absolutely. I give you my word."

The man's head fell back onto the pillow, the pain lines deepening. "Then what d'you say we get this show on the road."

An hour later—with an EKG and bloodwork confirming that Mr. Phillips had the constitution of an ox, even if he had the bones of the eighty-year-old man he was—Tessa shared an operating room with Clay for the very first time.

And the very last time, if she had her way. Her hands might not be shaking, but the rest of her certainly was as Clay stood across from her, working on the broken femur as she excised the skin tumor on the man's other leg. "It's not as deep as it could be," she said, unable to prevent herself from talking as she worked, something she'd always done. No one had seemed to mind it in the past. And Clay didn't seem to mind it now.

But for his part he'd been mostly silent as he worked on drilling holes for the pins that would hold the ends of the patient's bone together and allow it to heal.

Once she'd gotten clear margins, Mr. Phillips would have to undergo a PET scan to see if the cancer had spread. The tumor was large enough to make her uneasy, but things like this had surprised her before. She could only hope for the same good outcome. She glanced up. "How does his other leg look?"

Clay paused for a minute, before meeting her gaze. "I think he's got a good shot, if he's careful."

Keeping true to their word, Clay had made sure that Mr. Phillips's private parts were covered at all times, even though the man would never know the difference. And it made something inside her warm to know that Clay cared about his patient's dignity.

He was a good man. Even if he wasn't the right one for her.

And he wasn't. She'd done a lot of thinking over the past four years about her actions. Her temper—or maybe it was her pride—had gotten the best of her, and she'd ended their relationship in the worst possible way, mailing his gift back to him and basically telling him to get lost.

Yes, maybe someday she would find a way to apologize for that. She wasn't sure when or how, but now that they were working together, surely it was a sign that Fate was giving her an opportunity to make things right. Maybe they could at least become colleagues, even if they could never be friends.

She screwed up her courage, finding it took a lot more cranks of the handle than she'd expected. But she finally took a deep breath and succeeded in opening her mouth. "Do you want to go grab something to eat once we're finished? Unless you've already had dinner."

He eyed her for a second as if not completely trusting her motives. "Where did this come from?"

"If you'd rather not…"

Okay, now she felt like an idiot, but it wasn't as if she could withdraw her invitation.

"Tessa, Tessa…" He clucked his tongue. "I didn't say that."

So what was he saying? That he wanted to go after all?

Before she could ask, he went on, "Molly's staying at my folks' house tonight, in fact. So dinner it is." He put his head down and went back to work as if that was that.

The reminder of his daughter brought home the fact that Clay had a child with another woman. A supermodel, from the looks of his ex. What had happened between them, anyway?

Maybe he'd tried to buy her one too many gifts. Except the former Mrs. Matthews didn't look like the type who would have any trouble accepting gifts or anything else from him.

No, that was just her. Stupid, prideful Tessa, who just had to do everything on her own. She'd come to terms with Clay's parents and had come to appreciate everything they'd done for her. So why couldn't she do the same with their son?

Because she'd wanted to be his equal. Had wanted so badly to know that she could live and survive and thrive on her own, as her parents had done after moving to the United States. That she was every bit as smart as they'd been.

And then Clay had come along with his easy charm and old-fashioned attitude that said it was okay for him to want to take care of her…when she had still been learning how to take care of herself.

Was it his fault that he'd been born into a wealthy family?

No. But it wasn't her fault that she'd been born into a family who'd had to work hard for every single thing they had, either. And Tessa had wanted to prove that she was cut from the same cloth. That she could work just as hard and achieve just as much as they had. All on her own.

It wasn't rational. She would be the first to admit it. But it was what it was.

She finished up the sectioning of the tumor and dropped the last piece into the collection tray to be taken to Pathology. "How are you getting on?"

"Almost done." He glanced over at her surgical site to find her putting in the sutures. "I'm probably fifteen minutes behind you, if you want to go get cleaned up."

"Do you mind if I watch?" She smiled. "After all, you got to watch me a few days ago."

She wondered if he'd even remember what she was referring to, when he'd stood on that observation deck and made her feel so nervous. She'd started out today as a bundle of nerves as well, but had calmed down once she'd realized he had been just as engrossed in his surgery as she'd been in hers. It had felt almost good to be working side by side with him.

No. Not good. Just not crazy scary, as she'd expected it to be. Maybe even like the equals she'd wanted to be all those years ago.

It gave her more hope that they'd be able to come to some sort of accord, since it was inevitable that they'd see each other from time to time around the hospital, just as they had today in the ER.

So maybe she wouldn't have to avoid him, as she'd thought she would. Maybe she could just smile and walk on by when she happened to see him, instead of ducking into a room and hiding, as she'd resorted to a few days ago.

He smiled back at her, giving her a jolt when his teeth

flashed that slow sexy smile she'd once loved so much. "I don't mind at all, Dr. Camara. By all means…watch me."

A wave of heat washed over her at the words. Because she could remember a time he'd said just that. Only he hadn't been operating at the time. No, he'd been lifting her hips, getting ready to…

God! She physically shook her head, trying to rid it of the images that were now spiraling out of control. How he'd wanted her to watch as he sank into her. Slowly. Deeply.

And she had.

She finished her last stitch and tied it. Then had the nurse cut the suture before dropping her needle into the discard tray, her thoughts in a tizzy.

So…she could just grin and give Clay a happy wave whenever she saw him? Evidently not. He'd just shot that idea to hell.

She took a step back from the table, wanting nothing more than to flee the room. But to do that would look funny after everyone in the surgical suite had heard her ask to watch him complete his surgery. And they'd also heard her ask him out to dinner.

More heat poured through her, pushing blood into her head and making it pound with embarrassment. What had she been thinking? She'd wanted to set the record straight—apologize—but there had to have been a better way to do it than going out to eat with him.

Too late to do anything about it now.

And he probably hadn't even meant his words the way she'd taken them. He'd just been giving her permission to observe him.

Watch me.

Oh, hell. There it was again.

Think about something else, Tessa.

She focused on his hands, watching those long nimble fingers as they worked on Mr. Phillips's leg. Fingers she could remember running over her in passion, drawing forth reactions she hadn't known she was capable of.

Make this about his job. Not about what you once meant to each other.

She looked at him with new eyes. And what she saw impressed her. He was good at what he did. Confident. Unerring. Just as she hoped to be one day.

If she could just fix herself on those kinds of thoughts, she would be able to get through dinner, and he'd be none the wiser about anything. Like how she still turned to mush just looking at him.

Please, no. Just get through tonight.

Once they were done eating, she would slide back into her normal routine and forget this surgery—with all its terrible revelations—had ever happened.

CHAPTER SIX

"So you're going for a fellowship in Mohs?"

They were sitting in a small restaurant around the corner from the hospital two hours after completing the surgery on Mr. Phillips. Tessa had ordered some scans to make sure the tumor had not metastasized past the site on his leg.

She'd acted strangely at the end of the surgery, though, and Clay had wondered if she was going to back out of dinner. And maybe she should have. Or he should have. It didn't feel half-bad, sitting across from her. Some of the bitterness and resentment he'd had toward her seemed to have leached away over the years.

"Yes, I was planning on applying in the fall, hoping to get an early start."

The waiter interrupted, bringing their wine and taking their orders. When he left again, Clay leaned forward. "I know Dr. Wesley, head of Oncology. We're friends, actually. I could put in a good word for you."

There was silence at the table for about five seconds. Then Tessa's face turned pink. But it wasn't the soft color that had infused her skin in the operating room, filling him with a heat that had threatened to make itself known to everyone in the vicinity. No, this was a very different kind of red.

She was angry. At least he thought she was.

"Do you think I can't get the fellowship on my own?"

What the hell?

"I just thought since I knew Josiah, I could—"

"Take care of it for me. Help me out."

"Is there a problem with one doctor helping another?"

It was what doctors did all the time. Part of the politics of a hospital, whether he liked it or not. There were a lot more residents than there were fellowship slots. Most people he knew would welcome anything that gave them an edge.

"I don't need any favors, Clay. Or gifts. Or scholarships. Not anymore."

The soft words were said with such quiet conviction that they took him aback. They'd had many arguments about his gift-giving over the course of their relationship, but had their problems extended even further than what he'd thought? "Are you talking about my parents? Was that what our breakup was about…them helping you with a few expenses?"

And there it was. The bitterness he'd felt standing in front of the door of her dorm room was back with a vengeance. He should have known they couldn't have a meal together without getting into some kind of argument. The woman had a chip on her shoulder the size of Mount Everest.

"A few expenses? *Meu Deus!* It was more like my whole education." Her voice rose enough that a couple of people at nearby tables glanced their way. She closed her eyes, her chest rising and falling as she took a deep breath and let it out. "Look at it from my perspective. I thought I had earned that scholarship. I worked hard in college and applied for every financial aid opportunity under the sun. And then to find out that my scholarship had nothing to do with merit or anything else I'd done…"

His stomach tightened. "Why didn't you say anything while we were together?"

"Because I didn't know where the money came from. Not until the day of my graduation." She toyed with her fork, eyes not meeting his.

"You didn't know until…"

Everything fell into place in an instant: why she'd thrown their relationship away with a haughty look of disdain, why she hadn't wanted to talk about anything.

But it was only money.

"No, and you went out with me and never said a single word about it the whole time we were together." Her eyes did come up this time. "I felt so humiliated. My rich boyfriend's parents paid my way through one of the best medical schools in the country. Only no one saw fit to tell me."

When she put it that way, he could see why she'd been so upset that day. But his parents had certainly felt as if she'd deserved the scholarship—had seen it as an investment in the future. Yes, they had a soft spot for Tessa's folks—they were good friends, in fact—but they weren't the kind of people who threw money at a cause they didn't believe was worthy. They'd expected Clay to work just as hard as they did. And Tessa *had* made stellar grades. Better than his, even.

His anger faded. He reached across the table, touching her face. "My parents may have paid the tuition, but you're the one who earned that degree, Tess, not them. I know how many hours you put in studying. And if their scholarship hadn't paid your way, any other awards agency would have been happy to step up to fill in any gaps. Is it so terrible that it was my mom and dad who happened to set it up?"

Her gaze held his for a long second. "I don't know what to think. My parents didn't know about it, either. Wouldn't it have been easier if they had just told us about everything up front?"

"They probably thought your parents would refuse the money if they knew who it came from. They're proud. Very much like a certain young doctor I know." He took his hand away and sat back.

A small smile played about her lips. "I'm just a little proud."

"Oh, Tessa, if that's your definition of *a little*..." He sighed, then fixed her with a look. "You're going to be a damn good doctor. You already are, in fact. I saw you operate on Mr. Phillips's leg."

He hesitated about saying the next thing that came to his mind, but went ahead. "Your mother would be proud of all you've accomplished. And I know your dad is. Mom says he talks nonstop about you."

Tessa's eyes turned soft and moist, the green glittering like meadow grass covered with dew.

"Thank you." The words came out a shattered whisper. "My dad and I miss her more than words can say."

Suddenly his focus slid lower. To the pink lips that had once parted beneath his own. He wanted to part them again...to use his mouth to chase away the pain and grief he heard in her voice.

As if she heard his thoughts, something simmered in the air between them. An electric current that seemed to draw them closer and closer.

If not for the fact that there was a table and plates between them, he might have leaned across and kissed her right then and there—to see if the experience was as heady as he remembered.

But there *was* a table…along with a whole lot of baggage. So he picked up his fork and speared one of the meatballs on his plate of spaghetti instead. Just because she'd confessed the reasons why she'd broken things off with him, there was no reason to think they could pick up where they left off.

They couldn't.

Too much time had passed. He had a daughter and an ex-wife. He, more than anyone, should know when to leave well enough alone.

Tessa took a bite of her salad, her gaze now traveling around the room. Time to steer the conversation toward something a little more superficial.

"How is Marcos and everyone over at the studio?"

She smiled. "Still as ornery as ever. They're excited about the exhibition." She paused. "Which reminds me, I totally forgot to call him and ask which day would be best."

"Better sooner than later. Molly saw a movie a few weeks ago about a kid who learns to do all kinds of fancy karate moves. She's been going on about it nonstop. *Capoeira* isn't karate, but I think it would seem like it to her."

"I'm sure Marcos wouldn't mind her coming in. I'll try to ask him sometime tomorrow morning." Tessa's lips pursed for a second. "I'm sorry about your divorce."

The shift back to personal subjects took him by surprise, hitting a little too close to home. "Long-term relationships don't suit me, evidently."

She laughed. "You and me both. Your daughter is beautiful, though, so something good came out of it."

Yes, it had.

"She's my life."

Those simple words contained more truth than he'd handed to anyone in ages. They cut to the heart of who he was now, barreling past the flip replies that seemed to come far too easily these days.

He could only hope he and Lizza had spared Molly most of the ugliness that had gone along with their breakup. Those last few months hadn't been pleasant ones. Thankfully Molly had been too young to understand what the fights and arguments had been about back then—unlike now. He did his best, but he still got a sick feeling in the pit of his stomach whenever it was Lizza's turn to have her for the weekend.

He wouldn't put his daughter into a volatile situation like that marriage ever again. Remaining unattached was the best way to guarantee he didn't. Which meant no kissing of spunky redheads was allowed. Unless it was a single night of summer madness that lasted no longer than that.

Now that he'd settled that he could lean back and enjoy himself.

They ate for the next fifteen minutes, the silence broken only by comments about the food and how good it was. The tension that had filled the operating room and their initial meeting seemed to have faded away. Instead, it felt more like those periods of quiet companionship they'd once shared.

Only this wasn't four years ago. It was now. And where he'd once walked with confidence, he now needed to tread with care. For Molly's sake.

And his own.

Tessa's hand slid over his. "Hey. Thank you for understanding. About what happened all those years ago."

Clay wasn't sure he'd call it understanding in the sense

that she meant it. Instead, maybe it was an acknowledgment that mistakes had been made on both their parts.

It wasn't a new day exactly. But the warmth of her skin against his made him think about that single night of summer madness idea he'd had moments earlier. And how he might just like to experience a night like that.

Not smart, Clay.

That didn't stop him from turning his hand so that his palm was facing up and catching her fingers in his.

And then, opening himself to what could be madness itself, he lifted her hand and kissed it.

Shock went through Tessa's system at the firm press of his lips against her skin. Memories old and new swirled through her head and her eyes locked with his as he slowly lowered her hand back to the table. But he didn't let go.

His plate was empty. So was hers.

"Do you want dessert, Tessa?"

She did. Only it was the forbidden kind that she'd enjoy for a little while and then regret the moment she swallowed the last little bite.

She shook her head, still unable to look away.

Not bothering to ask for the check, Clay released her long enough to throw a couple of bills on the table and then stood, hand outstretched.

Her tummy began to twist and turn, half in anticipation, half in fear of what she might say or do.

She gripped his fingers and let him haul her out of her seat in a way that felt like old times—when neither of them had been able to wait for what came next.

Only Tessa no longer knew what that was.

He towed her through the restaurant, nodding at the hostess, who wished them good-night. Then they were outside in the balmy New York air and her back was against the rough adobe finish of the restaurant.

With Clay standing in front of her. Inside her personal space.

He was so close, and when his thumb swept over the back of her hand she jumped.

"Scared?"

Yes. But she knew when to lie. "Not at all. Should I be?"

His fingers gripped even tighter and he gave a slow, knowing smile. "Absolutely."

"Why is that?" Okay, now she was not only scared, she was dying for him to come a little closer, everything inside her coiling in readiness.

And desire.

Another couple went by them on their way to the front entrance of the restaurant, glancing quickly at them and then away again as if afraid of intruding on an intimate moment.

And they were.

Clay must have felt it, too, because he leaned next to her ear. "Exactly how soon do you need to be home, Tessa?"

Her stomach dropped to her feet. Was he asking if she had to be home, period? Because she had no idea what she was going to say if he asked her to spend the night with him.

Um... Okay, think this through for a minute.

He probably didn't mean what she thought he did. It had to be something else. Something different, and she was being stupid and naive.

Except he was still stroking his thumb over her skin with featherlight sweeps that were driving her crazy. And his breath was still warm against the side of her face.

She bit her lip, struggling against the need to close her eyes and just go with the flow. If he did mean what she thought he meant…would she say yes?

Yes.

"I don't have to be home right away. Why?"

How was that for prevaricating? She gave herself a high five for quick thinking.

"It's a beautiful night. I thought we might start with a walk in the park."

Start with?

Her stomach dropped a little lower. Central Park was one place they'd gone when they'd been dating. To either walk or study…or find a secluded spot.

They'd been kids back then, though.

So thirty-year-olds didn't make out?

He doesn't want to make out with you, Tessa. Get real!

"Do you go to the park a lot these days?"

"Sometimes. It's a good place to clear my head after surgery."

Had he gone there after she'd broken things off with him—walked around all by himself? Somehow that thought made her heart ache. But he'd never called again after that scene at her dorm, or even acted as if it had been a big shock.

They'd been fighting on and off for months before that. It had been inevitable that things would eventually come to a head. If he'd just heard the cry of her heart back then, maybe the end of the relationship wouldn't have been so bitter. They could have parted as friends and gone their separate ways with nothing but fond memories of their time together.

But, of course, that's not what had happened. And she couldn't take back what she'd said to him, even if she wanted to. She still felt justified in breaking things off, in some ways.

She hadn't wanted Clay's gifts or to have him fix things or take care of her. She'd just wanted his love and respect. He'd never been able to understand that. And maybe he still didn't, judging from his offer to put in a good word for her with Dr. Wesley.

Enough, Tessa. Let it go.

One thing she did want to do was go for that walk he'd suggested. Just to put to rest any animosity between them. Although she definitely wasn't sensing any from his side right now.

So she gave his hand a quick squeeze. "The park sounds good."

Twenty minutes later they were looking over the pond as a couple of runners glided past on silent feet. "I remember when I was a teenager," Tessa said, "Mom told me to stay out of the park at night. Things sure have changed over the years."

"My folks were the same way. In fact, I doubt my mother would come here after dark even now unless she had a police escort, and even then it's iffy." He gave a low chuckle. "I probably won't admit I came here, even now." Clay probably wouldn't admit it to anyone, actually. Especially his mom, who'd been stunned by the abrupt end of their relationship, although Clay had broken it to her in a completely different way, telling her that the decision had been mutual. There'd been no reason to poison his folks' attitude toward her, and at the time he'd had no idea that his parents' scholarship had had anything to do with how Tessa saw him.

Evidently it had.

He was doubly glad he'd handled it the way he had

with them. They'd be hurt. Devastated, actually, if they thought they'd had anything to do with her dumping him.

He wished she'd said something. Anything. Maybe they could have worked it out.

No, they couldn't have. If not because of Tessa, because of him. He'd failed at two relationships. There was no reason to think he'd be successful at a third. He had Molly to think about should things get messy.

And they always got messy. Especially when there was lust pumping through his veins that was as strong as it had ever been.

A police officer came walking by, pausing to glance their way as if mentally assessing the situation. Clay nodded at him and the cop returned the gesture, continuing on his way.

"That's why things are so much better," she murmured. "And it's been cleaned up. It's beautiful here."

It was, with the soft glow of the park lights gleaming off the water…and off Tessa's hair.

Hell, part of the reason he'd suggested coming to the park had been to give himself a chance to think about what he was doing. Kissing her…or anything else was sheer madness.

Yes, it was. The madness of a single summer night.

The words whispered through his skull, a terrible litany that demanded to be heard. Demanded an answer.

Kiss her.

The urge he'd had at the restaurant was back. Stronger than ever.

As if sensing his thoughts, Tessa turned her face toward him, and her eyes widened. Damn. She always had been able to read him.

And since she could…

He moved a step closer, waiting to see if she'd back

away from him. She didn't. So his fingers went to her face, tracing across her right cheekbone, her skin warm and soft, just as it always used to be. He couldn't remember feeling anything softer. Not even Lizza, who always had some kind of cream or ointment smeared over her skin.

Tessa's felt…real. That was the only way he could think to describe it. Flesh and bone, and the softest, silkiest skin known to man.

"Hey." Why he'd said that particular word, he had no idea, except it had always been a kind of signal between them. And it had almost always been followed by a meeting of their lips.

Right on cue, hers curved up at the edges. "Hey, yourself."

That was all it took. His hand went to her nape and drew her closer. It wouldn't be the first time people in the park had seen couples kissing—or more.

And as much as he wanted to just plaster his mouth over hers and grab at everything she'd let him take, he didn't. Instead, he barely touched her. Just a gentle press and release. When her hands went to his shoulders, he repeated the move, his fingers sliding into the hair at the base of her skull as their lips met again. Parted.

As if protesting his teasing, her teeth nipped his bottom lip, sharp enough to sting.

Okay, honey, don't say I didn't try to resist…

This time, when his mouth met hers, all hesitation was gone, and he let her feel the frustration and desire he'd been fighting for the past week. Out it came, spilling over him in a torrent, making him crush her to him as he continued to deepen the kiss.

A quick wolf whistle by another passing jogger almost made him smile. Almost.

Still holding her, he edged her back a little way until they were behind a stand of landscaping that was just tall enough to give them a modicum of privacy. If the cop came back, he'd probably scowl at them and send them on their way.

Clay was willing to risk it. And more. He crowded her against a tree as his mouth again took possession of hers. Tessa made a small sound at the back of her throat, the hands that had been on his shoulders winding around his neck instead as if she needed to burrow closer. Her breasts flattened against his chest. He ached to reach up and cup them—to see if the weight in his palms was as perfect as it always had been. But he didn't think Tessa wanted to risk a night in jail.

Although there'd been a time when neither of them would have cared. And they hadn't—Tessa coaxing him into the lush greenery of the park and making a few of his deepest fantasies come true.

Just the memory made his flesh leap.

It had been so long.

And when her mouth pulled away from his, he muttered a curse beneath his breath, only to have her laugh and kiss her way up his jaw. "The problem with the park being safer is there are also more people."

"I don't remember that being a problem before."

Her fingers floated down his chest, sliding over his nipples. He sucked in a quick breath.

She'd always been a daredevil at heart—not a hint of shrinking violet in her. Maybe it was the heated Brazilian blood flowing in her veins.

"Tess, I don't think you want to do this."

"Don't I?"

Her hands slid around to the back of his waist and ducked beneath the band of his slacks. She pulled him just a little bit closer, until there was no doubt that she could feel what she did to him. Because it was right there, pulsing against her, wanting nothing more than to shove her clothes aside and take care of business right then and there.

Not a good idea. Not only because of the venue but because if he was going to have her, he damn well wanted it to last more than a few seconds. He wanted to see every last inch of her, feel every secret dip and swell and run his tongue along all those soft curves.

He pulled back, gritting his teeth at the whimper of protest that tempted him to give in and start all over again.

"No," he muttered, his voice coming out rough and dark, even to his own ears. "Not here."

Green eyes blinked up at him. "What?"

Holding her back so he could fully see her face, he gave her a smile that held every lusty imagining he'd ever entertained about her.

"I don't want a quickie in the park. And I damn well don't want it on a night when you have to get up at the crack of dawn." He leaned in until his lips were against her ear, breathing in her scent and letting it slide back out. "It's going to happen at my place, Tessa. And I'm going to keep you there all night long."

CHAPTER SEVEN

CHOP-CHOP-CHOP.

Short little fingers connected with his shoulder in a sharp triplet that had him shaking his head.

Chop-chop-chop. The hatchet-like barrage was repeated for what seemed like the hundredth time.

Clay's mom, standing in the kitchen stirring a pot of pasta, laughed at the bloodcurdling shriek Molly gave for effect.

He gave her a sour look. "Don't encourage her."

Clay had tried a reward system with his daughter, had tried reasoning with her, but nothing seemed to deter her.

The girl spun around on her toes, her hands making various slicing motions that would make any masseuse proud to know her.

"I'm not encouraging her." His mom pointed the wooden spoon at him, eyes crinkling in the corners even though it was obvious she was trying her best not to smile. "Like I said earlier, the sooner you can get her over to that studio, the better."

It had been two days since he and Tessa had kissed in the park, and he'd railed at himself at least a thousand times since. What had he been thinking, promising her a steamy night at his place? He didn't take women there. Ever.

Chop-chop-chop. Molly turned her efforts to one of the bar stools, while Jack laid his head on his paws and did his best to blend into the beige carpet. With his black and white spots, it wasn't working out very well for him.

He patted the side of the chair, inviting his parents' dog over to him. Jack glanced at Molly and then with a low *woof* came over and plopped down on the floor beside him.

"You're not fooling anyone, you old softie," he said, scratching behind the Dalmatian's ears. "She's got you wrapped around her little finger just like the rest of us."

As if to agree, the dog pulled in a deep breath and let it out in a sigh, his brown eyes closing, lids flickering as he fell asleep.

If only he could go to sleep that quickly and easily. But lying in his bed was torture. Especially after telling Tessa he was going to keep her in it all night. Every time he started to drift off, images danced behind his eyelids and he'd jerk back awake.

Chop-chop-chop.

This time it was Clay who was holding back a smile. Just when he got too hung up on all that was wrong with his life, this little girl swooped into his field of vision and turned it all right again.

Getting up from his seat, he went over and caught her up in his arms. "Let's say we go get those little choppers all washed and clean for dinner."

Molly giggled and wrapped her arms around his neck. "When are we going to see *capo…capo…*?" Her tongue struggled over the pronunciation.

"Capoeira." He drew the word out slowly so she could hear it. "And we're going soon. Very soon."

I hope.

With that, he swept her down the hall, knowing that

as soon as dinner was over her little karate chops would start all over again. And continue on the drive home, until she finally fell asleep in her bed.

We're all friends here.

Were they?

Tessa had hoped Clay wouldn't come to the *capoeira* studio when she was there, but Marcos had made a scoffing sound. Right before making his comment about them all being friends.

Besides, he had something to run by her, he'd said. And by Clay.

That filled her with trepidation more than anything.

She pulled up to the studio to see that Clay's car was already in the parking lot, but he wasn't in it. Great. She definitely didn't want Marcos relaying some scheme while she wasn't there to mediate. She'd never told the director of the studio what had happened between her and her ex, and he'd never asked. But surely, since Clay had stopped coming in to train, he'd figured out they were no longer together. At least she hoped he did.

When she pushed through the door to the studio, she saw the man in question immediately. He was there in the middle of a swarm of *capoeiristas* with his daughter. Everything in her relaxed. He'd said he wanted Molly to see a training session, so it hadn't just been a line.

And after that kissing session in the park she'd halfway expected him to show up on her floor and start making plans about that night he'd talked about.

She'd had second thoughts about that. She could only hope his absence meant that he'd reconsidered, as well.

It had been a warm, dark evening, and the park had been beautiful. It had been natural that it would bring up old memories and emotions.

Emotions that had no place in her hectic life right now. She was getting ready to complete her residency and apply for that fellowship. The last thing she needed to do was rekindle a romance that was dead and gone.

Was it?

Of course it was. But she was also a young woman with normal urges. And it had been a very long time since she'd been with a man. Well over a year.

If Clay propositioned her, she couldn't guarantee she'd say no. But it would be with the understanding that it was just about the sex.

S-E-X. Nothing more.

That tick-tick-tick going on inside her chest was not some biological clock warning her time was running out. Her residency took priority. But once that was done she planned on looking into adoption. Or checking into in vitro fertilization, using a sperm donor.

Clay's blue eyes met hers and one side of his mouth tilted up in that crazy sexy smile. Okay, so she'd been staring at him as all those thoughts had gone wriggling through her head—just like a thousand swimmers all headed for the prize. Great. Clay was *not* a potential sperm donor, and she hardly thought he'd be amenable to dumping a sample in a cup and handing it over to some fertility expert.

No, he'd want his donation to be up close and personal.

She shivered for a second before realizing Marcos had said something.

Clay's brow went up, his smile widening.

Caught again! Damn.

She dragged her eyes away from him and found Marcos at the front of the room. "I'm sorry?"

"I said it was good to have Clay back in the studio, Tessita. Do you not think so?"

Tessita. Oh, no. He was already irritated with her.

"Yes. Of course it is." She kept her eyes off Clay and fixed them firmly on Marcos.

"Do you want to show him what you're working on?"

"What?" Oh, no. She hadn't planned on training in front of him. "It can wait. Really. I think he just wanted his daughter to see what *capoeira* is."

"And who better to show it to her than someone who has mastered the sport, *não é*?" Marcos held out his hand. "After all, he has seen you train before. He has trained with you."

I've done more than that, Clay's glance seemed to say.

She wanted to send Marcos a biting reply in their native tongue, but Clay would know they were talking about him. Or arguing about him. She didn't want him to think his being here bothered her at all.

Even if it did.

Marcos clapped his hands. "Form the circle. And we begin."

The *practicantes* gathered in a loose ring, Clay standing just a bit back, still holding Molly up where she could see.

Tessa hadn't even changed into her *capoeira* gear yet—she'd been running late from the hospital. All those recent night shifts had wreaked havoc on her concentration. She also hadn't expected to be dragged into an impromptu exhibition. So she was in yoga pants and a loose T-shirt.

Something in her wondered exactly what Marcos had up his sleeve.

She moved to join the circle of students, dragging her T-shirt to the side and tying a knot to hold it tight against her waist. The last thing she wanted was for it to ride up in front of everyone when she did some of the flips and twists she'd been practicing.

The studio's tambourine players started things off, snapping out the typical beat of the studio, while the stringed bow added its own unique twist. The rest of the circle joined in, clapping and chanting in time with the beat. Pointing at two of the studio members, Marcos signaled for them to be the first to enter the ring. The men moved forward and began the advances and feints that were typical of the martial art. One of the men fell as he attempted a single twist backflip, but leaped back to his feet.

"Ai caramba, gente. Força!" Marcos waved the man out of the circle and jabbed a finger at another participant, who took his place. The other *capoeirista* didn't miss a beat, just engaged the new guy. Back and forth they went in a perfectly synchronized dance that often came within a foot or two of crashing into the bodies that formed the human cage behind them but not so close as to be a real danger to anyone.

Tessa clapped in time with everyone else, but glanced back at Clay, who stood on the outside of the ring. She'd always stood next to him in days past, translating whenever Marcos had gone on a tirade about something in Portuguese. He nodded, indicating he got the gist of it, although with the way the fallen guy had slunk out of the center of the circle it was pretty obvious he'd been scolded. He shifted his daughter to the other arm and said something to the girl with a smile. She then started clapping along with everyone else.

She couldn't hold back her own smile. One of her earliest memories was of watching her dad in the ring, doing some of these very same moves, and the memory of receiving her very first cord—the *capoeira* equivalent of

a belt. It had been white. She'd rapidly worked her way
up the ranks, although her advancement had slowed once
she'd gone to medical school and had only been able to
come once a week rather than the usual three that most
of the serious participants trained. The purple and green
cordão she currently owned signified she could be an ap-
prentice instructor if she wanted to.

But she didn't have time to do anything except practice
medicine and come to the studio once a week.

Marcos treated her as if she were one, though, being
tougher on her than he was on a lot of the other students.
Since she was participating in the exhibition, he had good
reason to be. One mistake and the public demonstration
would be ruined—and, like most Brazilians, he would
see it as a reflection on his teaching abilities. And he
would not be pleased.

Marcos motioned for a new player to enter the ring,
the flow in and out of the circle seamlessly performed.
A few minutes later it was her turn.

Gritting her teeth, she forced her concentration to spi-
ral down to what was contained within the circle, not allowing it to stray as she performed a low bent cartwheel,
which moved her to the center of the area. She immediately went into a *cadeira* squat as the other player swung
his leg in an arc over her back.

Clay had once said *capoeira* looked like a form of
breakdancing. With the sweeping circular movements
and spins, she could see why he thought that. But a lot of
the moves were contained in other martial arts—they'd
just been modified a bit and put to a beat. *Capoeira* had
become a kind of art in motion in a lot of studios, rather
than outright combat.

She twisted her body and went on her hands, both legs

gliding over the other person's bent head. Keeping the rhythm pulsing in her brain, she swept over and around and circled her opponent, her body constantly in motion, gaining speed as she went.

Her rival matched her move for move until there was nothing but the leaps and vaults and spins that swept her into another realm. Tessa likened it to a trancelike state, except she was aware of everything. Even the small commotion currently going on somewhere outside the circle. Her opponent backed up a few paces, still sweeping and twisting and ducking in time to her moves, but she sensed a change coming. Then he was leaving the ring and another player was entering. Not a *craque*, as she called experienced *capoeiristas*, but a novice.

She dialed down her pace and with a backward twist came face-to-face with her new partner. She faltered, almost falling right onto her head in the middle of a handstand before catching herself.

It was Clay.

What was he doing? And where was his daughter?

Those two thoughts ran through her head before Clay jumped high into the air, one leg sweeping over her as she came out of her handstand. She countered him with a leap of her own, her foot coming within inches of his chest as he spun back and went into a low crouch, one leg going beneath hers as she leaped over it.

Her heart began pounding, her concentration slipping in and out as they continued to parry and evade, advance and retreat. It was as if somewhere inside Clay he'd retained everything he'd been taught. Still a novice, but sure and confident and never giving quarter if she didn't force him to. And she had to. She had to put an end to this or she was going to make a fool of herself in front of everyone. She edged in closer, still twisting and turning and leaning back whenever a foot or hand swished past her. She looked for an opening and found it within seconds. Making it look like an accident, she swept Clay's legs out from under him in the *batizado* move she'd taken him down with all those years ago.

And he did go down, his back hitting the mat with a loud slap that reverberated through the studio. Breathing heavily in the absolute silence that followed—since the drums and other instruments had stopped playing—she stood over him, only vaguely aware that he'd suddenly moved with lightning speed, his legs scissoring hers and jerking them out from under her. She fell right across his chest.

Argh!

She opened her mouth to yell foul, but instead found herself laughing. He'd learned a thing or two since leaving the studio, evidently. Because even though she'd gotten the best of him, he hadn't let that stop him from turning things right back around.

The sound of someone clapping in a slow, rhythmic way broke through everything else.

"This!" It was Marcos, and far from being angry at how she'd stopped the session he seemed delighted. "There is still that same fire between you. You must bring this to the exhibition."

What? Her eyes widened in horror, and she leaped to her feet with a clumsiness she'd never had in the ring before.

No, no, no!

This was Marcos's plan for the big finale he'd talked about?

There was no way in hell she was going up against Clay during that exhibition. She wouldn't have even done it now if she'd known her friend was going to throw him into the ring while she was there.

Clay stood as well, leaning down to her ear. "Did you know about this?"

Well, if Marcos wasn't angry, Clay more than made up for it. Because he was furious.

"No, I did not know." Her voice came out as a hiss that matched his.

Several other players came into the circle and slapped Clay on the back, everyone laughing and talking at the same time, completely unaware of the tension flowing between them.

"What better way to end the exhibition than to have two doctors from West Manhattan Saints enter the *roda* together?" Marcos smiled at both of them. "We will have posters made up with your pictures and—"

"I'm sorry. I can't." Clay's voice cut off the spiel in midstream. His easy charm was nowhere to be seen.

Tessa swallowed hard, trying not to let the pricking sensation in her gut mean anything.

Marcos countered, "But it will be perfect."

Perfect? A perfect disaster maybe.

She shook her head, agreeing with Clay, even as the jabbing in her midsection increased. "It won't work. There's not enough time to practice. The festival is only three weeks away."

"I will train you myself. And it will be a *good* thing if the moves don't look so planned. It will help people see that anyone can train in *capoeira*."

"Sorry. No." Clay headed out of the ring, going to where one of the other members held Molly and taking her.

The little girl, unaware of the tight lines of her father's

jaw, brought the side of her hand down on Clay's shoulder with a quick whack. "Fun!"

No, it hadn't been fun. Clay's outright rejection hurt more than she wanted to admit, but he was right. Her nerves were stretched to the breaking point just from being in the practice ring with him. If she had to go up against him in front of thousands of people...

She'd be a wreck.

No, Clay had made the right call. And if she knew him, nothing would change his mind.

Not Marcos...or anyone.

Peter Lloyd was seated behind his desk, writing furiously on a report, when Clay entered the room. He had no idea what the hospital administrator wanted. In fact, he'd only met the man a couple of times. Once when he'd decided to transfer to the hospital to be closer to his apartment and his mom and dad's place. And the other had been when he'd come in to fill out the paperwork. To be suddenly called down to his office made no sense. Unless there was something he still needed to do to finish his file.

"Ah, Dr. Matthews, come in and have a seat. I'll be with you in just a moment." True to his word, the man kept writing while Clay lowered himself into one of the leather chairs that flanked his desk.

Nothing like trying to intimidate your prey.

Only Clay wasn't intimidated. He'd done nothing wrong.

Mr. Lloyd glanced up from his papers and pulled another sheet in front of him. "You've heard about the yearly Health Can Be Fun festival we hold to fund cancer research by now."

Clay immediately tensed. He still hadn't volunteered to do anything. He'd meant to do it this week, but then the *capoeira* session had messed with his head. As had Tessa. She seemed just as anxious to avoid being paired together as he was.

Except in Central Park. She'd certainly seemed willing to be paired in a completely different way when they'd been there.

"If this is about the sign-up sheet, I know I haven't put my name on it yet, but I will. I fully intend to support the campaign."

Tessa's mom came to mind. How great would it be if someday cancer no longer took loved ones from their families?

"Good, good." The man pushed the paper away. "Glad to hear it because a special opportunity has just presented itself."

"It has?" Clay had no idea what the administrator was talking about. But he got the feeling he was about to find out.

"Actually, the opportunity is for you and Dr. Camara. It'll provide great exposure for the hospital."

His gut clenched. Had Tessa actually come back here and said something about the *capoeira* studio? She'd seemed just as against it as he was. Or had that all been an act?

He forced his mouth to say the words. "What exactly does this opportunity entail?"

Mr. Lloyd sat back in his chair. "I hear that you and Dr. Camara used to train together at one of our sponsor's studios."

He heard the words through a buzzing in his skull that was growing louder by the minute. "Are you talking about Traditional Capoeira of Brazil?"

"Yes. So you already know what I'm going to ask."

Clay shook his head. "Not really." Actually, he did, but he was hoping against hope he was wrong.

"The owner of the studio stopped by and made a convincing argument. He said this could be a huge draw to the festival. It would help the studio, and it would help the hospital. A win on both sides." Mr. Lloyd reached behind his desk and pulled out a rolled-up poster board. When he slid the rubber band off the tube of paper Clay's clenched gut tightened even further. It was an old snapshot of him and Tessa at his ceremonial induction, when his first cord had been presented to him.

Tessa's leg was outstretched and poised just behind his knee. It was right before he'd gone down. Only the image had now been blown up to gargantuan proportions.

Hell. He and Tessa looked happy.

Really happy.

Looking at her face, he could remember what they used to be like together.

"I don't think Dr. Camara is going to agree to this. In fact, I'm pretty sure this would not be a good idea."

The administrator frowned. "You're new here, aren't you, Dr. Matthews."

"As of a week ago, yes." That was when he realized he wasn't actually being asked if he would like to participate, he was being told.

"The studio has been one of our sponsors for a number of years. In fact, their exhibitions always attract quite a crowd." He sent Clay a smile that looked genuine for the most part. "Hell, even my wife went over and took a few lessons from them after seeing it one year. So what do you say?"

There was a pregnant pause while the administrator's eyes remained on his.

What choice did he have?

"I guess I say yes, provided Dr. Camara agrees." Tessa was going to have his hide. "Have you already spoken with her about it?"

"I thought I'd leave that to you. She was already planning on taking part in the exhibition, so this shouldn't be much of a surprise to her."

Oh, it was going to be a surprise, all right. And not a good one. He'd be lucky if he came out of there with his head intact.

"I'll see what I can do."

Great move, Clay.

He sighed. Surely they could work together for five or six hours without killing each other. And it would benefit the hospital and those in need. No big tragedy. They were both adults. They would get through this and come out stronger on the other side, right?

"Oh, and we'll want to get your and Dr. Camara's formal permission to use this poster. We'll put some of them up in the hospital entryway and some other places. It'll help get the word out about one of the highlights of the festival."

Highlights?

It just kept getting worse.

The last thing he wanted was to have a spotlight placed on that picture of him and Tessa together. Not because it was embarrassing or humiliating but because it hit too close to home—was too much of a reminder of what he and Tessa had once meant to each other.

She was going to blow her top when she heard about this. And his parents. They were going to get their hopes up that he and Tessa would get back together. At least his mother would. Of that he had no doubt. He was somehow going to have to figure out a way to nip that in the bud. Because there was no hope. No hope at all.

A single night of summer madness? Well, it looked as if the exhibition might turn into exactly that.

He left the office and headed for the bank of elevators. Once inside one of them, he punched the button for the third floor and leaned against the wall, waiting for the doors to open. When they did, he was surprised to see Tessa there. From the furrowed brows and flashing green eyes he gathered she was upset with someone. Well, so was he.

As he made to step off the car he found a hand planted flat on his chest, pushing him backward. She moved into the space and pressed all the buttons one by one.

What the...?

The doors closed, and it started moving up—with him and Tessa as its only occupants. She turned toward him. "What is going on? I just got a call from Marcos that you've decided to take part in the *capoeira* exhibition after all."

He tried to wrap his head around her words and failed. He'd only just come out of Lloyd's office. Surely word couldn't have gotten back to her or Marcos this fast.

"Did you already know about this?"

The doors on the next floor opened and, when no one got on the car, closed again. The elevator continued on its course.

"Know about what? That you were going to go to the administrator and ask him to put you into the exhibition?"

"No. That would have been you."

"Me?" Her eyes widened. "Why would you think...? Hardly. I thought you said you didn't want to do it."

"I don't."

"Then who...?"

"Marcos." They both said the name at the same time. Clay's muscles relaxed and he leaned back against the wall of the car. Lloyd had said it was Marcos, but he'd only half believed the man.

The elevator stopped again, the doors opened and then closed once more. He could have gotten off and walked up the two remaining flights of stairs to his floor, but he didn't. "So what are we going to do about it?"

"What can we do? Between Marcos and Peter Lloyd they've got us right where they want us."

He laughed. "And where is that?"

"Putting on a show for anyone who wants to watch."

For some reason a lurid image came to mind, of Tessa again sprawled across his chest. But this time, instead of leaping to her feet, he stopped her, his hand sliding into her hair and angling her head within reach of his mouth.

He swallowed hard, trying to banish the mental picture. It didn't work. So he trickled a bit of gasoline on the spark to make her aware that she was treading on dangerous ground. "Then we'd better make that show worth their while, don't you think?"

This time her face tipped up to look at him. Seeing what was written there, her lips parted and she blinked. "That could be awkward, Clay. Very awkward."

"Could it?"

Clay remembered playing these games with her many times in the past. Suddenly all thoughts of his mother getting her hopes up fled as those memories crept closer to summer madness. "They have a poster already made up. The one taken at my *batizado*."

"The one where I… And afterward we went to your place and…"

"That's the one."

Two more floors came and went. After the next one they'd be heading back down the way they had come. The doors opened and this time a nurse got into the elevator.

He nodded a greeting at the newcomer, who turned to stare at the readout, her head craning to the side, probably wondering why so many floors were lit up.

Tessa's cheeks turned a shade of pink he recognized all too well.

She was the one who'd pressed all those buttons. And he realized he'd squandered his chance to act on their time alone. Except that little camera in the corner—which he hadn't noticed until just now—would have caught them in the act. Good thing someone had interrupted or the poster the administrator hung on the walls might be even more suggestive.

Not the kind of staff behavior Mr. Lloyd would approve of.

There was silence for two floors, then the nurse got off, leaving Tessa and Clay alone once again. Despite the danger, he couldn't resist pressing just a bit harder. "So we'll have to practice," he murmured.

"More than likely." She flushed even more.

Hell, he'd love nothing more than to crowd her against that wall and mash his lips to hers. Instead, he crossed his arms over his chest. Time to cool things down a little. "What day were you planning on going over to the studio?"

The elevator stopped again, and this time Tessa pushed the button to hold the doors open. "This is my floor. But I'll be over there Tuesday at five."

"I'll see you there, then." Three days from now. "To practice."

She stepped off in a hurry, saying nothing more. Soon the doors slid back together and cut her off from view.

What the hell had he just gotten himself into?

This was crazy. Except the anticipation flooding his veins and infiltrating his thoughts said something com-

pletely different. That the only crazy thing was thinking about what would happen when the exhibition was
over and done.

And when he and Tessa finally went their separate
ways. Once and for all.

CHAPTER EIGHT

TESSA'S ATTENDING WAVED to her as he walked past the desk where she was reading through some of the newer protocols on melanoma. It seemed research was showing that the depth of the tumor wasn't always the best predictor of whether or not it would metastasize, rather it depended on the type of melanoma itself. So even very thin tumors could be deadly.

"Do you want to check on your patient this morning?" he called.

"Mr. Phillips?" The elderly gentleman was still recovering from surgery on his broken leg. "Have you gotten the results back on his scan?"

Brian backtracked until he stood in front of her. "I was just going to check the computer to see. We can stop by my office on the way."

"Sounds good."

She followed him down the corridor to where some of the staff offices were. Once there, he sat behind his desk and she slid into one of the chairs in front of it. Tapping the keys on his computer, he soon pulled up the file and turned the monitor so they could both look.

Flipping through the different slides, he soon got to one that made Tessa lean forward. "Oh, no."

Mr. Phillips's liver had a couple of hot spots on it, as

did his lungs. "I see them. We'll need to talk to the patient and then assemble a treatment team."

Tessa's heart contracted. The leg break was now suspect, as well—although it could be coincidental, due to his age. They wouldn't know for sure without a bone scan. And at almost eighty she wasn't sure what kind of intervention his body could handle. If they'd caught the cancer earlier…

Memories of her mom's fight came winging back. It had been a similar case, only her tumor had been deepseated, roots extending down to the lower levels of the dermis before it had been caught. By then it had been too late. It had spread everywhere.

None of that helped them right now, though. All they could do was come up with a plan.

Brian looked up. "Thoughts? He's officially your patient."

And this was where the weight of responsibility became heavy. It was one thing when you worked under someone and they made the final decisions. Tessa was rapidly coming to a time in her career where she would make those choices. As much as she might wish it were different, to have it any other way would be a cop-out. Brian was basically handing this case to her. She should be ecstatic. Instead, she was swamped by indecision. But she'd better snap out of it or she may as well hang up her scrubs right now. So she stiffened her spine.

"I concur with what you just said. His daughter flew in to see him pretty soon after surgery, and she's got medical power of attorney in the event that anything happens, if I understood her correctly."

The daughter whose name was Tessa. The memories of Mr. Phillips protecting his modesty seemed bittersweet now.

"Good," Brian said. "DNR order?"

The tightness in her chest grew. *DNR... Do Not Resuscitate.* "I don't know. I was hoping the section was all he'd need."

"I'll need you to check on that. Talk to the daughter."

She knew that Brian didn't mean to sound brusque. It was part of remaining objective enough to do what was best for the patient. And she should be grateful that he was guiding her through the necessary steps, because right now her head was spinning. She'd lost other patients, especially when she'd done her trauma rotation. But there was something about this one...

Maybe because she and Clay had worked side by side on him—as if by joining forces they could double their healing power. But there was an inferno raging within Mr. Phillips's body that would take a miracle to put out.

"I'll talk to her."

"I was going to go down with you, but the fewer people in the room when he hears the news, the better." He studied her across the desk. "Are you up to this?"

Was she? This wasn't going to be an easy conversation. And she could probably say the word and Brian would go down in her place and handle everything. She wouldn't ever have to see Mr. Phillips again. But sometimes caring about a patient meant having to relay difficult news and muddling through it the best you could. And if she was ever going to be able to do this job on her own, she was going to have to take the bad with the good. Walking with the patient, working together to make the very best choices, brought its own rewards—even if that reward was in bringing honor and dignity as they made end-of-life care decisions.

But they weren't there yet. The team would meet and

come to a joint recommendation. That was, depending on what Mr. Phillips wanted to do.

"I'm up to it." She stood. "I'll let you know what the feeling is from Mr. Phillips and his daughter."

"Call me if you need me." He glanced back at the screen, where those bright spots seemed to glitter an unspoken accusation at her. "And, Tessa, I'm sorry. I didn't expect to see this any more than you did. Sometimes these things just don't follow any pattern."

Maybe they did, though, in this case. The tumor hadn't been all that deep, and she'd gotten down to clean margins. But somehow those cancer cells had ventured outside that dark circle and burrowed deep inside Mr. Phillips's body. She wondered if Clay knew yet.

Probably not. He was an orthopedist. That's where his efforts would be concentrated. No need to even contact him with the news. Besides, he could pull the results up just as easily as she could, if he wanted to.

"Thanks. I'll let you know how things go." With that, she left his office. About halfway down the hallway she stopped and leaned against the wall, drawing a couple of deep breaths and trying to organize her thoughts. No sooner had she done that and gotten on the elevator that her time with Clay in this same space filled her head and made tears spring to her eyes.

The back-and-forth innuendos and laughter seemed crude now.

You're being ridiculous. This is part of being a doctor. If you can't handle it, you'd better get out now.

Someday she would take a patient's diagnosis in stride, as Brian did. As Clay probably did. But today was not that day. Not with the anniversary of her mother's death still clinging to her thoughts.

The elevator stopped one floor down and opened,

leaving her staring at the glare from the brightly waxed linoleum tiles. It took the elevator doors marching back toward each other to make her reach out to stop them. She stepped off and glanced at the board that listed the patients and room numbers. Mr. Phillips was still in room five, down to the left.

When she arrived she heard laughter coming from inside. Giving a quick knock and forcing a spring to her step to avoid looking like a funeral director, she entered the room.

Someone was sitting in a chair next to the head of the bed, a grin on his face that was as big as Mr. Phillips's. Two pairs of eyes swung toward her. But it wasn't the man's daughter who sat there. It was Clay.

He kept smiling, but a subtle shift took place as his eyes met hers. She made her own lips curl, although it took an enormous force of the will to get those muscles to tighten.

She glanced around the room, hoping his daughter might be there. But she wasn't. Just Mr. Phillips and Clay.

"What are you two talking about?" she asked. Her voice was light enough, but it had an artificial timbre to it that reminded her of those sweetener packets she used in her coffee.

Mr. Phillips's eyes crinkled around the corners. "Just comparing notes."

"Guy notes." Clay's gaze never left her face.

He knew. She could see it in the slight movements in the muscle at his cheek, in the firming of his glance.

And it was Clay who provided the opening she needed. "I was telling Mr. Phillips his break is healing just the way we like to see. Do you have news on that spot you removed?" He stood and motioned her to take the chair so she could be closer.

"I do. Do you want your daughter to be here?"

Just like that, the crinkles disappeared, dying a terrible death. "That bad, huh?"

Tessa could have taken the chart and studied it as if there was something important written there and avoided meeting Mr. Phillips's gaze altogether, but she wouldn't do that to him. She owed it to him to be direct and honest, without taking away all hope. "Your scan showed some areas that we need to look into."

"Where?"

"Your liver. Your lungs."

The man's breath exited in a soft sigh. "Cancer?"

"We need to do so some more—"

"Tessa." That single word came from Clay.

Mr. Phillips looked from one to the other. "I've been around the block a couple of times. Something's eventually going to get me. Why not this? I've outlived most of my friends. My brothers and sisters. My wife. So just give it to me straight."

Swallowing, she nodded. "Yes. We're pretty sure it's cancer that has spread from your leg. We're going to get a treatment team together and see what we come up with."

He looked at her for a minute or two. "You do your talking. But if it doesn't look like an easy fix, I'm going to have to turn you down. I can't do that to my daughter and son, and she's traveled a long way to see me already. At least I'll have time to say my goodbyes."

Mr. Phillips's wife had died almost ten years ago of a massive stroke. She'd been dead before she'd hit the ground.

Tessa wasn't sure which was worse for those who were left behind. Watching your loved one wither away before your eyes or having them snatched in an instant.

"Do you want me to speak with your daughter?"

"She'll probably want to talk to you herself, but I'd rather break the news to her." Mr. Phillips reached out and gave Tessa's hand a squeeze. "It's okay, honey. I've been ready for a while now."

She wrapped her fingers around his for a few seconds. "As soon as I know something more, I'll let you know."

"I know you will." Rheumy eyes moistened. "I don't mind telling you, I miss my wife. I'll be glad to see her."

Clay's hand landed on her shoulder, whether in support of her or Mr. Phillips she had no idea. But she was glad he was there.

"Don't make your reservations just yet, Mr. Phillips." If she could will someone's cancer to go up in a puff of smoke, this would be the person she did it for. But she couldn't.

"Can I talk to you outside, Dr. Camara?" Clay's low voice made her nod.

But before she got up… "Is there anything you need? How is your pain level?"

"I think it's better than yours right now." Her patient let go of her hand and gave her a smile. "Don't be sad for me, honey. It's going to be okay."

She gave one more nod, unsure she could force another word from her mouth, then stood to her feet, following Clay out of the room.

Once there, he turned to face her. "You okay?"

What was it with male doctors asking her if she was all right? She was a professional, just as they were. Her head went up, along with her temper. "Fine. Why?"

He made a tsking sound with his tongue. "You wouldn't be human if it didn't get to you. Especially with some patients."

"Brian seemed just fine." Her face felt carved out of stone.

A frown appeared on his face. "You saw him?"

"Um, yes. He's my attending. We just finished discussing this particular case."

"That's not what I meant. Did he mention them?"

"Them who? I don't understand." Sadness morphed into confusion.

"You don't know about the jars."

She blinked. "Jars?"

Taking her elbow, he led her a few feet away from Mr. Phillips's door. "It seems some collection jars have been set up at some of the nurses' stations."

Okay, now she was getting irritated. "They always put up jars before the festival. The staff contributes to whatever charity the hospital has chosen this year." It seemed a little weird for him to have pulled her out of a patient's room to tell her that. Unless he was trying to spare her feelings.

"Yeah, I don't think these are the kinds of jars they normally have out."

Glancing across the space, she saw the nurses' station was empty of personnel, but it did indeed have a jar. In fact, there were a pair of them. That was strange. Why would they need two?

She walked toward the containers and squinted at the writing on the first one. Someone's name… Her thoughts fell off abruptly.

No, not someone's name. *Her* name.

The second jar. Oh, Lord! Clay's name.

"What's going on?"

"It appears that news travels around West Manhattan Saints as quickly as it did at my former hospital." His voice came from behind her. "They're betting on who's going to come out ahead during our exhibition match."

Her head whipped around to look at him. "Our exhibition? But that hasn't even been announced yet."

"Oh, it's been announced, all right. And it looks like there's no getting out of it at this point. I have a feeling Peter Lloyd isn't taking any chances. If this is as big a draw as he claims it will be, it'll be something for him to crow about."

All Tessa heard was the part about there being "no getting out of it at this point." Had Clay been trying to think of a way to not go through with the demonstration? She thought he'd resigned himself to it, just as she had. Evidently that wasn't the case.

"He can't do that. Besides, what's the point?"

"It seems he can and he did. All the money is still going to charity. It's just an internal bet with no actual payout. I've even heard talk of the hospital matching the donations of the winner's jar, although that would have to be approved by the hospital trustees."

How had he heard all of this when she had known nothing? "Maybe it was Marcos."

"Possibly, but I would lay odds on Lloyd. And so far it looks like you're ahead by a long shot. It seems you've engendered some loyalty, Dr. Camara."

She had? That was news to her. She was normally so busy she barely had time to throw a hello here or there. Which explained why she'd missed noticing those jars this morning.

Her sadness over Mr. Phillips was still hovering in the background, but even she could see the humor in this situation. "Well, you know… I think I've won every match we've ever fought."

"Because we weren't actually *supposed* to be fighting."

"Mmm-hmm."

"You don't sound convinced."

She smiled. "Because I'm not." Gesturing at the jars, she shrugged. "If this earns more money toward a good cause, then we'll just have to make sure we really do put on that good show we talked about."

"Are you saying you're going to take me down?"

Reaching into her side pocket, she took out a few bills and peeled off a ten. Walking over to the jars, she stuffed it inside the one with her name on it. She turned back to look at him. "Oh, yeah, mister. You are going down."

Dodge, dodge, dodge…retreat.

When was she going to miss a beat so that he could gain some ground?

Time and time again Tessa had pushed him to the very edge of the circle with no more than a twist of her body. She wasn't aiming to hit him, since that wasn't the goal of this match. But she was making him move his feet. And they sure as hell weren't moving forward.

They were supposed to be putting on a show, but not one that had him stepping backward for the whole fifteen minutes of their exhibition.

Cut yourself some slack.

This was only their first training match. He couldn't be expected to whip himself back into top form all at once.

Except his top form had never been any match for Tessa's skill. And she now had those damn jars as incentive to make this a show everyone would remember.

Well, two could play at that game.

Concentrate.

He sidestepped, mentally keeping the circle of people around them in his mind. He didn't want to go back so quickly that he careened into them—the idea was to stay inside the ring. If something happened the circle would open, but whoever broke it would automatically give up his place. In other words, he would lose.

Okay. He did a quick flip, a few muscles protesting at how much of a slacker he'd become over the past several years. His brain still remembered the moves, but his body was giving him hell over the contortions he was putting it through.

Tessa actually stepped out of the way.

One for me!

Until her foot found the back of his knee.

Dammit!

Down he went. Right onto his back.

He glared up at her, only to find her eyes alight with wicked laughter. She'd done that on purpose.

Just because she could.

And he found he couldn't stay mad at her. Not with her face all bright and gleeful and happy.

Happy.

He hadn't seen her like that in…over four years.

"Tessita." Marcos entered the circle. Unlike Tessa, the man did not look happy. "This is not what we are looking for. It is okay for one of you to defeat the other, but you need to give him more than two minutes. Otherwise those watching will not see the true beauty of our *capoeira*."

Ha! True. Two minutes did not constitute a match. Although his body could swear it had been closer to an hour. Marcos said it was okay for one of them to take the other down, but the director and Clay both knew who would be left standing and who would be on the floor when all was said and done. And that person was still grinning at him in that old familiar way—despite Marcos's chiding words.

Except this time it brought back a not-so-happy memory from days past, when she'd said the words that had ended their relationship. He'd lain flat on his figurative back then, too, while Tessa had stood over him, scowling. He'd do well to keep that in mind.

Clay levered himself to his feet. Lord, he was going to be sore tomorrow.

He waited for Marcos to leave the ring and for the rhythm instruments to again pick up that hypnotic beat. All the other participants had run their matches just as they'd been programmed, entering and exiting the ring like seasoned pros.

And he and Tessa—the last match on the exhibition agenda—were gumming up the works.

"Ready?" he asked.

"Absolutely." She yanked down the hem of her close-fitting tank top, her skin gleaming.

This time Clay executed a series of moves that actually had Tessa swerving and doing some tricky maneuvers of her own to avoid him getting too close.

This was more like it. For three minutes they continued like that, the match feeling much more even all of a sudden.

She arched into a backbend and flipped out of it like an expert.

Of course it felt even. Because she was letting him gain the upper hand. Just as Marcos had suggested.

Time and time again she kicked and bowed and spun. Back. Away from him.

"Dammit, Tessa, you're not even trying."

She swept by him with another grin. "Because someone told me to keep it going."

Perfect. She didn't have to admit to it.

He pushed harder. Entering her space and then exiting it, his leg barely missing her head as he swept past.

But Tessa was good at what she did, able to calculate down to the last centimeter how much room she needed to give him in order not to get hit. Because, as Marcos had said, the goal wasn't to make contact but to show off techniques and the unique dance style, the give and take that went on in the ring. Clay had never seen anything like it in his life. And the real *capoeira* experts were as ripped and fit as athletes in any other sport. The timing was what made it what it was. Because in some ways it was harder to go at each other knowing you weren't supposed to strike them, but to sweep past, and over, and under, with barely any room to spare. That took skill and an ability to read your opponent. Something Tessa seemed built to do.

And she *could* read him.

He only hoped that some of his secrets stayed hidden, even from the great Tessa Camara.

Like how turned on he got by watching her arms and legs move with the grace and strength of a ballerina.

At least when he wasn't the one fighting her. And even now it was only his concentration that kept him from thinking too hard about her body and how absolutely flexible it was. In more ways than just training in *capoeira*.

Something hit the small of his back, and he lurched forward. Damn. He hadn't even seen that coming. And just like that he was once again on the defensive. Because Tessa had evidently decided enough time had gone by that she could really start fighting. And no way could he look down at his watch to see if the requisite fifteen minutes had passed. It probably had, though, because she would be keeping that internal clock ticking, despite gliding around the ring in time with the beat of the instruments.

His left knee gave way so fast that he thought he'd stepped the wrong way. He hadn't. Tessa had just stepped the right way. Down he went. For the second time that day.

Tessa once again stood over him, her exercise tank molding to her chest with each breath she took. "Sorry, Clay. You weren't concentrating."

No kidding.

Marcos clapped his hands. "This is enough for tonight," he said, his Brazilian accent a little thicker than it had been at the start of the evening. "Much better, Tessa."

Oh, yeah? And what about him?

As if reading his thoughts, the other man said. "You will improve next time."

Clay, from his spot on the mat, couldn't help but chuckle. This was the same old Marcos. Never pampering his students but giving it to them straight, without being ugly. But his attempt at encouragement said it all. He would improve. He needed to improve. And the director would accept nothing less.

Hell, he'd missed this whole scene. More than he wanted to admit.

Tessa reached down to help him up. He started to ignore her hand but something made him grip her palm, making sure to give a quick jerk as he stood so that she was momentarily thrown against him. He stepped back. "Sorry, Tessa. That's what happens when I forget to concentrate."

Her face flashed with color immediately because he'd used those same words in more than just a *capoeira* session. He'd used them once when he'd been so carried away with how she'd made him feel that he'd lost control, coming in a rush before she'd climaxed.

He'd made it up to her minutes later, though, until her eyes had squeezed shut with her own orgasm.

And Clay had said those very words to explain what had happened.

She'd liked it. Liked that she could make him forget everything but what was happening.

Releasing her hand, he gave her a knowing smile. "Shall we call it even?"

Before she could say anything, Marcos was telling the group that he'd made plans for them all to go out to a bar a couple of blocks away to celebrate their first official practice session for the exhibition.

Clay could feign being tired and needing to go home and rest before work the next day, or say that Molly was waiting for him, but she was with his parents. Besides, he wanted to go. He'd missed the camaraderie of this group and how they always seemed to start their sessions as friends and leave the same way, no matter what went on in the ring. Maybe because they left any hard feelings inside that circle. Or maybe because most of them were Brazilian, lapsing into their own language at times. And they always made him feel like an insider—as part of them. Clay had learned bits and pieces of Portuguese during his time with Tessa, especially since her folks spoke it at home—although they'd always made an effort to speak English whenever he'd been around.

In the excited rush of voices that followed Marcos's announcement he glanced at Tessa and saw a shadow of indecision in her eyes. "Come on, Tess. You owe me a drink or two for the way you manhandled me."

Her brows went up. "Manhandled? I went easy on you."

Had she? A shadow passed through his head. Maybe she had tonight, but four years ago? Not a chance. And that should be what he concentrated on, not the memory of those times they'd shared in the ring…and in bed.

If only he could convince his body to cooperate.

He shook his head to rid it of that thought.

Today was a new day. And they could very well go out and enjoy a drink together, dammit, without him turning it into a huge friggin' deal.

The group headed to the locker rooms to change back into street clothes. Since Tessa was the only woman in the room, she went to Marcos's office.

Something about how close she and the studio owner seemed to be struck him for the first time.

He looked at Marcos with new eyes. Were they seeing each other outside these sessions? The man wasn't married, and he certainly seemed to have a soft spot for Tessa, having used the diminutive form of her name quite a bit today. He couldn't remember if Marcos had done that in the past.

But he was in his late forties.

And that meant what, exactly? Tessa was thirty. Not exactly a May to December romance.

A shard of what could have been jealousy went through him, except it wasn't. It couldn't be. He and Tessa had been over for a long time. He'd married another woman and had fathered a child, for heaven's sake. He saw how that had turned out. Failure on a spectacular level. So whatever was going on between Tessa and her trainer was none of his business.

She kissed you.

The inner voice rumbled in his head, reminding him that either he was wrong about his speculation or their relationship was open enough that neither of them cared what the other did.

He couldn't see Marcos being that nonchalant about it,

though. He was a pretty intense man. And no way would Clay have ever allowed any man to touch Tessa without risking a permanently rearranged face when they'd been dating.

Again, those days were over.

He changed quickly and ran his fingers through his hair to put it back in some semblance of order.

Why? It was just Tessa and the old gang. They'd all just been through the same workout.

A few minutes later he was standing beside her as they made their way down the sidewalk. It had been decided it was faster to walk than to try to all pile into cars and meet there. Besides, The Pied Piper was only a couple of blocks away. And the way this group partied, it was probably better that no one would be driving himself home. They'd flag down taxis and return for their vehicles in the morning.

Clay intended to keep his wits about him, though, whatever the others decided to do. A night of drinking could cause problems and not just with his job.

"So is Molly going to come to the exhibition?" Tessa's question came out of nowhere.

"Probably. She seemed to like the studio a lot. My folks will be taking care of her during the festival, since I'll be a little occupied."

She immediately tensed, head coming up, eyes facing straight ahead. "That's nice. It's wonderful that they can watch her when her mother can't."

Yeah, which was most of the time, since Lizza was normally busy flitting here or there and focusing on her career. The funny thing about that was that Tessa was doing exactly the same thing. Working hard and putting all of her efforts into her job. But it didn't bother him that she did it.

Why?

Because if Molly had been her daughter, he had no doubt that she would somehow make time for her, just as he did. Sure, his parents cared for her while he was working, but he spent every second he could with her. Tonight was the exception to the rule. He rarely went out to do anything fun anymore because he had responsibilities and he took them seriously.

So did Tessa.

And so did Lizza, in her own way. Except Molly's mother seemed to check her responsibilities at the door when it came to her own daughter.

His teeth grated against each other.

He glanced at Tessa, and she seemed to have relaxed again, so maybe it was his imagination that she'd suddenly gone all stiff and nonresponsive.

They arrived at the bar to find the *capoeira* group assembled out front. Marcos waited for the last two stragglers to arrive. "Everyone good with doing his own thing and leaving whenever you want? If you want to share cabs, make those arrangements now before it gets crazy. You can pair up again on the way out."

One of the players grinned. "My wife is meeting me here, so count me out. I'm not sharing that cab with anyone but her."

A couple of laughs went through the group at the bald innuendo.

Clay glanced at Tessa. "Are you okay with sharing one?"

"Of course." She stopped. "Unless you're staying until the place shuts down."

"I wasn't planning to. How about if we leave whenever you're ready?"

She gave him a pointed look. "If you want to prowl

around, though, and find someone else to leave with, just let me know. You can text me."

"The only person I'm leaving with is you." He realized how that might have sounded when her face turned pink. But everyone was already moving into the bar and the sounds from inside were leaking out through the open door.

"I guess that's our cue. Shall we?"

He waited for her to enter, already ruing the thought of sharing a cab with her. Because it made him think of sharing other things. In a much more private and fulfilling venue. That single night of summer madness. The one he couldn't get out of his head.

A single night, he could probably handle. But any more than that truly would be madness.

CHAPTER NINE

SHE PROBABLY SHOULDN'T be dancing with him.

Especially not this kind of dancing. Cheek to cheek, her right hand cradled in his, the fingers of her left hand at the back of his neck. Except the entire evening had been leading up to this. She'd danced with Marcos for a whole dance before Clay had cut in with a smooth remark about needing to discuss *capoeira* strategy for the exhibition.

Only Clay hadn't talked strategy. He'd simply spun her into his arms as a slow dance came on, his warm fingers burning through the thin knit top she'd changed into. It wasn't nightclub wear, since she hadn't known they'd be going out tonight. But, then again, The Pied Piper wasn't a dressy kind of club. It was where professionals went after work to wind down from the day. And to possibly score a little company for the night.

Tessa wasn't interested in scoring anything. So she'd been more than happy to stick to dancing with people she knew. Even if that meant finding herself in Clay's arms all over again. They'd come to this club from time to time when they'd had a few hours free during med school, which hadn't been often. But when they had, they'd inevitably wound up in a bed somewhere. Once they hadn't even made it that far, driving Clay's little sports car to a secluded spot across the Jersey border and squeezing both of their bodies into the passenger seat.

Sex between them had always been hot.

Which was why she wondered what she'd been thinking to allow herself to fall right back into his embrace.

She wasn't. Thinking, that was.

It was the excitement of fighting him in the circle once again. The memories of how invigorating those matches could become later, in the privacy of the night.

Which made her next thought stop her in her tracks. What would it matter if they engaged in a little hanky-panky on the side? They were no longer involved—Clay had a young daughter he needed to concentrate on.

But she had needs. And she imagined he did, too—although Clay probably had those needs met on a regular basis. She wasn't made like that. But maybe she could bend her own rules in this case, since she and Clay weren't exactly strangers.

Her fingers tightened a bit on his neck. Clay's response was to grip her waist with a firmer hand. Or maybe that was her imagination wanting to make it so.

And, Lord, if he didn't smell good. Too good. Especially this close. The match and exertion should have washed away any trace of aftershave, so that couldn't be the source of the woodsy, yummy scent that made her breathe a little bit deeper.

It was just Clay. She recognized it—remembered going to sleep to it and waking up with it beneath her skin. And, just like in the past, it drew her to him.

Her nose brushed his shoulder before she realized how close she'd gotten to him. With almost no hesitation—except maybe in her brain—her head turned sideways and she pressed her cheek against him, allowing her eyes to close. To "feel." Something she hadn't done in a very long time.

Her days of med school and internship had turned her into an analytical machine, with cause and effect always at the forefront of her mind...her feelings tucked in a distant part of her brain, where they rarely surfaced. Except in instances like with Mr. Phillips, when they'd re-emerged without warning and threatened her objectivity.

Maybe she shouldn't even be a doctor.

Yes, she should. Her mom had been so excited for her when she'd been accepted into med school.

And if it had come with a price—her relationship to Clay—it was still worth it.

If she could help people like Mr. Phillips, then she would continue to make those sacrifices.

The hand at her waist slid backward until it rested on the small of her back. She might have thought he was trying to put some distance between them but, if anything, he was tucking her closer, his chin coming down to rest on top of her head.

Her breath caught at the familiarity that was slowly wrapping her in cords of silk.

Especially with the little hum of vibration that went through his chest, a sound she couldn't hear but that she could feel. And she felt it all the way down to her toes.

What was one night? Was Clay even thinking the same thing? Wondering if they could set the love machine for a quick tumble cycle that would heat up quickly, shaking out the wrinkles from their daily lives? Afterward they could fold everything up and put it back into a drawer. Out of sight. Out of mind.

Should she say something? Proposition him?

And just where would this sexathon take place? She could drag him back to her unit at the brownstone, where

Caren, Holly or Sam might overhear something. Her nose crinkled. No, if they got together, she didn't want to hold back anything, except her emotions.

They could go to his place—where he'd murmured he wanted to take her when they kissed in Central Park. His apartment was empty—at least according to Clay, who'd said that Molly would be at his parents' house for the night.

She tilted her head, dislodging his chin. He glanced down, a frown marring his brow.

"Do you think Marcos would mind if we left early?" she asked.

"Marcos?" His eyebrows pulled closer together as he studied her for a second or two. "Feeling okay?"

"Not really." That wasn't what she'd meant to say. She hurried to correct herself. "I'm feeling a little…"

Her courage gave out, and she let her voice trail away.

"A little what? You've only had a glass of wine, not very much, even for a featherweight like you." This time a slight smile edged one side of his mouth, although his frown was still there.

"No, it's not the wine." Wow, she was glad she wasn't a man, because she was terrible at this pickup stuff. They could have it. "I was just wondering if you might want to…"

She swallowed and forced the rest of the words out. "Leave. Go somewhere else."

His face went totally still, and she held her breath, praying that if he was going to refuse he would at least let her down easily.

"You're not going to believe this, but I was thinking the very same thing."

"Oh, God." She sagged against him. "It's stupid, isn't it? We shouldn't. We both know it."

"Yes. My head knows it." He hauled her closer, where she could feel the inner workings of a certain body part. "But other areas disagree. Vehemently, I might add."

"Ditto on both counts."

His hand slid beneath her hair and held her while his mouth came down and claimed hers.

Lord, she hoped no one in their party could see them now. But if Clay wasn't worried about it, why should she be?

She kissed him back, stretching up as high as she could in order to reach him better. It wasn't enough. What they both needed was a surface that put them on a level playing field.

Like a bed.

Something on Clay's body vibrated again. Only this time it didn't come from his chest but his waistline.

She broke free. "Clay…"

"I know. Give me a sec." He unclipped his cell phone with one hand while keeping her tight against him with the other. He put the object to his ear. "Matthews here."

The frown was back. Not of confusion this time but of concern. "Where are you?"

She thought at first it was his parents saying something had happened to Molly, except his face was up looking over the heads of the people on the dance floor. When she turned to follow his lead she saw a hand waving.

"Got it," he said. "We'll be right there. Call 911 as soon as you hang up."

He let go of her and shoved his phone back in its holder. He leaned down so she could hear him above the music. "Something's wrong with Marcos. Let's go."

Her heart in her throat, she kept hold of Clay's hand as he led the way toward the place where she'd seen the hand waving. As soon as they arrived, she dropped to her knees.

Marcos was having a seizure, eyes rolled back, muscles twitching in useless contractions. The connections in his brain were going haywire.

Why?

She went back into analytical mode as she tilted the *capoeira* master's head to the side in case he vomited, while Clay belted out question after question about whether or not anyone knew Marcos's medical history. More *capoeira* folks had evidently noticed that something was going on, because they slowly gathered around them, including the man who'd mentioned sharing a cab with his wife. He was the one who finally spoke. "He has epilepsy."

What?

Tessa looked down at the man she'd known most of her life. She glanced at his wrist, but there was no medical alert bracelet, something he should have been wearing. But Marcos was a proud man. And Brazilians didn't like to display weakness. She remembered one of her father's friends who'd severed his index finger at the second joint. He'd insisted the doctor reattach it, even though the digit would never bend again but would stick straight out. He'd just wanted to "be whole."

Clay asked their group to form a ring around Marcos just like during practice to keep everyone back and then knelt beside her.

She glanced at her watch, timing the length of the seizure. Two minutes from the time Clay's phone had rung. If it lasted longer than five minutes, they were in trouble. Right now, though, they were helpless to do anything except wait it out and hope that an ambulance arrived soon.

"What does he take?" Her eyes went to the man who'd voiced that Marcos had epilepsy.

He shrugged. "I don't know. I just saw something on the calendar on his desk about a doctor's appointment. I asked, and he told me. I had no idea until a couple of years ago."

Marcos went still suddenly, all his muscles going lax. Glancing at her watch again, she murmured, "Just over three minutes from the time you got the call."

Despite the medical emergency, the music was still playing and there was activity on the dance floor. Not everyone knew something had happened on this side of the room, which was probably a good thing, since she could just barely hear the sound of an ambulance in the distance.

A man in a tie broke through the ring and stood over them, introducing himself as The Pied Piper's owner. "What happened?"

Clay spoke up. "We're doctors and our friend had a seizure. There's an ambulance en route. If you can clear a path to the door and let the EMTs get through, we'd appreciate it."

All it took was a motion from the owner to get three beefy men to come over. He explained and they immediately opened up a swath of space. Within another minute a duo came through, wheeling a stretcher.

Marcos was just starting to regain consciousness, trying to weakly wave away their attempts to help.

Tessa leaned close to him and whispered in his ear that he needed to go with the EMTs and get checked out at the hospital. "Did you take your meds?"

He blinked at her as if he might deny taking anything, then nodded. "Yes."

The medical services pair quickly took her friend's

vitals and checked his pupils, asking a few standard questions about whether he'd hit his head and how much he'd had to drink. Marcos was still too confused to really answer much, so they put a collar around his neck just in case and bundled him back through the crowd on the gurney, with Tessa following close behind. Clay turned to talk to the other guys from the studio, probably reassuring them that he'd let them know what was going on as soon as he knew something. He caught up with her just as they reached the ambulance. The EMTs recognized her from the hospital, so they didn't question her when she said they'd meet them at the hospital.

Then the ambulance was off and Clay was flagging down a taxi.

There was silence on the way to the hospital. Her stomach churned in her gut as her thoughts raced. Marcos had epilepsy? He was a *grande mestre* in *capoeira*, a level that took many years and a whole lot of training to reach. She couldn't believe someone hadn't discovered this sooner, although most epileptics whose seizure activity was well controlled could live normal lives and do most of the things that other people did. Except drive. And even that depended on the type of seizure activity.

But Tessa had never seen any evidence of even a petit mal seizure.

A taxi pulled up to the curb and they both got in.

Clay wrapped an arm around her waist and slid her next to him. "Sorry, honey. He's confused right now. Maybe he forgot to take his meds this morning. And if he had anything to drink…"

"I know." She laid her head on his shoulder. "Anything could have triggered it. We'll have to wait and see what he says when he's a little more with it."

"I know he's special to you."

She closed her eyes. "Yes. Very."

Warm fingers cupped her chin and lifted her head. "How 'very' is very?"

What did he mean? "I've known Marcos my whole life. I've been at that studio since I was a kid. Marcos took over as owner when I was a teenager."

"Is there something more to it than that?"

"More…?" She sat straight up, eyes widening. "What the hell, Clay? Do you think I would have asked you to leave the club with me if there was anything going on between me and Marcos?"

His fingers tightened to prevent her from jerking away. Instead, she glared up at him, anger pulsing at her temples. "The way he talks to you…"

"We're friends. He's friends with my parents." She shook her head. "Just like your parents and mine are friends."

"Exactly."

She sighed, her indignation beginning to unravel at the seams. "He's almost twenty years older than me."

"Since when has that mattered?"

She could see his point. But her and Marcos?

It was true that she and Clay had originally met through their parents—at a Christmas party his folks had thrown years earlier. The second they'd seen each other it had all been over. And when they'd danced…

She and Marcos had never shared that same spark. Not when they first met…and not after all these years of working together. She saw him as a mentor. Someone to learn from.

"We're friends." She placed a little more emphasis on the words this time around.

They pulled up to the hospital, and she was the first to leap out of the cab, hurrying up the walkway while he had to stop and pay the driver for the short ride. Even so, he caught up with her before she reached the double doors of the emergency room. "Wait."

She slowed her pace. "You can go ahead and go home. He's my friend. I'm going to check on him."

"He's my friend, too." Once they were through the doors he stopped in front of her. "It was an honest question. If we were going to go back to my place, I wanted to know the score. I don't encroach on anyone's territory."

"I can't believe you just said that. I'm no one's territory."

He laughed. "No. You're not. You were always your own woman. Someone who knew exactly what she wanted out of life."

A flash of hurt went through her heart. At one time that "want" had included Clay.

"No more than anyone else."

There wasn't any time to say more because one of the ER doctors met them in the hallway, nodding a greeting at them. She quickly explained why they were there. "Marcos Figuereiro. The man who came in with epilepsy."

"Dr. Simon is back there with him right now. Exam room three, I think."

They made their way to the cubicle and Tessa called through the closed curtain. "Drs. Camara and Matthews are here to see Marcos."

"Come in. We're just getting some background on him." Randy Simon's words came through loud and clear. A large man with a booming tone and optimistic manner, he was good with patients and family alike.

Clay drew back the curtain and motioned her in first, then followed her. Dr. Simon draped his stethoscope around his neck and glanced up at them.

"He has epilepsy?"

Marcos growled, "I am right here."

"So you are." Randy's brows went up an inch, but he smiled down at the man and went back and forth with him about his diagnosis and medical history. It was like pulling teeth, though, to get anything out of the man.

But they did eventually. Dr. Simon decided to hold him overnight and check the blood levels of his meds. Marcos grumbled about it all, but Tessa got the feeling the episode had scared him as much as it had those around him. Which meant it wasn't something that happened every day. So, yes, it was better to make sure nothing had changed or that there wasn't something else insidious going on inside her friend's body.

"You two might as well go home." Marcos crossed his strong arms over his chest. "I'll probably get the worst night's sleep known to man, but I would rather do it in private than have someone hover over me for the next eight hours."

"Are you sure?"

"I will call if I need something."

Tessa managed a smile. "Hope you don't mind if I don't believe you."

She reached into her purse—realizing for the first time that Clay must have retrieved it from their table at The Pied Piper, as she'd forgotten all about it until they were in the cab. But there it had been. She found a business card and wrote her cell phone number on the back of it, handing it to Dr. Simon. "Will you have someone call me if something changes?"

He glanced from her to Clay, probably wondering what they were doing out and about together. Those damned jars. She vaguely remembered seeing a pair of them in the ER, as well.

Perfect.

"I'll give you a call," he assured her.

Clay shook the other doctor's hand while she leaned down to kiss Marcos's cheek.

"You get some rest," she said. "We have a lot more practicing to do over the next couple of weeks, and we need you strong and rested."

He grumbled about them needing a lot more than a couple weeks, but since that was all they had…

They left, and Tessa wasn't sure what to do. Did she hang around in the waiting room to see if there was any news? Or did she go home?

Now that the scare was over, she was wide-awake. There was no way she'd get any sleep tonight.

A vision of herself wrapped in Clay's strong arms shimmied through her head, bringing with it the knowledge that she'd never had insomnia when they'd spent the nights together. Instead, she'd slept like a baby.

Clay, as if reading her thoughts, said, "You can't do anything by waiting around, Tess. Randy said he'd call if something changed." He glanced at his watch. "Besides, it's almost eleven."

Too late to do anything besides sleep? Yes, he was probably hinting that his better sense had put in an appearance after all and that he wanted to go home. Alone.

The least she could do was be graceful about it if that was the case, although now that Marcos's doctor had her cell phone number she would love nothing more than to go to sleep with Clay next to her. But she wouldn't.

"Well, I guess I'll see you tomorrow, then?"

They stepped through the emergency room doors into the balmy night air. "That depends on how long you plan on staying over."

"Staying over?" Said as if her heart had not just leaped

in her chest at the idea that he might not be saying good-night quite yet after all.

His eyes narrowed. "Nothing's changed, Tessa. And if I know you, you won't get any sleep." He wrapped his hand around her nape. "I still want you to come home with me. Will you?"

He was asking. Not demanding. Not assuming, as he might have when they'd been together before.

Relief washed through her. "Yes. If you're sure."

"Honey, I'd like nothing better than to be pinned down by you in circumstances other than standing in a room-ful of men watching our every move."

Capoeira.

She grinned, her eyes holding his as her fears over Marcos began to fade. "You just don't like to lose in front of a bunch of people."

"I don't like to lose at all. But what I have in mind has two winners and zero losers. And no one around to see the outcome except for us."

He drew her a little closer and then bent down to give her a light kiss.

Unfortunately, he didn't move to deepen the contact, and considering they were standing outside the hospital, that was a good thing. For both of them.

He didn't release his hold on her, however. So his next words were whispered inches away from her lips, giving them an intimacy she was dying to explore.

"My place. My bed." The promise from a week ago flowed over her skin, making her shiver.

"Your car?" She didn't have a vehicle at the moment, preferring to zip around the huge city on public transport or her own two feet.

"I think we can make it to the apartment."

Only after he'd said it did she realize he'd taken her

question about how they were going to get to his place and expanded it to include whether or not they would even make it that far. Or whether they'd have to park his car and consummate things inside. As they'd done before.

An ambulance pulled into the circular drive in a blare of sirens and Clay finally lifted his head and backed up a pace. But he didn't leave her totally without contact. Reaching down, he grabbed her hand, tugging her to his side. "Ready?"

She made a sound of affirmation that found her being towed behind him, his long steps requiring two of hers for every one of his. She didn't care. All she knew was that she was going to feel him around her in a way that she hadn't in four long years.

And she couldn't wait.

Maybe they wouldn't make it back to his apartment after all.

She managed to climb into his car with shaky legs and settle into place. She even managed to keep her hands to herself, although she couldn't say the same of Clay. Because once they got out of the parking lot and onto the street, they were immediately caught up in a snarl of traffic that slowed to a crawl.

"Damn," he muttered.

Double damn, she echoed in her head. Balling her hands together in her lap, she tried not to squirm on the leather upholstery beneath her thighs. Or dwell on the warm ache between those very same thighs.

Clay let go of the gearshift and dropped his palm onto her left leg, just above her knee. "This wasn't quite what I had in mind, but…"

Her breath caught in her throat when his thumb brushed over the loose, gauzy fabric of her long skirt. The ache grew a little stronger.

The car in front of them crept forward a couple of inches, and Clay followed it, the slow pace evidently not requiring him to shift, since his hand stayed right where it was. In fact, his fingers ran in little waves of motion along her inner thigh in a way that caused the hem of her skirt to rise almost to her knee, where he caught it with his index finger and lifted it higher.

"Clay?" His name came out a bit strangled.

"Shh…" This time when his fingertips came back in contact with her it was against bare skin. "Who knows how long this ride is going to last? Just keeping you interested."

Interested? She didn't need him to do anything to hold her enthralled. And the only ride she wanted right now was one where she was straddling his hips and moaning.

His windows were darkly tinted, and between the streetlights and headlights she doubted anyone could see inside the vehicle. Still, when his hand changed legs and bunched the fabric up until it was halfway between her knees and her hips, her stomach tightened in anticipation, along with everything else.

He dragged his palm with painful slowness up her skin, raising goose bumps in its wake, his eyes never leaving the road. And yet, even without glancing at her once, he seemed to know the havoc he was wreaking on her mind…and her body.

Traffic moved forward another couple of feet, and suddenly Tessa wasn't in such a hurry to arrive at their destination.

He continued to tease with light strokes up…down… across, never quite reaching his destination. Eventually, she couldn't take it any longer and her eyelids slammed shut, unable to concentrate on anything other than what Clay was doing, how he made her feel.

And it was incredible. She trusted him not to go so far that he would get them both arrested, even as she turned her body over to him, allowing him to do things she never would have let anyone else do.

Because she did trust him.

Wanted him.

Despite their past.

And when he got them home she was going to show him exactly how much.

His fingers slid between her thighs and urged them a few inches apart with a gentle pressure that she immediately responded to, although she did have enough common sense to reach down and flip the fabric of her skirt down over his hand and her knees.

"No fair, Tessa." He ventured higher, wringing an unwilling moan from her throat, her head lolling back against the seat. "I'm beginning to think I should have chosen the car option."

She felt the vehicle move forward again. Each time it did, Clay seemed to grow a little bolder.

When he withdrew his hand completely, though, her eyes jerked open in disappointment.

"Truck," he murmured, as a big vehicle rumbled forward and moved twenty yards ahead of them.

Thinking she'd give him a taste of his own medicine, she twisted on her seat and moved her hand to the gearshift, sliding her fingers over the top of it and then down its stem, watching him. He wasn't looking but she knew he was aware of exactly what she was doing—of the game she was playing.

"Dangerous."

"No more dangerous than what you were doing," she whispered.

"I'm driving."

Yeah, driving me insane. She didn't say it out loud, though, because it sounded stupid, even to her own ears. But it was true. And Clay knew it was. He always did somehow, even when she'd tried to hide how devastating his touch was to her. And when he'd shown up at her dorm room she'd kept the door between them, knowing that if he touched her it was all over.

It always would be for her.

That fact should make her wary, should make her back away from him emotionally, even now. That's what she was trying to do, actually. Accept that they'd always been more than compatible physically, even if they weren't good as life partners.

She needed to be self-sufficient. He'd tended to smother…trying to take care of her, even when she'd longed to do things herself.

Traffic opened up suddenly, and Clay spent the next few minutes threading his vehicle through the congestion, making several turns before finally veering into the parking garage of what looked like an exclusive apartment building.

Of course it would be.

Even as the thought ran through her mind, she banished it. The brownstone she lived in wasn't exactly a pauper's abode, thanks to Holly's family. Besides, tonight wasn't about houses or money or anything else. It was about her needs and Clay's needs and how they could come together to find a mutually satisfying solution.

The second he pulled his car into a space and shut off the engine he threaded his fingers through her hair and turned her face up for his kiss. And as soon as his lips met hers she knew there was no turning back. She and Clay were destined to reignite the fires of the past. She just hoped that when it was all over she'd have the strength and courage to put them out again.

CHAPTER TEN

TOUCHING HER MADE something inside him come alive.

And at the moment he wasn't touching anything except her hand as they rode up in the elevator. But she was gripping back as if her very life depended on maintaining that contact.

If someone had told him four years ago that he'd find himself riding to his apartment with this woman, he'd have said they were crazy.

But maybe he was the crazy one. Setting himself up for another big knock to the gut.

Nope. No gut involved. Just that single night of summer madness he'd been craving for what seemed like ages. Nothing below skin level would be involved. Because anything she touched would be on the surface. No emotions. No longing. Just skin-to-skin contact that he could wash off with a single quick spray of his showerhead. Just like soap or shampoo. Once applied, he would simply rinse it all off again.

But didn't most of the instructions on those packages say "Lather, rinse...*repeat*"?

Maybe one night should become two.

He tugged her closer, until their arms were touching. As long as he was smart about this, he could have sex with her as many times as he wanted and not be affected.

After all, when Lizza had finally filed for divorce, it hadn't hurt that much. In fact, he'd been relieved in some ways, except for the fact that Molly had been left without a mom for the most part.

He'd had superficial sex since then. Not very often, because he did have a daughter to think of. But the times he had, he'd been able to roll from beneath the woman's sheets and get on with his life without a backward glance.

Except he hadn't brought them to his place. He and Lizza had never even lived in this apartment. His home had become sacrosanct…a place reserved for him and Molly only.

So what was different now? He was about to violate his own unspoken rule: no liaisons of the sexual kind happened in the apartment. Ever.

Madness.

To keep from trying to rationalize things beyond that one word, he let go of her hand and draped his arm around her shoulders, allowing his fingertips to glide across the bare skin of her arm. On the second pass he moved the contact forward just a couple of inches, so that he was still on her arm, but the backs of his knuckles grazed the outside of her breast as he made his way back down. A shiver went through her.

The elevator stopped on his floor before he could do anything more.

And there was still a whole lot he wanted to do.

He spun her out of the elevator and against the door of his apartment, settling his mouth on hers in a way that he hoped left no question about what they were going to do. It wasn't as if he thought she was going to angle for a cup of coffee and then flee for her life. But why take any chances?

When her palms landed on his butt, fingers splayed

apart and urging him closer, he combusted, a flame shooting from his groin to the top of his head. She was evidently taking no chances, either.

He obliged her, pushing one knee between her legs and settling his stiff flesh against her thigh. Digging into his pocket for his key, he managed to get it into the lock beside her waist and twisted. The door gave way, and so did Tessa, tumbling to the hardwood floor and dragging him down with her. He was somehow able to keep from crushing her as he landed, her husky laugh washing over him in a flood he just couldn't resist. So he stayed there, pushing the door shut with the sole of his shoe as he sank deeper into her soft curves, his aching flesh wanting nothing more than to yank her skirt up and be done with it. To hell with all the formalities.

But if he hurried it would be over.

As in…no second chances.

So he tried to rein himself in, thinking he would stand up calmly and lead her to the bedroom. But Tessa's hands were on his ass again, only this time they'd somehow wormed their way beneath his waistband and briefs and were now on his bare skin. Her mouth found his at the same time, and he knew it was all over, because her kiss was warm and thorough, shot through with sensual promise.

He gave it one last shot. "My bedroom is just down the hallway."

Her fingers traveled lower, setting off another set of explosions within his skull. Then she pulled her hands free. But before he could protest she shoved him up and over, until he was the one on his back and she was straddling his hips.

"Damn, Tess, if you wanted to be in charge, all you had to do was ask."

She leaned over, elbows beside his shoulders, her breath washing over his lips. "I prefer to keep my opponent off guard."

Hell if she hadn't done that the whole time he'd known her. When she leaned over and gave his lower lip a quick bite, sucking it, his eyes closed as a wave of ecstasy swept over him.

"So I'm the opponent?" His voice came out rough, sounding very much as he felt—that what little control he had was rapidly crumbling.

She sat up and pulled her shirt over her head, revealing a tiny black bra that barely covered the tops of her breasts. "If you fight me on this, absolutely."

"Honey, I have no intention of fighting anything." He decided to have some fun of his own, reaching up to take hold of the fabric barely holding in her curves and tugging it down to expose them completely. "I just thought you might want a soft bed to do this in."

Her fingers trailed along his jawline and one brow edged up. "I don't want a soft…anything."

To prove her point, she widened her legs and settled fully against him, shifting her hips along his length.

No softness there. Just a pulsing need that wouldn't quit.

Tessa balled her skirt up and allowed it to rest on the tops of her thighs, baring them, while she reached for the button of his slacks.

"Wait." He gritted out the word. "I told you I don't want this to be a quickie. I want to enjoy you."

"After getting me all worked up in the car as we drove here? No chance. And, believe me, I intend to enjoy it. Fully. Deeply." The button popped free, and his zip went down. "And I somehow think you'll manage to come along for the ride."

At the rate she was going it would be a very short trip. But if that's the way she wanted it, who was he to turn her down?

Then she had him in her hands. Squeezing. Stroking. Driving him out of his mind.

"Condom."

"Pill."

"In that case…" He took hold of her butt with both hands and lifted her slightly, waiting for her to hold herself in that position. Then he reached beneath her skirt and found her panties. Moist heat met his touch as he edged aside the silky fabric. "Let's see just how fully and deeply we can go."

He guided himself into position. She immediately pushed down hard until she was fully seated, a soft sound coming from her lips as she paused there. "Damn."

Damn? *Damn?*

"Too deep?" Afraid he was hurting her, he started to reach for her, only to have her wave away his hands.

"No. Too good." She sat very still, her bared breasts rising and falling as she breathed in and out, mouth open, eyes closed.

Hadn't she just suggested that she was going to make him pay for what he'd done in the car?

Too late for you to try to draw things out now, darling.

And he was going to make sure she suffered as much as he was suffering. One hand went to her breast and the other beneath her skirt, both finding their targets within seconds.

Her eyes flashed open. "Wh-what are you doing?"

"Keeping my opponent off guard." With that he pressed up deeper with his hips and used his thumb to glide over that most sensitive part of her.

Tessa moaned. "No, I won't be able to—"

"Don't, then, baby. Let it go."

He kept up his assault, stoking with his hands and pumping with his hips, until she joined him, riding him, her hands on his shoulders.

A few seconds later her movements became jerky and erratic, fingertips digging into his skin.

Yes!

She cried out, and her flesh clenched down tight on him, sending a searing stream of pleasure through his system that he no longer tried to fight. Instead, he released his hold, his own orgasm breaking free with a violent series of spasms that made his vision go dark for several long seconds.

When he finally came back to himself Tessa was half lying across his chest, one arm curled around the top of his head.

They were a tangled mess of clothing and limbs.

And Clay wouldn't have had it any other way.

Or maybe he would. Because he wasn't done with her. Not yet.

So, keeping the contact between their bodies, he rolled her beneath him, his body already responding to the thoughts that were beginning to filter through his head. "Let's say we try that again. Only this time in my bed. And without our clothes."

She smiled up at him and the pure contentment on her face sent a twinge of warning through him that he ignored.

"What fun would that be?" she murmured.

"Oh, I bet we can figure something out. And I promise I can make it a whole lot of fun."

Tessa actually laughed. "Then lead the way. And if you think I'm not going to hold you to that promise, buster, you're very much mistaken."

* * *

They had a small going-away party for Caren, just the housemates. But it was hard to concentrate on sending her friend off when her mind was on what she'd done last night with Clay. They'd made love several times and it had taken her until tonight when she'd opened up her packet of birth control pills to realize there were three extra pills in her little round compact.

She'd missed taking them the past three nights.

Three!

That had happened a couple of times over the past six months, but as she hadn't been sleeping with anyone she hadn't worried about it. Her night shifts always threw her schedule off, and it had been a crazy couple of weeks. Every other time she'd simply caught up with her dosage and gone on with life.

She swallowed as the implication hit her.

This wasn't "every other time."

Clay had offered to use a condom.

Why hadn't she let him?

She'd been too caught up in her own greedy need to get him inside her, and she had no idea if the condom he'd talked about had been in his wallet or in another room of the house. And she hadn't wanted him to get up.

Besides, she was on the Pill! Or she had been. And she hadn't planned on spending the *entire* night at his place. She'd figured she'd just take it when she got home.

Panic flashed through her system. What if his sperm had already made its way to an egg?

Would taking a Pill now undo it all? Maybe.

Which is what you need to do!

Or there *were* morning-after pills. That might be the best route.

But hadn't she been thinking about adoption or in

vitro once her residency was completed? The image of herself holding Clay's baby began growing in her head.

What if this was fate's way of telling her to go for it? That now was the time?

And what about Clay? Did he have no say in the matter? She didn't know. Her emotions were a huge jumbled knot in her stomach.

She needed to give herself a few hours or a day to think this through. It wasn't as if she had to decide in the next fifteen minutes.

Really?

God, she was setting herself up for a disaster. She was almost at the end of her residency—there was no way she could afford a pregnancy right now.

And especially not one with a man she'd ended things with four years ago.

What a mess.

Caren touched her arm. "Everything okay?"

"Yes. Of course it is." She searched her mind for a believable reason for being so distant. "I'm just thinking about the festival. There are only two more weeks to get ready for it."

"I know. You must be nervous. And it's weird about those jars, but I'm sure it's just some dummy playing around." She winked.

Holly nodded, lowering her voice so that Sam, who was busy pouring their drinks, wouldn't hear. "You know how things get blown out of proportion."

"What things?" She had no idea what either of them were talking about.

The two women looked at each other. "The jars. The ones of you and Dr. Matthews," Holly whispered. "Someone added something to them."

"Added what?" Tessa had been far too distracted, her head racing with other, more pressing, worries.

Caren's brows went up. "You haven't seen them yet?"

She'd been too confused today to even look at them. Actually, she'd been avoiding looking at them like the plague. Because she somehow had to get up the nerve to keep on practicing with him or she'd have a lot of explaining to do to Peter Lloyd. And to Marcos. No way did she want to tell anyone what had happened between them last night.

Clay's mom had shown up at eight o'clock this morning with Molly in tow. Tessa had been in the shower, still in a blissful haze after waking up to Clay's lips on her neck. Only the Clay who'd poked his head into the bathroom had been a different man from the one who'd sunk into her two hours earlier. "My mom is here with Molly."

Her heart had shuddered to a stop. "*Meu Deus.* What do you want me to do?"

She'd expected him to tell her to hide under the bed until he could sneak her out of the house. Instead, he'd shaken his head. "Nothing. I told them we had an emergency at the hospital and were exhausted. That you slept over." He gave her a smile. "You were expecting to hide in a closet?"

Yes.

She brought herself back to the conversation at hand. Which she couldn't seem to remember for the life of her. Oh, yeah. The collection jars. "We found out that the hospital administrator set them up. Are they overflowing or something?"

Holly glanced again at Sam, who was now headed toward them, juggling four glasses. "Just look at them when you get to the hospital in the morning, okay? You'd think that you and Dr. Matthews were dating."

She sucked down a shocked breath, but before she could say anything else Sam was handing her a cranberry juice—she'd refused the wine, saying she wasn't feeling all that well. Poor Caren. This wasn't exactly the send-off she'd been looking to give her. And she would genuinely miss her.

"So when does Kimberlyn arrive again?"

"She's supposed to start moving in the day of the festival, so I figure it'll be a good way for her to see some of the hospital staff in a more laid-back setting." Caren looked around at the group. "Make her feel welcome, okay? She's been putting a lot of pressure on herself lately. If she doesn't get that fellowship…"

Tessa laid a hand on her arm. "Don't worry, we'll make sure she feels at home. We'll put up a sign and everything."

Holly smiled, dropping onto one of the plush striped sofas that flanked the fireplace and taking a sip of her wine.

"I can tell her where all the cool shops are, or go with her if she needs anything. You just make sure you don't catch any tropical diseases, or we'll have to come down and rescue you."

"I'll be careful. Don't get rid of my room or anything. I plan on taking up where I left off when I get back next year."

This time Sam spoke up, his eyes glinting. "I'll try to keep Holly from redecorating it while you're gone." Their male housemate might be quiet but his dry humor sometimes came out of nowhere, surprising them all.

They all laughed right on cue, and Sam emptied his glass of the last of his wine. "I can't stay but, seriously, take care, kiddo. And keep in touch."

"I will." She gave him a hug. "I need to go, too. Would

you mind lugging those two bags to the bottom of the stairs while I call a cab?"

"Will do." Sam took his wineglass and set it on the counter by the sink. To Holly and Tessa he said, "See you sometime tonight."

With that, he picked up their friend's luggage as if it weighed nothing and headed out the door.

Tessa's eyes moistened. "I'm going to miss you. More than you know."

"I know. Me, too. But I'll be back before you know it. Give Kimber any help she needs, okay?"

Holly gave Caren a quick hug as well, turning away quickly, probably on the verge of blubbering, just as Tessa was. "I'll call the taxi service for you."

Moving forward, Tessa gave her friend a long hug, feeling sadder than she should under the circumstances. This was a fabulous opportunity for Caren, and she should be glad for her.

She was. She was just feeling weepy and out of sorts for some reason today.

"Email me as soon as you can. And call if you need anything."

"You can count on it, honey. Don't go and get married or anything before I get back."

That was one thing she could reassure Caren about. "I'm not planning on marrying anyone for a long, long time. Maybe even never. I have too much to prove to myself first."

If things hadn't gone south between her and Clay, she might already be married. But their relationship might have wound up on the rocks, like his other marriage. Part of Tessa wondered if she was even marriage material. She squirmed at the thought of a man wanting to protect her. Or pay her way.

She felt for any guy who ended up getting involved with her.

Caren glanced at her face and then smiled. "Be careful about saying never. And definitely look at those jars when you go to work tomorrow. And I hereby deny all knowledge."

Something about the way she'd said that…

"Knowledge of what? Caren, what did you do?"

Holly came back over. "Taxi is en route."

"Saved by the cab. Okay, I'll go stand with my luggage so Sam doesn't have to wait around. Love you guys."

"Love you, too," Tessa and Holly said.

Holly turned to her. "I need to run by the hospital and check on my schedule for next week."

"I'll straighten up." Tessa was actually glad to be by herself for a few minutes. She'd been running on nerves since she left Clay's this morning. Maybe she could take a bath in peace for once. It had been a long time, in fact, since she'd had a day off. It was sorely needed today of all days.

And it might give her a chance to figure out what to do, or at least work up the courage to do something that would make sure she wasn't pregnant.

She waved the girls off and slumped into one of the chairs, where she sat for several minutes, just staring at the empty fireplace in front of her.

Her eyes closed and her hand slid across her tummy. "Please, God, don't let me have to make that choice. Anything but that."

A gust of wind blew against one of the windows, making it rattle in its frame. Somehow she couldn't get it out of her mind that the Big Guy might just be looking down at her and laughing.

* * *

Clay was in the lobby when she arrived at work the next morning. And the man did not look happy.

Her stomach clenched, but she forced a smile. "Hi. You're here early." Tessa had purposely arrived a half hour before her shift. Obviously, if she'd been trying to avoid Clay, her plan had failed miserably.

And she still hadn't started taking her her birth control pills, because she didn't know if it would do any good at this point. But what she *had* done was decide to make an appointment with the head of Maternal Fetal medicine here at the hospital and see what she had to say.

You would think as a doctor Tessa could formulate her own professional opinion. And she could, medically speaking. But it wouldn't be objective. And that's what she needed right now, someone to talk her off whatever ledge she was standing on.

Clay still wasn't smiling. "I need to warn you about something."

This time it wasn't her stomach muscles that reacted but her heart, the organ racing within her chest. "Warn me about…?"

Surely he didn't know about the Pill fiasco.

No. How could he? She'd told him she was on them, and he'd obviously believed her. And she had been. She certainly hadn't been lying or trying to pull any kind of funny business.

And if she wound up pregnant…would he still believe her then? That it had just been a fluke?

"Come with me."

She shied back from him as if he was going to grab her hand, which of course he wouldn't. Not here at the hospital.

They did have practice today, so they would have seen each other at some point anyway.

His eyes narrowed as he studied her for a minute, then he simply spun on his heel and walked toward the bank of elevators. Left to her own devices, she followed him, assuming that's what he wanted. He pushed the button for her floor. "You might want to do something about it."

Again her heart skipped a time or two.

Stop it, Tessa. He has no idea that you missed taking your contraceptives.

She didn't ask what he wanted her to do something about, figuring that's why he'd come up to the floor with her. Maybe there was a problem with a patient. Or maybe even the one they'd worked on together. Except he wouldn't be on this floor.

"Is Mr. Phillips okay?"

He glanced back at her. "As far as I know. I haven't checked on him today." He motioned at the desk.

Her eyes skipped across it, seeing the two collection jars.

Wait. The jars. Caren and Holly had mentioned them, and Caren had denied any wrongdoing.

She walked slowly toward the desk, her eyes on the clear glass containers that were now lined with green bills. They were both stuffed almost full.

And then she saw it.

The labels had been changed.

Oh, God.

The simple names the jars had sported before had morphed into hand-drawn likenesses of them. Only these were no ordinary pictures. They'd each been made to look as if they were puckering up. And the jars been turned so the lips met...so she and Clay appeared to be kissing.

Each other.

She made a low sound of distress, and Clay moved to stand beside her. "It's obvious that someone saw us outside the hospital."

"Are they all like this?" she whispered.

"Every single one of them. It isn't Lloyd's doing this time." His breath whistled out in a long pained sigh. "And the worst thing is, we're not the only ones who've seen them."

Since the jars were in an open area on every floor, that stood to reason. "I guess the whole hospital knows about that kiss, then." She groaned, knowing there were going to be endless comments and speculation about what was going on between her and Clay.

And if she suddenly wound up pregnant?

She swallowed hard.

"Yes, the whole hospital knows." He turned to face her. "And so do my mother and Molly."

CHAPTER ELEVEN

TIME TO DO some damage control.

Practice that afternoon had been a bust. Clay hadn't been able to keep his mind on what was happening in the ring, and neither could Tessa, evidently, since Marcos—back in royal form after his hospital stint—had excoriated both of them. Publicly. And had told them to be back tomorrow for a private session.

Everyone else was off the hook.

There'd also been no end to the questions from Clay's mom, who'd believed him when he'd said that Tessa had merely slept over. He'd even let her assume that he'd spent the night on the couch, although he never actually said that he had.

Now she thought he'd lied to her, of all things.

And had warned him about letting himself get too involved, reminding him that they'd already tried that path once and it hadn't worked out. She didn't want to see him get hurt.

He was no longer a little boy, but he was still his mom's son. She was worried about him. And probably with good reason. He'd been shocked by the depth of his response to Tessa the other night. As hard as he'd tried to keep things on an even keel, telling himself that it was all about one night of really good sex, somehow he knew it wasn't. That was as much of a lie as letting his mom believe that he and Tessa had spent a platonic night together.

As if he and Tessa could ever remain platonic.

She drove him insane. And not in a good way.

The worst thing had been when she'd peered a little bit closer at one of the jars and seen the check his mom had made out and slid inside it. It should have grated on him that his parents had voted for Tessa and not for him, but they knew how good she was at *capoeira*. It would be crazy to bet on anyone but her.

Tessa's face had blanched, turning as white as one of the paper sheets the hospital used to cover the exam tables. She hadn't said a word, just backed away from the jars.

He had a feeling her reaction had something to do with that discussion they'd had a couple of weeks ago about his parents paying for her education.

But this wasn't paying for anything. They were simply contributing to a worthy charity.

But Tessa might not have taken it that way.

Clay had been so worked up about his mom getting the wrong idea that he hadn't bothered to see Tessa's reaction as anything other than petulant. But maybe it was more than that.

Tessa was proud. Very much so. Maybe because she hadn't been born here, she felt as if she had more to prove.

But he wasn't a mind reader, neither did he have the time to worry about anything other than the well-being of his daughter. He was not going to drag her through another one of his failures.

Which meant he needed to cool it with Tessa. Big-time.

Only he didn't want to.

He wanted to sleep with her. Again. Despite everything that had gone on with the hospital and with his mom and Molly.

He and Tessa had always been great together in that way. And she was a hot, giving lover who made him reach for the stars. The two of them had had some wild times together.

His body couldn't be blamed for remembering what they'd done and wanting to grab at more of the same. Especially since his love life with Lizza had been lukewarm at best. Once they'd married, she'd tolerated his advances, but beyond that she'd seemed perfectly content to keep to her own side of the bed. The only thing she'd really seemed to like had been when he'd complimented her on an outfit or admired her beauty.

And she was beautiful.

But Tessa had a quality that Lizza could never touch.

A raw, honest sensuality that went to the very core of who she was. And Clay couldn't believe no other man had snatched her up.

Then again, maybe she hadn't wanted to be snatched up. Tessa was so driven to succeed. Maybe that was enough for her.

Except what he'd experienced in his bed said she wanted more.

He ducked into Mr. Phillips's room to check on the man's leg. Brian Perry was there as well, reading the patient's chart. He nodded to the other doctor, who returned the gesture. Tessa had mentioned that the care team had met about his melanoma, and the recommended treatment was a grueling course of chemo. Mr. Phillips had said no.

"How's our patient?" Clay asked. He wouldn't admit that he was disappointed it wasn't Tessa in the room. At least, not to the other doctor.

Mr. Phillips was the one who answered. "I'm ready to go home, that's how I am."

It was said with a smile but, still, he could hear a little note of impatience in the man's voice.

"I'm sure it won't be much longer. But you're going to need to visit a rehab center to get back on your feet. You realize that, don't you?"

"I think I'll skip that, if it's all the same to you, Doc."

Clay looked at the patient's face and saw a tiredness and grim resignation that made his chest ache.

In the end, it was Mr. Phillips's decision, and Clay had to respect that. "Is your daughter still here?"

The man nodded. "She's going to stay for a while. Her kids are grown, and she said she's wanted to take a vacation for the past year." He shifted on his bed. "I don't think this was quite what she had in mind."

Maybe not, but Clay was glad someone was going to be with him. Maybe she would even talk her dad into moving closer to them.

"I'm sure she's just happy to get to see you for a while." He did a quick check, measuring function in his damaged leg. Dr. Perry stood a few feet back, watching the proceedings without saying anything. Clay assumed he'd already done his own assessment on the site where they'd removed the melanoma. But maybe not.

Once he finished and told Mr. Phillips he'd return tomorrow with news about when he'd be released, he left the room, only to have Brian follow him.

He turned toward the other man. Maybe he'd been right the first time he'd seen Dr. Perry and Tessa doing surgery together. He'd gotten a funny feeling that the other man might like her. Could be that he was going to ask about those damned jars or warn him off.

To which he'd offer a warning of his own: that the man

needed to mind his own business. He was in no mood to spare anyone's feelings at the moment.

"You and Tessa know each other from…before, right?"

The question took him by surprise, and yet it was along the lines of what he'd expected. "We knew each other in medical school, yes."

He was not about to admit that he'd been ready to propose to her back then.

"Did she ever express any interest in obstetrics while you were in school?"

His brows came together. "Obstetrics? No. Why?"

Brian leaned against the wall. "I expected her to apply for a fellowship in either cutaneous oncology or Mohs, but Faye Powers mentioned Tessa had an appointment with her today. When I asked her what it was about, she said she assumed it was about the fellowship positions, since applications are about to start coming in. Faye's still officially the head of the department, at least until she retires next week. She's decided to accept paperwork until they appoint a replacement, although she won't be making the actual decisions about who gets the fellowships."

Brian scuffed a toe on the linoleum. "Tessa did a rotation in Obstetrics, but I didn't think she was headed in that direction."

Clay tried to wrap his head around that.

"Obstetrics? Are you sure?"

The other man shrugged. "I can't think of any other reason Tessa would want to speak with the head of Maternal Fetal medicine, can you?"

"No." Tessa was always full of surprises, but he couldn't imagine her wanting to change specialties midstream. Especially not with her mom's illness driving her in the other direction. But what else could it be?

Something clicked in the back of his head, a few gears engaging the problem.

If she hadn't been on the Pill, he might have wondered if the appointment had anything to do with the night they'd shared together. But she'd assured him she was.

Could she have been so caught up in the moment that she'd lied?

He couldn't imagine her being that irresponsible. Besides, he'd wanted to use a condom, and she'd countered by saying she was on the Pill.

He hadn't argued, accepting the unspoken message— they were both clean, and she was protected.

Brian moved away from the wall. "Well, I thought you might know something. Our department would hate to lose her. She stands to be one of the best we have. I'm already hearing murmurs that the hospital wants to make sure it keeps her."

Clay already knew she was good, but he had no idea why Brian thought he'd know anything about what she was planning.

Those damn collection jars. If his mom thought they were becoming involved again, even knowing their past, everyone at the hospital probably thought the same thing. Or worse. "I'll direct her your way, if the subject comes up." Not that he expected it to.

Except something in him wanted to make sure. *Had* to make sure.

They parted ways, Clay heading down the hallway toward the bank of elevators. The first car opened its doors, and he got in just as the one coming down opened. Tessa emerged from the pack, heading with purpose down the hall toward their patient's room. Putting his hand out, he stopped the elevator doors from closing and murmured his apologies to the other passengers as he stepped off.

"Tess."

His voice stopped her in her tracks, but she didn't turn around right away. When she finally did, her face was pink. What the hell was going on?

"I just checked in on Mr. Phillips, if that's where you're headed. Brian Perry was there, as well." No reason to beat around the bush, but he certainly didn't want to do it standing here in the hall, where anyone could overhear them. "Would you come to my office for a minute? I'd like to talk to you."

He thought she was going to refuse, but then she nodded.

Leading the way, he was careful not to touch her as they got back on the elevator and made their way up to the fifth floor. Neither of them said anything as there were a few other people in the car. Finally they got off and headed down the corridor to Clay's small office. Once inside, he shut the door and motioned her to a seat, while he perched on the front of the desk.

"Like I said, I saw Brian Perry while I was in Mr. Phillips's room."

"Oh?" She looked up at him, clearly confused. "That's what you wanted to talk to me about?"

"In part. He's worried you might be changing specialties."

"Changing specialties? What gave him that idea?"

He crossed one ankle over the other. "Your trip down to the obstetrics department."

Her mouth popped open for several seconds before she closed it again, her teeth sinking into her bottom lip. Then she sat up a little straighter. "I—I'm not sure I follow. Why would he think I was changing specialties?"

She hadn't denied going to Obstetrics. It was more as if she was avoiding the word altogether.

"Maybe because you had an appointment with Dr. Powers, who's collecting fellowship applications until she retires."

Every ounce of color leached from her face. "How did he find out about my appointment?"

"She thought you were applying for a fellowship as well and mentioned it. If Brian Perry knows, others probably do, as well." He leaned forward a bit. "What's going on, Tessa?"

"Nothing." Her voice shook the tiniest bit, belying the word.

His brief moment of suspicion flared back up, finding new fuel and licking at it for all it was worth.

"Does this have anything to do with the other night?" He gripped the edge of his desk with both hands. "We still have *capoeira* practice to contend with, so we're going to have to work to get past this."

"I know. It's just awkward. I don't think either of us expected what happened."

"I certainly didn't expect to hear about you running down to Obstetrics within days of our encounter."

"What do you mean?"

He studied her for a moment or two then decided to be blunt. "You said you were on the Pill. You are, right? Your visit to Faye Powers had nothing to do with our time together."

"Clay, I…" He thought she was going to say something else, but she simply shook her head.

An eerie premonition began to march up his spine. Lizza had gotten pregnant with Molly unexpectedly, and he'd asked her to marry him to make things right. But Tessa hadn't wanted to be married to him back when they'd been dating, and he didn't expect her to want it now. Not that they'd need to.

She's not pregnant.

Time to get that thought out in the open and verify it for his own peace of mind. "Did you take your Pill the night we were together?"

Her hands twisted in front of her. "I—I'd been so busy over the past week and had several night shifts. By the time I got off... I was exhausted. I should carry them in my purse, but I haven't been involved with..." She shook her head. "The short answer is no, I missed a few days without realizing it. I didn't do it on purpose, Clay, I swear it."

A field of white danced in front of his eyes. He had no doubt she was telling the truth. He could see it in her face. Hear the anguish in her voice.

She might become pregnant. Hell, she might already be. And she'd said nothing.

"That was what your appointment with Faye was about?"

"Yes."

She wanted to know what her options were. They ran through his head. Start back on the Pill and hope for the best. Morning-after pill. Abortion. Adoption.

Each of those made his gut churn and his throat tighten. But it wasn't up to him. Although he damn well would have liked some kind of say in the matter. "What did Faye say?"

"She said since I missed several doses at this point..." Her words trailed away.

A few tense muscles relaxed. Did that mean she hadn't gone back on the Pill?

"What about Plan B?"

Her brows came together. "I'm right at the limit for time. I need to do it now, if I'm going to."

Something made him lean forward. "Don't take it,

Tess." In that moment a crash of realization had him off the desk and reaching for her, hauling her out of the seat and into his arms. He loved her. Had never really stopped loving her.

She wrapped her arms around his neck, unaware of the thoughts veering around inside his head. "I don't know what to do. Please, believe me, Clay. I never meant this to happen. Any of it. Not that it has."

"I know." He pulled her tight against him, memories of the other night chasing him down a fast-moving stream. One he couldn't seem to get out of. Tipping her head back, he kissed her. And just like that, things exploded between them. Mouths sealing together, hands traveling over each other's bodies in a mixture of anguish and desperation.

Clay turned with her still in his arms and pressed her against the desk, not even attempting to hide what she did to him. He pulled his mouth free. "Say yes."

He had no idea what he was asking for. Say yes to having sex with him in his office? Say yes to having his baby? He didn't care. He just wanted to hear the word.

Her hands went to the back of his head. "Yes," she whispered, just before she hauled him back to her.

Holding her against him with one hand, he swept papers and a pencil cup onto the floor and lifted her onto the desk. She leaned back, her light blue scrubs the only thing stopping him from finishing the job. He would soon remedy that. But first no more misunderstandings. "Stay right there."

He grabbed his wallet out of one of the desk drawers and removed a condom. If she wasn't already pregnant, he sure as hell wasn't going to purposely try to make it come true. No matter what his heart was saying.

He pushed down the front of his own navy scrubs,

sure there had to be some kind of rule against attendings having sex with residents, but he and Tessa weren't just any mismatched pair. They had history. One that had repeated itself a few days ago.

Ripping open the condom, he frowned when Tessa sat up.

Rather than leaping off his desk and hightailing it out of his office, she simply took the packet from his hand and set it on the desk. "I know we have to hurry, but give me a second."

She palmed him, her eyes closing as she gently squeezed then trailed her fingertips down the underside and slowly back up to encircle him again.

His breath hissed in his lungs. Yes. This felt so right. So good.

Before he could move to stop her, Tessa slid off the desk and knelt in front of him, her lips sliding down the side of his erection in a slow, languorous journey. Then she came back the way she'd gone, opening her mouth and taking him inside. Yellow lights flashed in his head at the bevy of sensations that crawled over every part of him, threatening him with imminent meltdown.

Pushing his fingers deep into her hair and closing around the silky strands, he allowed himself the luxury of closing his eyes and pumping into her heat, once, twice, before slowly pulling free. He sucked down a couple of breaths then reached to bring her back to her feet. It had to be now or he wouldn't find the strength to stop.

Setting her back on the desk once again, he eased her back in an act of reverence this time rather than a rush toward completion. Her arms curled above her head, eyes on his as he reached for the condom and rolled it down himself. He wrapped his hands around the backs of her knees and tugged her toward the edge of the desk, her hair fanning behind her. Rather than wait for him to pull the bottoms of her scrubs off, she rolled over until she was on her stomach then pushed the garment down her hips, baring her luscious bottom to his view. A much more practical—and quick—solution than getting undressed all the way.

"You sure?" he gritted.

She wiggled her ass. "Does it look like I'm sure?"

Leaning down to nip her neck and trail his lips up to her ear, capturing it between his teeth, he muttered, "Tell me you want me, then."

"I want you."

With that he found her, amazed that she was already moist and ready against his tip. With a hard push he entered her, going deep and holding himself there while he absorbed the tightness of the fit—the heat he could feel even through the protective barrier.

Her muttered *"Meu Deus"* in her native tongue said the feeling was mutual.

Gripping her wrists, he moved them above her head and held them there with one hand as he began to thrust inside her. Lord, she fired him up as no other woman ever had, bringing him immediately to the brink of release whenever he touched her.

He slid the fingers of his other hand beneath her right hip as he continued to press deep, finding that sensitive little bud between her legs and stroking gently. He wasn't going to be able to hold on for long, no matter what he did.

It didn't look as if it was going to matter, because Tessa began moving her hips as he continued to manipulate and squeeze, hoping he could at least hold on long enough for her to...

Just then, she pushed up against him in a couple of

hard, fast thrusts and went off with a raw whimper that reached deep inside him and set him free. He came in a series of disjointed bursts that only slowed when the hands he still held went lax.

He leaned down and kissed her neck, allowing his tongue to travel up it.

It evidently tickled, because she squirmed, letting out a strangled laugh. "Clay, I need to get up."

Aware that he might be crushing her, he hurriedly stood, pulling out of her and wincing when he immediately missed the contact.

He removed the condom, aware of her scent clinging to his body, despite the fact that he'd been mostly covered in clothes.

Tessa was slower to move and he couldn't help but admire the view, his hands itching to cup her butt and absorb the firm softness—two words that should have been at odds with one another but somehow weren't.

When she finally did get to her feet and pulled her panties—black lace, he noted—and scrubs back into place, she turned toward him with a smile. "I certainly didn't see that in the residency tips manual."

He relaxed, surprised at how tense he'd been a second ago.

"Didn't you?" He smiled back. "I'm sure I saw it listed somewhere in there. Maybe in the FAQs."

She came over and lifted her hands to his face, rubbing her thumbs along his cheeks. "Thank you for not freaking out about everything. I'm sure it'll be fine."

Oh, he was freaked out, all right. He was just good at hiding certain things. Sometimes even from himself. Surely they could work something out. Especially now.

"What did Dr. Powers say about the festival—about training? Did you ask her?"

"We don't even know if I'm pregnant yet, but she said there shouldn't be any problem as I've been doing the workouts for years. Sitting at home and doing nothing would be the worst thing I could do. I just need to make sure my core temperature doesn't climb too high."

"Good to hear. And if you do end up pregnant—" he leaned against the desk "—we'll figure something out. I can help with expenses—"

"No." The hands on his face went still and then fell to her sides as she backed up, her smile fading in a second.

"Tessa…" His patience dried up just as fast. "I'm not asking. I'm telling."

"Excuse me?" Her eyes turned to frost. "If I am pregnant—and *if* I decide to keep it—I can take care of the baby on my own. With no help from anyone. Not you. Not your parents."

A reference to them paying her tuition? That was just damned ridiculous. That was years ago, and Tessa had done a great job proving she could do a lot of things. But taking care of a baby while tackling the crazy hours that went along with residency? Why would she, when people were willing to pitch in and lend a hand? Besides, it was *his* baby, too. And his parents would want to know that they were about to become grandparents again.

"Why are you being so stubborn? You're still doing your residency, for God's sake." He tried for a more conciliatory tone. "Let's meet for dinner and talk about this."

"I've said all I'm going to say." She ran her fingers through her hair, no longer looking directly at him. "I won't keep the baby from you, if there ends up being a baby. But I don't want any financial help." This time she did look at him. "Please, Clay."

Anger washed over him, reminding him of all those fights they'd had in the past. Nothing had changed. She was still as unreasonable as ever. He put his hands up. "Have it your way. I guess I'll see you at practice this afternoon."

"I guess you will."

With that she opened the door to his office and strode out with an air of confidence. As if she hadn't just been sprawled across his desk.

He slowly walked around and picked up the items he'd scattered in his haste to have her, shaking his head. She might not be willing to let him help her but that didn't mean he had to listen to her.

And if he couldn't help her directly, he could always help their child, if there was one.

Surely she wouldn't stop him from assuring himself the baby had the chance for a bright future.

He plunked the pencil cup back onto his desk and sat down to come up with a plan.

One not even Tessa could refuse.

CHAPTER TWELVE

SHE COULDN'T CONCENTRATE.

No matter what she did, Tessa couldn't seem to get the upper hand on Clay during practice. They'd come to a kind of uneasy truce over the past week and a half, coming to practice and performing in a way that even Marcos seemed happy with.

Only not today.

Because her period was late. It was to be expected that her system would be messed up, as she'd stopped taking the Pill, so one day was no national tragedy. But she couldn't shake the feeling there might be another reason behind it.

If so, what was she going to do? Neither of them had spoken about the issue since that day in his office, and they certainly hadn't slept together again. But there was a nagging sense of disquiet inside her. If she was pregnant, she was going to have to let him know. It was only right. He was bound to find out, even if she tried to hide it from him. And then all hell would break loose.

And rightfully so.

She'd told him she wouldn't try to keep the baby from him, and she wouldn't.

But what that would entail she had no idea. She didn't

want him to start back up with the gifts…with always needing to take care of her.

She misjudged a jump and slid sideways, falling to the mat. For the third time today.

"Tessita." Marcos clucked his tongue. "What is wrong?"

"Nothing." Her voice came out a little too shrill, making both the studio head and Clay look sharply at her. Hell. If she kept this up, she might as well hold up a sign and let everyone know: *I missed my period, and I'm terrified.*

Clay touched her arm. "You okay?"

The words were said with such compassion that her eyes stung. Blinking quickly to rid them of the sensation, she went back into the "ready" stance. "I'm fine. Let's try it again."

"I think maybe that's enough."

And so it began. "Clay, I said I'm fine."

Everyone else in the studio had already finished, and Marcos had sent them home so he could work with just the two of them. So there was no beat to drive her forward, no supportive murmurs from the circle of participants to help center her.

Just keep telling yourself that, Tessa. You know it has nothing to do with that.

Maybe she should let Clay help her. Not financially, but emotionally. There was nothing smothering about that. If she was pregnant, Molly would be this child's half sister. And Megan and Frank Matthews would certainly want to see the baby from time to time. It was selfish to think she could cut Clay's parents out altogether.

And her own dad would want to help, as well. They both had busy schedules, but that could change. This would force them all to slow down. To rely on each other.

It wasn't charity. It was a village raising a child. Wasn't that the right way to go about it? She had to believe it was.

Yes. She would talk to him about it after their session was over. *Abre a mão*—open her hand—as Brazilians liked to say and compromise just a little bit.

As long as he didn't go overboard, they should be fine.

She might not even be pregnant.

Yes, but shouldn't she be prepared if the possibility arose?

"Ready?" she asked him.

He nodded. "If we're going to do it, let's do it."

This time, when she swerved, Clay matched her, move for move, step for step. It was the best session they'd had the whole time they'd practiced.

Fifteen minutes later, Marcos called time and gave her a quick hug, handing her a towel. "*Perfeito.* I don't know what that last part was all about, but do not change one thing before next week. I'm counting on both of you to put on a good show. One as good as you just did. Can you do that?"

Her eyes clipped Clay's and smiled when he nodded. "Cross your fingers, Marcos. Because that's as good as it's going to get."

"That's as good as I need it to be." He tossed Clay a towel, as well. "I'm going to lock up and make sure everything's secure before I leave. I'll see you at our last practice."

The second Marcos was out of earshot Clay turned to her. "You're late, aren't you?"

Her eyes widened, although she should have realized he would figure out why she was off her game. "Yes, but only by a day. That could be because my hormones are out of whack."

"Possibly."

He didn't look convinced and suddenly Tessa wanted to make sure things were okay between them. She hadn't done that during their breakup and it was something she'd regretted…not really talking to him about things. Touching his arm, she said, "I'm so sorry for making a mess of this. If I'd just let you use protection—"

His mouth went up into a half smile. "You're not the only one to blame. You didn't expect me to keep you at my house and ply you with wine and kisses."

"I don't remember the wine, but I definitely remember the rest of it."

Linking his fingers with hers, he gave her hand a squeeze. "It'll be okay, Tess. No matter what happens."

He truly believed that. That fact filled her with hope. Maybe it *would* be okay. "Will Molly be upset if I do end up being pregnant?"

"I think she'll be thrilled. Especially if you give us a chance to be involved in the baby's life."

She glanced back to make sure Marcos wasn't coming and nodded toward the front door. She wanted to drop a bombshell and see what happened. *Open your hand, Tessa, abre a mão.*

Once they were outside, she turned to him. "You talked about wanting to help." She licked her lips. "If it comes down to it, I think I'm going to need it. I can't expect my dad to shoulder everything on his own."

"Of course. I already said I'd—"

"I don't want money. I'd just like the baby to have a support system. And to know his or her sister."

He touched her face. "You won't regret it, honey. I promise."

Leaning into his touch, she tried to make herself believe that it was all going to be okay, just as he'd said. Because she'd made her decision, even if she hadn't voiced it yet. She was keeping the baby, if there was one. She just had to figure out how to have a child and still reach for her own dreams.

Letting someone help didn't have to mean being a charity case. She would keep telling herself that. There was a world of difference between bags of used clothes and a new life that needed to be nurtured and loved. This was her way of starting down that road.

Clay's thumb curved under her jaw. "Molly's with me tonight, or I'd ask you to come home with me."

"It's okay." She thought for a minute or two. "How would you feel about the three of us doing something together?"

"You, me and Molly?"

Tessa nodded.

"I think Molly would be thrilled. Are you sure?"

"Yes. A close friend just left for a medical mission, and I'm feeling a little lost these days. Although I think she's the one who changed the labels on those collection jars."

"I told you you had some loyal fans. Okay, let me call Mom and let her know we're on our way."

Tessa hesitated. "Will this make things awkward with your mother?"

"She loves you, Tessa. Nothing will ever change that."

Warmth bloomed inside her that spread to every square inch of her being. "I was pretty awful when we broke up."

He shrugged. "I never told her most of what happened. Just that we decided it wasn't right. And if things change, she'll be over the moon."

"You're a good man, Clayton Matthews."

"Maybe not so good, because right now I'm wishing that Molly was spending the night with my mom."

She wrapped her hand around his upper arm as they

crossed the street and made their way down the sidewalk. Traffic rushed by at a frenetic pace, a harsh reminder of what they shouldn't do. "Let's not be in a hurry, Clay. We'll just take everything slow and see what happens."

"I'm up for that." He dropped a kiss on top of her head.

Maybe time had dulled the pain of the past. She didn't want to get her hopes up or think that they could go back to what they'd been before. But maybe they could forge something…friendship, or even a little more out of the ashes of the past.

She'd never really gotten over him, she could admit that to herself now. It still didn't mean they should go back in time or start dating again.

Dating?

Hadn't they already gone light years beyond that? They'd made love more than once at his house and again at the hospital. There was evidently something still sizzling on the burner between them. And maybe those sparks had created a tiny new human. She didn't know yet. But within the next couple of weeks Tessa was sure they'd have their answer. Whether they were ready or not.

"Me next!" Molly watched Tessa go down the plastic slide at Family World and clapped her hands in glee.

Clay wouldn't have believed Tessa had this in her, but the kids' outdoor park and eatery had been her suggestion. And she'd claimed it had been one of her favorite places to go as a child. Bright stadium lights illuminated the place as if it were still daytime.

Molly seemed to like it, that was for sure. She'd barely let go of Tessa's hand long enough to try any of the rides herself, so Tessa had been forced to go with her on most of them. Which was fine by Clay. Something about seeing the pair of them together gave him a taste of what it would be like to see her with their child—and created a funny little ache in his chest that was getting harder and harder to ignore.

It was strange how he'd gone from "if" there was a child to hoping there was one. Tessa would be nothing like Lizza. She put her heart and soul into people... not into things. It was probably one of the reasons she'd wanted to become a doctor so very badly.

And the fact that he hadn't needed to finagle his schedule around to be with her only added to the enjoyment of spending time together. It seemed as if they were on the verge of the breakthrough that had eluded them during their years together.

But he would take it slow, just as she'd asked.

Tessa laughed as Molly tugged her toward the next attraction, a huge trampoline area, sectioned into large rectangles so multiple people could bounce at one time. The whole thing was then surrounded by a net and rubber bumpers.

"Wait." He slowed her with a touch to the arm. "You're not going on there, are you?"

"It's fine. Dr. Powers said I could follow my normal routine."

"That looks normal to you?"

"Absolutely." She gave him a smile and a wave and got in line with Molly, leaving him to head up to the elevated viewing area.

The attraction was busy, and they had to wait until two people exited before they could go in. Then they were climbing up the stairs and onto the taut canvas surface toward the available rectangles. Holding Molly's hands when they reached the first one, Tessa bounced up and down and side to side, the woman's hips swinging as the pair did some goofy things.

Goofy to his insides, as well.

Then Tessa moved to the other free rectangle, while Molly continued to jump in the one they'd just shared. To his surprise, Tessa did a test backflip, landing right on her feet. His daughter stopped to watch, eyes wide as she proceeded to execute a series of moves that would have made Marcos proud. She added twists and rolls and *capoeira* moves that became even more impressive when performed on the elastic surface. Within a minute or two a small crowd had formed in the viewing area, but Tessa was oblivious, the concentration on her face blocking out everything but Molly and what she was doing for the little girl.

In a flurry that reminded him of the last few moments of a fireworks display, when the operators let loose everything they had left at their disposal, Tessa went into a series of arcing jumps that moved closer and closer to the dividing line where Molly was standing, her little body bouncing in glee, her laughs echoing, as with one final leap that ended in a forward roll, Tessa stopped right at the edge of her canvas, facing his daughter.

Murmurs went up from those watching and someone whistled. Tessa glanced to the side, blinking in apparent shock. But she quickly recovered and, holding Molly's hand, directed the girl to give a little bow along with her.

His chest swelled with pride. Hell, he loved that woman. If he could only get her to see how good they could be together. How good they *were* together.

They could be so much more.

Their romance from years past had been a whirlwind affair, seeming much like that blast of moves she'd just performed on the trampoline. This time around he had to respect her wishes to go slow, focusing on steady progress that didn't scare her or make her want to bolt.

Only Clay had no idea how to do any of that.

Maybe he shouldn't try to plan it. He could just take things one day at a time. One moment at a time, starting with getting through the festival…seeing if she was pregnant or if all of this was a false alarm. And if it was? Would he still want to move forward?

Tessa stepped onto the ladder, making sure Molly was the first one on the ground. She paused to shake the operator's hand with a smile.

Oh, yes. He wanted to move forward.

The crowd dissipated, and when he joined Tessa he found her holding his daughter's hand, her cheeks flushed with exertion and enthusiasm. The woman was gorgeous.

And he couldn't help but lean forward and give her a quick kiss on the lips.

Her eyes registered shock but she didn't pull away and his daughter seemed to take the move in stride, the way kids did, already talking about what to do next.

"I think I need to take a few minutes to rest, if that's okay," Tessa said.

"Are you okay?"

She rolled her eyes. "I'm fine. Just tired."

Molly nodded. "Me, too. Maybe we can get a corn dog or something."

The rest of the evening went better than he could have planned and when he dropped her off at the brownstone where she lived, this time it was Tessa who leaned over and kissed his cheek. "See you at work tomorrow, handsome."

His throat tightened as a wave of emotion swept over him. The old endearment had seemed to flow from her lips with almost no effort at all. He forced a smile that he hoped looked more casual than he felt and tweaked her nose. "See you."

* * *

"Well, Mr. Phillips, I guess this is goodbye."

The elderly patient sat in a wheelchair flanked by a nurse's aide, Tessa and Clay as they waited for his daughter to bring the car around. He'd stuck by his decision not to undergo chemotherapy, saying that at his age he just wanted to enjoy the days he had left. Tessa couldn't blame him, but all the same she wished there was something more that could be done.

Sometimes there wasn't, and you just had to acknowledge that fact. It didn't make it any easier to accept, and she couldn't imagine a time when she wouldn't feel that crushing blow when a patient's cancer was discovered too late. But at least Mr. Phillips had lived a full life, unlike her mom. He was ready to go and would be surrounded by loving family members. His daughter had even convinced him to consider selling his house and moving back west with her.

"Thank you for being a straight shooter." He held out his hand, and she shook it, giving it a gentle squeeze. This would probably be the last time she ever saw him. And that was hard.

Clay came forward and also shook his hand. "Make sure you continue doing the exercises they showed you. You want to maintain as much mobility as possible in that leg."

She realized that somehow Clay had learned the art of compartmentalizing, dealing with the things he was able to fix and pushing aside those things he couldn't.

Not a bad trait for her to learn, as well.

Like maybe putting their past mistakes in a compartment and leaving them there? Allowing what was here and now to be what she focused on?

Surely they'd both learned from what had happened. She knew she had. At least she hoped that was true.

Mr. Phillips's daughter pulled up and Clay helped their patient move from the wheelchair into the front seat of the vehicle. Then the door closed, and he was waving goodbye through the glass of the window.

Goodbye, dear soul.

She closed her eyes for a second or two and felt a hand touch hers. Just enough for her to know it was Clay and that he was lending her support.

Taking a deep breath, she opened her eyes and smiled up at him, noting the nurse's aide had already taken the wheelchair back inside, leaving them alone on the sidewalk as the van pulled away.

He moved to stand in front of her. "I know you asked me not to put in a good word for you with Josiah Wesley. Would you reconsider that? He has several residents interested in applying for a fellowship, and I want to make sure you're in a good position to get one of the spots."

Don't overreact, Tess. Stop and think for a second.

Before she could, Clay went on, "I know you can do it on your own, but most applicants are going to have a list of references. I'm simply asking to be one of yours."

That made her blink. When he put it like that, it sounded much more reasonable. And she knew Dr. Wesley's reputation well enough that she was sure he wouldn't hand her a fellowship based solely on Clay's word, friend or not. She'd done all the hard work in getting ready and making sure she was up to speed on the newest techniques. Clay was just acting as a reference. And he knew her better than almost anyone, despite their rocky past. He knew her character. And that's what a reference was all about.

So she nodded. "Thank you. I'd appreciate that." The

relief on his face was almost comical, and it made her smile once again. "Am I that hard to get along with?"

"No. But you are that proud. And I don't mind telling you I'm damned impressed by everything you've accomplished."

"Thanks. I'm getting off in a few minutes. When does your shift end?"

"Same time, actually." He hesitated. "Mom is watching Molly at my apartment today, though, or I'd ask you to come back for dinner."

"My place is free."

"I thought you had three other people living there."

She laughed. "I do, but Caren has already left for her mission, remember? So that leaves two. And I think the only one off today is Sam. So if we tiptoe past his door, we might be able to sneak in unseen."

His finger hooked around hers. "But what about all that noise you'll be making."

"Wow, that sure of yourself, are you?"

"No. That sure of you."

Her brows went up. "Oh, now you've just throw down a gauntlet I can't resist. I bet you tickets to the ball game of your choice that I'm as quiet as a church mouse."

"You're on, Tess. But just in case, I think you'd better turn the speakers on your MP3 player way up."

Tessa fell back onto the bed, her breath heaving from her lungs, the strains of jazz still blaring in the room. She laid a hand on her bare stomach and stared up at the ceiling, trying to get her racing heart back under control. "Okay, so maybe the church mice were throwing a party today."

Clay rolled onto his stomach and bracketed his arms on either side of her shoulders. "That must have been some party, with all that shouting they were doing."

"God. You don't think Sam heard anything, do you?"

"Does it matter if he did?"

She punched him in the chest. "Only if I want to be able to look him in the face again."

"He didn't see me come in. He'll probably assume it was a show on TV."

"Jazz punctuated by moments of moaning and crying. I see how that could become a whole new trend."

Gripping her waist, he flipped back over, dragging her on top of him. "Don't knock it until you try it."

"I just did."

"And did you like it?"

She slid up his body until she was perched on a certain part of him. "So much that I'm thinking about repeating the experience."

"Hell, woman, you're going to kill me."

Only it didn't feel as if she was killing him. In fact, if what was happening beneath her was any indication, she'd say that he was up to the challenge.

Forty minutes later, dressed back in her street clothes, she headed out to the kitchen to get them both a glass of wine. Stuck beneath a magnet on the door of the huge stainless-steel refrigerator was a note penned in a decidedly masculine hand.

Interesting choice in music. Headed to the hospital, so don't bother sneaking him out.

She grabbed the note and scrunched her nose. *Gads! And you can't have wine, ninny. You still haven't had your period.*

Another little something she was going to have to deal with at some point.

Making her way back to her unit with one glass of

wine and one bottle of water, she was slightly disappointed that Clay had also gotten dressed while she'd been getting their drinks. She set them on the scarf across her dresser and waved the note under his nose. "I blame this on you. You can't get me all sexed up like that in front of people."

He glanced at the words then wrapped his hands around her waist and reeled her in. "It was hardly in front of him. But if that's the kind of thing you like…"

"Stop it. I'm already going to have a hard time not turning beet red the next time I see him."

"I'd like to be there to see that." He glanced at the drinks with a slight frown. "It's been almost a week. And since we just had sex, I'm assuming you still haven't seen any sign of activity."

"Not that kind of activity, no." She pulled away and sat on the bed. "My emotions are all mixed up about it right now."

"So you're still planning on keeping it?"

"That's the plan." But beyond that she had no idea what she was going to do.

He uncapped the water bottle and handed it to her then took a big sip of his wine before sitting down next to her. He slid his hand across her belly, sending a shiver through her. "I don't mind telling you, I'm already starting to think of this as a reality."

Pressing his hand against her, she linked fingers with him. "This isn't at all what I'd planned on. But now that it might be a possibility…" She shrugged. "A million things have been going through my head, like names and whether it might be a boy or a girl."

"A girl." He leaned over and kissed her temple. "One who has red hair and is as proud as her mama."

"Or a boy, with a big heart like his daddy."

Clay's thumb rubbed across her stomach. "I want to talk to you about something."

Everything in her tensed up. *Please, don't ask me to marry you, Clay. Not like this. Not for this reason.*

She was being stupid. Of course he wasn't going to do that. They didn't even know for sure if she was pregnant. And he had a daughter of his own to think about.

"Okay, what is it?"

He didn't look at her or get down on one knee, so a part of her relaxed.

"I know it's still early and this could all be a false alarm, but I've been thinking. You don't want any financial support, right?"

Her jaw tightened. "We've already been over this."

"And I'm willing to respect that. But this baby will be mine as well, and I want to make sure he or she is provided for. What if I set up a college fund that would be used just by the child?"

Tessa's heart turned to ice in her chest. "You mean pay for everything? Kind of like your parents did for me?"

She hadn't meant the words to come out with the harsh edge they had, but there was no way she could call them back now. Not when all the walls she'd just let down started to go back up, block by block. She knew him well enough to know that he would just keep pushing, trying different angles in order to get his way. *She* wouldn't accept his financial help, so he would just bypass her and give it to their child instead.

Was that what she wanted? For herself? For the baby?

As if sensing her thoughts, Clay pulled his hand from her stomach and stared straight ahead. Then he took a drink of his wine. Then another.

He stood to his feet and set the glass back on the dresser.

Just when she thought he was going to leave without saying another word, he turned to her. "If you think I'm just going to sit back and not participate in my child's life, you're wrong, Tessa. You can't expect me to help Molly get an education someday and do nothing for this child."

"But it's different with Molly—"

"No. It's not." He sent her an angry glare. "Even if she lived with her mother on a full-time basis, I would still want to contribute—to have some say—in what happens to her. It's the same for any child you and I might have. I would want to take care of him or her. How can you not see that?"

I want to take care of him or her.

At those words, all the anger from the past bubbled out of the compartment she'd built for it and tainted everything they'd shared over the past couple of weeks. His constant need to take care of her years ago—to give her things—had become a point of friction, rubbing at her until she was raw. Well, she could read the writing on the wall. He was about to start doing it all over again, and if she gave in on this point he would start pressing her to give in on other areas.

"That's not your choice to make, though. I think I'm perfectly capable of taking care of myself and any child I might have."

His face closed, turning to stone. "That might be true, but you can't stop me from setting up a fund like the one I have for Molly. Neither can you stop the child from using it once he or she comes of legal age."

Horror went through her. Would he actually go against her wishes like that?

"Don't draw this line, Clay. Please." All her hopes for making things work between them shriveled in an instant. Nothing had changed. Nothing.

"I'm not the one drawing the line. You are. And if you think I won't step over it, you're wrong. I just did."

With that, Clay picked up his wallet from the nightstand and shoved it in his back pocket. Out came his car keys. And without another look in her direction he let himself out of the door and, very probably, out of her life.

CHAPTER THIRTEEN

TESSA STOOD IN the circle of *capoeiristas* without a partner.

Clay had not shown up for practice. Not that she could blame him after the bitter words they'd hurled at each other. Fifteen minutes had gone by and Marcos was beyond frantic.

"What did you say to him?"

Her? Why did he assume she was to blame?

Maybe because she was. She'd reacted badly to Clay's words, throwing them away before she'd had time to sift through them rationally.

Of course he'd want to provide for any child he had. For her to expect that he'd be hands-on with everything except his money was ridiculous. But she wasn't exactly sure how to fix it. Or even if she should.

It could be this was the confirmation she needed that she and Clay were never meant to be together.

Except the problem had always been much more on her side than on his. He was a caring, generous man. He always had been. And she'd hurled it back in his face time and time again.

Over two bags of hand-me-down clothes?

People all over the world would have been happy to have gotten those clothes. So why not her? Did she see herself as so much better than everyone else?

Hadn't she gathered her own bags of clothes over the years and put them in the receptacle of a homeless shelter just down the road?

Yes. She had.

But right now she had more immediate issues to think about. Like what she was going to do about the match. It was possible she'd just ruined things for everyone, including all those people at the hospital who were expecting to see her go head to head with Clay.

Well, she already had.

And she'd come out the loser.

Maybe it was time to change that. She wasn't sure how. But she'd figure it out after this practice.

"I don't know where he is, but we should come up with a plan B, just in case."

She cringed, realizing that was the common name for the morning-after pill. The one she'd thought about taking after their first night together.

Only she hadn't been able to bring herself to do it.

Marcos let out a long wounded sigh and let off a string of Portuguese words that probably had his mother rolling over in her grave. "I'll be your partner. It's the only way."

But if Clay didn't show up, Marcos was holding her personally responsible. He'd left the words unsaid, but it didn't take a rocket scientist to hear the subtext coming through loud and clear. She had no doubt he would try to call Clay after they were done tonight.

That thought made her stomach churn.

They went through the motions, and they were actually better partners than she and Clay had ever been, since they were closer in skill level. But she knew right away that the fire and passion that had punctuated her sessions with Clay were missing. Marcos did his best to cover for her, but her moves were lifeless caricatures of what good *capoeira* should look like. Even the people keeping time with the drum and instruments seemed to sense it and it came through in their playing.

If this match was ruined, it was her fault.

Unless she did something about it.

But what?

The idea came to her just as Marcos made his next move. She spun away, the energy she'd been looking for coming back with a vengeance.

It had worked once before, maybe it would work again. At least she could try.

This might be her only chance to fix the mistakes of the past—and of the present. With a little luck and a whole lot of praying.

She just hoped it worked.

It had taken Tessa two days to get up the courage to send out the gold-foiled invitation. And she'd gotten no response. At all. As the week before the festival went by in a whirlwind of activity and patients, Tessa's days began to run together in an endless stream, punctuated by a definite lack of sleep.

No word on whether Clay had even received her request. All she could do was hope he'd remember the invitation she'd sent at the beginning of their relationship and see this for the olive branch it was.

She loved the man, she now realized. Wanted a second chance.

Only the festival was here, and time had run out.

As she changed into her white outfit and cinched the purple and green *capoeira* cord around her waist, she wondered if he'd *ever* forgive her for being so intractable and arrogant.

And if he didn't? What did she do then?

She had no idea. And a tiny wave of nausea had hit her this morning, similar to the one she'd felt during practice the other night. It hadn't lasted long, and at first she'd attributed it to nerves over the match today and what had happened with Clay. But now she wasn't so sure. Her period was still nowhere to be seen, and her doubts about everything turning out okay were growing by the second.

Marcos, already suited up and ready, came back to the dressing area and found her. *"Pronta?"*

"I don't know. I've never had to do the top match before." During their other demonstrations her spot had always been tucked somewhere in the middle.

Her old friend laid a hand on her arm. "It's not going to be any different, *querida*. You'll be surrounded by friends, enclosed in our circle." He moved on to more practical issues. "The match area has been moved down the hill a bit so that people will be able to see into the circle."

"Okay." She took a couple of deep breaths and then blew them back out. "Do you want to run through anything before we go out there? Practice?"

One of the other players came over to where they were standing, and Marcos held up a finger to tell him to wait. "We're not going to practice any more. We don't need to."

Since when did the *capoeira* master not want to practice? Never, that Tessa could remember. Maybe he was responding to her nerves and didn't want to make them worse. Or maybe he was worried about his epilepsy showing up again. He hadn't said anything about that attack, and Tessa had gotten the feeling he didn't want to talk about it.

He tapped her under the chin. "I'll see you over on the field in ten minutes."

"Okay."

His epilepsy wasn't the only thing Marcos had failed to mention. He hadn't talked about Clay, either, so she guessed he hadn't called to confront him after all. What was going to happen with all those collection cups? Or to Clay's job, for that matter, since they'd given the administrator their word that they'd put on this match? And the hospital trustees had approved matching the money in the winning jar.

Well, she and Clay had tried. And it hadn't worked out any better this time than it had the last time.

All because of her.

She checked her appearance once more before walking out of the space and down the hill, following other members of the *capoeira* studio as they grouped by the staging area.

Trying to shake the nervous energy from her hands by wiggling them at her sides, she joined the *roda* of participants as they waited for the signal that would send the first pair into the ring. She and Clay were supposed to be the last to perform, the whole exhibition taking about thirty minutes. She glanced around the area. Spectators were already starting to gather in the designated spot, which was just as Marcos had said, high enough that they'd be able to see into the circle. It really was a smart move on his part, because the action would be hard to see otherwise.

She caught sight of her housemates standing together at the front of the crowd. She sent them a quick wave. Caren had already gone, but Holly and Sam were there, along with a woman she didn't recognize. She tilted her head. Was that Kimberlyn? She *was* supposed to arrive today, and from the picture that Caren had left of her... yes, she thought it might be. It was nice of her to come out, although, knowing Holly, she probably hadn't had much of a choice. She made a note to herself to help the new arrival get settled in.

Marcos caught her eye and gave a slight nod.

They were ready to start.

The tambourines began setting up the basic rhythm, while the third man with a long curved *berimbau* added the deeper bass notes, using the single string stretched from end to end along with the *shoop-shoop* made by pebbles in the gourd at the base of the instrument. A minute went by while everyone absorbed the acoustics and then joined in with claps and a lilting chant they used for every match. Soon Tessa would feel the kind of euphoric state that drove the participants forward. It was all natural, powerful and earthy.

The first two *capoeiristas* entered the ring, their sinuous weaving steps carrying them forward and back, arms sweeping in wide arcs that carried their whole bodies along with them. Each bout was programmed to last two minutes, except for Tessa's, which was fifteen, so they didn't have much time to demonstrate their skill. The pair was doing a phenomenal job, however, both going into joint handstands, their legs bent at the knees, bodies perfectly still for several beats before coming back down at the same time.

They transitioned smoothly into their next group of moves, their cords swinging at their waists. Each pair of fighters had been geared to highlight different skill sets, moving from beginners and going up the ranks to advanced—with like cord colors entering the *roda* together.

Tessa and Clay were to have been the exception. Her cord was two steps below Marcos's, so they were closer in skill than she and Clay.

Not that it mattered. Her heart ached as pairs of

capoeiristas entered and exited the circle, getting closer and closer to her turn.

There was nothing to do but go through with it and act as if it was all part of the plan. Then afterward?

Well, first she was going to have a good cry. All by herself.

Next, she was going to hunt down Clayton Matthews and plead her case in person. Maybe sending an invitation hadn't been such a good idea. Men didn't take hints, right? Well, she would just have to be more direct the next time around: she would accept whatever help he wanted to give her.

The second to last participants entered the ring, and Tessa tried to get herself to a place where she could concentrate on what needed to be done. When she went to catch Marcos's eye, she was surprised to find him looking elsewhere. She frowned, continuing to sing along with the rest of the group. Normally the pair would make eye contact and prepare to go forward.

Something was wrong. His epilepsy?

Her nerves went on high alert, trying to figure out what she should do. She really didn't want to enter that ring alone and go through a series of moves that had no purpose except to show off. One partner fed off the give and take of the other.

And if Marcos was sick, she wanted to be there to help take care of him.

Just as Clay had wanted to be there for her. For the baby. God, she'd made such a phenomenal mess of things.

The participants currently in the ring were slowly backing toward their spots, the signal for her and Marcos to move forward.

She had to do it. She'd given her word. Maybe he'd

arranged for one of the other members of the studio to take his spot. If so, she'd soon find out.

Stepping forward with the low ducking side steps that kept to a strict beat, she glanced again to see that Marcos hadn't budged from his spot at the perimeter of the ring.

What was going on?

Then someone moved just beyond the edge of the *roda*, and the group parted to let whoever it was pass.

Her heart stopped in her chest, and for a second she thought she might fall to the ground. It was Clay. He was dressed in his white *capoeira* gear, his yellow cord knotted at the side of his waist. And he was moving toward her in those familiar crouching strides.

Tears formed in her eyes, making it hard to focus for a second. She blinked them away, sure she was seeing things.

But Clay was still there, passing to her side, leaning to and fro as he did, reminding her of a cobra. Only his eyes didn't have the dead look of a snake. They looked alive and warm and…

"Got your invitation," he said, just as he slid past again.

He had! And he was here.

She arched her spine and placed her hands on the ground behind her, powering into a back flip that carried her away from him, before pivoting on her heel, the need to see him—be close to him—overwhelming. "I'm sorry."

He bounced forward, leaping into the air, one leg curving high over her head as she went into a crouch. "For the invitation?" He landed. Spun toward the other side of the circle.

She had to wait for him to return to give her response. "No."

They advanced and retreated again and again, demonstrating kicks, turns and other techniques, but each time they came together, one of them brought a new message.

"Sorry for what?"

"Being stubborn."

"You are."

"I know."

The next time Clay passed, his hand brushed across hers, making the move look planned. "Why am I here?"

Come on, Marcos. Call time. I need to tell him the truth.

He came by again. "Why, Tess?"

She couldn't do this. Not anymore. So she stopped dead, right in the center of the *roda*. No longer moving to the beat. No longer putting on a show. Her eyes were centered wholly on Clay, who took one look at her and ceased all movement, as well. They stared at each other across the circle as the rhythm instruments faltered, the clapping and singing dying away a section at a time.

Then Clay was striding over to her and taking her by the shoulders. "Tell me, Tessa."

"You're here…because I want you to be. I love you."

The whole circle went silent.

"God. I never thought I'd hear you say that." His hands cupped her face. "I love you, too. But we need to be able to help each other—both of us. I need to be able to do things, without you considering it charity and pushing me away."

Hope soared in her chest.

"I know. I'll try. I'll have to, because I think I really am pregnant." She gave him a wry smile, knowing she would be battling herself about accepting his help but knowing it was a fight she had to win. And she would.

Because Clay was worth it. And so was the precious life that might be growing inside her.

"You are?"

"I think so."

His eyes closed, and he pressed his forehead tight against hers in a way that made her eyes sting and her breath stick in her lungs.

"I want marriage," he said.

"Can we discuss it?"

An exasperated chuckle met her ears. "Can we compromise?"

Slowly, very slowly, she hooked her right foot behind his calf and swept his legs from under him. Down he went onto the mat, with her right beside him.

"Yes," she whispered. "We can compromise." With that, her lips met his in front of God and everyone, handing him a promise that was stronger than any legal document. She knew he'd want to marry her eventually—Clay was old-fashioned that way. But they could talk about the timing. She wanted to get through her residency first, but after that…

After that, she'd gain not only a husband but his sweet daughter in the process.

In the background, she became aware of a dull roar that began to gather strength. The sound of clapping, and shouting. Not just from the circle of *capoeiristas* but from the crowd, who'd watched the whole strange scene unfold. She pulled her lips from his with an embarrassed laugh, only to have him slide his fingers behind her head and draw her back down. "Don't worry, Tessa, I'll wait until we get back to my house to finish this. But I fully intend to."

A shiver of anticipation rolled over her.

"Where's Molly?"

"With Mom and Dad. They're here somewhere, but they've promised to keep her for the night." Clay climbed to his feet, helping her up and then swinging her into his arms. Members of the crowd hooted its delight at the unexpected turn of events.

If she'd thought those collection jars in the hospital had been outrageous after a simple kiss, she hated to imagine what would be drawn on them next.

It didn't matter. Because, whatever it was, it would be the truth.

The musicians suddenly began beating out a frenzied rhythm while the rest of the group reacted by doing volleys of leaps, handstands and whatever other acrobatics they could fit in the now-crowded ring. From across the staging area Marcos gave her a quick wave and Brazilian thumbs-up sign of victory, just before Clay turned and carried her away from the crowds. Away from the music. Toward a future filled with fresh beginnings.

This time their match would be a lasting one, because it would be built on hard work, mutual respect and compromise. And soon, very soon, she hoped another adventure would come their way.

A new little *capoeirista*, ready to join the world of music, *rodas*…and love.

* * * * *

SURGEONS,
RIVALS...LOVERS

AMALIE BERLIN

To my real Cousin Karen:
1. Sorry about the spelling change…
2. Thank you for all your support
and enthusiasm for my books!
3. Childhood would not have been
the same without you in it. Xoxo, Duh

CHAPTER ONE

THE SOUND OF screeching tires stabbed Dr. Kimberlyn Davis's ear. One by one every one of her major muscle groups seized, stopping her cold on the Manhattan sidewalk, tensed for impact. One burst of sound, then another and another—rubber on asphalt, metal on metal—her every heartbeat shuddering in time with each bone-rattling sound.

Teeth gritted, she twisted toward the street in time to see a body arcing through the air, arms and legs flailing for purchase in the already warm morning sun. A man. A motorcyclist. He tumbled, rolled and came down chest first on the grille's edge of a still-moving black SUV. The second impact tossed him back—a human pinball thrown and battered far more than flesh and bones could stand.

Her clamped jaw held back sounds she couldn't control enough to stop, a whimper that burned like a roar—searing her throat and blazing a trail down her chest to the still-bothersome scar that would forever mar her cleavage.

She should've run when she'd heard the first sound of squealing tires. Away from the danger. But she had taken an oath.

Before the cascade of car horns died off, before the vehicle he'd flown into had even managed to stop moving, Kimberlyn forced herself to start. One stiff step, then another, each step loosening her muscles and allowing the next to come easier, faster. Off the curb. Onto the street. Within three paces she was running.

Moving cleared her mind. One act of willful defiance in the face of her fear, her memories, let the next one came easier.

"Someone call 911!" she shouted over her shoulder.

Please, don't be dead.

She kept her gaze before her long enough to plot a course, then through the windows of every car she passed en route to the man.

She's okay.

They're okay.

Awake with head laceration.

Okay.

Okay.

Of course this was how her first week in New York should start.

By the time she reached the motorcyclist he was wholly beneath the SUV and several feet from where he'd landed. Dragged by the front bumper. The driver looked stunned through the shattered glass. He had a gash on his chin and another smaller cut above his left eye, but he was awake, moving...

Over the past year she'd gone from running from accidents to running toward them—but it always felt wrong. Even the times she'd come on the scene after the carnage had been wrought, her very soul had vibrated with the wrongness of it.

Wrongful death. All her fault.

From the first wreck she'd passed on the highway after her accident—when she'd been three months post-op, still in a cast, and on the way to yet another session with her physical therapist—she'd forced her mother to stop the car so she could get out and help. And she hadn't stopped since that accident. Couldn't stop.

Only the top of her current patient's helmet showed his

location under the SUV and the only thing she could feel at all good about was the lack of engine noises. It must have shut off during impact.

"Check breathing," she whispered to herself, words slipping in a steady stream through her lips as she talked herself through the things she needed to do. Order of operations. Mental checklist for emergency scenarios. Only action could keep her focused, let her ignore the tangle of emotion rotting in her gut.

It was also the only way to try to block out Janie's face, always with her—cut, battered and swollen—at the back of her mind. It became harder to ignore in situations like this.

"Bashing damage to chest. Get to his chest…"

If his heart still beat, he had a chance. If she got to him fast enough… Nothing could guarantee survival. Even if he appeared stable, some injuries just took longer to kill you than others.

"If the patient can't come to you, you go to the patient. Gotta get under the car…"

She dropped her backpack as she fell to her knees and scrambled over broken glass. Craning her neck, she looked under the car to see if anything besides the helmet had been snagged.

She couldn't see much besides that he wasn't moving. To try to take control of her mouth, she began to narrate on purpose—the habit drilled into her as an intern so that the patient knew what you were doing. And on the off chance that he could hear her…

"Sir?" Sir, because this patient wasn't Janie. Sir. A man. A man she didn't know. Not her fault. Not her fault, not this time. "Keep still, I'm going to come under there with you."

Her voice sounded shrill even to her own ears. Anyone would know she teetered on the edge of panic, but she wouldn't fall headlong into it. She had control. Always. Always. But if her patient could hear her, she should be comforting him. Making him confident she'd help him, not squeaking like a cartoon mouse. Her throat refused to loosen, but she forced a few more words through. "I'm a doctor... We're going to get you out of there."

Her heart banged a couple times, popping out of rhythm as it tended to do when dosed with adrenaline. It would settle down. It was nothing, a flutter. Pay no attention...

"Not answering...not moving..." The whispering started again, and something new—the slow, hard beats of her heart, an insistent reminder of the emotion she tried so desperately to ignore. He was never coming out of this. There was nothing she could do.

Be optimistic...

Straightening, she looked around the street to the closest group of people, eyes skating from figure to figure. No police to help yet...

Get under the car. Take a light.

Ripping open her backpack, she fumbled inside for the kit, glad for once that she had to keep it with her.

Once the dented silver case was in her hand, she flipped it open and snatched out the penlight. With only her light clutched in her hand, she looked around again for help.

Running toward her through the scene she saw a figure in ceil blue, the color of the scrubs she also wore.

Someone with appropriate skills coming to help...

She flattened to her belly and crawled under the SUV with her patient. When she was beneath far enough to reach his wrist, she felt for a pulse. Present...but weak. She continued to narrate, as she'd been taught to do. The practice was supposed to help patients manage their own fear in emergency situations, but it saved her from drowning every time. Even now, when the man didn't move or answer her.

She ran her light up and down the motorcyclist's body, looking for points of contact with the vehicle. Nothing. No snags. No parts of his body pinned beneath wheels. It didn't look as if he had any points of contact with the underside or the vehicle, except for where the bumper had snagged his helmet.

"Is he trapped?" a man's voice yelled from beside her, his words only just registering above the noise of the street and the roar in her ears.

Kimberlyn backed up carefully, doing her best not to bloody herself on the broken glass. When she finally got out, she took the light out of her mouth and straightened to look at her helper. The embroidery on the left breast of his scrubs showed the name of her hospital, where she'd been headed for her first day.

The name DellaToro stood out on the tag beneath the logo for West Manhattan Saints.

Him. Enzo, her cousin Caren had called him. At least she knew he was knowledgeable and skilled. He'd help her.

From the narrowing of his gaze as it rolled over her own embroidered name, he recognized who she was, too.

Neither Caren nor her new friend Tessa had told her how good-looking the man was. Dark hair and olive-skinned, deliciously scruffy. Shockingly dark blue eyes beneath eyebrows built for brooding... No wonder he was so used to people doing what he told them to. Difficult to argue with a jaw that square—made him look hard and unyielding. Like granite. Sexy, sexy granite.

Perfect time to think about the man's attractiveness. *Goodness, what was wrong with her?*

The answer hit like a slap in the face. His face had blocked out Janie's. That was why she'd noticed, and why her cheeks tingled.

What she needed was for her patient's face to replace Janie's. He deserved all her attention. But DellaToro's scruffy good looks would serve as a guilt shield until she could get that helmet off.

"The helmet is wedged under the bumper." Breathlessness replaced her shrill tone. Was that better? "But it doesn't look like there's any crushed areas or snags. We have to get him out from under there."

"But the helmet is wedged?" He bent to look, then felt around to where it was caught, apparently coming to the same conclusion she had: there was no foolproof way to get him out from under there. "We need to be careful of his spine."

"I know, but a perfect spine never did anything for a dead man. I can't even tell how he's breathing like this. Or if his eyes are open." Or show her inner demon that the motorcyclist wasn't Janie, even though she logically knew that couldn't be the case. "We might be looking at head trauma, too. We have to push the car off him." She turned toward the sidewalk and the closest pedestrians and called, "Guys, we need some help pushing the car."

DellaToro straightened to look at the group she'd called to. The group that wasn't moving at all to help them. He then knocked on the hood and yelled to the driver, who had found cloth in his vehicle to put pressure on his bloody wounds. "Put it in Neutral."

The man nodded, still mentally with it despite the blood on his face. Should she check on him? He could die from lack of attention while they worked on one man whose chances were much slimmer, by appearances.

She had to stop finding points of comparison. This wasn't her wreck. That man wasn't Janie, either.

Then, in a far more commanding voice, Enzo faced the rubbernecking pedestrians and pointed to two specific men. "You and you, help us roll the car."

The authoritarian edge to his voice seemed to work. The men who had ignored her just moments before came down onto the street, shedding jackets and dropping whatever they carried to come to the front hood.

Figures. Also not worthy of examination right now.

Ignore the handsome doctor's jaw, help the patient.

His attention turned to her and he continued giving

orders. "Reach under and get your hands around the edge of the helmet. We'll push it. You hold his head in place as well as you can."

Kimberlyn maneuvered herself to the man's head. With her cheek mashed against the front bumper, she strained under the car to get her hands around the edge of the helmet. "Got it." A pause. "Don't let it rock."

If it rolled forward even an inch, it might also snap both their necks.

"We won't."

At least Dr. Granite Jaw had a plan for this. All she had was grime from the street, a lurking wave of panic and glass shards sticking to her scrubs.

With the three of them pushing the SUV, they managed to roll it smoothly back. Pressure was released from the helmet. She eased her hands loose and when his head held position she flipped the visor open.

Finally. Another face to quiet guilty echoes in her mind.

Young. Very young. Closed eyes. Fast breathing. Still no response.

Had that been how she'd looked? Blood loss sped up respiration and heart rate as tissues and organs became deprived of oxygen, so it stood to reason that it was. Except she'd been pinned inside a vehicle, and the blood loss had been mostly visible, not hidden inside the chest cavity.

As the SUV continued to roll, revealing the man's body, she reached for her bag again and her kit.

DellaToro joined her, unzipping the man's protective leather jacket. At least he'd had the protection of sturdy clothing.

"His breathing is labored," DellaToro announced.

Of course it was. She'd take comfort in him still breathing if she didn't know how quickly that could change, and give them all a really bad day. One heartbeat to the next, things could turn, and the person you thought was most stable…

Focus.

"I've got some..."

She stretched to where she'd dropped her backpack and then tore into it. "Here, Dr. DellaToro." She produced a stethoscope and handed it to him.

"Thank you, Kimberlyn. Heard you were coming." He used her first name while taking the instrument.

Was that some kind of dominance display?

Not the time. Correct later.

She dug into the engraved silver kit again. The fact that she could act now steadied her. Those images of her wreck were still there, always there, even a thousand miles away—but now they lurked on the periphery. The rabbit hole she never wanted time to go down.

Just a little longer.

She extracted the gauze scissors and began cutting down the front of her patient's T-shirt, exposing an already forming bruise. Deep purple stippling slashed across pale flesh, right over the sternum. Bad bruise forming. No way would it be unbroken, and a broken sternum didn't protect what was inside very well. Bruising organs at least. Heart. Lungs, maybe. Bashing damage could be more destructive than bullets.

She bent forward to listen to her patient's breathing as Enzo listened to his heart.

Enzo. She could do it, too.

"Steady, but fast and faint..." he announced, pulling the stethoscope from his ears to hang from his neck, and bending to grab for the penlight she'd been using under the car.

"Faint?" She repeated the word—as if she didn't already expect that exactly to be the case. As if it could be anything else.

Her fingers searched his wrist, and she could barely feel anything but her own thundering pulse. "You're sure it's beating?" She fumbled beneath the edge of the helmet to find the carotid, looking for a stronger throb. Her fingers tracked over corded vessels. The jugulars stood out as if he was straining.

Distended veins in the neck. Symptom number two that she'd both expected and dreaded.

The carotid didn't stand out at all and she felt nothing pulsing in the general region. Blood backing up in the veins and not pumping through the arteries—reason for the distended veins.

"Pupils responsive," Enzo announced, then listened again. "Faint, but still fast. Maybe speeding up."

She should be doing that, announcing her findings as she went. Just one more second, one more symptom… Make sure…

He hadn't picked up on the diagnosis yet. She'd share as soon as she confirmed the third. Even if she was already certain what her fingers and eyes told her, she needed something solid to reference.

Her hand shot into her backpack again, but books and sundries blocked her search. She upended it and dumped the contents onto the pavement. The wrist BP cuff she still carried with her rolled free—her second guilty security blanket. She grabbed it and wrapped it around the man's wrist.

"You carry a cuff?" Enzo asked, but he was listening to her as he went back to the abdomen and began prodding gently, looking for injury.

Kimberlyn didn't answer, just pressed the button to start the automated machine and leaned forward to listen to his breathing again. "We need an ambulance. Did anyone call an ambulance?"

A beep announced the measuring of vitals had finished and she looked at the small display.

Pulse one twenty-nine. Pressure ninety-five over seventy-five.

"Crap. Crap, crap…"

Enzo's eyes snapped to her and then to the display on the little cuff. "That's not good."

"No," she said, looking around again. "Did anyone call 911?" Repeated it louder.

No one answered. The ones who'd helped push the car had already abandoned them. Enzo fished his phone from his pocket and dialed.

"We need a large syringe, and I don't have one of those in my bag."

Either he wasn't worried by the situation or he didn't realize the extent of what was going on.

"Enzo, listen to me." She used his first name this time to capture his attention. When his eyes met hers, she had to force the words through her clenched throat. "Cardiac tamponade."

Attention captured. "How do you know?"

"See the veins in his neck? Fluid's coming on fast, filling his chest, and there's no time for the pericardium to stretch and accommodate it to let his heart beat right. Either blood or serum. Probably both. Preferably more serum than blood." More blood would probably mean a tear, but serum could just be trauma.

A cold pit opened in Enzo's middle. They were close to the hospital, but that was the kind of diagnosis you wanted to say *after* remedying it.

He barked their location into the phone and followed it with, "Possible cardiac tamponade." After demanding two additional crews and the NYPD, he ended the call and stashed his phone again. The borrowed stethoscope replaced the phone at his ear and he listened hard. The faintness bothered him. "You think pericardial effusion from the impact?"

She nodded, and from the lack of color in her face he believed her. No one could go pale for show like that.

He hadn't had a cardiac tamponade patient in his four

years of residency, but she sounded certain and had the look of someone with first-hand knowledge.

Something had to be blocking the sound of the heart. If anything, the man was underweight, nothing else made sense besides a wall of fluid muffling the sounds.

Sam Napier, his best friend in the residency program, had warned him that one of the many women in Sam's House of Gorgeous Roommates had a cousin transferring in to chase Enzo's fellowship. He'd expected…well, someone sunnier in disposition and appearance. A duplicate of Caren's golden-blond curls, dimpled cheeks and the too-cheerful smiles that made it hard for him to be around her before at least two cups of coffee. Not this soft-spoken, dark-haired creature with the delicate features and soulful brown eyes.

"He was hit chest first," she said, taking the blood pressure again. "As in he landed with his chest on the front top edge of the grille of the car. Then bounced off. I've seen this before in another crash. Three big symptoms, Beck's Triad. Muffled and faint heartbeat. Distended neck veins. A narrow difference in the blood pressure readings… One, two, three." She pointed as she counted, chest, neck and the cuff. "There's barely anything between the systolic and diastolic."

The cuff beeped again, the new results darkening the screen. Pulse one sixty-two. Pressure eighty over sixty-five.

Damn. She really was right. He was either bleeding out or something else was filling his chest.

The sound of sirens close by caught his attention. They were only a couple of blocks from the hospital, and the sound came from the right direction. Closer than Dispatch, and coming toward them now. Lucky.

They'd have a defibrillator, and other tools…

He could hear her little cuff running again, beneath the blessedly loud siren of the ambulance as it rolled to a stop just ahead in the intersection. "You." He jabbed a finger at a woman in a power suit who still stood nearby, watching, "Meet the ambulance. Tell them we need a huge syringe." He placed the stethoscope on the patient's chest again, doing what little he could do to monitor the situation as help arrived.

Before the suited woman even got to the ambulance, the medics came running with a bag of tools, defibrillator and a large hypodermic syringe they slapped into his hand. His order had done the trick.

"Have you aspirated a pericardium before?" Enzo asked, looking at Kimberlyn. He hadn't. Normally he'd like to try, but she'd made the diagnosis. Even if it weren't a professional courtesy, he wanted to see her perform so he could gauge her skill level. It was the best way to ascertain if she was simply another trauma resident or an actual threat to his fellowship.

Whether she had ever done it before or not, the small brunette crammed her hands into the gloves presented by the medic and indicated an area on the right side of the man's chest, "I can do it. Swab around and between the fourth and fifth ribs." She joined him on the patient's right side.

He ripped into the alcohol prep and broke the canister within the squeegee to disinfect the area.

"Tell me if his heart starts sounding louder or if there's any other change."

Would chest compressions even work if the pericardium was full of fluid? It'd be like trying to squeeze a water balloon inside a larger, overfilled balloon...

Even with the stethoscope buds in his ears, he could hear the tremor in her voice. Still scared. Was she steady enough to perform the aspiration?

"I will." He listened and directed the EMT, never taking his eyes off Kimberlyn, "Get him wired up and on the monitor."

Cardioversion was possible now at least.

With the extra-large hypodermic in hand, she braced one elbow on her knee for support and explained. "I'm going from the right side because the heart juts to the left, and I don't want to hit it."

Yeah. Don't hit the heart...

She looked steady enough now. Whatever had her fighting panic, it came and went in waves.

Enzo backed up enough to make room but stayed close enough to keep the stethoscope in place to listen while the monitor was hooked up.

This might have been a bad call. She seemed competent except for those nerves. Her nerves triggered his. If she ended up doing more damage... Maybe they should just move him now and hope he lasted another five minutes, or however long it took to get to the hospital.

With her arms steadied and braced, she waited patiently the long seconds it took for the electrodes and wires to be placed.

He listened hard, holding his breath to cut out as much sound as possible. His own pulse sounded in his ears louder than what he was hoping to listen for...

Closing his eyes helped, cutting down the external stimuli. Without vision in the way, he could hear the heartbeat faintly in the background. Fast. Very fast. And with an abnormal rhythm.

This heart didn't just inch toward failure, it galloped. The man would never make it to WMS.

What kind of fibrillation—atrial? Ventricular? He opened his eyes and craned his neck to see the green line denoting the rhythm tracing across the black screen of the monitor.

The line swung wildly in an undulating wave that told him nothing.

Check the leads.

Okay, check the placement of the electrodes.

He grabbed an extra electrode and placed it beside the

one that looked somewhat off-center, then reattached the lead. The line settled into the regular, horizontal position, allowing him to really see the points.

Ventricular fibrillation. And tachycardia. He listened again, with his eyes following the line. The sounds were almost too faint for him to hear—something that backed up her diagnosis: there had to be a massive amount of fluid compressing the heart. "He's in V-tach."

"Thought he might be. His time is running out." She breathed in. When all hands were still, she breathed out slowly as she pushed the needle into the man's chest.

She could've done this a thousand times. Smooth and slow enough to be cautious but quick enough to feel the texture of the different tissues she penetrated. Her eyes had taken on that out-of-focus quality that came with pinning all your attention on feeling your way to a site unseen. He'd seen that look on the real pros so many times—an amazing ability to visualize the path through and the imagination to picture the diagnosed problem. It almost felt like sorcery.

As she drew back the plunger, bright, arterial crimson began to fill the clear tube. As pressure was siphoned off, the heartbeats became a little louder, a little more distinct.

She withdrew the full syringe and looked at him, those eyes dark with fear...not the exhilaration he'd expected. But, then, he'd never been in this situation, either. Exhilaration was hard to come by. Something entirely more primitive took its place.

"No change?" So hopeful.

"Still in V-tach." Enzo listened a few more seconds to give him time to convert. He tried counting beats but found it impossible and shook his head. "No change." He gave the heart a few more seconds, listening again, then shook his head, "Clearer, but still distant-sounding and out of rhythm. Drawing off the fluid wasn't enough to convert him to normal sinus."

She paused another few seconds, pinned by those soulful

eyes. Dr. Ootaka, his mentor, counseled distance. Emotions clouded reactions. Enzo had never had reason to doubt this mantra, though right now he couldn't claim to have that distance. He wanted to give the hope her eyes begged him for.

Hoping wouldn't get the job done. "I've never dealt with this. How did they do it at your old hospital?"

"The only one I saw treated was done in the hospital and they used imaging equipment to verify the diagnosis and location of the fluid before they aspirated." She answered quickly, her focus returning, and her voice firmed as she spoke. One word led to the next, and she focused on the EMT. "I need another hypo. Bring two, just in case."

She'd only seen it done once. Ugh. At least she didn't look it. Move past it. Enzo gestured to the defibrillator and she followed his gaze.

"Not yet. He's already banged up enough. Let's give him one more chance to convert. Honestly, it's not electrical, it's the pressure in his chest. I doubt cardioversion would do any good for him unless his heart stops entirely."

She rose on her knees and shouted toward the back of the medic, "Bring epi if you have it! Enzo, start the cuff again. I want the pressure before and after each draw." With a fresh alcohol prep she swabbed the area where she'd just gone in, readying the chest for another puncture.

Long, torturous seconds passed and the other medic arrived. As soon as the pressure was displayed, she pushed through with the second needle.

Enzo watched another rush of bright red fill the tube. It looked thinner and more translucent than it had before. "It's part serum, or he's filling with more serum than blood now."

"Good. The pressure might stop his heart still, but maybe it's not an aortic dissection. Buys us some time."

If it was only a small cut in the aorta rather than a hole through it, they had a chance of getting him stabilized and to the hospital before he crashed.

He concentrated on what he was hearing—the monitor couldn't tell him how loud the heartbeats sounded so the stethoscope was still needed. It was easier to look at the monitor—or even the dark, eggplant-like bruise on the man's chest—than at her worried face. He could tell from her complexion that she was normally a warm tan, but today she looked pale and fragile. Not a great look for a trauma surgeon. Even a trauma resident.

With the second round of pressure relief, the speed of the man's heart slowly decreased and the rhythm began to convert to something closer to normal. First, a few normal beats amid the pre-ventricular contractions. Then louder. Then steadier.

"It's working." He pressed the button on the cuff again and then leaned back to place the stethoscope in her ears, holding the chest piece over the heart again. He let her listen as she was the one performing the procedure.

After a few seconds she nodded. "I don't want to go again, I might hit the heart. The less fluid that's in there, the closer the pericardium is to the heart, the less balloonish padding to protect it." And they didn't have the luxury of imaging equipment here to see how thick that fluid balloon was.

"Agreed." Enzo checked the cuff again. "One hundred and forty-three over eighty-one." The tension that had held him stiff and hard in the preceding moments left in one rushing wave, so swift his shoulders slouched forward briefly.

Without thinking, his nearest hand landed on the back of her neck to lightly squeeze as he directed her gaze to the cuff. Her skin felt hot beneath the ponytail she wore, and his palm prickled where it touched her.

"Blood circulating again," she whispered, her breathless smile hitting him square in the chest. Shared relief. Before he could think it through, he pulled her into his arms for a hug. She sagged against him, her hands fisting in the back of his scrubs.

Apples. Her hair smelled faintly of apples, and something earthier. Clean. Sweet.

The comfort was fleeting as within seconds she'd stiffened. Her hands released the material of his shirt, reminding him it wasn't the time to be hugging this stranger with the soft womanly curves, or smelling her fruity hair.

He let go and put a little distance between them. What was worse, looking overly familiar or overly emotional?

Color had returned to her face and was focused on her cheeks now. He'd definitely crossed some line.

Right. "Get a line in him, and we'll ride with you." He redirected his thoughts to the paramedics, who really didn't need to be told what to do except that they'd come to a scene with two surgeons running things.

Kimberlyn left the cuff in place but went about gathering the contents of her bag as if the contact had never happened. He reached for his cell again.

Ootaka answered on the first ring. "Dr. Ootaka, there was an accident a few blocks from the hospital. Assisting with a cardiac tamponade. Thought you might want a heads-up to meet the ambulance."

The conversation was brief. A neck brace and helmet removal later, they lifted the man onto a backboard, then the stretcher, and trotted for the ambulance.

"He's on call today?" She climbed into the ambulance after the stretcher had been rolled in.

Enzo nodded, keeping his hands off her even though his natural instinct was to help her into the ambulance. "He's going to meet us." He stashed his phone and jerked his head in the direction of the hospital. "I'm running. Keep our patient alive. It's only a little way to the hospital."

Some physical exertion would help. So would avoiding any enclosed spaces with her. Good for all concerned. Or good for him, which was the important bit. And she

wouldn't have to worry that he was about to hug her again.
What the devil had that been about? He was happy about
the patient, but still—weird.

Probably some kind of natural instinct in the wake of
all that fear and hope warring on her face roused his protective instincts. Unfortunately.

He closed the doors, banged once to let them know it
was safe to drive and then took off at a run for a nearby
alley. Three blocks by vehicle, one on foot.

After her showing up on the scene, even if Ootaka
would've been put off by the emotion, he still would've
been impressed by the woman's knowledge. Which was
okay, so long as Ootaka remained most impressed with
him. Enzo hadn't fought his way through school and years
of residency to lose it at the eleventh hour to a little scared
Southern nobody...

If his luck held, Ootaka would meet him at the ambulance bay and he'd have a couple of minutes to speak with
him before the ambulance—and his shiny new competition—caught up.

CHAPTER TWO

ENZO MET DR. TAKEO OOTAKA at the ambulance bay doors. Normally, sprinting a block would do very little to his heart rate. Not today. Today he was winded by the time he jogged through the automatic doors. Winded and annoyed. Off his game.

The older Japanese surgeon stood waiting, leaving Enzo no time to work out his problem. He barely had time for a good breath. Ootaka stared past Enzo to the empty ambulance bay, a look that demanded answers.

During the past four years, and especially the past year when he'd largely been Ootaka's primary assistant, he'd become used to anticipating Ootaka's questions from his expression alone. So he answered, "I ran ahead. It was faster on foot and I wanted a better chance to brief you."

And it's hot, he wanted to say. Hot and muggy, which no doubt contributed to his elevated pulse and respirations.

He took another deep, cleansing breath and launched in, giving the pertinent details even as he heard the sirens drawing closer to the building. "Massive bruising, likely fractured sternum, probably some ribs, too, but structure mostly intact."

From where the ambulance bay was located, he could see the vehicle turning into the parking lot. If he wanted to ask, it was now or never.

"I expect that there will be a need for surgery." He

waited only long enough for the usually taciturn surgeon to nod, and added, "I'd really like to stay with the patient and assist you."

Underhanded? No. Smart.

She'd been the one ahead of the curve with the diagnosis and field aspirations. While he wouldn't ever claim the spot of underdog, or let himself be relegated there, winners made their own fate. Preemptive maneuvers. Offense, not simply defense.

Besides, Davis had to learn sometime that the laid-back Southern lifestyle wouldn't fly in the city—something she clearly needed to work on, in addition to learning some leadership qualities. Let that be her second New York lesson: if you want something, you have to fight for it. Everyone wanted something, so chances were if you wanted something, then someone else wanted to take it away from you.

And that was enough justifying. What in the world was wrong with him?

He blew out a steady breath as his vitals came back under control.

"Let's see what we have, then." Ootaka finally spoke as the ambulance rolled to a stop, triggering the automatic doors. They moved off to one side to clear the route for the stretcher.

Ootaka stood with his hands at his sides, placid and waiting attentively. No indication anything was amiss.

Never in his entire career so far had Enzo ever felt this rattled in front of his mentor.

Only one person in the hospital had ever been able to rattle him, and they had an unspoken agreement of avoidance.

Even while watching his fellow residents fall out of the grizzled surgeon's favor, Enzo had always been the one in control and confident in his abilities. He knew Ootaka's rules. He understood the detached perfectionism that made up nearly the entirety of his operating-room demeanor. His professionalism, steadfast confidence and resolve were perfection in Enzo's eyes. Ootaka was precisely the kind of surgeon Enzo wanted to be. The best. Second to none after Ootaka retired. There could be no better place to learn that than Ootaka's OR.

Tension rolled over his shoulders and down his arms. Not like Ootaka's relaxed stance. In the reflection of the glass doors he could see his own arms…hanging at his sides, but stiff, ready for a fight. He rolled his hands at the wrist and settled. Shaking his arms out would only look even more affected.

He couldn't avoid Davis as he did Lyons. Did he even want to? He took an inventory of his goals. Staying on top would mean a better understanding of whether she truly was a threat or just another future ex-contender. Having a good understanding of his obstacles was the only way to overcome them. It was the not knowing that had him rattled. Once he had figured out the situation, there wouldn't be any weird emotional responses to taint Ootaka's opinion of him.

Whatever it took. Even if it meant angering a new colleague when she figured out he'd outmaneuvered her. But what did that matter to him? Another fact for her to get used to. She would've had to anticipate the sharp learning curve to come into the program this late in the game, and there was zero chance of her assisting on her first day anyway.

Ootaka never trusted one of his patients to anyone with untested skills. In that light, his request wasn't anything more than a formality when you got down to it. Asking first just showed initiative, a good practice. He wouldn't feel guilty about it.

Bonus: it'd give Ootaka an easy out if Davis came in asking, because she'd definitely want to assist. Helpful, like someone he'd want around for the next two years. As she exited the ambulance, Enzo added, "There was another resident on the scene. The transfer, Davis. She rode in the back with the patient."

"I wondered why she wasn't here yet."

In addition to untested surgeons in his OR, Ootaka also hated tardiness. The man kept an updated list of sins that could get you banned from his OR forever. She probably hadn't a clue about them. His action now might actually save her career—give her time to learn the rules before she went in blind and violated them. It was a good-guy thing to do. The idea that her competence might come into question because she'd been late saving a life didn't sit well. He could throw her a bone, let Ootaka know she'd made the call and aspirations.

"She—"

As the first word came out the two EMTs, Davis and the gurney rolled in, the little motor on the wrist cuff whirring to take another reading.

Ootaka cut in, "Who diagnosed the cardiac tamponade?"

"I diagnosed Mr. Elliot's tamponade, Dr. Ootaka." She immediately answered the question while still passing through the sliding doors.

All the mousiness he'd glimpsed earlier was gone. That was something at least. She recognized Ootaka on sight, which really shouldn't surprise him—she'd transferred in for his fellowship if the rumor mill was to be believed. She'd have done some research.

Though Ootaka was hard to miss. He had a kind of forbidding quality to his expression, even when he was in a good mood. Smiles actually involving his mouth were rare. Ninety percent of his expressions were in the eyes.

"The aspirations are what stabilized Mr. Elliot." He rolled with the name they must've discovered on the way. "Brought him back into normal sinus rhythm. He was in V-tach before the serosanguineous fluid was drawn off."

She still wouldn't be asked to assist, but she deserved to observe. It'd be the honorable thing to do, help her get a

foot into Ootaka's OR in a way she probably couldn't unwittingly screw up.

At the scene he'd noted at least three behaviors Ootaka
would cut her over: inability to speak with authority; lack-
luster leadership skills; and visible displays of emotion.
From the sidelines she'd be able to get a feel for things
without being in the spotlight.

"It had stabilized him, but he's popping more PVCs than
he was, and his blood pressure range is narrowing again,"
she added, directing all attention to the patient and the display on his wrist. "One hundred over seventy-five."

Enzo had gotten used to being the main one to answer
questions or brief Ootaka on patients. It was only to make
sure that he knew the whole situation that Enzo tacked on,
"Pressure had normalized to one hundred and forty-three
over eighty-five after the second aspiration."

"One hundred and forty-three over eighty-one," Davis
corrected.

Right. No more giving her credit. Those four measly
points didn't make any difference to the situation, other
than highlighting that he'd made a tiny mistake. Not precisely underhanded but kind of snotty all the same. Apparently she was capable of a modicum of backbone. But
squabbling over insignificant details wouldn't impress Ootaka, so he held his tongue.

Ootaka nodded in the direction of Trauma 1 and led the
way. In less than a minute the stretcher was locked into position amid the equipment in the trauma suite, all gloved
hands on deck.

"Davis," Ootaka directed. "Another aspiration."

Davis? *Damn.*

A larger hypo than the ones she'd used on scene landed
in her hand. A nurse took over the job that Enzo had performed earlier, swabbing the chest.

Again he watched Davis carefully position and guide
the needle into the man's chest, then another flow of bright

blood pulled back into the hypodermic. Not so watery as it had been on the second draw.

"For the third draw, it's a lot thicker than it was even the first time."

Enzo locked his jaw to keep quiet. Something he never did with the other residents...but this was Davis's show.

Davis withdrew the needle and concluded, "His chest isn't simply filling with serum again. There's bleeding. He's got a tear somewhere."

"He does," Ootaka confirmed. "Going to have to go in. Correct call, DellaToro."

Of course it was. Enzo stepped forward again. Before Enzo could do more than nod, Ootaka turned to Davis. "Welcome to West Manhattan Saints, Dr. Davis. An OR has been prepped. You're with me."

Enzo's head jerked back as if he'd been slapped.

Ootaka had invited her to surgery.

A slower step back to get out of the way again and Enzo found himself blinking, as if clearing his vision would do something to clear up what he'd just heard. But nothing had changed. The situation settled like lead in his belly.

Ootaka was definitely impressed with her.

The man told all the first-year residents they couldn't assist him until he'd seen them in the OR to weigh their ability. They observed, he gave them small tasks, and gradually built up to assisting. Usually other surgeons did much of the initial surgical instruction, Ootaka was next-level surgery. And if you didn't meet his expectations...

It wasn't so much that Ootaka made a production of letting the resident know they were no longer welcome—big displays of emotion were the same as big displays of drama—he simply stopped extending invitations. It usually took the resident a few weeks to realize they were no longer welcome or even on his radar. Enzo had even seen the man forget the name of residents once he'd stopped shining attention on them.

Davis wasn't precisely a first year, but it was her first year at WMS. Ootaka had never seen her perform.

A pericardial aspiration by hypodermic, while tricky, didn't compare to using a scalpel...

The team wheeled Mr. Elliot out of Trauma 1 and down the fastest hall to the OR, leaving Enzo to find something else to do.

A now-familiar Scottish brogue came from just outside the door. "Kimberlyn got Ootaka already? Caren said she was good." He looked around the door frame.

"Don't make me hit you, Sam." Enzo stepped out, uncrossing his arms to let them hang, feigning the relaxed appearance he'd rather others see. He just couldn't get his shoulders to loosen up. "What are you doing down here anyway? Aren't you supposed to be with the babies?"

"I came to make sure Kimberlyn had made it, actually. We were going to walk together today, but I ended up needing to leave early for an errand."

"Miss Scarlet needs an escort?"

Sam gave a low chuckle. "She really did get under your skin."

"She's not under my skin. It was a quick reference to that dark-haired Southern pretty girl thing she's got going on." Enzo had lied, and he wasn't a liar. It was a point of pride that he could be blunt and honest about anything. She'd thrown him off his game for a third time. "It takes more than a strong base of medical knowledge to impress Ootaka. She's got steady hands, but her leadership is non-existent. Couldn't even rally some rubberneckers at the accident to call 911 or to push the vehicle off the patient."

"Want to grab a pint after your shift? You can find some pretty lass to take your mind off Cricket."

"Yes," Enzo answered, because a beer sounded good, as did the idea of finding a *pretty lass*. Someone more his flavor. Not dark and soulful. Davis probably wrote poetry and wore black all the time when she wasn't in scrubs. Also not a lass. That sounded entirely too much as if it could fit Davis, and he'd rather have someone real. Overly emotional just didn't do it for him, either.

Hold on. "Did you call her Cricket?"

"It's her nickname. Don't tell her I told you."

Enzo snorted, but nodded to his friend—Dr. Cricket's new housemate—and headed off to look at the surgery board. Maybe they'd be in one of the surgeries with an observation gallery so he could at least watch...

A short walk and he stood, looking the whiteboard over. Head of surgical residents Dr. Gareth Langley had taken one of the rooms with a gallery. The name Lyons stood out on the list. He looked only long enough to determine he wouldn't accidentally walk in on that man's surgery, then moved on. Ootaka had indeed reserved the last gallery.

If he hurried, he might even avoid accidentally running into Lyons on the way. That had been the other bit of information to stand out on the board: times and approximate duration. His father was the last person he wanted to see today. Or any day. The fact that they frequently shared a hospital made it impossible to avoid him altogether, but Enzo did his best. Always did, and he imagined Lyons did, as well. In four years they'd managed to avoid saying even a single word to one another and that level of avoidance couldn't happen without two people actively working at it.

He relaxed only when he'd stepped through the door leading up to Ootaka's gallery.

In his time in the program nearly all of his competition had fallen by the wayside. Winning this fellowship was a marathon, but Davis was here to sprint the last leg. An immediate invitation into Ootaka's OR definitely meant she had started the sprint and he felt as if he was standing still, which was ridiculous. She couldn't cover that much distance in one surgery.

Time to get his head back in the game. Observe the new surgeon. See how much of what Sam had said was actually correct. See if she really was a threat to his goal or if his mind was playing tricks on him. However unlikely the possibility might be, he needed to judge for himself. If her backbone wasn't full-on displayed, it didn't matter how much she knew. She wouldn't threaten his position as favorite horse in the race for Ootaka's final fellowship.

But it might do the pit in his gut some good to see her getting the unavoidable dressing-down coming her way.

God, he sounded like a petulant child wanting Daddy's approval. His stomach churned.

No one could survive Ootaka's surgery without learning his particular rules. He should feel sorry for her.

If her arrival hadn't felt like another shadow he'd have to fight his way out of, he might actually muster some sympathy.

The only way to find whatever was bleeding inside Mr. Elliot's chest was to crack it.

Kimberlyn had been in a few thoracic surgeries since the accident, during the last months of her first year back… but seeing a chest open still made her scar burn.

This was someone else's sternum, someone else's pain.

The words danced through her mind on repeat every time she started to feel her chest tighten or her heart speed up.

Mr. Elliot deserved undivided attention, and the likelihood he'd one day have his own scar to fixate on hinged on the talent and skill of his surgical team. Mainly Ootaka, but she mattered.

Luckily, Ootaka was the best. One day she'd be that good—another mini-Ootaka to save those poor wretches who had to be cut out of ugly car crashes. Just as she had.

Ootaka's fellowship was the reason she'd come north. He announced last year that it was the last fellowship he was going to do, which was why she had ended up transferring to West Manhattan Saints when she'd been set up perfectly and had enjoyed her former hospital.

Waiting two years to apply for his next fellowship? No longer an option.

The intention toward trauma hadn't really existed before her accident. She'd thought about it but had floated between cardiac, cardiothoracic and plain old general surgery, too.

Her life had become a series of dominoes that day...

As much as she hated what had happened to Mr. Elliot, his pain was her good fortune. It had gotten her noticed immediately. Now she just needed to perform well in this surgery. Keep Ootaka's attention. Build his appreciation and belief in her. Do everything in her power to make this year count. Keep her promise: save the good people like Janie from the bad people like *her*.

Or, better, save the victims so the idiots who'd caused the wreck could learn and avoid turning into her. Normal lives for all involved. Two birds, one stone. That was a worthy goal. That would make her worthy.

Which meant outshining Ootaka's star pupil, Dr. I'm-Running-Ahead...

"Suction."

So Ootaka started her with the basics. Minding the blood was important enough. Suctioning it off where he needed to see what he was doing, keeping an eye on the pressure to alert him when they needed to give fluids...

Which was now.

"He's lost a...bit of blood," she began. Assisting a surgeon for the first time always meant getting used to the way they liked to do things. Very few things were standard when it came to OR etiquette. Hence her needing to ask, "At what point do you like to hang blood?"

"Are you saying that you believe we should be doing so now, Dr. Davis?" Ootaka never took his eyes off the patient, but movement in the corner of her eye pulled her gaze up. Someone in the gallery.

Enzo. Could he hear them up there?

Okay, she was being paranoid. Why would that matter? If he could hear, maybe he'd just pick up on how to be professional and not sneaky with a colleague.

Focus on the OR, not on who lurked above it.

"Yes, Dr. Ootaka. I would like to give him some packed red now."

"Better. In my operating room, do not couch your concern for the patient in question. You're a surgeon. Asking questions you know the answer to makes you sound uneducated. Save your questions for when you really don't know the answer."

Right. She could do that. Most of the surgeons she'd worked with preferred deference, but maybe that was their way of keeping a hierarchy in place. Ootaka's air and reputation did that well enough—maybe he had no need to force protocol through some etiquette dance.

"Yes, Doctor. I'll remember that." While she usually handled change well, not knowing how she was to behave wasn't one of those changes she could just float with. If she wasn't supposed to ask questions, did that mean she should just do what she thought was best? Mr. Elliot was Ootaka's patient now, not hers.

He did glance up long enough to look her in the eye. "Yes?"

"Does that mean for me to go ahead with what I think is the right decision, or—"

"No. Announce first with clear intentions and reasons. Always reasons." He'd started to sound a little annoyed, so she was happy when he immediately switched back to the subject. "Why packed red cells?"

As far as reprimands went, it wasn't much of one, but all corrections made her cheeks burn. Luckily, the surgical mask kept anyone from noticing, even if the inside of her mask was getting a bit stuffy.

Before moving to carry out the task of replenishing the

man's blood, she answered Ootaka. Minimize chance of rejection or reaction. Saline could do the job of plasma for now. Oxygen depletion to traumatized tissue was best avoided, so red cells were her choice. Reasons anyone in medical school would know, let alone a fifth-year surgical resident.

But at least there was some comfort in the sameness— questions and answers accompanied all lessons, no matter what hospital or surgeon you were with. She looked up at the galley again, and this time Enzo was looking at her. Not just watching the table. When she looked up, his gaze was locked on hers. Her belly trembled.

How was she supposed to keep her eyes on the patient with him staring? Correction: staring and smirking? Or was that a grimace?

Ignore him.

With the Q&A finished, she ordered the packed cells and another bag of saline.

So he could hear them. Whatever. Not that she expected any less from her competition. Caren had warned her he could be a jerk. He'd wanted to assist. She'd seen it in his eyes when Ootaka had invited her into his OR. And what was that about him being right about the need for surgery? She had to wonder what else he'd told Ootaka after running to get there first. She should've run with him. Only that would've meant leaving Mr. Elliot—and even for a couple of minutes she couldn't have made herself do so, knowing that neither of them would be with him.

What she needed to do was not think about him as an attractive man. Focus on the jerk, not the jaw. The arrogance. And all that jaw did was frame a smirking mouth.

Jerky, not to mention manipulative. *Keep our patient alive* indeed. Those words had assured she'd stay put.

But, worse, they'd made her feel important enough that she'd hardly questioned why he wasn't riding with them in the ambulance.

They'd made her underestimate him…

Later she'd send Caren a crankygram—an email she'd no doubt check in a couple of weeks. Maybe she could find Tessa after the surgery ended to get information. See if her new friend knew Enzo's tactics. Plot some ways to outmaneuver him, or at least figure out his usual manner of manipulation. It would certainly behoove her to know what his weaknesses were. Aside from arrogance.

Or maybe just vent. His attempt to maneuver the situation hadn't worked out so well for him this time. Maybe she didn't need to try to learn to do that. Maybe it was just a case of where the cream rose, and she just needed to focus on herself and…stuff. That's what she'd like. Avoid confrontation. Be pleasant and easy to work with. Be the person that everyone liked, or at least felt no overt hostility toward.

Be exactly who she'd been before the accident. That'd be awesome.

And impossible.

Think later. Pretend Caren had been overreacting when she'd focused on how hard Kimberlyn would have to fight for the fellowship.

CHAPTER THREE

Six hours of surgery later, Kimberlyn edged onto a stool that one of the post-op nurses had been kind enough to place beside Mr. Elliot's gurney.

This wasn't her usual routine. She usually avoided Post-op due to the confined quarters, activity and motility required for the staff to attend all the patients. Although her feet and back ached from the long day, and although she could swear the screws she would always carry in her femur buzzed and itched from standing in one position for hours, the manner of their meeting made it impossible for her to leave his side yet.

Distance was already an issue with this patient. Something she should work on.

Within the past year there hadn't been many patients who'd delivered gut punches like this, but she could still recite the names of each one, along with the big facts. How they'd presented. How they'd been injured. Procedures required to save them. Major complications. Length of hospital stay...

And she could recite even tiny details from the chart of the patient who hadn't made it.

"So, you were at Vanderbilt before transferring here?"

There was so much activity in the ward she hadn't even noticed him entering. The surgery had become like that at around the two-hour mark, when Ootaka had given her bigger tasks. They'd taken up more space in her brain, letting her stop worrying whether she was going to make some etiquette mistake or what Enzo thought about her performance.

Part of her wanted to know why Enzo had come to Postop now, the other part just wanted to sit and rest. And stop thinking. Stop comparing. Stop bracing for impact…

Sometimes people pulled through open-heart surgery only to die in Recovery or the surgical ICU—the reason she sat there. The first few days were the most tenuous. But here he was distracting her—her new and annoyingly attractive nemesis. Or possible nemesis. Working that out right now required too much brainpower.

"Yes." There. She'd answered. Maybe he'd go away if she wasn't chatty.

Obviously he could find out information about her from other places, much as she'd done before arriving. He'd known who she was on first meeting, after all. And now he was spouting questions about procedure at her alma mater. He knew she had her sights set on Ootaka's fellowship. The grapevine didn't just extend from Caren and Tessa to her. It went the other way, too. Enzo had a grape on the vine.

And he could just go squeeze that grape for juice.

He rounded the gurney to stand on the other side of Mr. Elliot, giving the monitors a look, though he continued speaking quietly to her. "And you're Caren's friend."

"Cousin," she corrected. Correcting him was surprisingly satisfying. No doubt a holdover from the irritation she'd been nursing about his *run ahead* and *smirky looming* stuff.

He turned his eyes to her. "Did she give up her spot in the program specifically to free up space for you?"

"Of course she didn't." The hotly whispered denial sprang from Kimberlyn's lips so fast she hadn't even really considered whether he was correct before speaking.

Had Caren done that? It was like her cousin to do something altruistic and then lie about it to salve people's pride, but... "She said she wanted the opportunity to go into the field with that professor and his mission to Cameroon."

A nurse approached to get vitals—as she must every fifteen minutes—and Kimberlyn became all too aware of how crowded Mr. Elliot's bedside had become. Her being there had been fine, but two surgeons bickering definitely wasn't fine.

With energy granted by indignation, she stood, pushed the stool back out of the way and headed out of the ward. If he was going to grill her, he could do it somewhere else. The patient needed rest, and the nurses didn't need the distractions in the already tight quarters.

He followed her out.

Once the door swung shut and they were alone in the hallway, she turned to face him.

"Why did you ask me that? It's a...really...rude thing to say. Insinuating that I'm taking advantage of her good nature and maybe wrecking her career or something." Confrontation. Yay. Was it too much to ask that they maintain a civilized competitive atmosphere based entirely on merits and...positive junk?

"I just want to figure you out."

He didn't look bothered to be called on his machinations. He looked relaxed, no longer smirking, and also as if his question wasn't rude or anything to get worked up over. He didn't even stand at attention now, leaning with one of those broad shoulders propped against the wall, arms crossed and weight shifted to one foot. A lazy angle made from his...admittedly nice...athletic lines and other angles.

Not what she was supposed to be focusing on. Kimberlyn forced her gaze back to his.

"And I want to believe that you are a decent guy despite having been told otherwise, but the only reason I can think of for you to ask me that is because you want to put me on the defensive. Make me uncomfortable in my new program."

Mission accomplished. That, along with the sudden realization that she was doing exactly what strange men did to her: ogling his body. But that was her making *herself* uncomfortable.

When her eyes locked with his again, his brows lifted a little. Busted. But at least he didn't comment on it.

"I'm curious about you. Most people don't change programs in the final year. It's too hard to rebuild your support system and reputation in a new hospital. Makes this seem like some kind of impulse decision. A short-term goal. Not a career choice."

"Choosing trauma as my specialty, or choosing this fellowship as the one I wanted?"

He nodded. "Both. You just decided a couple months ago, right?"

"No. I decided before I began my fourth year in residency." When she was in the hospital for other reasons besides work. The very thing she'd spent the whole day trying not to think about, and which she had no intention of revealing to him. Her stomach crunched and growled in a way that was part hunger, part nausea. Perfect. "But I really don't owe you any explanations about my or Caren's motivations. I'm here. I'm not leaving. You can't intimidate me or scare me into changing course."

"I'm not trying to do either, Davis."

"You're just trying to figure me out," she repeated, disbelief making her fling her hand through the air. "Fine. Here's all you need to know about me—I'm good at what I do. In fact, I'm so good at what I do I'm not going to play games with you. I'm not going to scheme or run ahead to try to get to Ootaka first to get what I want. That's not who I am, and it's not who I want to be. You want to help me figure you out? Because right now, after having had a day to think about it, I'm having a hard time being charitable in my assessment of your character. You were great on the scene. Actually, I was extremely thankful that you were there. But then you spent the day smirking at me from the gallery. And now this?"

Once she'd started, it got easier to say what she thought about his behavior, too easy. She'd feel guilty, but her words looked to bother him about as much as a sunny spring day bothered daisies. She knew that people were blunter up north, but dang...

Before she lost her gumption, she whispered hotly, "And just for the record, I know what DellaToro means. From the bull, or of the bull...and obviously it's missing a final word." The half-whispered words could've passed for a two-year-old with her first introduction to whispering.

He smiled at the end of her tirade, uncrossing his arms as he chuckled, which was at least better than all the smirking. "Feel better?"

"No!" A bit mean and snotty, actually. And immature, and ridiculous that she'd taken the long way around saying the *S*-word... Lame.

"Did you see that condition a lot at Vandy?" He asked again.

Back to digging for information...

"No." Again she denied first and then had to pause and consider. He'd managed to rile her up, but that didn't mean she had to stay riled. She could chill out. If she let that little fire he'd built in her gut go out, he might not see how emotionally battered the whole day had left her. Depriving him of information had started to seem like a valid survival tactic.

To give her mouth a chance to chill, she took her time leaning against the wall facing him, across the several foot divide framing the doorway bay into the SICU. "I saw it once at Vandy. But I have the symptoms etched on my brain. It was in the back of my mind before I even reached him. I expected it the second I saw him coming down chest first. You shouldn't feel bad about not knowing at the time. It's really easy to miss."

There. That was more like her. Nice. Helpful. That's the kind of person she wanted to be.

Enzo watched Davis's expression go from angry to gentle in the space of a few statements. Too smooth and practiced to be real. "So I'm rude, and I'm guessing *jerk* also wouldn't be far off your definition, but you're still trying to make me feel better about my mistakes?"

She smiled at him, a real smile with just a hint of something bratty twinkling in her eyes. And it was adorable. "Just because you're a jerk doesn't mean I have to be one, too. Besides, you didn't make a mistake. You just didn't know the answer. There's a difference."

No difference. If she hadn't been there, he would've made a mistake. That single thought had weighed on him throughout the long day. He had to do better than that. He had to be better than that. The only thing worse than standing in Lyons's shadow was the idea of never exceeding it.

On a personal level, Enzo already knew he was a better man than his father—he took care of his family and had started trying to do that at four years old and hadn't actually learned how to do it until his mother had remarried—but he had to be better than Lyons professionally, too. That was what the world judged a man by: his prestige. That's why Lyons was known the world over, but the world had barely blinked a year ago when his stepfather had died.

It wasn't so much he wanted Davis to make mistakes, but before today he'd always been the one with the answers. If he hadn't known something, none of the other surgical residents had known it, either. And maybe none of the thoracic residents, or cardiac residents.

A successful trauma surgeon had to know a great deal about a number of specialties to handle whatever might come up in surgery. Like today. Cardiac tamponade… He wasn't sure that a cardiac resident in his final year would've even gotten that—but she had and it had impressed Ootaka. And him.

"You're sweet. You shouldn't give everyone the benefit of the doubt. Sweet doesn't survive long here. New York chews up sweet people and spits them out." The words— the very idea—left a sour taste in his mouth. Right now, he was the main predator circling her because he had to have that fellowship.

He didn't want to be the one to chew her up and spit her out.

It was in that second that he realized he was attracted to her. When she'd been pale beneath her tan at the scene, he'd still noticed she was pretty but not in a way he'd had time to think about.

During the hours watching her in the surgery, he'd had few physical details to form opinions on—most of her had been covered in the protective gown, mask and cap. He'd been able to see she had a fluidity of movement that spoke of control and precision...grace. And she had the mental endurance required to focus on a task for hours.

Seeing her now, when she was tired enough that her defenses were down and she was no longer concealed by OR green, he could appreciate the delicate quality of her features and the hints at the shape hidden by baggy scrubs.

"Is that a warning of your stance on this fellowship?"
No.
"Yes," he said.

Ootaka's fellowship was the best anywhere. He wasn't just a trauma specialist; he'd completed separate fellowships in several subspecialties. Spending a couple years as his single student was like a crash course in Everything That Can Go Wrong in the Human Body and How to Fix it.

"So you sought me out to warn me about yourself? Or was that part of your study methodology to learn more about the condition and Beck's Triad?" Okay. Now she wasn't buying that she should see him as a threat, even though he'd admitted it. Either she was as confident in her abilities as he was, or she was playing with him. "I'm still kinda surprised you haven't seen the condition in the past year."

Earlier, at the accident and throughout the surgery, her accent had been suppressed. Now, tired after a long day, the more she talked the more he expected her to hand him a lemonade and invite him to the front porch swing.

Which was also adorable. He had to stop thinking those kinds of things... She was the enemy. In theory.

"It has happened in the ER here in the past year, but never when I was on duty. I'm sure no part of the city is cardiac tamponade deficient, but I haven't actually treated that condition before today," he assured her, and then backed up, something she'd said earlier refusing to stop echoing in his mind. "Symptoms etched in your brain from a condition you've only seen once? Makes it seem like you have some personal connection to the condition. Is that why you were expecting it?"

Her smile disappeared and she leaned off the wall, eyes leaving him to track to the door again. She didn't want to answer that question. It had roused the wariness his warning had failed to do. Good.

"I read and study a lot to keep sharp."

Lying. They were both lying, but he was just better at it.

"So all symptoms of emergency scenarios are etched on your brain?"

She plucked up the badge that had been left for her during surgery and got ready to buzz herself back into Postop. "That's my goal."

Not lying.

"And I'm sure that they'll be etched on your brain from here on out," she added.

Still uncomfortable. Uncomfortable enough to flee.

"How long are you staying?" He nodded to the ward door, allowing the subject change.

She hesitated, fishing a watch from her pocket and putting it on. "I don't know. I might not go home... There's an on-call room, right?"

He nodded then extracted his card from the thigh pocket of his scrubs. "My cell's on the back. If Elliot takes a turn while you're here, would you text me?"

The way her brows lifted said that he'd surprised her. She hadn't expected him to care that much about the patient. Maybe his warning had done a small amount of good. With her hand outstretched, she stepped forward to take the card. "You're worried about him?"

Her words confirmed it.

"I do that on occasion."

Before he put the card in her hand Enzo took the little outstretched palm in his own. Small. Delicate like her features. Nice skin, soft, but she was obviously tired. "Your hands are cold."

Resisting the urge to rub some warmth back into them, Enzo placed the card on the upturned palm and curled her fingers over it. "If you're going to go home, get someone to walk with you. Our part of Brooklyn isn't bad, but it's safer in pairs or groups. At least until you get some city smarts, Country Mouse."

She couldn't slaughter Sam for that nickname.

A ghost of her earlier smile returned.

He let go of her hand and let her buzz herself back into the ward before heading the other way.

"Hey, before you go..." she said, from behind him.

He turned to look back at her.

"Really, thank you. For charging into the fray to help me and Mr. Elliot. Not everyone is willing to do that, put themselves out there when it's dangerous—physically dangerous—and also because of the litigation-happy society we live in. If it had been just me on the scene, Mr. Elliot would've died under that SUV. Doesn't matter who got to assist Ootaka. You saved a life today, Enzo."

Still being kind.

If Country Mouse wanted the position, she'd have to fight for it. She might yet figure it out. This was only her first day.

Kimberlyn adjusted the hang of the shopping bag on her arm as she walked beside Sam, one of the two remaining roommates at the brownstone that Caren, Tessa, Sam and Holly had shared—and Holly owned.

Holly was loaded and well connected, and both those things encouraged Kimberlyn to keep her distance for now. She already had enough stress to deal with.

Tessa had recently moved out of the house and in with her boyfriend, Dr. Clay Matthews.

Caren had left for Cameroon, leaving Kimberlyn to sublet her unit.

She hadn't seen much of anyone but patients over her first week, so an outing with Sam was just what she needed, and the green market was the clincher on her decision to come out. Spending time with someone else who didn't sound as if they were native to the area—or in Sam's case sound as if he was from anywhere but Scotland—was the perfect way to try to let go of the week's stresses.

Organized tables and stalls stretched far out in front of them, each one lined with small baskets filled with produce and fruits to tempt. It looked fresh, but fresh off the truck rather than fresh off the vine. Appearances could be deceiving, and this country girl could spot a hothouse tomato at twenty paces.

"This is the most orderly vegetable market I've ever seen. Our farmers' market is usually staffed by old men with beer bellies and overalls. They look like they hand-picked every vegetable, and sometimes they smell like they did it that morning. Though it's better to go out back in Mamaw's—er, my grandmother's—garden."

Since relocating, she'd been making a concerted effort to try to ditch the twangiest part of her accent, but if she wasn't vigilant, it kept slipping through.

"That sounds entertaining at least."

Entertaining, like listening to Sam talk, spending time with others rather than in her own head...where all she could do was think about Mr. Elliot.

Despite his body stabilizing after they had operated and repaired his problems, he had yet to wake up. His body was on the road to recovery, but his EKG had stayed depressingly flat. Not the rocketing recovery she'd hoped for him.

If he didn't wake up soon or show signs of activity, his family might have to make some hard decisions. If she hadn't been on the scene, they wouldn't have that unpleasant possibility looming in the future, a possibility that felt more certain every day.

But maybe he'd still come out of it. Wake up. It could happen. He was still recovering from the anesthesia and the powerful pain medications that went with the kinds of surgeries he'd had. He might wake up. Though even if he did, chances were slim that he'd be the same.

Worrying about him wouldn't help him. Wouldn't help her. But this trip to the market would, as long as she found a suitable topic soon.

"Sometimes. There is one old farmer who goes to the market we frequented...and everything he said sounded like a Southern preacher. Booming and dramatic. Even just talking about vegetables, I always kind of wanted to add to the collection plate..."

Sam's expression said he didn't know what Southern preachers sounded like. Right. Their different geographical histories gave them a misleading feeling of sameness.

Trying to make a new friend, and this was the best she could do?

What else? Enzo and the fellowship were pretty much the fixation of her every waking hour, but she couldn't talk about that, either, with Sam. Enzo and Sam were friends, and since Sam was her roommate she wanted him to be her friend, too… There could be no drama. Only niceness. And the quiet, neurotic worry that came with having an overactive imagination—whose imaginings now centered on all the ways Enzo could screw her over while she listed about, not knowing how to compete.

Sam led them off down the first aisle of Brooklyn's green market, and she yawned for the third time in the few blocks they'd walked to get there.

"Not sleeping well, Country Girl?"

Country Girl. Country Mouse…she might as well be wearing bib overalls and chewing straw…

"Not so far. All the noise. I thought I liked noise to sleep by, but with all the horror stories I've heard from everyone back home about the dangers of New York City—don't go getting a big head when I tell you this, but the only way I've been able to trick myself into sleeping is by imagining that I am safer in the house because you live there. My inner feminist really hates that I feel that way."

Sam grinned down at her, and was she imagining things or was he standing just a little taller?

"Strut all you want, Braveheart. If someone breaks in, I'll remind you about the strutting when you fail to go rushing in to defend us, or at least scare away all the would-be robbers or probable serial killers in a manly fashion."

"You're entitled to your fantasies." He didn't comment on the likelihood, but got back to her problem. "Get earplugs, maybe a fan or some kind of ambient noisemaker. Before too long you'll be too tired to notice the noise anyway."

"I'm already tired enough that if I didn't have to eat, I'd be uneventfully thrashing around in bed right now. I'm sure that my poor diet isn't helping me sleep better. Everything

I've eaten since I got here has either come from a vending machine, a box, or was served with fries on the side. My body is screaming for something leafy and green. And fruit. And possibly some manner of stimulant-infused ice cream. Energy drink companies should make ice cream. Comfort food and caffeine to help get through the transition. They have everything else in New York..."

It was all different. Different and scary. According to the rumor mill, Enzo had run off two different contenders for Ootaka's fellowship in the past year.

Run them right out of the program, and they'd switched specialties. Two in one year. So obviously it wasn't just her who found him intimidating and a jerk. And annoyingly handsome, though that probably wasn't what had run off the other contenders.

In all the times that she'd spoken to Caren about her transfer into the program over the past year, she could have mentioned those specifics. Maybe her cousin hadn't wanted to scare her off. Or maybe she just hadn't thought Kimberlyn actually had a shot at it. There were other trauma residents in the program. She could blend in with them and still get a darned fine experience and go on to a great fellowship. It just wouldn't be Ootaka's.

"I'll never get used to the heat," Sam muttered.

Small talk. Small talk. More small talk... Because this was how people made friends. At least, when there was no shared misery to bond them together.

"We have hot and muggy most of the year. Only when we have it, there aren't these enormous buildings blocking the view of the horizon. I never have to go far to see whether black clouds are rolling in, so I can tell if there's a storm coming to cool things down. Or I can see trees, and they let me know."

"Trees tell you if it's going to rain?" A male voice came from behind her.

Speak of the devil.

She'd only spent any measurable time with Enzo for one danged day, and Kimberlyn could already recognize his voice. And it had nothing to do with how nice a voice it was…though it did have a kind of velvety rumble that made her ears tingle. It was more about being alert, and that voice came attached to someone she'd really like to stop sneaking up on her.

She'd seen Enzo here and there, but she'd mostly seen his name on the surgery board. Despite Ootaka giving her a shot with Mr. Elliot, she hadn't been in any other surgeries with him since. Enzo had. Maybe not a bad thing for her, but definitely not helpful, either.

"Hey, man. She's in tune with nature. Just because the only green you've seen is in Central Park, or that weird girl with the green hair you dated last year…" Sam turned but Kimberlyn kept her eyes on the tables of veggies and fruits. There was a basket of tomatoes that wanted inspection, and if she didn't engage, the market might remain a nice diversion.

It probably shouldn't bug her that he was there, or that Sam was friends with him. But all the time she'd spent fretting and worrying this week came surging back. She'd nursed it through hours of surgery, staying by Mr. Elliot in SICU until the wee hours, through the phone calls to Tessa, scheming and digging for info, and reading yet another stack of journals to try to know everything—right now!

"She was a freak, but she was fun," Enzo said. She could hear the smile in his voice. "So how do trees tell you about rain?"

She turned and immediately regretted it. Out of scrubs, wearing blue jeans and a black T-shirt, he had that simple, manly, doesn't-give-a-damn-about-fashion-and-still-looks-amazing thing working for him.

"If you know what to look for, there are lots of signs in nature to give information. Like moss growing on the north side of trees. That kind of thing," she explained without explaining and then stopped and turned back to the vegetables. The more she talked, the more ammunition he'd probably have. Who knew what he could use? Maybe someone better skilled at duplicity. Someone who wasn't her.

"You're still generalizing. Specifically, how do trees predict weather?" He sounded interested, though it could be a cover for trying to make her look dumb.

But Sam also seemed interested. Sam was a good guy. She'd heard enough from Tessa and Caren to know he wouldn't be trying to set her up. And just like that, the air shifted and her annoyance started to subside.

"When the barometer and the winds change just before a storm, the leaves of many deciduous trees—the trees that lose their leaves in autumn—like to turn over. You look at the tree canopy as a whole, and if there's lots of patches of light green amid the deep greens of the top side, that usually means rain," she explained. "It's not foolproof, sometimes they flip over when the winds are blowing from something other than the usual direction, but in the hours leading up to a good storm in the warm months, it happens a lot. More accurate than the weatherman during winter."

"Sounds like superstition or old wives' tales," Enzo announced.

"Our wives' tales are more colorful than that." Kimberlyn put down the basket of tomatoes she'd picked up. They were much too perfect. Perfection meant hothouse. "Like if you need rain, kill a garter snake and hang it in a tree. But I've never heard of anyone actually trying that one. You know, since the 1800s."

"Could be true, though. The leaves, not the snake," Sam argued, though in a noncommittal way, and then shifted the thrust of the conversation. "I thought you usually went to your mom's for dinner on Saturday."

"I do. I am. Just thought I'd grab some strawberries for my girl on the way. She loves them."

His girl. Good. Dr. Sexy McSneakyFeet had a girlfriend.

She could ignore his attractiveness now as a matter of sister solidarity. Not that it really mattered. Dating was off the table until she got through her fellowship and got a practice established. Her training and education had to take at least 95 percent of her waking hours. Even if that meant listening to lectures in the shower and reading while she ate.

"You know you're always welcome to join us. Mom makes way too much food." Enzo and Sam talked food, too, which set her stomach growling.

"You know I'll come. Your mum's a much better cook than any restaurant I can afford."

They both turned to look at her. Was that an invitation?

Kimberlyn smiled to cover the nervousness coiling within her and pretended it didn't sound as if her stomach had given up waiting for food and was fixing to just digest her instead.

"Hungry?" her sexy nemesis asked.

Wasn't there some old saying about eating with your enemy? Technically, observing Enzo in his natural habitat could be related to her training. Eating with him and his whole family and the strawberry-lover? Yeah, that sounded like a bad idea.

"Don't worry about me, Sam. I can find my way back. You two go on. Get your strawberries there before they go mushy in this heat."

"You don't want to come?" Enzo asked, stopping her from actually running away yet.

"I'm sure it's really great and I appreciate the offer, but—"

"You're afraid we're going to poison you?"

"No." It felt as if she answered all his questions with *no*. "Don't be ridiculous. If anyone poisons me, I'm sure that Caren will tell the police to come straight to your house. So it'd be silly for you to try." Picking at him, acknowledging the conflict that had been flying between them since day one, somehow made it more bearable. It was actually kind of fun in a completely messed-up way that felt like playing... Something she should not enjoy.

Seeing his girlfriend started to sound like a better idea. Maybe that would help diminish his attractiveness, and making friends with his girlfriend so that maybe he wouldn't be too scheming over the fellowship was pretty much the extent of her manipulative abilities right now.

Enzo grinned. "Most of my family are Sicilian. We're not big on subterfuge."

"So, I wouldn't get poisoned, I'd get..."

Sam dragged a finger across his throat in dramatic fashion, making her laugh. "No, seriously, you should come. Enzo's my friend. You're my roommate and my new friend. I know you're both going after the same fellowship, but I like both of you and I'd hate to be stuck in the middle. Come. Eat. Call a truce for the day. You were just complaining about eating food from a box..."

"Yes, I was."

"And your stomach was complaining about eating nothing," Enzo pointed out, triggering another protracted growl.

She looked at Enzo, giving him a few seconds to shut the idea down. When that didn't happen, she pointed to a flower vendor in the next row over. "Okay, but I'm bringing flowers at least. My grandma would skin me alive if I showed up empty-handed."

CHAPTER FOUR

"OH, HELL."

Sam's expletive cut through whatever he and Enzo had been speaking about, not three feet away from the white wrought-iron fence circling Enzo's mother's home.

Enzo and Kimberlyn stopped walking and looked at Sam.

"I forgot about something I needed to do today. I have to go to the hospital."

"You don't want to go after you eat?" Kimberlyn asked, her gaze shifting from Sam to Enzo. They hadn't known one another long, but surely he could recognize a pleading look when he saw one. No way did she want to go in there alone, but she'd been hungry before even leaving for the market, before the walk of several blocks to get here. If she didn't get food soon, she might knock down Enzo and steal his strawberries. Maybe they'd pair well with chrysanthemums and daisies.

"I really need to go now."

Enzo accepted this with a quick shrug, "I'm sure Mom will send food home with Kimberlyn for you."

But that left her alone to talk, say dumb things and give Enzo ammunition, completely upsetting her plan to sit silently, smile, eat and listen to other people talking.

It was easier to listen. Easier on her nerves, and also a good way to learn about these people who were now inside the small circle of her life in New York. As much as she appreciated being included, her generally introverted, social survival mechanism was to blend into the background. Not having to talk facilitated that.

Sam had other ideas. After quick goodbyes, Enzo turned to Kimberlyn, gesturing her to follow him. "Let's go on in. You can meet my girl." He led the way through the gate and around the back of the house.

Right. His girl. How would his girl feel about Enzo bringing home another girl to meet the family? This day just kept getting better.

The back door opened straight into the kitchen and a sea of people. Was it a family reunion weekend?

Kimberlyn smiled to swallow her panic and closed the door. She'd never seen so many people for any sort of dinner besides the reunions her mother's family held, picnicstyle, every other Mother's Day at a park in the Smokies.

Enzo wove through the people. Kimberlyn stayed at the door. She might be able to run still... Maybe everyone would just be so happy to see Enzo that they wouldn't notice her sneaking back out the door.

"Mom, everybody, this is Kimberlyn." Enzo spoke loudly enough to be heard over the crowd, and suddenly the sea parted and loads of people—many of whom had those pretty dark blue eyes—looked at her.

Right. Speak now.

"Hi." Kimberlyn waved the flowers, reminding herself that they were in her hands, and slowly inched through the rapidly closing wake Enzo had left. "I hope you don't mind the extra mouth, ma'am."

She stopped near the older woman and held out the flowers, smiling to cover the fear scratching at her insides.

"Not at all. Thank you, Kimberlyn," Enzo's mom said, graciously taking the flowers and handing them to one of the younger women in the crowded kitchen to put in water.

The house had obviously been remodeled since it had

been built, with an eye toward making the kitchen as big as possible. It took up almost the entire first floor, as far as she could see. In the places where walls had provided support there were now simple wooden pillars to keep the house structurally sound.

Relieved of her cargo, Kimberlyn edged toward a pillar—her gateway to somewhere with a little more elbow room.

Although Enzo had been living in his own place for years, his mother's house still felt like home. Smelled like home. Smelled like dinner, too, thank God.

"You should've brought Sam with you, too," his mother said.

Enzo kissed her cheek and once Sophia was finished with the flower vase, he took his berries to wash. "I tried. He got all the way here before remembering something he had to do. Kimberlyn is his roommate. Just transferred into the residency program and the trauma track. Sam would be happy if you sent him a plate home with Kimberlyn."

That said, he looked to see that Kimberlyn had scrammed to the far side of the dining-room table, where she could sit and not have anyone directly nearby—everyone was either in the kitchen or in the living room, with the dining half of the great room in between.

He didn't see who he wanted, though. Raising his voice, Enzo bellowed over the crowd, "Okay, where's my girl?"

From the sunken living room, he heard the call, "Jo-jo-jo-jo..."

"Joe?" The look on Kimberlyn's face went from confused to amused as his baby niece barreled in his direction, crawling fast enough to silence anyone who said she wasn't as strong as any other baby her age now.

With the largest, reddest berry in hand and paper towels, he met Maya halfway in the dining room. Once he'd swooped her up and given her a kiss, he headed for Kimberlyn and the table. "She can't say my name yet. Zs are hard." She was never going to learn to say it properly if he didn't correct her, and he didn't care at all.

With skinny little arms around his neck, Enzo bounced her to one of the dining tables and sat near Kimberlyn.

"She's beautiful. Is she yours?" Kimberlyn tilted her head to get a view of Maya over his shoulder, where she'd been squeezing his neck. "I thought you were referring to your girlfriend. You know, at the market."

He laid the towel and berry on the table so he could maneuver the little wriggler with both hands, letting Kimberlyn really see the niece who'd stolen his heart. "This is Maya, and she is my girlfriend, aren't you?"

"She's mine," Sophia said from the kitchen. "Enzo just likes to pretend he did the heavy lifting when she was born."

"She's beautiful," Kimberlyn called back to Sophia, then focused on the two of them again.

Enzo picked up the berry and held it up. Maya seized it with two grabby hands and set about gnawing at her favorite fruit.

"I delivered her," he explained to Kimberlyn, whose brows rose in unison.

"She's your...?" She pointed to Sophia.

"Sophia is my sister. Maya is my niece, and she is my special girl so I bring her strawberries to buy her affection."

Kimberlyn smiled at him, widely and without even a hint of the apprehension he'd seen on her face since he'd gone to Post-op to talk to her and made sure she knew he was a threat. Suddenly, he wanted to give her a strawberry, too.

But that would not happen. If she wanted one, she could get one herself. He shouldn't be happy that she once again looked at him as if he could be the good guy, or someone she could be friends with. He sure as hell shouldn't be sitting at his mother's dining table with her, showing off Maya…

"I think your cunning strawberry plan is working, Dr. DellaToro." She shook out the damp towel, folded it and placed it back on the table, where he could get to it and wipe the red juice off the baby before she became unalterably sticky.

The softness in her eyes when she looked at Maya made Enzo want to like her.

"You thought I must have come from a family of ogres, admit it."

She smiled again. "I suspected you were raised by wild dogs, but maybe that's just what you want your competition to see."

"You think you're my competition?"

"I know I am." Her smile took on a cheeky edge that demanded he grin back at her, especially as she turned in her chair so she could watch the baby gnaw the berry and ooze pink drool everywhere. "And you know it, too, or you wouldn't be…well, the way you are with me at the hospital."

"Maybe I like to put on a scarier mask than is real."

"Maybe. Or maybe this is a trick, too. You could have bought that insanely adorable baby, for all I know. She certainly seems to like you well enough to be a paid actor."

Maya picked that moment to offer Enzo a soggy bite of her strawberry.

He mimed eating it and made *nom-nom* noises that made the baby laugh, and probably lost him some of his power of intimidation with Kimberlyn. But when he looked at her he found a wistful image that bordered on adoring.

His mother approached the table, laughing in her usual manner, and saving him from saying the wrong thing and simultaneously redirecting them both to the baby while singing his praises in one fell swoop. The woman could multitask.

She always could, as far back as he could remember.

Though maybe it had started when Lyons had walked out on the four of them and she'd been forced to raise three kids and hold down two jobs... It had been years before she'd remarried and their family had grown again.

Kimberlyn said something that shot past him. The next thing he knew, she'd reached out to touch Maya's big dark curls. "I'm sure if you brought this one into the hospital, she'd be the best PR in the world."

"All the people in the hospital who matter know Maya already," Enzo tossed out there, but didn't get a chance to say more. A hand fell into his hair and what started as a loving pet to the back of his head became the kind of tug that only mothers could get away with.

"Does Lorenzo have a bad image at his hospital, Kimberlyn?"

"Oh, no, ma'am. He can be just a bit intimidating to his peers. Not me, of course." And if he'd had any kind of winning hand before, he'd shown his cards when he'd gotten Maya on his lap.

"But maybe people who haven't seen him with such a doll on his knee..." Kimberlyn said, her accent slipping in as she joked with his mother, or maybe flirted with him?

That could be a suitable swap for powers of intimidation.

"Honestly, he's thought of as the top resident in the trauma rotation. I'm currently waging a war with him, though it only started Monday. We have a truce for dinner, but I make no promises he won't pelt me with peas or lob a spoon of potatoes."

Kimberlyn turned her attention back to the baby and felt something soften in her. Did he know what it was like, seeing a stupidly handsome, brilliant, successful man holding a baby? Like a mule kick right to the ovaries. So unfair.

It made it completely impossible to view him in the same manner she had, even as late as coming through the back door of his mother's house.

He loved his family, and he was completely different around them.

He loved his niece, too. He'd be a wonderful father.

And she had been totally flirting with him a minute ago. *Shoot.*

All that aside, it still felt like a foreign country to her. She'd been around people with big hands-on families back home, but she didn't have that.

Enzo's mom said something and headed back to the kitchen, leaving her with Enzo, the most beautiful and adorable yet slobbery baby in recorded history and the distinct feeling that she'd just been set up.

"You're a very hands-on uncle."

A powerful urge welled up inside to smack him on the back of the head and take his baby away. She'd accuse him of faking all this, too, if Maya didn't clearly adore him.

"I'm not the one who's special here. Maya is our little miracle. She was very premature, which is why they know her well at the hospital."

Kimberlyn looked at the baby more closely. She was small, and she had a more slender build and face, but she seemed normal despite that. Bright-eyed and rosy-cheeked, even before the strawberry. "How old is she?"

"Just coming up on a year."

Okay, she was very small for her age. "How far along was she?"

"Twenty-six weeks and three days. It was a couple of weeks into the start of my fourth-year residency at Saints and in my free time I was doing a ride-along one night a week with the local squad to get field experience. A call came in for Mom's house. I knew it was something to do with Sophia…and my squad responded. The baby was already coming when we got here. I delivered Maya over there in the living room."

Twenty-six weeks wasn't the death sentence it had been a couple of decades ago, but outside a hospital setting?

"Pretty terrifying," Enzo confirmed, reading her expression right apparently. "If she'd been born in a hospital at that time, her odds would've been great, but..." His expression firmed, and she knew he'd been transported back to that time. He'd have been calculating the same odds she was now calculating. At that point in development every day mattered, every day added a handful of points to the chances of survival.

You never want someone in your family to have roughly equal odds for survival or death...and especially not a baby.

Her throat thickened. She knew how the story ended up—she could plainly see that it had been a happy ending—but the emotion in his voice kicked her in the heart. And she knew better than anyone that someone could look perfectly normal and healthy but have myriad health problems beneath the surface.

He never looked at her, his gaze absorbed by the tiny baby girl in his lap gnawing on a strawberry and leaking pink drool everywhere. "We got them to the closest hospital, and about a week later I managed to get them transferred to WMS. She was in the NICU for a long time."

Which was how he and Sam had become friends, she understood immediately. In that moment she knew with just as much certainty that she'd definitely been set up to come to this dinner without him.

"That's why your mom asked where he was, right? Sam's got a standing invite?" Maya drooled on Enzo's arm and Kimberlyn picked up the paper towel to swipe it up before they got stickier. "I think we've been set up, Enzo."

"Sam?"

She nodded. "He's your friend, he's my roommate and one of the handful of people I know here. He outright said that he didn't want to be in the middle of us earlier."

And she could appreciate his position. She didn't want him to have to choose sides, either. Her longest contact with anyone in the brownstone had been a simple phone relationship until she'd finally gotten to the city and met Tessa in person—but she wasn't in the house any longer. She could see that kind of friendship between Enzo and Sam being a strong one. She could also see someone like Sam being the loyal type…

Enzo could've had a hand in the manipulation—it was a great way to let her know how much the fellowship meant to him: his family was his motivation. But he'd be playing it up if that were the case, and he'd looked as surprised by Sam bowing out as she had felt.

"You've gone quiet," he said.

"Just thinking." Not worth talking about, because even if Sam hadn't orchestrated exactly this situation, she just couldn't look at Enzo as the shark in the goldfish tank anymore. He was more than she had been giving him credit for. He had depth, and if he used every weapon at his disposal, she couldn't really blame him.

Change the subject.

"And I was also thinking about whether or not I should ask any questions…"

"About Maya?"

"She looks very healthy."

"She is very healthy now. Her lungs were the biggest problem, lagged behind as is normal. But she has no heart or digestive issues so we were very lucky. She needed help breathing for the first few weeks and had to have her system nudged to start producing surfactant. But we were incredibly lucky." He kissed the top of his niece's dark, curly head, and she grinned then showed him that her berry was all gone, nothing left but the stumpy bit at the end that no one liked to eat.

"All gone," Enzo said, refocusing just like that. He captured her drooliest hand and held it out for Kimberlyn to clean off. "We'll have another one after dinner."

Dinner had better be worth all this. How in the world was she supposed to keep her guard up when he was shar-

ing a well-gnawed strawberry with a miracle baby and involved in cleaning tiny sticky hands?

"You have a nice family. It's not even a holiday and
you're all getting together to eat. You said weekly dinner
when we were at the market, but I guess I didn't expect...
well...like, twenty people at a weekly dinner."

He finally looked up from the baby and shifted her so
that she leaned against his chest and he could turn his
chair to face Kimberlyn. "You're not close to your family?
I thought you and Caren were close. Of course, I thought
that family values and togetherness was big in the South.
Along with cotillions and hoedowns."

She snorted, "No way. Hoedowns are so overrated. To
Nashvillian's of culture, it's a hootenanny or nothing."
When she was rewarded with a chuckle, she answered a
little more seriously, "They also still have cotillions, but
they're like the fancy-dress equivalent of civil war reen-
actments. Cotillion clubs exist, but I never had any desire to join one. And I think your definition of close and
mine don't necessarily line up. My parents are pretty busy,
I guess. They do their own thing. I largely did my own
thing, too. We see each other on holidays. I call once or
twice a month." She paused and looked toward the living
room briefly before asking in a quieter tone. "Has your
dad passed?"

It wasn't a subject Enzo liked to talk about, though for different reasons than why he didn't want to talk about Lyons.
"Ernst died last year. About two months before Maya's
birth," he answered, realizing in that moment just how
near it was to the anniversary. Which would bring everyone down if he pointed it out. Maybe she wouldn't pick up
on that. It would definitely change the flavor of the afternoon for her. For all of them.

But he should probably say something about Lyons. She
obviously didn't know Lyons was his biological father yet,

but chances were good that she'd find out. Rumors circulated through the hospital like a soap opera, and even though they didn't share a name—or anything else—someone would tell her about him. "My father..." He hated explaining this to anyone. "Ernst was my dad. My father is still living, but we don't have contact with him."

"Oh."

No, it didn't fit with what she was now seeing of his family, and maybe that's why his father had bailed—he hadn't really liked the idea of a close-knit family. Or maybe he had been, and still was, just a selfish monster who didn't want to know anything about them and resented reminders that they shared his genes.

The first year after Lyons had left there had been gifts delivered for birthdays and Christmas, and thereafter just extra money in the child-support payments to account for gifts. He'd found out that Lyons had even stopped asking about them around that time, despite his mother always reassuring him that his father was going to come visit soon... he was just very busy...

"I'm sorry. I didn't mean to pry."

"It's not a big deal." He jerked his thoughts back to the present. Talking about Lyons always did this to him. "You'll probably meet him before long, though. He's got privileges at Saints." He bounced his knee a little, refocusing on Maya—she was a happy addition to his family, and Lyons was neither wanted nor needed. Time to shift the subject away from the bad parts of his family history back to Kimberlyn. "No siblings?"

"No siblings. But you're right, I was closer to Caren. I had family in the area, but they were mostly older. Caren was the only one my age who lived moderately close, and between visits we were like pen pals, then phone buddies. Probably unsurprising, since we're the same age."

"Same?"

"Yep, our birthdays are less than a month apart."

"She's a year ahead of you."

"Yes," she answered, her expression becoming more guarded. The same look he'd seen on her face outside Post-op. Hiding something. Cagey. A hint of fear in the midst of sadness. Definitely hiding something.

"She was a year ahead in school." Kimberlyn's words came slowly, as if they were carefully picked.

Something happened. "Did you get held back a year?"

"No!" The shrill pitch her voice took on gave her expression the kind of transparency that Enzo always avoided. He'd just upset her inner perfectionist by even asking that question. "I was valedictorian. I decided to take a year off...a couple years ago."

What kind of driven professional would take a year off in the middle of their residency? No kind. Not someone with a choice in the matter at least.

"You took a break in the middle of your surgical residency?"

Kimberlyn sat back in the chair, her mouth suddenly dry. How could she explain it safely?

When she'd come back to her residency program after the accident people had treated her differently. Not because they'd thought badly of her—although they probably should have done—but everyone had watched her as if she was going to fall apart, physically or emotionally. Even if she wasn't wary of Enzo knowing too much about her past, she wouldn't want everyone at WMS knowing her medical history. She'd worked hard to get back on her feet, and they were now firmly beneath her. It wasn't a weakness to exploit, or wouldn't be if no one knew about it.

But she had to tell him something. Truth was, she didn't want to be the sort of person who always suspected other people of malfeasance. The only thing that could make sense here would be the truth. Besides, what kind of hypocrite would a surgeon have to be to fault someone for taking time to recover from several big surgeries?

In front of her was a man with a baby on his knee, surrounded by family and a pervasive feeling of goodness—a still-scary *abundance* of people who loved him. She wanted to tell him. Ignore the shark-shaped shadow he cast behind him, which everyone had warned her about.

Which was the real him, the one she could be friends with or the one who would see her as chum in the water?

Ugh, subterfuge. She sucked at this. "You're probably getting strawberry drool on your shirt." Trying to change the subject might be cowardly but it was the only truly safe thing to say.

The squint of his eyes said he saw through her tactic, but he went with it for the moment. "Strawberry drool would be the best thing I've had on my shirt all week."

He smiled, his eyes connecting with hers, and she looked deep. Gorgeous eyes, really. Intense. Sexy. Deep oceanic blue with a thread of golden amber toward the pupils. That gold gave them warmth…and she wanted to be suckered in by it. Being so far from home, immersed in the new hospital and a completely alien culture, she'd felt adrift. But as she looked into those beautiful hazel blues…

A loud clatter from the kitchen broke into her thoughts—she really didn't need to be thinking about him in the vicinity of the word *beautiful*. One metal pan on the floor triggered another fall, and the noise scared Maya. The baby let out a howl that proved beyond any doubt that her lung function was excellent.

Kimberlyn took advantage of the commotion and stood, gesturing around the large, open room. "I need the ladies' room." Lies, half-truths, covers for her limping sanity… She just needed a few minutes of solitude to try to figure out the best course of action before he started demanding answers. And he needed to comfort that baby.

This scheming and manipulation business was going to be the death of her.

Enzo gave directions while standing and cradling the screaming baby against his shoulder.

She slipped past him and the family at various seating areas through the house into the cool half bath for guests. Small, but a sanctuary.

Enzo didn't seem to be in on the scheming but it would've been a dastardly brilliant way of putting her off her game. But if he knew what drove her it could only hurt *her* cause.

He'd managed to run off two residents, and no one could tell her exactly how that had happened. They couldn't even confirm for sure that it had happened, only that they'd been there, they'd been competition and then suddenly they had been somewhere else. Since then no one else had gotten that close. People didn't run off or switch focus without a reason, just as she would've never taken time off if she hadn't had to. No sane person intentionally sabotaged their schooling, especially after all the effort required to make it that far.

Despite that year of therapy and recovery from the accident, the extended routine to get back up to fighting trim after the accident, her endurance still wasn't where it had been. Some surgeries could last well over twelve hours, and if she were asked to perform one of those today, she might not be able to.

She didn't honestly know if she'd ever get to that level. Her heart was in good enough shape to be considered normal, but she still had brief spells where it would go out of rhythm for a couple of beats. Not enough to be diagnosed or on medication, but it served as a constant reminder of what she'd lost physically in the accident. If this race came down to one of stamina, he'd win for sure.

But she couldn't live with herself if she didn't try. It was the only thing that made it okay that she'd survived that day when her best friend hadn't. Not okay, it could never be okay, but it could be bearable. She could become someone worth the sacrifice Janie had made for her.

When she came back out, people were gathering around the table, and the conversations continued as if she weren't there. Just the way she liked things. Eat. Blend into the background. Go home. Figure everything else out later.

Maybe call Tessa and harness some extra brainpower, since she obviously couldn't make up her mind about anything with regard to Enzo.

CHAPTER FIVE

THE FOOD WAS GREAT, the cheerful atmosphere even better, and by the time Kimberlyn said goodbye she had a basket with food for Sam and an escort home.

What she didn't have was an idea of how to respond to or even process the evening. With a handful of blocks to travel, she'd have walked it alone if Enzo hadn't insisted on driving her. A quick car ride later and he pulled up in front of the stately brownstone.

She turned to look at him. "I have to ask you something. Did you run off two other contenders for Ootaka's fellowship? Because there are so many rumors floating around, and I thought that they fit the man you are at the hospital, but you're completely different with your family."

"Aren't you different with your family?"

Kimberlyn shook her head. "I guess. I don't know." And then she squinted at him. "Was that part of your plan, to bring me to your family's house and make me watch you carry around an adorable baby to make my love petals go all dewy? Because that's a dirty trick."

"Love petals?" He laughed suddenly, shaking his head. "That phrase should be struck from your vocabulary, Mouse."

"You didn't answer the question, Rat." Hah, Rat. Not the world's best comeback, but she was new to this verbal sparring thing. "For the record, an attractive, successful man carrying around an adorable baby is like a sucker punch in the ovaries for almost any straight, single woman. Probably even those who don't want children. There's just something alluring about a big manly man and a tiny help-less baby…" She shook her head and then faced him. "It would be like me showing up at your door in crotchless panties…and then taking your picture!"

"Taking my picture?" Enzo watched her with barely contained amusement. Not exactly the emotion she'd been looking to rouse in him.

"You know, flashing you." She grumbled. "That's what my grandma called it…when a woman didn't sit in a lady-like manner while wearing a dress. Off the topic."

"And the topic is?"

Kimberlyn squinted at him. "That you with the baby was a dirty trick. And it's not going to make me go easy on you just because you're sexy."

"You were planning on going hard on me before?"

He baited her—repeatedly—and she kept falling for it. Time to put a lid on that. "I was planning on being my best, and that's still my plan. I can be really obnoxious about knowing everything and answering every question. I know this about myself and usually I try to dampen it a little so that other people have a chance, but I'm not doing that with Ootaka."

His amusement faded a little, but not enough to show he was taking her seriously. "Noted." He lifted one shoulder, the half shrug of an unconcerned man.

She stopped with a sigh.

Enzo watched her deflate, but his mind still stuck on the idea of her showing up anywhere in lingerie. "Just for the record, lingerie allegories are not going to help clear anything up. All they do is muddy the water."

"Fine. So does a handsome man cuddling a beautiful baby." She went back to that subject with a resolute nod. "So if that was a tactic, it was completely unfair."

If she wasn't attracted to him, it wouldn't have bothered her. Though, really, it didn't go the other way. The idea of a gorgeous woman in lingerie would have sent his mind off track. It didn't have to be particular to this woman. The urge to torment her, though...definitely particular to this woman. "Are you trying to tell me that my holding Maya made you attracted to me?"

"No!" she blurted out and then sighed hard enough to fog the windshield. "Kind of. Yes. Just put me out of my confused misery. Are you the man I saw today, or are you a shark swimming through chum-littered waters? Did you—"

"I didn't run them off," Enzo answered, though why he didn't know. He'd encouraged those rumors in the past. They did the work for him and kept people wary of him and more easily intimidated. But after spending an afternoon with her, the idea of her thinking badly of him...

"What happened, then?" She leaned forward, picked up Sam's basket and settled it on her lap. Readying to make her escape.

"People need someone to blame when they fail." He shrugged. "I let them blame me, but I wasn't any worse to them than I am to any other resident. I pride myself on knowing the answers and performing at my best, just like you do. When someone screws up, I make sure they know why they screwed up. Some people don't take correction well."

"Is that it?"

"I may not have been very nice when I corrected them, but I've got no more authority over any other resident than I do over you. I've never chewed anyone out publicly, but I have privately ripped into anyone who jeopardized one of my patients..." As he spoke he could see, even in the low evening light, the war on her features as she tried to decide what to think. "And I don't see anything wrong with that."

She was quiet a moment and then gestured in a half-hearted way designed to express disagreement, or maybe just frustration. "Presentation matters."

"Not more than the message."

The quiet resumed. "I guess not," she said eventually, then asked, "So, where does this leave us? I know you warned me off you, but…"

It was Enzo's turn to choose his words carefully. He could feel the weight of those soulful brown eyes on him. The day had changed things…but the realization hit him that so had his opinion. It had been a nice day, and he was going to have to ruin it. "I want to put this nicely because I do actually like you, and I respect your skill and knowledge…"

Kimberlyn nodded when he paused, giving another gesture for him to continue. "I hear a *but* coming."

Do it quickly. Be honest. If he lied about this, it might save her opinion of him, but it wouldn't save his opinion of himself. "But I don't see you as competition for the fellowship."

Kimberlyn let the words sit for a moment, her brows pinching as she worked over the words. "You mean at all? It's only been a week…"

"I'm sorry." Why was he apologizing for this? Because she'd been with his family, she'd been great with Maya… and he owed her courtesy if nothing else. "It was a week that started with a bang. I admit it, you had me on my toes from the moment we met. I was very concerned."

"But I did something wrong," she filled in, the slight wobble to her voice letting him know that she was working to keep her words and voice level.

"Not exactly…" Enzo grimaced. "You haven't made any mistakes that I know about. And I am sure that Ootaka is impressed with your ability to diagnose and perform the steps that kept Mr. Elliot alive, and you did a good job in surgery, outside that one thing."

"Get to the *but*."

"But…you're very gentle." Gentle. It felt like some kind of slam against women to use that word on her in that fashion, which he didn't like at all. He tried again. "Your natural inclination is to be sweet and deferential. Those aren't leadership qualities. When he takes on a fellow, Ootaka is looking to remake himself. He's looking for someone commanding and self-assured."

"It was my first day and the first surgery. Do you think I won't have any other opportunities to perform with him before the end of the year so I can tell if I'm…improving?"

She didn't take his choice of words like macho rubbish but, then again, someone sweet and deferential would give him the benefit of the doubt in that. An example of what he'd meant, which he'd feel like a jerk pointing out.

"I don't know if you'll have other surgeries with him or not. You might. You might not. If you do, keep in mind that he's not going to correct you on the same thing twice. And you're probably going to be left with as many questions about whether you are doing better in his eyes after future surgeries as you do right now."

"I see." Kimberlyn said the words as a kind of verbal pause. She didn't really see, but she'd never been somewhere that being deferential was a bad thing before. Her upbringing had drilled into her the importance of respect. She'd even given her stuffed animals the appropriate deferential titles. Her stuffed walrus was Mr. Waldo, not just Waldo.

Without deference as her go-to position, she wouldn't know how to behave at all. It was in her to always try to be kind first…but she'd never had a combative support team in an operating room. Outside a general sense of leading the team, she couldn't even picture a situation where she'd have to throw her weight around with her surgical team.

The scent of food that she'd found delicious only a couple of hours prior now smelled heavy and made her feel a touch queasy. Kimberlyn shifted the basket out of the way and opened the car door. "Thank you for telling me. Your advice. Dinner…" She was waffling. It sounded like a pathetic cut and run even to her own ears. "And the ride home! Don't want to forget that. I'll make sure that Sam drops the basket off at your mom's."

Kimberlyn closed the door before he could say anything else and headed for the brownstone's steps at a trot.

She hadn't reached the first step before hearing the other car door. She kept going. "What are you doing?"

"Walking you in." His voice sounded closer behind her.

"Unnecessary. I'm almost to the door already." The weight of the basket in her left hand lifted as he commandeered it.

He'd probably just call Sam to invite him inside if she said no. And he had invited her to dinner with his family… Swallowing a sigh, she unlocked the door and stepped inside. He followed.

The common areas of the house were extremely nice and tidy. The kind of elegant niceness that made Kimberlyn hesitate to put the food down anywhere but the kitchen. The food he was carrying anyway.

He followed to the kitchen.

"Obviously you can see that I'm inside. So what is it you really want?" She turned and propped her hip against the counter, arms crossing.

For the first time since she'd met him Enzo looked uncertain. Even when they'd met at the accident and he hadn't dealt with a cardiac tamponade before, he'd still never looked uncertain. He'd been unflappable. And now, of course, it didn't last, but it was there, a fleeting furrow of his brow that said words he'd probably never admit to.

"You're upset," he said.

"So? You aren't responsible for my happiness." For someone who avoided confrontation, she sure ended up arguing with Enzo a lot. "Don't expect me to cut tail and run to obstetrics because you don't think much of my chances with Ootaka. I'm here to try and I'm going to do that to the best of my abilities."

"Good. I want you to. But you have got to grow a thicker skin. Become a crocodile." He closed the distance between them and placed his hands on her shoulders, keeping her facing him and holding eye contact. "And just so you don't have any room to run this around in your mind later, I don't usually give pointers to the competition."

"Like you said, I'm not the competition," she muttered, realizing as the words came out how childish she sounded. She usually did so well with accepting criticism in order to improve. Her skin was usually thick, like a rhino's.

"Hush. I'm trying to say that I like you. Even when you're…" He stopped, his gaze going from her eyes to one of her shoulders, where his fingers were tracing over the thin cotton of her shirt and the still-thick and welt-like scar crossing her shoulder. "What's this?"

"It's…nothing. It's just…"

He pulled the neck of her shirt to one side, exposing the site of one of her incisions. "What was this?"

"A knife fight," she joked, because making up a story felt entirely more fun than talking about her actual trials, tribulations and the barbed-wire, booby-trapped obstacle course she'd run the past two years. "But it was one of those plastic knives you take on a picnic. So it took a lot of sawing back and forth to make a substantial enough cut to scar like that."

Before he held the shirt to the side to cause the neckline to bag and reveal the meatier, more worrisome scars, she pulled the fabric from his hand and covered herself again—neckline up to her eyebrows, just how she liked it. "Repair of a torn rotator cuff. And it's healed now. I had lots of therapy and it's fine. Didn't affect my dexterity at all."

She held the affected hand out for his inspection, steady as a rock. No shaking. Surgeon's hands, and an injury that had worried her sick for months wondering…

Shake it off. Prove to him that it was steady. She went through a series of arm motions to show the range, twisting her hand, forearm and full arm at the shoulder. No catch. No issues. Proof.

He lowered his hands, let his arms hang at his sides, then apparently thought better of it and crossed them. The muscles down his forearm corded, echoing the sudden tension in the room. "That's not why I asked."

If he didn't consider her competition, would it even matter if he knew a little bit about the accident? Outside him maybe treating her differently. He'd been the one to start the relationship off on the wrong foot. Not relationship. Well, professional relationship. Which was where she was going to file that thing he'd said a second before discovering the scar. He liked her. As a doctor and colleague. Not in a sexy way. And she didn't like him in a sexy way, either. And didn't even want to, no matter what her emotions had been saying at dinner.

If she just came clean—or cleanish—it would definitely save her from having to come up with some reason for the injury that he might not even deem acceptable anyway.

All the subterfuge, weighing words and jockeying for position, could make her give up before she even really got going with the year.

"Okay. The truth is that I've seen both sides of the trauma table. I was in an accident. There were some surgeries that patched me back up. I'm better now."

"That incision site is still pink. Not quite the angry red of an immediately recent scar but definitely not more than two years old. Is that why you had the break mid-residency?"

"Yes."

More truth.

"What other surgeries?"

"Does it matter? I'm fit now. If I don't have a completely clean bill of health, then it's just a little dingy. Like a coffee dribble on your scrubs in the morning."

She gestured to her chest, realized that she'd more or less pointed him at the evidence of having her chest cracked at around the same time, and quickly gestured at her thigh instead—where he'd find another scar if he looked. Darn it! If she didn't give herself away with words, it was with body language.

"You're the one hiding surgeries, so you tell me if it matters," Enzo muttered, taking a step back away from her to lean against the counter, rather how he'd leaned outside Post-op. His jaw bunched as he apparently gritted his teeth...out of sync with that lazy lean.

"It doesn't matter to the job," Kimberlyn said quickly, looking him in the eye steadily, willing her words into him. "Yes, I've had some obstacles to overcome on my way here, but we all have our obstacles."

He wasn't buying it. She could tell from the way those dark blue eyes became little more than squinty slits. "Why wouldn't you want anyone to know that?"

"Because there are always consequences to obstacles you have to work through. Funny me, I thought one of those consequences might be that you used it as a reason to limit me. And you know, you told me right out of the gate not to trust you, so why would I tell you any of this?" She grabbed Sam's food basket and went to shove it into the refrigerator. If nothing else, she could save him from some dreaded spoiled-food disease. "All that matters is I've recovered. And I don't want anyone thinking that I can't do something before even giving me a chance to do it."

"And you thought I was the bogeyman, that I'd use a torn rotator cuff against you."

Not even a question, he'd just made worrisomely accurate deductions about her motivation to keep things secret.

"Yes," she confirmed, for once starting a response to him with something other than the knee-jerk *no*. "Again, not entirely my fault. You warned me, and you *do* have that reputation for being lethal to the careers of competitors.

And before you even say it, I know you don't consider me competition right now, but that'll change. I didn't come all this way to fail."

He didn't need to know how far she'd actually traveled. Not just the hours and hundreds of miles she'd driven to get from east Tennessee to New York City, the metaphorical road had been even harder to travel.

When she turned to look back at him his features had relaxed again and now matched that lazy lean a little better. "Okay."

"Anyway, the consequences are personal. I grew up keeping personal stuff personal. I don't have that big beautiful family background where hugs abound, and everyone talks and laughs and catches up with each other on a weekly, if not daily, basis. I don't know how to be that... sharing. Especially with virtual strangers."

"Okay."

"Okay?"

They eyed one another warily.

Kimberlyn was the first to crack. "What does 'okay' mean?"

Enzo stepped closer and reached out to take one of her hands, forcing her to look him in the eye just by the way he focused on her. "I'm not going to use your trauma against you, okay? I'm going to help you."

"Why?" Her voice broke over the short word, the deep eye contact and warm hand holding hers overwhelming her senses. Her skin buzzed where they touched, and the physical sensation grounded her even as his gaze skewered her. It all added up to a connection that made it seem as if he truly did care. Lord, she wanted to believe it. And that was wrong, too.

"I like you." A rueful light shone in his eyes, making her believe him.

He did like her.

If a simple touch could make her insides tremble, how

would it feel to have his arms around her? To be skin to skin down the length of her body?

It couldn't happen but, oh, she wanted it to.

"So, I'm going to tell you something I've learned in the past four years. You know Ootaka's guidelines he keeps on the bulletin board in the locker room?"

He was still talking. And this was supposed to help her.

She nodded, trying to concentrate on what he said rather than the feel of his larger, warm hand in hers. How much bigger was it? How would his warm olive complexion look against the rosy tan she'd inherited from deep Cherokee roots? Her eyes tracked down to look and watched his square thumb stroke the back of her hand, firm but tender. A manner of touching she recognized, even if she hadn't felt it in a long while. He wasn't lying. It wasn't a trick. He liked her.

And was truly trying to help. "I know the list," she whispered, her voice refusing attempts at any volume. She had to stop this hand-holding thing. What was she, twelve?

"Memorize it."

"What?" Kimberlyn pulled her gaze back up to his as she extracted her hand. This touching and talking thing could not work. One or the other. And the talking she needed.

A crease appeared between Enzo's brows as she pulled her hand away, but he got on with what he was saying, clearly not as affected as she'd been. "Memorize Ootaka's guidelines. Really think about what each one means. It's the reason I said I didn't know if you would be invited back to his OR. He really is trying to remake himself every time he takes a fellow. And when the other surgical residents failed to live up to his expectations—the points on that list—he stopped inviting them to his OR. That's why there are so few people I consider competition. He's not going to choose someone who doesn't follow his guidelines."

Without the connection, her brain started working again,

clicking through what Enzo had said as it applied to her situation. She'd violated that list her first day in the OR. Before she'd had a chance to read it.

It put him running ahead in an entirely new light. If he'd been the one to assist she'd have been angry—she'd been angry even when she'd gotten to assist—but Ootaka wouldn't have had to give the admonition. Maybe she'd misjudged him.

She stepped in and leaned up on tiptoe, arms stretching toward his neck. A hug would be all right. He was a hugger. He came from a family of huggers... That's what normal people did. He'd hugged her that first day, and she'd been so thrown she hadn't really enjoyed it.

Slipping her arms around his shoulders, she pressed in close. For a second it seemed as if he might not hug her back, but then the firm warmth of his arms wrapped around her, complementing the strength and heat of his chest warming her.

She couldn't remember the last time someone had really hugged her. In the past couple of years people had always tried to touch her to convey support, but every touch had been gentle. Hugs that had been more air than substance. As if she was made of eggshells already riddled with cracks.

Enzo didn't do that. His arms around her felt solid and real. There was nothing between them, really—maybe friendship? But he held her as if she might get away from him if he loosened his grip. Everyone else's hugs felt more like...a cage of arms. Protective, maybe, but distancing. Lonely. *Cold.*

Somewhere in the back of her mind her promises echoed and bounced around. They always did, swirling and waiting for any sign of weakness to pounce. Janie hadn't had any hugs, be they cagey and cold or full of heat and... something else, some nameless want she didn't have time for and didn't deserve.

She should let go of him. But both arms stayed locked

around his shoulders, not ready to let go yet. Kimberlyn leaned back far enough to look into his eyes again so that if he looked troubled, that would give her motivation to put some air between them.

So blue, but that golden thread highlighting the pupils pulled her in like a miner with gold fever.

Her gaze drifted down over a nose with a slight crook around the bridge—speaking of fights in the past—to a sensual mouth framed by that scruff he wore so well. So close. Oh, man, was she going to kiss him?

The butterflies suddenly swarming in her stomach said yes. Yes, she was. Just one kiss.

The last thing she saw before closing her eyes was the surprise in his as her intention registered.

His head tilted to meet her. Warmth and gentle, firm pressure settled against her lips, a slow, leisurely kiss, as if he sensed that's what she needed.

In preparation for her transfer, her first year back in the residency program went by in a blur of studying, lingering physical therapy and work. She'd distanced herself from everyone, refusing any attempts others had made to improve her social life. Her education had become her everything. And that just couldn't change. Not yet. She'd promised Janie, or at least Janie's memory. Janie, the one who would never get to have another first kiss, or feel this desperation to get closer that Enzo's touches inspired in her.

The scent of strawberry lingered on his shirt, and the soft scrape of at least three days' growth of beard contrasted with all that was soft and sweet-smelling about him.

Her heart stuttered and sped up.

His hands slid down, kneading her hips and then cupping her backside. A lift, a turn, and she sat on the counter. He slipped between her legs and pulled her close against him, then his hands traveled back up to cup the back of her neck and deepen his kiss. Open mouths, stroking tongues, thundering hearts, breaths that came shallow and quick, and heat blooming between her legs where he'd pulled them together.

The anatomy of a perfect kiss. It was just kissing. Kissing was not naked stuff, no matter what her hips wanted. Kisses didn't constitute a relationship, but it warmed a cold, hollow place inside her.

Until his fingers pressed just a little more firmly where they curled under her jaw, and he broke the kiss to look down at her, his brows pinching. "You've got an irregular heartbeat…"

Her eyes came back into focus and she saw a frown in his.

Great, so now having someone cup her jaw could give everything away? He'd been feeling her carotid.

She leaned back swiftly, cracking the back of her head against the cabinet behind her. "It's okay. I'm okay." A couple of deep breaths and the fluttering feeling in her chest passed. "I get a little bit flip-floppy at times. It's nothing to worry about."

He leaned back just a touch more, though his hips still rested against the counter. "Is it A-fib?"

"Not sufficient for a diagnosis or medication," Kimberlyn whispered, adding, "It really only happens…" When she got excited. Something else she didn't want to admit. That might lead him to thinking this kissing business was more than a mistake…

"When your heart speeds up?" He grinned, showing how pleased he felt with himself for making her heart speed up.

"Yes." She breathed the word on a sigh.

"Consequences of the accident?"

"No." Another quick denial, as per protocol…

He lifted a brow, and might've well called her a liar out loud.

She tried again. "My heart's in good condition. It's really fine. A mild electrical issue from time to time."

"The cause?"

She shoved lightly at his chest, opening enough space to bring both legs to one side and slide down from the counter. There was probably some rule about using the counters for anything but food-related activities anyway. Once both feet were on the floor, she put some distance between them. "It's fine now. Steady and normal. Really, I don't need to be diagnosed or worried about. I run all the time, give it a good workout. It's not a problem."

Skeptical eyebrows stayed in place and suddenly the idea of him thinking it was because of the kiss sounded much better than the idea that she wasn't fit for the job or the fellowship...

"It happens when I get excited, okay? And you can just shut up about it, Mr. I'm-Kind-of-a-Jerk-but-the-Ladies-Don't-Mind-Because-I'm-a-Great-Kisser."

Yes, it happened when anything got her too excited. It had happened briefly at Mr. Elliot's accident—from fear that time, but the result was the same. And he didn't need to know that, either.

That smile returned and he snagged her arm to pull her back to him, closing up that gap she'd put between them. "Want me to kiss you again? A test to see if we can replicate conditions? I'm happy to do so."

"You're offering to kiss me just so you can monitor my pulse?" She rolled her eyes, shaking her head. "Oh, take me now, smooth talker."

"Actually, I was planning on monitoring your hips, or possibly inspecting the areas closer to your heart. They are...beckoning."

Kimberlyn lost any idea of whether they were fighting or flirting. "We were just arguing."

"But you kissed me and I came up with a cunning plan on getting information from you."

Enzo's hands stayed at her waist, holding her to him so she had to crane her neck to look up at him. "What's your plan?" She really shouldn't be encouraging him. A fling—

because it surely couldn't be anything else—was not part of her five-year plan. One day she might have that, and maybe a husband and children…when she deserved them. When she'd earned them by keeping her promises.

"I'll pay you in orgasms."

She laughed despite her mental reminders. "You're pretty confident. How do you know you could deliver?"

"Are you kidding?" he asked, hands kneading her hips as he slid her back to him. "I'm a master of anatomy. I know the female form intricately and have devoted at least half of my life—probably more like three-quarters—to observing it in its natural habitat."

There it was, the rascally charm she'd witnessed at dinner with his family, only naughtier alone with her. She flushed to the tops of her ears while a more insistent heat settled lower in her belly. It'd be inappropriate if they hadn't just been kissing a minute or two ago.

"You sound like you've been studying gorillas in the mists with Jane Goodall." She tried to sound grumpy. What she should be doing was putting space between them, but what actually happened was her sliding her arms around his waist and leaning her cheek against his chest. Dumb, but…it felt necessary.

He chuckled and leaned down to kiss the side of her neck, causing her pulse to soar.

How had this started? Oh, yeah, she'd kissed him.

A dang good decision. Or a really awful one. "I think you're making promises you don't know if you can keep."

"I didn't say they'd be your orgasms." Enzo kept up the flirty banter, his words tickling her neck. Coupled with the heat spreading through her limbs, if she didn't stop this soon…

She hadn't felt this good in such a long time. Which was probably how it should be, but it was hard to turn away from. Playful flirting almost left her feeling nostalgic. "So it'd just be orgasms in my honor?"

"Maybe. Maybe not." Leaning back, he looked her in the eye again, his face scant inches away. "I'd certainly do my best to make sure it was the other way, but I left some wiggle room in my wager so I can fulfill the letter of the agreement if you had any sort of performance issues."

"So there will be orgasms for someone, eh?" She should stop this. "It's somewhat less convincing that way."

But no less tempting.

Only she'd have to take off her clothes for sure then, and exposing the physical signs of trauma would expose the emotional traumas...and those were the ones that could really hurt her.

Right. That did it. She shoved against his chest until enough distance opened that she couldn't feel his heat through the air. The warmth of his arms around her, the firmness of the chest and shoulders beneath the black T-shirt, the deep kisses and playful banter had all felt too good.

It might have been better when she'd been viewing him as a viper out to ruin her.

It was going to be harder to compete now that she actually liked him.

CHAPTER SIX

ENZO STOOD AT his locker, changing into fresh scrubs, when Kimberlyn rushed in. The front of the light blue scrubs she wore were soaked in what he could only be a little envious of: in the rock-paper-scissors of viscous scrub splatter, blood always beat barf. And his scrubs, the ones he'd just removed? Barf City.

Her shoulders curled forward and she pinched the front of the scrub top, pulling the saturated fabric out to create a hollow at her chest—no doubt an attempt to keep the long-sleeved, white Spandex undershirt she always wore from becoming soaked, too.

Once inside the door, she whisked the blue top off, revealing the sanguine splatter saturating the white beneath.

Attempt unsuccessful.

Since their kiss Enzo hadn't seen much of her. Ootaka had been called in during the night a couple of times, which had meant that Enzo had been called in, too. It had messed up his schedule.

If he was honest, there was more to it than simple conflicting schedules. He hadn't really been avoiding her, as he did Lyons, but the urge to see her, flirt with her, hadn't diminished at all over the week. A week in which he'd had time to really consider the ramifications of kissing her. Or, more precisely, what could happen if he gave in to the urge to kiss her again.

He already had the urge to help her with Ootaka, already had the urge to protect her. And the way she'd clung to him when she'd hugged him might've stayed with him even more than the kiss.

After tossing her scrub top into the hamper for hazardous materials, Kimberlyn maneuvered in front of a mirror to look at her bloody chest again. Then at the sink. The paper towels. Weighing up...

She didn't want to take that top off, and he knew in an instant what that was about.

Scars. She'd seen both sides of the trauma table, and orthopedic surgeries weren't really what the trauma table was about. Surgeries to repair broken bones and torn ligaments waited until the life-threatening stuff had passed. So the trauma table would have dealt with the torso. Organs. Hemorrhages...

Something else that had been on his mind since the kiss in the kitchen—he wanted to know, and he also didn't want to know.

A nice guy would probably go somewhere else, let her keep her secrets, but Enzo wasn't feeling particularly nice.

As closed-lipped as she could be, if he stormed ahead and demanded to know exactly what he wanted, she wouldn't budge. Start small. Innocuous questions.

"Looks like you've been into something more exciting than barf basin patrol."

"Gunshot," she confirmed, her frown deepening as she stared back at the shirt.

Definitely more exciting. "With Ootaka?"

"No." She turned away from the mirror and frowned more deeply. "I can't wear this."

Not Ootaka, but still surgery trumped being the master of being puked on by sick children. "Are you going to jump in the shower? You really should get that cleaned off your skin. I could bring your fresh scrubs to you if you want."

The offer was another difficult one to make. His instincts were more wild man than civilized in certain situations—work and sex being right at the top.

Work meant the competition.

The competition meant there shouldn't be any sex. But sex was right at the top of his thoughts when her name or anything remotely related to her popped into his head.

And he wanted to see those damned scars. That was where his wild man went even more animalistic: Kimberlyn's scars might be where work and sex overlapped. Competition, concern and an inability to deal with not knowing something he wanted to know.

Not many people ever told him to stuff it when he asked a question, but Kimberlyn pretty much did. Half answers, diversions, while he wanted specifics, details. As much as he'd enjoyed the intimidating reputation he'd earned over the past four years, when she failed to trust him with this information that had been—and continued to be—very important to who she was, it really set his caveman off.

"I..." Her cheeks puffed and she looked toward the showers. "Yes. But the only undershirt I have in there... Well, I spilled my yummy mocha on it yesterday so I wore my spare and didn't take everything home to wash. It was late and I forgot..." Another puffed sigh and she rattled off the combination to her locker and dashed for the shower stalls.

By the time he'd gotten his shoes back on and gotten to her locker she was calling from the bay, "Enzo?"

"The combination isn't working," he called back, rotating the dial again and giving the thing a jerk. Nothing.

Oh, lucky. She'd have to come out...

She yelled the combination again, and Enzo repeated the numbers back as he worked the dial to the respective numbers. Two turns to the right, blah-blah-blah, number, number, number...

Nothing.

"It's not working," he called back.

Caveman or gentleman? Caveman would go to the shower and make her come out. Gentleman...would get her scrubs from the machine.

With a grunt, he grabbed an extra towel—as far as he was willing to go in the gentleman direction right now—and went to meet her at the shower.

The curtain still closed, the water turned off, and he could see her feet facing the curtain. She wanted to come out. And she really didn't want to come out.

"Are you sure you did it right?" she asked from behind the curtain. "Two turns to the right, one to the left, back to the right?"

"I'm sure," he said and then chuckled a little. "I know you think I'm sneaky—which I will admit is my fault after our first meeting—but I'm not that underhanded."

"You want to see my scars," she pointed out, still hidden behind the flimsy curtain.

That was true. Why bother denying it? "Yes, I do. Just to be clear, I also want to see the rest of you, but I'm not lying about the combination not working. I also promise that I was at the locker bearing your name on tape."

He thrust the towel through the side of the shower curtain farthest from her feet and felt cold, damp hands grabbing for it.

It would be so easy to jerk that curtain out of the way, but there wouldn't be a shred of honor in the act. Even his caveman had some restraints. "Do you want me to go get you a set from the machine?"

"They don't have the... I need the Spandex. The..."

Enzo filled in, "The undershirt you always wear."

"They don't have those," she muttered in between grunts as she wrestled with her towels. God, what was she doing in there?

"No, but they have the tops and the bottoms."

"And I have to wear something. This will teach me to put off doing something. I should keep two extra shirts..."

She sighed and gestured through the curtain to the bench. "My badge is in my shoes."

He retrieved the badge, verified that he knew what sizes to get for her and headed out. When he came back she had finished drying and had snagged a third towel to fashion herself some kind of towel outfit…top, skirt and some kind of wrap? Just how many freaking scars did the woman have?

Enzo laid the scrubs on the bench along with her badge and headed back out.

No scar-viewing yet. It had only been a couple of weeks. Needing to know only felt important… Her health seemed fine, aside from those skipped heartbeats. Knowing wasn't critical. Not knowing wouldn't kill anyone.

He paused at the door and looked back at her, transfixed by her neck-to-knees terry-cloth covering. "Whatever your scars are, I'm not going to use it against you, Mouse." He'd used the nickname again, but it had started to sound like an endearment even to him—which was why he probably should stop using it. "I can understand being worried about it, but it's not going to happen. The only kind of old injury I might think could impair your ability to treat patients would be located on your head or your neck."

"Neck?"

"As in spinal-cord damage that kept you from being able to control your arms. Or seizures. Narcolepsy. Something dangerous."

She nodded, but still didn't offer any big revelations despite the thoughtful frown that confirmed she'd heard him.

"I might be a bastard sometimes, but even a bastard has some lines he won't cross." It might only be a teaspoon of honor, but it mattered. "But if your hesitation is about some kind of body shame, get over it. Having to cover yourself from head to toe every day is no way to live your life. It's limiting. You don't swim, do you?"

"No," she answered, and for once the *no* didn't sound fueled by reaction—a different emotion echoed in her voice. She knew he was right, but she wasn't quite ready to change yet. "I'm working on it. I think it'll be better next year, after this is over and after they've faded."

The smallest fragment of information. An opening.

"How long ago were your procedures?"

"Eighteen months since the last one. But they've been fading more slowly than most people's I know. I don't know why. Maybe my collagen is extra-colorful."

Six months before she'd resumed her residency. Not much of a clue—nearly anything healed in that time. He managed not to ask how many procedures she'd had. She might answer him, but she wasn't going to give locations and reasons to him today.

Seemed like a condition a surgeon wouldn't suffer from—shame over surgical scars—but maybe it was something more. It was enough for today, even if he really wanted to know. Take it slow.

Maybe sooner if he worked a little of his magic to assure her some OR time with Ootaka in the near future.

"Are you heading to one of the ORs?"

"No. The other guy, not Ootaka, has the gunshot. I was just helping in the trauma room."

The other guy. Exactly how he thought of Langley—"the other guy." Not Ootaka. Only Ootaka really mattered in their universe.

"Langley." He supplied the name, then headed out. He'd already been too long off the floor; surely somewhere there was some vomiting child who needed a target…

No matter how much Enzo told himself that he should just get back on the floor, he still found himself loitering outside the locker room, waiting for her.

The locker room was coed and the residents changed clothing in front of one another all the time, but waiting for her in the room would've been too aggressive. She never changed in front of others. She'd likely have changed in the bathroom if the shower hadn't been necessary.

The door opened and he had to step away to keep from getting smacked by it.

Kimberlyn stepped out, her face pale and one hand plastered over the V-neckline of the scrub top, covering the skin.

"I… It's not very concealing," she whispered, and Enzo pulled his gaze from her hand to her eyes.

Scrubs were anything but revealing…

Hand over that part of her chest? It wasn't cleavage she was hiding. As nice as her curves were, they didn't make cleavage up to her clavicle. If she had a scar beneath her hand, it could only be for one reason.

He wrapped his fingers around the slender wrist and pulled her hand firmly away from her chest, revealing a cord of scar tissue tracking down the center of her chest. It looked even angrier than the one on her shoulder had.

"Your chest was cracked?"

He hadn't needed to ask the question. He knew already that it had been, but the idea that she had been injured so badly in her accident made something feel hollow and haunted inside him.

She looked away, swallowed and nodded.

Enzo wasn't really prone to randomly hugging people. Yes, his family was like that, and he hugged when it seemed like something a sibling or his mother needed. And he hugged Maya all the time because the first months of her life had been such a scary time, and during much of it she had been sequestered in an incubator, starved for contact.

But he'd never hugged another colleague.

He pulled open the door again and tugged Kimberlyn back into the relative privacy of the locker room.

As the door swung closed he tugged her into his arms and clutched her to his chest, as if having her there would relieve the sudden tightness there.

The thing was, she was right. This made him feel differently about her.

Not that she couldn't do the job.

Not that she was less than any of the other residents, not that she was handicapped at all...

The strength he hadn't questioned at the scene of Elliot's accident now seemed precious and transient. She felt dainty, but he knew her to be determined. Until then he'd never questioned her endurance. She looked completely fit with her clothes covering the scars.

Now she felt fragile. She felt to him the way Maya's tiny body felt—as if she could be snatched away by a strong breeze.

"I don't want to know what happened." The words croaked out before he'd even given them much thought.

His hoarse confession was further muffled by the instinct to press his nose into the hair at her crown.

"You don't?" she whispered back. Then tacked on, "Good."

Regular volume would have made this conversation worse somehow.

It also would've increased the chance that anyone who happened to come into the locker room might overhear them.

"Just...don't tell me right now." He swallowed, pulled back enough to look down into those dark, hurt eyes. "Not because I don't care." He pried his own arms from around her, trying to regain some ground. "It's just a lot for work."

A lot of emotion. A lot of worry. A lot of nothing he could even do to fix this situation. He couldn't change her past, whatever it was that had happened to her. He felt helpless, and he was a fixer, a protector...

"Bolt cutters." He blurted the words out as the thought came to him. "Stay here. If you get called, delay for a few minutes. I'll be right back."

Having seen the scar, at least he knew she'd been under

the care of a cardiologist to take care of whatever had happened. Someone had fixed her. Someone was keeping track of her, or had been before she'd moved north. If she said the irregular beats were nothing to worry about…if she was being honest with him…he should feel better about that.

Doing something would help. He hurried to Maintenance.

Kimberlyn watched Enzo leave while pulling at the back of her scrub top so that the V in the front inched up to her collarbone. Covered. As long as she didn't move. She sat on the bench in front of her locker.

He didn't want to know. That was strange. But good. For her. Maybe he'd stop asking questions now. He'd probably keep his distance, too. Definitely good for her that he felt that way.

So why did she feel as if she'd just lost something?

Clearly her priorities had become clouded.

He was helping her with the lock, which was certainly a victory. He had learned about the big scar and he was going to help her hide it. All good. She didn't even know where to get bolt cutters at the hospital.

Good things. Victories. The only way her week could be better was if Mr. Elliot regained consciousness. He'd been transferred to a care facility that morning, never having come round. They had taken him off the machines, and his lower brain function was enough to sustain him for now, but that could only go on for so long.

The highlight of her time in New York so far had been the weekend, the dinner with his family, and the kissing and flirting that now jockeyed with her guilt for control over her thoughts during any minutes her mind had time to wander.

Someone came in, greetings flew in passing and she moved to the other side of the room and sat again—kept sitting, kept waiting, kept quiet… Maybe anyone else coming into the locker room would stay on the other side of the locker wall divide and never know she was there.

Before she had to make excuses Enzo returned with the bolt cutters and headed for her locker. One loud crack announced the severing of one side of the lock, and then another and the body fell away.

She opened the door and dragged out the long-sleeved, white Spandex undershirt that was a necessary part of her uniform and whisked the other top off, not waiting for Enzo to leave.

He made no show of shielding his eyes or giving her privacy now. With the intensity of his gaze she was probably lucky he hadn't forcibly stripped her to look for the other scars. As she pulled the shirt over her head, he circled her, taking in every inch of flesh on display.

Thank goodness she'd not picked some lacy, sexy bra to wear today. It had been a sports bra day.

"Rotator cuff. Chest..." He listed two places that had needed to be repaired and then reached to touch the third scar on her belly. "What was this one?"

He could ask about that, but not about the heart. "It was a bit of metal."

"What did it hit?" he asked.

"Perforated the jejunum," she explained and heard him swear.

"Anything else where you're covered?"

"Broken left femur. Three screws."

"What happened?" he asked, then quickly followed it up with lifted palms. "No, don't tell me."

Someone from the door called to him, and he stepped that way, then right back. Indecision? She'd never have thought him possible of it.

"Tell me. And move your things to my locker." He gestured to her locker, which she'd now shut, lockless. A few quick turns of his combination lock and it came open. It figured that *his* lock would work.

"What if I need something today?"

"I'm going to give you the combination."

He had already dug out his notebook and pen and scribbled down the numbers.

She moved her things over, especially her bag and electronics…things she needed to not be stolen.

"You're not talking," he pointed out, tearing out the sheet with his combination and folding it once before he handed to her.

"It was a car wreck. We flipped. A couple of times."

"Hit other cars?"

"Hit a large piece of tire that flew off a tractor trailer on the highway, lost control and went off the side of the road into a… If I say the car went off a bridge, then it sounds like a big bridge over a huge river, which isn't accurate. It was a small bridge over a creek, mostly just bridging a gap between the banks…maybe about twenty-five feet across. The car didn't get all the way to the water, just to the bank leading down."

She pinched the fabric of her pants between thumb and index finger, then slid the material back and forth. Something physical to focus on. That coping mechanism was how she kept from being sucked back to the scene anytime she had to talk about it. Sometimes the physical focus was more vigorous than just worrying the fabric to make scraping sounds. Sometimes she had to pinch herself…or dig her nails in until she left tiny, half-moon bruises.

He was too quiet, but it was a heavy sort of quiet.

"Please, don't hug me again right now." She was definitely going to cry if she got hugged right now, and that wouldn't help her terrible day at all.

His phone beeped and he reached for it, then turned away to answer it, giving her the perfect window for escape.

She slipped out the door while he spoke in short, clipped tones to whatever angel had interrupted.

* * *

Kimberlyn spotted her lunch date across the crowded cafeteria and made a beeline for Tessa's table in the corner. Out of deference to Kimberlyn, Tessa had chosen the table with the best view of the room, and one that also gave the most privacy.

She set her tray on the table and dropped into the seat opposite. "I don't have a lot of time, but I needed to see someone uncomplicated."

Tessa grinned, "I don't know that I've ever been called that, but I like it that you think so."

"You're not Enzo. And you're not Ootaka. And that's about the limit of my brainpower to make comparisons right now. I called Mr. Elliot's facility to check on him again today. They're going to think that I'm the worst doctor in history, but I keep hoping that the upper level brain function will return. Stupid, right?"

"Not stupid, but maybe the hope would be better spent somewhere else."

Something that Kimberlyn appreciated about Tessa, she was warm and kind. She felt like someone from back home, as if they could have been friends for ages or gone to high school together. It was no wonder to Kimberlyn that Caren and Tessa were close. With her cousin out of the country, Tessa had become the closest confidante she had.

"I know you're right. I know talk of miracles is usually looked at askance in our occupation, but unexplained recoveries happen. I guess I just feel like…why was I the one on scene with him—me who recognized his symptoms and such—if I wasn't supposed to save him? It's just upsetting."

Tessa nodded. "Wish I had an answer for that."

She knew a little more about Kimberlyn's history through Caren and their discussions prior to her move, but she didn't know everything. And Kimberlyn didn't have the heart to talk about that right now, either. The words always scalded her tongue coming out. They were the kind of words best kept bottled.

"There's number one, Dr. Complicated." She nodded to Enzo, grabbing coffee instead.

"What's going on with Enzo?"

"I don't know. Stuff. Nothing. He confuses me, too. And I don't think he ran off those other residents." She lowered her voice. "I think Ootaka did."

Tessa's brows shot up and she leaned in to keep the conversation quiet. "Why would he do that?"

"Not on purpose. But you know his big list of guidelines for the type of behavior and decorum that best serves a surgeon in and out of the operating room?"

Tessa nodded.

"Well, you can't tell anyone this. It's just Enzo's theory—which he actually shared with me—but I think he's onto something. We think that if you violate Ootaka's guidelines in his OR, he just stops inviting you to assist. Now, during the fifth year, there are very few old trauma residents who get to practice with him. Enzo is mostly it. And I haven't been invited back into the OR since my first day with Mr. Elliot.

"Which apparently is because I wasn't...forceful or commanding enough? That leadership thing he has? I didn't do it well enough on my first day. Still not sure how I was supposed to be leading him, and really that first week was kind of crazy for me, trying to figure out how everyone liked to work...but my deference made me seem wishy-washy. He's not invited me back."

"So you think people are just realizing that they are not going to be in the running for his fellowship and transferring out?"

"I think so. One went to Cardiothoracic, right? And I want to say that the other one just decided to stick with general surgery without additional training after."

"Right." Tessa leaned back, her shoulders lifting slightly

as she considered what Kimberlyn had shared. "So Enzo told you this? That doesn't seem like him, either."

"I think he's got image issues and he lets them perpetuate so people are a little bit intimidated by him. He's not really a bad guy. He's kind of blunt and aggressive at times and, yes, he is arrogant as heck, but he's not blindly mean. He just doesn't really curb his tongue when he's got something to say. But you should see him with his family. He's completely different."

"You like him?"

Kimberlyn sighed. "Yes." It was only a month or so into the year and she had a big whopping crush on her competition. Mortifying. "You should see him with his baby niece. It's just so unfair. I don't know what it is about big handsome men carrying babies around. They might as well make that illegal. It's as potent as a drug." She remembered that she was supposed to be eating and set about remedying that with her broiled salmon and steamed veggies.

Tessa's knowing look compelled her to continue talking. "It doesn't really matter if I like him, but maybe it's a good thing. We've come to some kind of unspoken agreement that we'll fight fair up until January, when Ootaka makes the announcement." Yep, if it sounded like stupid reasoning to her own ears, she could only imagine how it sounded to Tessa. "And then one of us will have to chop the head off the other one and absorb all his power, just like on *Highlander*."

"Should've saved that zinger for Sam."

"Enzo's probably more likely to have seen it." And he liked to joke. And flirt. And...darn, she really did like him.

Kimberlyn stabbed a bunch of broccoli on her fork and shoveled it into her mouth.

Why couldn't he actually have been a jerk to her? Her life was complicated enough without adding something else to feel guilty about. If she gave in to temptation, that meant giving him time. Time she should be spending studying or observing surgeries from the gallery suites.

She should never have gone to that house, met his family or seen him with that baby...

CHAPTER SEVEN

A RINGING PHONE woke Kimberlyn about three hours into the thirty hours of sleep she really wanted.

Fifteen minutes later, she was up, teeth and hair brushed, standing at the foot of the brownstone stairs, waiting for Enzo.

When all hands were called in for surgery in the middle of the night, something big was happening. Something big meant Ootaka would be involved. Something big with Ootaka meant she might get to impress him more than she apparently hadn't impressed him on her first day, if Enzo was right.

Enzo pulled up in his sporty black something or other just as she scrubbed her face with the emergency cleansing cloths she kept on hand for the times when she slept in the on-call room, or got called from sleep and emergency hygiene conditions were a thing.

No makeup at all today. She didn't usually load up with the stuff, but she liked it when her eyelashes had some semblance of a presence. Men did it without mascara, a grossly unfair cosmic irony, and she'd actually spent time looking for the reason in medical texts in the past…because every question needed an answer.

"Morning," he said as she climbed in.

"It's not morning. It's two—"

"In the morning," he finished.

She buckled in and stuffed the used cloth into her bag. The last thing she wanted to do was to primp in front of the man, though that mirror she knew would be atop the sun visor tempted her with the siren song of her mascara wand…

No. She'd already been neurotic enough about her appearance in front of him. Besides, something big was going on at the hospital so no one was going to notice or care that she was not well put together at 2:00-freaking-a.m.

"Do you know what is going on? I didn't get a chance to ask when they called in." Or maybe she hadn't had the brainpower to form words in the fifteen seconds after waking when she had been listening on the phone.

"Organ harvest," Enzo said, working through the gears as he got the vehicle up to speed…and maybe a little past the speed limit.

"Was it someone who just came in tonight?"

Enzo shrugged, then mumbled, "I don't know. I didn't ask who the donor was."

Something else he didn't want to know? Just as he hadn't wanted her to tell him what they'd been treating when they'd cracked her chest?

Well, she wanted to know, and prayed it wasn't one of her patients.

At least it wasn't Elliot, he'd been gone from the hospital for a couple of weeks. She laid her head back, closing her eyes. Enzo was the one driving. She didn't need to think or take responsibility for anything right now, and sometimes she needed that space.

By the time they arrived Ootaka was already talking to the group of residents he'd pulled in to get ready.

As with everything, Ootaka had a very well-organized manner of conducting harvests. Their patient was a DNR who'd been revived enough to sustain life, no doubt with machines. A cadaver with a heartbeat, folks liked to say.

Appropriate and inappropriate at the same time. Also, something she'd never been involved with before.

Since it was up to him to orchestrate the harvest, Oo-taka used the trauma residents first. Enzo was given the liver to assist with removal and readying for transport. She was given the kidneys. Lungs to a third resident... with the heart coming last before another surgical team swapped in to recover tissues that could be taken after the heart was removed.

She got the second spot. That had to be worth something. Maybe Ootaka's opinion of her wasn't so bad. Maybe he just hadn't had a surgery he'd wanted her in on before. She could still be competition.

Or maybe she was just the most favored of those rejected from Ootaka's OR.

Enzo and Ootaka worked in tandem to get the donor onto the heart bypass pump before removing the liver. While he worked, she was tagged to scrub in so she'd be ready when Ootaka was. When she was at the table, the third resident would scrub in to be ready to remove lungs, and so on.

As she dragged the brush over her nails and creases in the fingers where bacteria might congregate, she watched through the glass partition separating the scrub room from the surgery going on.

She'd not been given the opportunity to watch Enzo perform much yet, and while her vantage point wasn't the greatest from the scrub room, she could see the concentration in the furrow of his brow, or at least the way it bunched under his scrub cap and the careful, confident way he moved and anticipated Ootaka.

When Enzo had shared his theory she'd doubted him a little. Not his concern, not the fact that he had been being honest with her—it hadn't been an act to throw her off—but she'd figured that warning her after one surgery with one small correction had been overestimating the importance of the guidelines. But today was the first time she'd been invited back, and that probably wouldn't have even happened if it hadn't been for the all-hands nature of the procedure.

She scrubbed more vigorously. Get done, get all the nooks and crannies and then get out there where she could better see and hear how the two men operated, and the way they complemented one another during the procedure. There could be no better instruction than witnessing what Ootaka would consider a well-orchestrated surgery. Who knew if she'd have another chance to try to dazzle after this?

She stomped on the sink pedal to turn off the water and headed out to the nurse to get gowned and gloved, then moved into position where she could see but didn't crowd. The patient's head was suddenly visible to her and a wave of cold prickles washed over her face and down her chest to where her heart stuttered in that way it liked to do when she was hit with a boost of adrenaline...

"Mr. Elliot," she whispered his name.

Enzo looked over at her briefly, letting her know with just a glance that he was right there with her. And that she'd said the name out loud.

A display of emotion in Ootaka's OR. She clamped her mouth shut and tried to focus.

She knew the ethics of all organ harvests and had read about the steps taken to vet a potential donor, the therapies required for the family, diseases and infections to be screened for...

She just hadn't known all that could happen without her knowing about it. It had only been a day or two since her last call to the care facility to check up on him. No one had said anything, but maybe he hadn't been through the screening then? Or maybe no one had told her because... he wasn't really her patient anymore. She was just the doctor who called more than was acceptable, the doctor who couldn't let go.

She'd known he'd had limited brain function after the accident. His body had sustained itself, but there had been no upper-level function. He'd just stayed alive. And in that condition, without a "Do Not Resuscitate" order, the family could've left him with a feeding tube in a care facility indefinitely.

Something she'd been purposefully not thinking about. She hadn't wanted him to die, but she hadn't wanted others to suffer or harbor the impossible hope that he'd wake up. She'd avoided thinking about the whole situation, avoided talking much about him...

If she wanted to get through this surgery with her professional decorum intact, she needed to continue not thinking about the fact that the man they'd worked so hard to save her first day was physically dying today. Another phase of the denial she'd been going through since the man had failed to regain consciousness in Post-op that day.

Pay attention to Enzo, the way he worked to augment Ootaka's actions and anticipate them. The removal of the liver ended with a tray and Enzo off to another area of the operating room to prepare it for transport.

As soon as he stepped away, she stepped in, breathing through her nose slowly and deeply. Controlling her emotions began with controlling her physical reactions to them. Deep breathing kept her heart rate more or less even.

"I'm glad you made it in tonight, Dr. Davis," Ootaka said to her, meeting her eyes over the donor. "We will give him a chance to help others. It is fitting that we do so together, yes?"

She swallowed and nodded, "Yes, Doctor. I want to be able to do what's best for him." And if helping get his organs to others was the only way to keep him alive in some small way, that's how she would do what was best for him.

Even if it meant disconnecting from the whole damned situation to get it done.

She offered a number twenty-two scalpel to Ootaka and when he took it she grabbed clamps and got ready to do what was needed. Anticipate. Be certain when she ordered the associate staff to do something. Make decisions, don't seem uncertain...

Don't think about Mr. Elliot until later.

After the liver left his care, Enzo retired to the lounge so he could suck down as much coffee as they'd let him have.

Heck of a morning.

And Kimberlyn's eyes when she'd realized who the donor was...

He'd hoped she wouldn't, but the bruising and the freshly healing incision on the man's chest had assured she would. Even if his face had been concealed, she would've known.

He could only pray that it wouldn't affect her performance with Ootaka. When she'd said Elliot's name, Ootaka had given no indication that he'd heard her.

Two kidneys to remove, twice as much time needed. She would be in there longer than he had. Her physical endurance wasn't a question for him—it wasn't that long a procedure—but her emotional endurance? That was the wild card today.

His phone buzzed and he fished it out of the pocket on his thigh.

Transplantation of kidney at seven. You're assisting.

The number was one he didn't recognize, so he thumbed through the numbers to find Langley. Not his number. He tried a few other guesses, a growing sense of dread filling in his middle as he found and eliminated number after number.

If it was Lyons...no way was Enzo assisting.

A few more calls and he'd reached the answering service for Lyons's practice…and confirmed that the number did indeed belong to his father.

Perfect. The only way to make this god-awful morning worse.

He hadn't spoken directly to his father since right after the high-school graduation he'd failed to attend…so Enzo texted back.

Not interested.

There. He'd responded without any swearing or name-calling.

He slammed back the coffee and went to get a refill. When he'd sucked that one down, too, he texted Kimberlyn.

Find me when your surgery is done.

He could do that at least, check on her. And she'd probably want to know that one of Elliot's kidneys was going to a recipient today. Even if he wanted nothing to do with the surgery or the surgeon, she probably would.

Besides, even if he was in the running for World's Worst Sperm Donor, Lyons was an exceptional surgeon—a large part of the reason Enzo would sooner carve out his own spleen with a broken spork than let his father come anywhere near his career. He'd gotten this far on his own, and when he got where he was going he wanted no one to be able to even hint that he'd done so by riding coattails.

She didn't need to know that garbage. But witnessing the transplant would be a good opportunity for her. Sometime over the past couple of weeks, since he'd discovered much of what she'd overcome on her way to the current fellowship, he'd stopped wanting to win at all costs. Oh, he still wanted the fellowship. He just also wanted to preserve a friendship with her. It wasn't pity, and it wasn't wholly attraction, either—though that played a part in it, he'd have to admit…

He'd just found a line he wouldn't cross to get it. Another line, rather. The Lyons line had been established long ago, but if he had to cut Kimberlyn down in any way to get there, he didn't know that he could do it, either. That included sabotaging her. She could gain something from assisting, and she also deserved it. It might even help her deal with Elliot's death.

He texted Ootaka to suggest that the trauma surgeon recommend Kimberlyn to assist his father in his stead.

CHAPTER EIGHT

"I DID THIS without your support or your money, and I'm going to finish it the same way. I don't need your help. I don't need your current suspicious favoritism. I don't need you."

Kimberlyn stopped dead in her tracks, hearing Enzo's raised voice around the corner of one of the long basement hallways peopled by staff and generally only patients en route to and from the surgical suites. Raw, undisguised disgust turned his tone to acid. No matter how blunt she knew he could be in his opinions, she'd never actually heard anger in his voice before.

Had they heard her walking? Who was Enzo fighting with? He'd wanted her to come find him…

Ootaka's voice reached her ears next, loud enough to recognize, not loud enough to hear the words.

Was he *yelling* at Ootaka?

Even if he wasn't, Ootaka would be unhappy to find Enzo yelling at anyone. That would clash with his mission statement of making an Ootaka ditto…one without displays of emotion.

She peeked around the corner, as unable to keep from doing so as she was to keep her heart in perpetual rhythm.

No, another man. Silvery-blond hair. Green scrubs. Fair. Trim and athletic.

Exact same stature as Enzo.

Seeing movement, Enzo looked toward her and gestured her toward them. "Here, this is Dr. Davis. She was the one who saved Elliot on the scene, making certain he lived long enough to get to the hospital in the first place. There'd be no kidneys harvested for your lifesaving operation if it weren't for her. She also assisted in harvesting the kidneys. She's the one who should be assisting you."

Her feet refused to obey. Instead of purposeful walking, she tracked forward slowly with no sudden movements. The same way she might approach—or creep past—an angry canine.

Should she shake the man's hand? What was the proper reaction when there was yelling? Kimberlyn grinned without showing teeth as she approached. Habit.

The unidentified surgeon looked toward her and her heart kicked again. Deep blue eyes. She took a couple more steps forward, needing to verify what instinct was telling her: that there'd be a matching thread of gold running through them, just like in Enzo's hazel blues.

"I'm sure Dr. Davis is a fine surgeon, but the invitation was specially for you," the man said, turning his attention back to Enzo.

Father. She'd lay money on it. His golden looks didn't mesh at all, but the stature...and those eyes... Someone not obsessed with them might not even notice.

Her feet stopped moving about five feet away. Should she approach further? Should she leave? Family drama, in public... But at least it was only the four of them in the hallway. Maybe this scene wouldn't go any further if no one else happened by, though gossip spread like an infectious disease within the close confines of the hospital. Enzo might not care if anyone heard him giving his father the finger, but the man already had gossip dedicated to him that he liked and rarely let people see anything deeper.

"So considerate of you." Sarcasm dripped from Enzo's words as he laid a hand over his heart. "Don't extend me any more special invitations. I prefer the old universe where I pretend you don't exist and you pretend that we don't."

We. Family. Not just him… From what she'd seen of him with his family, she'd wager that the pronoun selected hadn't been accidental. Enzo might've been able to forgive if his gripe was just about him, but it was about "we"…

Enzo headed for her, and as he passed he took her hand so that she was forced to spin and scramble after him, off down the hallway, with his long, purposeful strides eating up the distance.

She heard Ootaka backing Enzo's suggestion about her, but Enzo wanted to get out of there and he apparently wanted her to be with him. So she went. He wanted her with him, and that was enough. She would've gone even without witnessing that bitter display.

After the ache she'd been feeling in her chest since she'd realized it had been Mr. Elliot on the table she'd needed to see Enzo, too. It had been a relief to come out of the OR to his text.

And now there were even more messy emotions in the mix.

"Is that your dad?" she asked as he tugged her through a door into the stairwell and beneath the flight leading up.

"He's not my dad. He's my father. I told you, Ernst Marino was my dad. Don't let your tender heart feel sorry for Lyons. He's got everything else he wants."

Her back touched the cool brick wall behind her and he pressed in against her, his free hand capturing her cheek as he leaned in.

His kiss came without any other preamble, no flirty dance up to the heat, no real warning—unless having her hand held for the first time in two weeks and being half dragged down a hallway by an angry, glowering man counted as a warning.

This wasn't about her. He wanted to blot out the earlier exchange, and she was there. Not a relationship. Not a danger to her five-year plan, either. Janie would have said that she was acting stupidly, all these rules shutting down her emotions and possibilities in life. Caren said it, too. The plan that had been so clear before had become clouded with Enzo in the picture.

The hand that held hers turned to slide his fingers between hers, hot palms melding together the way his hips pressed into her. He was claiming more from her than a salve in the form of kisses.

She'd object if she didn't need him, too. They were alive. She was alive. It might not be right that she was here and Janie was not, but suffering alone would never bring her friend back. The rasp of his stubble against her lips only made his kisses sweeter.

Something had already changed in the way she thought about him and the situation. The guilt she felt for giving in to temptation had even started to slack off.

Her free arm slid around his shoulders, where she could knead the corded muscles in the back of his neck, anchoring him to her, keeping him close. Firmness, strong shoulders and lean hips, heat and strength holding her against the hard wall.

The other time he'd kissed her it had been playful and full of teasing. Passion contained, hinted at but not explored. But this was raw and full of need.

Coffee and spice, and not a hint of the bitterness she'd heard moments before in his voice and his words. And she needed this. She needed to touch, to feel connected to someone… They both needed this sweetness.

If he could make her feel better, that should help her stay on course. Just as long as she didn't get comfortable. Maybe if they both acknowledged their connection as being of a transitory nature, one meant to serve some higher purpose, then that might be okay.

Except Enzo didn't seem to be all that torn about a desire to spend time together.

She'd been asked out once since her accident and had agreed without thinking it through, but before they'd gone out the neckline of her shirt had gaped open, he'd seen the incision and had gone running the other way. People got involved with an eye toward the future, and someone who'd had open-heart surgery before thirty might not have much of a future. Even if the man hadn't been looking for marriage, it had still spoken of activity-limiting illness. Since then she'd counted out the prospect of dating or getting close to anyone. After the scars faded, she'd told herself. After she got through her residency. After she'd finished her fellowship. After she'd kept her promise.

After she deserved happiness.

And Enzo hadn't wanted to know. So in the back of his mind he must be thinking the same sort of thing: that knowing what had happened, and what her future might look like...limited things. But, God help her, she still wanted him in a way that made ignoring logic so easy.

Slow, deep kisses could blot out logic. Blot out the sadness she knew he shared at Mr. Elliot's passing—and further deepened their connection. If it helped him get through the years of hurt and apparent neglect from his father still lingering with him, or temporarily soothed the ache in her chest that never really went away, no matter how well-healed the bone and tissue beneath the still-red stripe...it had to be a good thing, on some level.

She didn't care that he wanted to live in denial where she was concerned. It meant that he wanted to be with her at least for today. Maybe he saw no future—really, could she see a future, either? One of them—probably him—would get Ootaka's fellowship and that was a special, one-person deal. She'd have to move on, probably to another city. Learn another new hospital and be one of a few in a less special fellowship where she'd still learn enough to do the job she was called to.

At the end of the year they'd go their separate ways and probably never see one another again.

That was reality. That was the future, regardless of her health or long-term prognosis.

She threaded her fingers through his silky black hair and clung tighter, feeding bad feelings into the furnace his kisses stoked low in her belly.

Just for right now. Just to get through.

Since no one but Enzo had been invited to assist in the transplant, Kimberlyn sat with a small number of other residents in the gallery to observe. Enzo was not among them. After he'd kissed her to the point of frenzy he'd urged her to watch the transplant and had left her gasping beneath the stairs…

Rather than give the impression that he cared even a tiny bit, he'd deny himself the experience of watching a transplant.

Pride was one of the seven deadly sins for a reason. It did his father no real harm for Enzo to miss this. If he truly cared about his Brooklyn children as little as he seemed to, then it wouldn't matter one bit to him if he drove his son away from something that would be to his benefit.

The problem was she cared. Things were so confused between them, but if she knew nothing else she knew that this was just a symptom of the big, angry, father-shaped scar he was hiding. She hid scars all the time.

Phone held in her lap, she watched through the window to the scene below, her fingers tapping the edge with the itch to summon him. Get him here… Or just maybe make him feel better somehow. A burden shared and all that.

Caving, she woke her phone and texted.

You should come sit with me in the gallery. We can do a running commentary on his technique.

Less than a minute later, he sent back: Wouldn't be fun if others got to witness my family drama.

We'll whisper. I'll start... You call that a functioning sub-cuticular knot? My mamaw could do better w/ a sewing needle and she's half-blind!

Pretending that she was fine was a stepping stone across the gully of *not fine*. Flirty banter with Enzo? Fun and less traumatizing than thinking about Mr. Elliot's passing and the tissue recovery still going on with the second surgical team.

It also kept her from examining why Enzo had put her name forward to assist, even if his father had declined his advice.

Ha-ha. He's already stitching?

No. I lied. I can do that so you'll fail when Ootaka gives us a pop quiz on the procedure. I'LL WIN.

He doesn't do pop quizzes. This isn't high school.

Fine. I'll do sports commentator then. No! Chess commentator! Nasal voice "It seems he's selected a number twenty-two scalpel. Let's see how his opponent deals with his opening..."

Who's the opponent?

His patient. Duh.

How's his opponent handling it?

It seems his patient has gone for some impressive obfuscatory technique to up the difficulty of this classic opening gambit!

Which means?

Blood. Duh.

I suck at this.

She smiled at the phone. He wouldn't play along with her if it wasn't helping at least a little.

I noticed.

I can't believe you texted the word obfuscatory.

I have mad tiny device typing skills.

I noticed.

He's going heterotopic, looks like.

Where?

Cradle of the pelvis.

It had been a surprise to her in medical school that transplanted organs didn't have to be planted in a mirrored position to where they'd been extracted from. She'd heard of the technique, but this was the first transplant Kimberlyn had ever witnessed. And considering the way he loathed his father, she imagined that Enzo hadn't witnessed any, either.

Well, she didn't want him to miss it. She also didn't want to appear weird and clingy with all the texting.

His silence spoke volumes.

Minutes ticked by and she texted again.

Did you fall asleep?

No. Just in a bad mood.

You should come up. Everyone's tired and leaving... Plus totally great way to flip BD the metaphorical finger. You still get to learn and you've made it clear you don't need his stupid overtures.

BD?

Bad Dad.

BF. And I'll pass.

Bad Father. God, she had to break that habit. His mother's second husband was the one who deserved the honor of the title *Dad*. Last time that mistake would happen. It was obviously important to him, the distinction between words.

What else are you doing that's better?

Lying in the on-call room.

You're in bed?

Yes.

Alone?

Yes.

Did I mention that transplants turn me on?

As soon as she hit Send she regretted it. They may have just been making out under the stairs, and they may have that other time, too, but there had been a long spell in between. She could just be a way to alleviate boredom.

No. She was more than that. He wanted her, even if he didn't want to want her. She just wasn't used to making such obvious moves...

I'll bribe you with orgasms.

Ahh, a strong bargaining position.

Don't you want to ask whose orgasms?

No. I'm good with them being yours as long as I get to participate. Or watch.

Heat flooded her cheeks. Was there anyone else in the gallery? She looked around to make sure she was, in fact, alone. The last observer had slipped out sometime since she had started texting...

You're taking me seriously? I may need some convincing to follow through.

Picture me naked. You've seen most of me already.

Yes, I have! It was nice.

Nice?!

I mean it was the BEST THING EVER. Are you coming now?

Coming? We haven't even started yet.

CHAPTER NINE

JUST AS THE KIDNEY was placed into the newly created spot, Enzo made it to the gallery.

Kimberlyn smiled when she saw him, stashed the phone she'd been texting with and sat up a little straighter.

True to her word, the gallery was empty.

He sat beside her and wrapped an arm around her shoulders, giving in to impulse simply because she felt good to touch.

"I'm glad you came." She snuggled in a little, taking comfort from him, as well.

That should have gotten him there sooner. The sadness he'd seen in her eyes during the organ recovery hadn't gone anywhere. She was just doing a good job of hiding it from most people. Including him, with the act she'd put on that had been all flirty and fun in the gallery. That had been for his benefit, to tempt him there.

He let his hand curl over her small shoulder, and against the hollow of his palm he could feel the scar from her rotator cuff surgery.

That wasn't a fun surgery, either, if any surgery could be called fun for the patient. But the shoulder was a painful thing when it healed. He couldn't imagine having that alongside a broken femur on the same side, a broken sternum from having his chest cracked and a bowel perforation.

She might feel delicate and fragile to him—and no doubt

she was more fragile now than she once had been—but she had to have been strong to make it through that and dive right back into her training.

Most people would have opted for an easier path after that kind of physical trauma, but she'd picked the hardest one she could find.

"Did you choose trauma because of your accident?" He still couldn't bring himself to ask what had meant her chest be cracked. He had the vague idea that the reason symptoms of cardiac tamponade had been etched on her brain was because she'd been diagnosed with the same at her accident. The same as the patient they'd officially lost this morning.

She nodded. "My primary surgeon was one of Ootaka's."

"Your trauma surgeon in Nashville was one of Ootaka's fellows?"

She nodded again. "One of his first, before he completed the last fellowship, the vascular specialty, and became the god of trauma surgery."

All trauma surgeons started out as general surgeons, which was what surgical residency was about. They went on to fellowships in trauma and critical care. Most stopped there, with licensing and practice.

Ootaka had gone on to several other fellowships—thoracic, cardiac and vascular. And all those would have come in handy when treating Kimberlyn.

Learning from Ootaka wasn't the same as obtaining all four separate fellowships, but it was the next best thing. Ootaka's fellows could go anywhere they wanted with the one fellowship.

He could see why she wanted it.

"I need to ask you a question, and I don't want you to get mad."

Enzo pulled his gaze from the surgery table—not that he had actually absorbed anything he'd been seeing the past several minutes. "Why would I get mad at a question?"

"Because it's to do with him, BF." She gestured with a flick of her finger to his father.

Enzo nodded for her to continue.

Her voice became quiet, gentle even. "What if he invited you to assist him as an overture to building a relationship?"

The question he'd been trying to ignore since the showdown.

"I'm sure it was," he said after the urge to shout settled down again. After the shouting match in the corridor, every time he opened his mouth he wanted to yell. But Kimberlyn didn't deserve his wrath. "But I still don't give a damn. I spent years seeking his approval, or even proof that he gave half a damn about me and my sisters. If he wants a relationship now, why isn't he also reaching out to them? Why didn't he even come by the hospital or send flowers when his first grandchild was in the NICU? Because he knew she was there. I guarantee he knew."

It was a good thing that the gallery was nearly deserted as his volume had started creeping up again at the end. It was even harder to moderate when speaking about Lyons's actions, or lack of actions. And it burned him even more that the only one of his children Lyons deigned to acknowledge was the male, and the surgeon. What about his little sisters? What about tiny Maya? How could he not want to know about his granddaughter?

"How did that happen? Why did they split up?" She watched the window, but Enzo could see that she was actually watching his reflection rather than the procedure below. Indirectly, probably so he didn't feel stared at.

"Lyons walked out on us when I was four. Mom, Sophia, Beth and me. Because he was tired of slumming it in Brooklyn."

"Slumming it?"

"He's Manhattan royalty. We're Brooklyn trash."

She scowled, angry on his behalf and apparently still unsure what to think. Her gaze tracked back through the glass to the surgeon below, her soft lips drawn into a flat, tight line. "And his name is Lyons. But your name is Della-Toro, and your mom and siblings are all Marinos. Where did DellaToro come from?"

That he could smile about. "Mom's maiden name is DellaToro. I filed for the name change on my eighteenth birthday. By then, she'd remarried Ernst, and you have met the second wave of siblings. He was a good man and we have a big happy family because of him. Ernst was the one who taught me how to be a good son, how to be a good brother."

"Good uncle," she said softly, the praise making him smile a little. "But you didn't take his name."

Enzo shook his head. "I wanted a blood tie with my name, and, as much as I loved Ernst and my younger siblings, Marino wasn't a name I felt ownership of."

All this talk about his last name reminded Kimberlyn of her words that first day. She looked directly up at him. "I'm sorry I said it was missing a word." She'd really been hateful to say that. The memory of the words rose like bile in her throat.

A quick head shake told her not to worry about it, but when he kissed her temple, it drove the sentiment home. Don't worry. About that. The arm around her shoulders loosened as his fingers tracked to the high, round neckline of her undershirt and then directly under it. He traced the scar on her sternum like braille that could tell him something he didn't want to ask.

Logically, she knew that the nerve endings in that seam had been severed and now no longer functioned. Since her sternum had healed beneath, there hadn't been any pain from touching it or pressure of any kind. No pain because there was no sensation.

That meant that every time it burned, the sensation was entirely in her mind. Knowing that didn't stop it from burning. Just like knowing there could be no sensation now didn't stop the rush of heat tracking over her chest and down her arms. Didn't stop the effervescent cascade from the imagined friction of his fingers on the tortured flesh anyone else would have avoided touching... No one but her and her doctors had ever touched it.

When she shivered, he looked down at her.

Did her cheeks glow as they felt they did? Had her pupils dilated with her faster breathing and heart rate? Desire had a very specific look, and this close... The look in his eyes confirmed it.

It was a familiar, intimate touch. His hands were soft, and the stroke of his long fingers so gentle. Tender even. Though they firmed in an exploratory way...

He was going to ask.

"Enzo..."

"I still don't want to know," he said quickly, withdrawing his fingers and curling her more firmly against his side, his gaze fixing once more on the gallery window. "You know, the name's not even really DellaToro." His voice rasped but gained strength as he spoke. "Mom's grandfather was a DellaTorre when he came through Ellis Island. DellaToro was a transcription error from Immigration."

He didn't want to know. Bad typists at Ellis Island had changed his name.

Who cared? Kimberlyn didn't even really want to stay and watch the surgery anymore. She was even having a hard time remembering why she should avoid those feelings. But God help her if she was going to pretend. She couldn't shrug it off as he did. "Torre means?"

"Tower."

She looked at him again, watched the corner of his jaw bunch and relax as he paused. No quick, easy flirting now. At least summoning words was hard for him, too.

"But he was a tiny man, preferred the idea of being linked with a bull... And ran with it. Remade himself into what he wanted to be."

She could see that trait as being inherited. Enzo came

from a blue-collar background and was intent and focused on reaching the top without help from someone who could've honestly done a lot to help his son if both—or either—of them had been so inclined.

She could use some of that strength of will right now.

Thinking about this, learning about him…it had all gone wrong somehow. Once he'd become more than a competitor, it felt as if every day she was coming up with a new way to cheerlead herself into some semblance of a belief that she could still prevail. That she still even wanted to. Because Enzo wasn't just a man on a personal mission, he was motivated for his whole family. It was noble. He actually was one of the good people she just pretended to be.

And maybe more deserving of the fellowship than someone just trying to clear bad debt from her moral ledger.

The mental back and forth exhausted her already overworked mind and heart. Something was going to happen between them, and she was going to let it. Because she wanted to. Because she was tired. Because she hurt, and somehow she hurt a little less those brief periods when she let his face block out Janie's.

"Look, he's tying it into the iliac and renal arteries rather than the aorta," Enzo said.

She laid her head against his shoulder because it hid her face and the tears suddenly threatening. The transplant was easier to talk about so she went with it. "Be harder to tap the aorta there. BF must have had some good vascular training, too."

Her parents weren't the most present people in the world, but they would never abandon her.

His angry words from the downstairs corridor came back to her: *I did this without your support or your money, and I'm going to finish it the same way.*

She'd thought he was just driven to do well for his family, but it went deeper than that.

Even metaphorical scars could burn your chest.

* * *

The good thing about watching someone else perform surgery from the gallery? Being able to leave whenever the urge struck. And after it was done, no lumpy mattresses in the on-call room that always smelled a little like feet no matter how frequently staff changed the bedding.

That had been part of the reasoning Kimberlyn had spent the remaining hours in the surgery convincing herself that she shouldn't drag Enzo to the on-call room to violate some rules. At least during those times when she hadn't successfully thrown cold water on her own mood with too many deep thoughts.

Now that they'd reached his car, now that he was driving her home, her list of reasons not to act on that desire shriveled. Kimberlyn paused with her hand on the passenger door handle.

She could take the subway home. That would immediately remove her from temptation. Then, maybe after she got some sleep, she'd feel...remotely sensible about anything pertaining to the man. The subway would allow her to put a damper on things before they got out of control.

And sounded like a terrible idea.

They'd controlled the lust three times now, but the first time he'd immediately left and she had gone to bed. Today's doubleheader left her feeling needy in a way that wasn't even simply about desire. That made it more dangerous to spend twenty minutes in his car, submersed in a cloud of his manly citrusy scent and the memory of firm heat still tingling in her side from having sat tucked against him for hours. Impossible to do and keep her sanity intact.

While she'd stood undecided at his car door, Enzo had gotten in. He leaned over now to catch her eye and asked, "Do you want to stay?" His words, while muffled by the raised window, were still understandable.

She shook her head, then shrugged and sighed.

He rolled down the window, the motion asking her for words.

"I'm just wondering if it's smart to keep hanging out, or whatever it is we're doing." The words rolled out, and she couldn't have said whether she wanted him to talk her out of it or not.

Enzo thought a moment and straightened. The hand resting on his knee moved up toward the ignition. Her stomach bottomed out and she snatched her hand back from the door. He was going to just go? Leave her standing? That would certainly send a message about how much he wanted her. Maybe earlier really had just been about feeling better in the moment...

He plucked the keys from the ignition before she reached panic stage. With one fluid motion he hefted himself from the car. Wherever he wanted to go, whatever he wanted to do, she was going. Even if he didn't say it, she was going to. She couldn't keep treading water around him.

A quick stride brought him around the car and he leaned against her door before speaking. "It's not smart at all."

Maybe he intended to talk her out of it? The look in his eyes was caught somewhere between a lusty smolder and a dare. A look she couldn't pull off if she tried.

He caught one of her hands and tugged until she'd taken the two steps separating them, and found herself chest to chest with him, heart rate soaring. "But I still want to do it. Whatever we're doing."

And more. He definitely wanted more. Thank goodness.

"How bad an idea do you think it is?" Why was she asking him questions? What could he say that would relieve the worry that wasn't going to stand in her way anyway?

What would it do to their relationship? How could he know?

How much would it screw up all their plans?

Could she do one night and return to the trenches the next day?

Had she even been in the freaking trenches yet?

"I need to rate it?" He asked his own question, breaking through the mental wall of flying questions, that flirty demeanor coming back over him, along with a lopsided little-boy grin so at odds with his hands sliding around her waist and down. Soon large hands cupped her rear and squeezed her so close she could feel the jut of his hip bones. So close she imagined she could even feel that delicious V of firm muscle leading down to the heat and firmness she knew she wasn't imagining.

How would he feel? What kind of lover would Enzo be?

Realizing she'd started breathing faster through her mouth, she closed her lips and tried to focus on what he was saying.

"Okay, let me think. On a scale of one to ten, with one being...ice cream for breakfast and ten being...getting hammered before you go to your first chain-saw juggling lesson, it's probably...somewhere in the middle."

A cute smirk followed that completely noncommittal answer.

She had to grin at the flirty fool, both for his examples of bad choices and for sharing her inability to nail down how bad the idea was. "Six?"

He shrugged, and rather than say anything else his hands lifted to her waist, then in one fluid movement dived down below the waistband of her scrubs and the thin cotton panties beneath.

Kimberlyn's breathing stuttered. It had been a long time since she'd been with a man. Before her accident. Well before. So far before that she was having a hard time thinking.

Hot, firm hands squeezing her bare cheeks would've been enough to set her brain to tilt, but Enzo didn't do anything in half measures. His hands slid and gripped, cupping and exploring the flesh.

When he tilted his head, hers fell back, so mad to kiss him that when he stopped with his lips barely brushing hers to whisper, "No scars here," she grabbed his head and kissed him before his words processed, then giggled into his kiss.

Playful. That's what kind of lover Enzo would be. And that was perfect. Playful sex would probably be easier to bounce back from than deep, soul-wrenching sex.

After another few kisses he lifted his head and smiled at her. "Do you really want me to put a number on it?"

Kimberlyn shook her head.

Long fingers tucked around the bottom curve of each cheek, stretching beneath until he had as much sensitive flesh in his hands as he could get, then he squeezed while tilting his head to kiss the side of her neck. Even if she'd demanded a number, that would've effectively shut her up.

Deep in the dark levels of the hospital's parking structure no one would happen upon them. She could probably tear his clothes off right here on the hood and...

Before her intentions crystalized, he slid his hands free from the baggy material, leaving her skin cold, and the rest of her way too aware of the damp garage.

He pivoted her to the side, opened the door and maneuvered her into the opening. "Get in. I demand privacy and somewhere I can take my time. But don't lose that thought."

"Not a chance." She smiled to cover the excited tremble that she was certain he'd see with one look, and did as instructed. Sit. Seat belt. Wait. Don't think about how deliciously aware she was of her body at that second.

In minutes they were out of the parking structure and on the street, heading for the Brooklyn-Battery tunnel.

She couldn't reverse completely, but her sex drive needed to downshift at least a little. And something about their earlier exchange hung around—Enzo avoided. That's how he was going to get through this, by not thinking ahead of time about what the consequences might be. Or maybe he just didn't foresee consequences.

"I have to ask you a question."

"Is it a sexy question?" he asked, and she didn't need to look at him to hear the grin in his voice.

"Not really. I'm just curious about something. You don't seem like the kind of guy who avoids tough subjects, but you kind of do," she said as they entered the tunnel. Dark underground places seemed like the right venue for talking about the subject they'd been circling for weeks: out-of-control attraction and what letting it run wild would mean to them when push came to shove. Or Ootaka began to really push...

"No, I don't. Not without an objective."

"Doesn't everyone who avoids tough subjects do so with an objective? Like the goal of not being scared, worried, sad...or some other unpleasant emotion?"

"Probably."

How was she supposed to react to that? He was good at answering questions in a way that still left her confounded.

"So, by avoiding the subject of how bad an idea it is for us to continue...growing closer, your objective is...?"

"You want to know my intentions, Country Mouse?"

That nickname. Most people who found her name objectionably long called her Cricket, a holdover from a childhood nickname. But somehow, when those words tumbled past his lips, they sounded like an endearment, not like the city slicker making fun of the bumpkin.

"Yes. I want to know your intentions." As all country mice should.

"I intend to take you somewhere private, deprive you of your clothes and ply you with wine and good food until you let me have dessert. I don't even care where. Your place. My place. A motel with a heart-shaped bed and magic fingers. I don't care. It just needs food, a bed and maybe a hot, steamy shower."

The blatant statement gave her another rush of good tingles in all the right places.

She wanted exactly that. "My place. I don't want to go to a skeevy motel."

"Good choice."

Yes, it was. Good choice because she was going to ignore logic. It was a choice that would mean staying with him longer, sharing something that would give them both peace, for a little while at least. She'd just have to take a page out of his book and not question the future for once.

After their long hard day they deserved some good. Something to counter today's heartache. Some way to stop thinking about Mr. Elliot's accident. Stop comparing his accident to hers. Stop wondering if it would have been better for him and his family if she'd failed to recognize the symptoms that had saved him and thus forced them into making such a hard choice after the seemingly good news of his survival.

Stop wondering whether, if the paramedics had made that decision at her accident, Janie would have been the one to survive instead of her.

Kimberlyn fumbled with the door handle as soon as Enzo threw the car into Park. By the time she got out he'd climbed out, shut the door and bounded around to her side. After an obligatory beep to lock the vehicle he grabbed her ponytail in the back, holding her steady as he swooped in and pressed her against the car.

She'd been thinking about kissing him for the past twenty-seven minutes, no matter what else she tried to think about. One more minute until they got inside was entirely too long to wait.

Her heart paused and then galloped hard. His soft lips and demanding tongue, the scrape of the three-day beard he wore like a three-piece suit. Heat, sweetness and need.

The long day had left her raw and hollow, despite the show she put on for him and anyone who looked her way. His hand left her hair and skimmed her body, around her waist to dive into the back of her scrubs.

Someone whistled. Outside. Still outside. "Inside," she panted against his lips, and he nodded, pulling his hands free and turning her in one motion. He walked behind her, propelling her up the stairs with his body.

His breath hot on her neck made her spine curl, and she bumped her rear end ever so slightly against him before she managed to straighten up and not fall.

Falling wouldn't be sexy. At least, not falling outside on the stairs.

She'd never been so thankful for her neurotic tendency to plan for everything—she'd gotten her keys out while still in the car. Now she just had to get the damned thing in the slot.

The end jabbed the dead bolt and slid off to nick the wood.

"Shoot."

He nosed her ear, purring the words so that the baby-fine hairs on the back of her neck stood at attention. "Don't worry, I've got much better aim than that."

He didn't take her keys but he took control of her hand and glided the key into the lock. God help her, he was making unlocking the door sexy, and she was aroused to the point that she was just happy to be more or less in control of her balance.

When it was seated, his hand left to stroke down her body to the heat between her legs. Through the fabric, his strong hands stroked along the seam, those deft fingers pressing firmly to mold the damp material to her.

Sandwiched between him and the door, she managed to click the lock and turn the knob. They staggered through the door. She dropped her bag to free her hands. The door closed somehow, and in three wide strides he'd propelled her backward to the stairs.

"No one here." He leaned back and ripped his shirt off and dropped it on the floor.

The man was fit, lean muscle and definition, short black

hair dusting the olive skin and trailing down over his belly, a path she let her fingertips travel, tracing every dip and swell of the hard muscle beneath.

He knew she had scars, but the filter he'd seen them through before had been clinical, curious. The sexy filter was a lot different, as was seeing them all together rather than one at a time. From the front, she was riddled with scars. When her shirts came off, what would he think? Would he be disappointed? Men were visual creatures...

Thoughts she'd never let herself consider before because of her five-year plan. It didn't include men. Before her accident she'd never considered whether she could please her partner. It annoyed even her that she oscillated between being plagued by guilt or plagued by insecurities.

He leaned back in, arms sliding into the triangle made by the stair at her back, his lips and tongue at the hollow beneath her ear when his hot breath would've been enough to have her arching against him.

She had to say something before her clothes came off and he was confronted with the ugly truth. Seeing it in his eyes might add more emotional scars than she could abide. "Enzo...you're beautiful. I don't have a pretty body anymore..."

He leaned back enough to look at her, his brows pinching in that brooding fashion before he shook his head. "Shut up, Mouse. You're smarter than that."

As soon as the words were out he moved against her, the hard ridge of his barely concealed erection grinding with enough strength to massage the rapidly swelling nub between her legs.

Okay. Point made.

"Not here... Upstairs," she panted, her words breaking over a single spasm of pleasure. Not an orgasm but close already, and if that was any indication...

His answer was another deep, drugging kiss. With every plunge of his tongue he rocked his hips against her.

When another of those prophetic spasms hit her, she cried out blindly.

Enzo could have stayed on the stairs. Hell, he could have stayed outside with her, or in the garage, or in his car pulled to the side of the road.

Anyone else and he might have. But Kimberlyn deserved better. Even if she hadn't been worried about her scars, the idea of someone else catching a glimpse of them together... more like the idea of someone seeing her body...set his teeth on edge. He didn't even want anyone hearing those special cries of pleasure that belonged to him.

And by the sound of things she had already neared orgasm.

Anchoring one arm around her waist, he rose and lifted her with him. "Up."

Her legs didn't want to carry her. She wobbled and grabbed his shoulders and the railing in equal measure, the wild heat in her eyes making the stairs and hallway seem like a thousand-mile journey. They'd never make it like this, and he didn't want her to calm down enough to make it on her own. He wanted her wild-eyed and panting, wanted to be the man who could knock her legs out from under her with her clothes still on.

Knocking her legs out from under her would get them upstairs faster. Bending, he anchored his arm around the backs of her knees so she fell forward over his bare shoulder, and he was off.

"Enzo?"

"Faster." He took the stairs at a jog.

When he reached her unit—another door to get through—he set her down and she handed him the keys, not even attempting to steady her hands enough to get the key in this time.

He kept her in front of him, her back to his front, the sweet curve of that soft little rump almost wrecking his coordination. She waited for him to click the lock, then turned the knob to push into the room.

He looked around enough to orient himself in the low evening light. Clean but the bed unmade, reminding him of how many hours ago they'd been called out of bed to the surgery. His bed remained unmade, too...

"Caren likes pink stuff," she said, curling her fingers in the waistband of his scrubs and pulling him to her from the front now, misinterpreting his expression.

"I like pink stuff, too," he said, unable to keep the little tease in. The door closed with more force than he'd meant to close it. But it was closed.

He reached for the hem of her scrub top and pulled it and the Spandex undershirt off in one motion.

The scar on her chest pulled his gaze, bringing a worry with it. "You've been cleared for sex, right?"

"I'm cleared for normal activity," she mumbled, flipping open the clasp at the back and pulling off the simple white bra and tossing it to the floor. Having her breasts free for inspection and adoration took his attention from the scar... which was just want he'd wanted.

Wrapping one arm around her waist, he kept her moving toward the bed.

She was self-conscious about her scars, and he didn't know whether to pay attention to them or ignore them. What would she prefer? There was plenty to keep his attention without those physical reminders of what she'd been through.

He lay between her legs, her soft breasts mashing against his chest. He wanted to feel the length of her against him, but her legs had wrapped around him and that felt amazing. Until a sneaker hit him in the back, breaking the kiss.

"Sorry." She toed the other one loose and kicked it away from them.

"Don't be sorry. I want you naked, too."

Shoes wouldn't slow them down. He undressed her in

another quick, smooth rush of fabric and then stood back to look at her.

No tan lines. She was naturally tan, and she no longer went out in public in a bathing suit. That shouldn't bother him, but it did.

It didn't make him want her less, but...questions. About her accident, and how she'd been since then. Questions he had no business asking. Willful ignorance could only help him right now. The more he knew, the more he wanted to know. The more he cared. The more confused everything got.

The scent of her skin, the way she arched and moaned when he took one of her nipples into his mouth. That was enough to know for now.

By the time a condom had been secured and rolled on, he was hard to the point of pain.

Go slow. He should go slow. Who knew when she'd last had a lover...?

He stroked the swollen head of his shaft through the slick folds and pushed into her.

Her body opened, wrapping him in heat and clenching hard enough to send shivers racing over his body.

He had to move.

Light-headed and panting, he withdrew and thrust, reveling in every gasp he wrung out of her, in every involuntary twitch of her body, in the way her toes curled against his thighs.

Every second in her was a struggle not to come, and when her eyes screwed shut, blocking him out, that struggle got easier.

And much less satisfying. He wanted to see the unfocused dreamy wonder in her eyes. "Look at me."

Even if his endurance couldn't hold out, he needed the connection. No, he wanted it. It wasn't need. He wanted the connection. He wanted in. Not just inside her soft body, but her—the intimacy that let him feel her pleasure, too. How much he pleased her.

She teetered on the edge, hit-and-run spasms crashing over her like miniature orgasms and threatening his sanity.

When the big one hit and that hot little core began to pulse, his heart thundered in his chest and he trembled from head to toe.

The first wave of climax hit like a thunderclap, stronger than anything he'd ever felt, breaking his rhythm. He'd swear he'd heard it...

One of them cried out.

Her legs clamped around his hips, pulling him into her again, urging him to move, each jerky thrust of his hips rewarded with another shock of pleasure—one he saw reflected in her dazed eyes. A look that no doubt mirrored his own.

When the storm passed, he flung himself onto his back, gulping down air like a drowning man.

She rolled to him and climbed back atop him, tucking her nose under his jaw and whispering, "Hug me. Hug me hard like you did."

When had he hugged her hard? He swallowed, mouth dry, but he couldn't do anything but what she asked. Both arms slipped over her back, squeezing her tight so she'd know he held her.

Her trembling eased as he squeezed her, but his insides still quaked like gelatin.

Grabbing the blanket at his side, he pulled it over them and closed his eyes.

He'd think later. The only thing clear to him right now was that his plans had changed.

He didn't want to think about how.

Kimberlyn awoke hours later, blankets and pillows scattered everywhere, still warm despite only the sheet remaining. Sometime in the hours since they'd fallen asleep they'd rolled. Enzo's big body now nestled behind her.

Although they'd moved, both his arms stayed wrapped around her—one beneath her head looped to rest his hand on the opposite shoulder, the other flung over her waist. Loose, but still around her. Heat at her back, breath in her hair... She could get used to this. Not that she should, but she really could.

The clock on the bedside table cut through the dark. Two in the morning. Right around the time they'd been called in the night before.

Should she wake him up? It would be sweeter if she went to the kitchen and made sandwiches first. Not usually something she'd do. She'd never been the girlfriend who baked or tended. She'd always had something of her own she'd been immersed in. There had been boyfriends, but she'd never felt compelled to take care of them. Probably unsurprising as her mother and father weren't that sort, either. They seemed to love one another, but it wasn't... consuming.

The word fit on so many levels right now.

Carefully, she lifted the arm draped over her and eased out from under it. Even in the dark she found her robe quickly, threw it on and slipped out of her unit to head for the kitchen.

The shirt he'd lost in the foyer was draped over the banister. She winced. Busted. They certainly hadn't taken the time before heading upstairs, and considering the standard of embroidered names their *thing* was no longer any kind of secret. Made it...what did it make it? In not talking about possibilities, they hadn't talked about whether or not they wanted others finding out.

No signs of life in the house. She made the sandwiches, grabbed some water and went back up with his shirt over one shoulder.

The light under her door was on. Enzo had awakened.

She slipped in and found him tying his shoes, dressed except for the top she carried. "Hungry still?" She showed him the plate.

"Yes, but I figured I'd head home and sleep a couple more hours before my shift in the morning." He rose and stepped over, taking his shirt off her shoulder.

Was it walk-of-shame time? She'd been worried about the consequences, but she'd thought they'd be more about work. And happen at work. Not that he'd take off as soon as he woke up.

She must have looked pitiful, because he looked down at the plate. His shirt back on, he gestured. "But I can stick around for a sandwich first."

Definitely crossed the line into Patheticville. This was what regret looked like. Enzo was unhappy they'd ended up here, even if he'd been so certain about everything earlier.

She sat on the edge of the bed and placed the plate to her side. He sat so it was between them, took the water bottle and started eating.

"If I hadn't come back so fast, would you have gone without telling me?"

"No," he answered quickly and then, as if to convince her this was just business as usual, added, "this is none of my business, but when was the last time you were with someone?"

Ah, the reason he'd been eager before and was less eager now. It hadn't lived up to his expectations. Or she hadn't.

The growling in her stomach faded, the sandwich no longer looked good. Maybe after she got this over with, after he'd gone, she could eat it.

"It was before my accident." Tell the truth. Get it over with. "I know it was fast. I'm sure it was…not as fun for you as it could have been. Sorry." Her gaze fell to her lap and a sigh slid out.

"Hey."

He wanted her to look at him, not something she was

keen to do. The only thing faster than his exit was how awkward the aftermath was becoming.

Just smile through it. Let him off the hook.

She straightened, her lips curling up slightly at the corners, she imagined. Or maybe they were just a straight line. Anything was better than turned down or wobbling.

"It's okay. I know this wasn't something that could ever happen again anyway. And it probably wouldn't have if yesterday hadn't been so difficult for both of us." She stood up and tightened the belt on her robe, willing it to be longer. Why had she gotten the short robe? Robes were supposed to be concealing and warm, not with a bouncy hemline for spring. Stupid.

"You didn't disappoint me. I just was thinking about how things were at the hospital, and that it could be messy. For us. Could upset plans, and neither of us wants that."

She forced herself to make eye contact with him, even though she wanted to shove him out the door, then maybe have a lobotomy or find someone to wash her brain. "You're right. We'll go back to business as usual. It's not a big deal."

It was a big deal if someone like Enzo could see past her scars and all her stupid issues. Which he had, she thought.

And none of that was the right reaction to have. A relationship wasn't in her plan. No men. The plan said no relationships. A one-night stand? Well, that could make it through on a technicality. But, still, he could have made it a whole night. This was more like a half-night stand.

She was still fuzzy from days of sleep deprivation. Not her best thinking state. At least not when emotions got into the mix.

"I need sleep," she said, to start him moving again. "I'm on the afternoon shift tomorrow, so I'm going to inhale the sandwich and get back to sleep. The door downstairs will lock when you close it. It always requires a key to come in."

He nodded, picking up the other half of his sandwich in one hand and his keys in the other.

His gaze tracked to the bed behind her, and for a second it felt as if he might stay. As if he might just say to the devil with all the things that had been said and stay.

"I'm on the morning shift," he said instead, the words shutting down her train of thought. It was just as well. She'd have let him stay for sure…because of pride? What was that?

Enzo stood there a moment, watching the angry tilt of her chin and the way her arms crossed and her brow furrowed. He could make her smile if he stayed. Go back to bed. Not sleep… Let things get messier than they'd already gotten.

He didn't even know at what point the line had been crossed, but it had been. For both of them. It hadn't just been sex. It hadn't just been comfort or need. She'd felt something. He knew she had. And he'd known it when she'd rolled with him. It had been in the hug she'd begged for. That hadn't been about desire. It had been something much deeper, something she thought he could give her.

Not daring to kiss her goodbye, Enzo nodded and stepped toward the door. As soon as it swung shut, he heard the lock.

Message received: unwelcome.

Good. He should be.

CHAPTER TEN

ENZO FOUND KIMBERLYN in the locker room, staring at the posting Ootaka had made earlier. It had been six whole days since he'd slunk out of her bedroom. Six days of not speaking. Six days of barely making eye contact. It had felt like six months of Herculean effort to pull it off. It felt almost as hard to approach her now...

That morning Ootaka had posted an announcement that the deadline for application to his fellowship had been moved up. Rather than them having until January, he was going to post his decision in three weeks.

Three weeks could be a really long time—but under a time crunch, time perception changed.

"Hey," he said behind her, since he'd managed to walk up without her noticing again. The woman was disturbingly easy to sneak up on. Anytime she was alone she was often so absorbed in her own thoughts that everything else went on without her.

And right now he knew what those thoughts were. For a fleeting few seconds he was glad that the deadline had been moved. At least now she didn't have to think about the ways he'd disappointed her.

"You okay?"

Because, of course, that wasn't a stupid thing to ask.

Kimberlyn turned to him and shrugged, not making eye contact again. "Do you really want to know?"

The same question he'd asked her before, the same question he asked himself all the time.

"I want to know."

Shaking her head, she moved on. "Do we know why he's moving it up?"

Still not looking at him—and not answering his question—she sat on the bench and studied her fingernails, picking at them as if there was a speck of something she just couldn't get rid of trapped beneath the carefully tended manicure.

"He has to go to Japan. Someone in his family is ill. When you have one the world's best surgeons sharing your gene pool, if something goes wrong you get to call in favors," Enzo said, tension eating at his shoulders again.

"And he'll be gone a long time, I guess."

"He might be." Still trying to relax, he sat on the bench beside her. His knee touched hers and he slid a couple of inches back. Too close. No touching. "He doesn't like to leave things unfinished."

She nodded, her brows as pinched as her lips were pursed.

Unlike Ootaka, he'd left whatever was between him and Kimberlyn unfinished. But this time his avoidance wasn't because he didn't want to know anything that might change his plans. Because he had no plans for once in his life. He didn't know what to do. One of them was going to be disappointed soon, and the way things were going with her...

"There's not a lot of time left for you to catch up." He didn't quite know how to phrase it so that it wasn't offensive. Being blunt was so much easier, but somewhere along the way he'd started using the same temperance with Kimberlyn as he did with his family. He didn't do that with any other colleagues, or even friends in the hospital. He certainly didn't do that with Sam, and Sam was a good friend.

"It's not, but I can still do it. I've always responded well to a ticking clock."

"Not me." His hand itched to touch her. She was right there, and no one else was in the locker room to disrupt them. "I tend to become a—"

"Hyper-focused jerk?"

"That," he agreed, trying and failing to smile.

"So are you here to warn me or am I still not competition?"

"No." But this was why he shouldn't have asked. "I think you're more competition than anyone else in the program."

Competition enough to make him feel awful. She'd definitely have the spot if he weren't around.

"That's something, I guess."

"I want to know about your heart now." The words had come out before he had even consciously thought about them. Had just appeared in his head and dashed out before he could consider the ramifications of asking right now.

"You mean my surgery?"

He definitely didn't want to know any more details. But he still asked, "Why was your chest cracked?"

"Aortic dissection."

What Elliot had suffered.

"Did it show with tamponade? Did they catch it during your bowel resection?" Please say yes. Make it as uneventful as possible.

She shook her head. "No, I didn't have the tamponade. The tear was small, and the blood wasn't leaking much into the chest cavity at that point."

"How did they find it?" Why was he even asking this? It was in the past. He couldn't fix her past. He couldn't fix anything for her.

"I went into shock in the ICU," she murmured. "But Dr. Anderson got me into an OR just in time."

His stomach churned just knowing how close she'd come to death. How close he'd come to losing her or never having known her. "You've come back from a lot." Maybe she could pull this off in the eleventh hour.

"I'm trying."

He watched her. She answered his questions. She wasn't yelling at him for the worst after-sex exit in history. It'd be better if she did. It'd be better than talking about this stuff. And people said talking helped problems… "You're succeeding," he argued, at a loss for anything else to say.

"Not as well as I'd like," she murmured, standing suddenly to pace around the locker room. Any second she'd be gone, maybe even just to get away from him.

"Have you thought about any other programs?" He dug into the pocket of his jacket to fish out his tablet. A couple of ticks and he turned it toward her to read.

She squinted at the tablet and the small colorful image of the whole document, "You have a spreadsheet of other trauma fellowships?"

He nodded. "Listed by desirability and the habits of the board to choose from pools outside their residency program."

Unlike Ootaka, who only chose from those he'd witnessed in the OR.

"So you made that when you were deciding where to request placement?" She crossed her arms as she finally fixed him with that squint that was becoming a scowl.

Her indirect way of asking if he'd done that for her or for him. "No. I did it a few days ago." Because he needed to try to fix things somehow.

And maybe he was working on his guilt after they'd banished a hard, long day by falling into bed together.

"For me," she said.

It wasn't even a question now.

"I care about you, Kimberlyn. I know you're not making a backup plan, and I was going to talk to you about it in a while, but now that Ootaka has moved things up it seemed like the time."

She unfolded her arms long enough for her cool fingers to touch his wrist and push away the hand holding his device. "Gee, thanks. I care about you, too, even though I think you're extremely arrogant and blind in this matter. It's not over just because he announced it will be decided sooner rather than later. I still have time."

"You have time to try." He tapped a couple more times on the tablet, emailing her the spreadsheet, since she refused to look at it now. "But I can't let my standing carry me. The next three weeks you're going to be working to catch up, and I'm going to be working to increase my lead."

"And your point is?"

"My point is that you should at least make a backup plan." Please, just let him fix something.

"Have you applied anywhere else?"

He dropped the tablet back into his pocket. "Not yet."

"But you're going to?"

"I haven't decided." He also hadn't decided until that second that he had to go back to maintaining that distance from her for the next three weeks. Not just avoidance. He... needed to treat her like Lyons. She made him soft.

"I'm not giving up, but I will apply for a few others. Ones I've already decided are my backups. Because I have to go somewhere, and I'm practical enough to know that even if I want this, I should spread my eggs among many baskets." She stood up, a tug of her top straightening her appearance, and headed for the door.

"Where are you going?"

A short laugh and she called as she kept walking, "To start crafting my plan for world domination."

"Wait." He caught up in a few strides and grabbed her elbow to stop her sassy exit. "I need to say something else."

She groaned. "You're in a hole, Enzo. Stop digging."

"It's a warning."

"Fine. Warn away." She crossed her arms again and watched him work out what he wanted to say. She'd spent the week regretting the sex, and now it was only worse. She'd been an idiot to think she could do a one-night thing without getting wrapped up in it. No doubt this was what she deserved for getting relaxed with him.

"I said I don't respond well to a ticking clock. I don't." He shrugged, as if he had more to say but didn't know quite how to say it. "Having my plans and my schedules messed with makes me more focused and competitive."

"Warning received—you're going into hyperactive jerk mode, like when you ran ahead to Ootaka."

"Don't take it personally."

"Of course not. You know, if you're going to be nasty or ignore me, like you have been, then just do it all the time. All this flipping back and forth between being a flirty smooth talker and a bastard is giving me motion sickness. If you have a decent bone in your body, or even if you just want to give a nod to fair play, pick a personality and stick with it." She really was getting used to the city if she could have a fight like this and not throw up afterward. "And just so we're clear, whichever personality wins, let him know that there won't be any further naked stuff with me."

Enzo had known this talk wouldn't go well. How could it go well when his instincts were at war? Like the ones that said he should ask her questions constantly at odds with his self-preservation instincts that told him to shut up. He couldn't blame her for thinking of him as a Jekyll and Hyde character.

But that didn't mean he had to like it. His lips firmed and his gaze slid down to her elbow where he'd stopped her flight, where he'd been stroking the skin in a classic comforting maneuver. That instinct to comfort always rose back up, but he was still the kind of man she should be warned about.

She pulled her elbow free and he let her. It was harder to think straight when they touched in any fashion, but especially flesh to flesh. "Good luck, Dr. DellaToro. And don't go complaining to Sam about me, either."

"I wouldn't do that."

"Good. He doesn't want to be in the middle, and he deserves that consideration."

His ears were probably lucky that the door she stormed out of couldn't slam.

Kimberlyn went directly from the locker room to Ootaka's office, where she found him doing paperwork. A short knock announced her and he looked up, motioning her inside.

"Dr. Ootaka, I know your mind must be going a million directions right now, but I need to say a couple of things. First, I'm sorry to hear that your family is having a difficult time. It's the right thing for you to go to them, and everyone understands that the deadline has been moved up."

He nodded, gesturing to her to sit in the chair on the other side of his desk, but went back to writing whatever he'd been working on—some form or another. "You want to ask about your chances with the fellowship, Dr. Davis?"

"No." She sat as invited but didn't relax, keeping her posture as straight and rigid as she'd always been taught to do. Situations like this demanded formality, that she be the proper and polite lady physically, even if her mouth was about to go a different direction than deferential etiquette drilled into her.

"I want to assist you in surgery. I understand your custom is to go slowly and let the other surgeons vet the residents before they are invited into your OR, but I've proven myself already."

She took a breath. Should she bring her personal history into this? It might seem like a request for him to take pity on her when her motivation was entirely the opposite. She wanted to show him she could take charge, prove her spine existed, and telling him everything—or almost everything—would demonstrate that. He didn't need to know more than that she was motivated. "How much do you know about my time and residency at Vanderbilt?"

"I have received a recommendation from Dr. Anderson. He speaks highly of your skill and focus."

She smiled when she heard the surgeon's name spoken, her resolve firming up. "He's had a special view of my focus."

"How so?"

"Dr. Anderson put me back together after a catastrophic car accident six weeks before my fourth year of residency was supposed to start." Her voice hadn't wavered at all. No emotion. She could do this.

That made his pen stop. He lifted his gaze from the paper and gave her his full attention. "I did not know you'd had an accident."

Think about the wreck as if it was one of her patients. Not her. Faking distance was something that had worked moderately for her in the past. "I had an obvious serious bowel injury when they cut me from the car. A piece of metal that had gone through my jejunum. He removed it and repaired my bowel. I also had a broken femur and torn rotator cuff. The structural orthopedic repairs that take a backseat to the life-threatening ones. While I was in ICU after the bowel repair I crashed. He had to crack my chest. I had a small aortic dissection that was taking its time bleeding out."

She took a deep breath. She should have stopped using *I this, I that*. She really needed to work on a narrative that could give her distance. Talking about the accident always left her feeling bare.

"How far behind your classmates are you?"

"Just one year," she answered, then drew a deep breath. "I'm not telling you this because I want you to think that I'm in need of special consideration. I just want you to see how hard I can fight for something that I want, and how motivated I am not just to succeed but to succeed spectacularly. I deferred my residency for a year to heal and work through the physical therapy necessary to come back from that. Vanderbilt let me defer that a year—it was my school and the hospital where I spent so much time recovering.

"But in all the time I spoke with Dr. Anderson in those first weeks I understood that sometimes fate interacts with our lives and changes the course forever. I know that I survived because of one of your fellows. And I know that I want to be that doctor for others. Give me another chance in your OR to prove myself."

Her knee started to bounce. She stopped it. She'd gotten through all that with a strong voice, clean...mostly free of emotion. Not the time to blow it now. Thinking about the emotions crossing Ootaka's face, as subtle as they were, could blow it for her. He had the kind of poker face that would clean up in Vegas.

"The next surgery is yours, Dr. Davis," he finally said.

She hadn't expected him to make a decision now. She'd expected that he would say that he'd heard her and that he would bear her request in mind—something that deflected from having to commit to a course of action. But he really didn't deflect.

She should've listened to Enzo on that one if nothing else—he didn't like to leave decisions hanging.

"Th-thank you," she managed, though a small stammer at the start probably gave away some kind of emotion. Was surprise a bad emotion to display?

"I had already intended to invite the top trauma residents into surgery in the coming weeks as a testing ground, but I appreciate your directness. I expect no less than that on the floor."

Nodding, she stood and offered her hand to him, repeating again, because she just didn't know what else to say, "Thank you."

It had been a brisk pace to learn the difference between the attitudes of the two different hospitals, but she was finally getting it. And there was something to be said for the direct route. While it didn't aim to spare the feelings of anyone, it also didn't build false hope. The cuts were quick and clean, and she could appreciate that.

When he'd shaken her hand, she headed out. He didn't comment on her accident, and she was thankful for that. As good a face as she'd just put on for him, it was faltering.

Once in the safety of the hallway, she scrambled to the nearest stairwell for a moment of solitude. She just needed to catch her breath, let her hands steady and her heart slow down before it started to feel as if it was doing somersaults.

Her heart, like the rest of her, would have to get used to the new normal eventually. Probably sometime after the blunt, quick-cut method of dealing with others came a little more naturally to her.

Though it kind of felt as if she'd already done that with Enzo back in the locker room.

In the lead-up to Ootaka leaving, the older surgeon had decided that the best way to test his top two candidates was to pair them off in surgeries where one led and the other assisted, then switch it around for the next surgery.

Starting tonight, Enzo and Kimberlyn were both on the evening shift with Ootaka so that they could be around for the busiest times for trauma surgeons. Enzo had never had a shift where something interesting didn't happen, but his hairiest nights were always on the weekend. Friday could be counted on to bring the hairy.

Since their quarrel about backup plans, something had gone down between Kimberlyn and Ootaka, resulting in her being his primary assistant for the past eleven days. And he was going to hold the line and not ask her any questions even if it killed him. Now, if he could just stop thinking about things…and her.

His phone buzzed. Text from Ootaka.

Time to work.

Enzo hit the door of the on-call room at a jog and headed for the OR he'd been summoned to.

He would be the first one to lead surgery. He'd been around longest, he'd had the most time with Ootaka in the OR and it probably said something about how much Ootaka trusted him that he gave him first crack.

It didn't do much to improve his mood.

Kimberlyn was at one of the sink bays, scrubbing in, when he arrived. "Bashing trauma," she said to him as soon as he entered.

He tied on his cap as he stepped to the second sink bay. She'd have to talk to him for the surgery. And the other way around. "From what?"

"Fight in Central Park." She shook her head. "He's young, Enzo."

Fight? Young? If it was a kid... "How old?"

"Fourteen."

His dinner felt like lead in his stomach. Not a little kid but young enough. He'd seen his fair share of fights in his neighborhood, but now that he knew exactly how much damage a fist could do to internal organs, the violence he'd grown up around and accepted as a matter of course sickened him.

That insensitivity to violence was part of the cultural divide he'd always been aware of with his father's departure from their lives—so aware of it that by the time he'd become a teenager he'd gotten into fights to reinforce that difference. Yelling at him as he had over the transplant was just a step away from throwing punches, but a step he'd learned not to take if he could avoid it.

"You okay?" she asked, the first personal thing she'd said to him since he'd bailed on her while inhaling a sandwich.

"I hate violence. Medical school ruined boxing for me. Ruined a lot of my enjoyment with sports of all kinds, but violence is especially disturbing. People think that if there isn't a weapon involved, nothing too bad can happen."

"Tree limb," she said, throwing him briefly. "That was

the weapon. Over by the carousel, they said. I don't know where that is, but…"

"You haven't been to Central Park since you've been here?" He asked the question as if he didn't know how busy she'd been, even before she'd become Ootaka's new toy. The reading and the studying could be done in Central Park, but maybe not if you were new to the city.

"No. But I went to the Statue of Liberty and the Empire State Building."

Enzo groaned. "I thought you'd flock to the green places, Country Mouse."

Damn, he shouldn't have called her that.

The tiny smile she gave him cracked him in the chest. He'd missed her.

Professional distance and avoiding anything else couldn't continue. He had to come up with some way to make things work out well for her, even after the fellowship was announced. He'd give his left kidney if Ootaka would just take them both on…

When they exited to the OR, nurses met them, gloved and gowned them. Ootaka had already scrubbed in and was in the OR, waiting for them both.

No instruction, but he took a position beside Enzo and waited, watching.

Enzo didn't even need to palpate the abdomen. He could see distinct swelling in the right quadrant of the boy's belly. Liver damage. And the only way to verify if it was bleeding, shattered or merely bruised and swollen was with visual inspection.

"Number twenty-two scalpel," he announced and made a diagonal incision below the lower curve of the last rib.

Kimberlyn was there immediately with retractors, helping to open the boy's belly so that he could get eyes on it. They could do this much together, at least.

"Narrate, Doctor," Ootaka instructed.

"Lots of blood," Enzo announced, and Kimberlyn was

there with pads to help absorb the blood. "Coming from the liver." He examined more closely and announced, "The organ has opened in two fissures."

"Action?" Ootaka prompted.

"Trim it and assure blood supply," Enzo answered.

Standing across from her now, while better than total avoidance, still wasn't enough. He wanted her in his life. The whole situation would be so much easier if he could just point to their relationship fissures, trim off the damaged parts, make sure the rest was fed... Was that possible? Was that how people healed damaged relationships?

Kimberlyn swapped the saturated pads with fresh ones as Enzo worked, working to not only anticipate his needs but also to keep her hands out of the way. Every now and then she felt his eyes on her over their patient. Not lingering, just a glance she was so aware of it might as well be a touch.

The rest of the team worked on the periphery, mostly silent like Ootaka, but it felt like just the two of them. She should be managing the team, too, not replaying him calling her Mouse again. The warmth in his voice and that rascally way he flirted always muddied up her thinking.

Like now. Manage the team. She checked vitals, blood, and had one of the techs reposition the light so that it lit up the body cavity better.

"I'd like to give him blood, Dr. DellaToro," she announced, because that lesson would never leave her. As he worked on trimming away the shattered parts of the boy's liver, she swapped the pads again, still trying to control the bleeding. "He needs clotting factors."

"Agreed." Enzo looked at the monitors to get a reading on the blood pressure, which was much lower than he wanted it to be.

Normally, in the case of extreme abdominal trauma, they went in multiple times to make repairs with periods to stabilize in between. First, stop blood loss. Close lightly.

Wait. Go in again after the patient had been stabilized to avoid shock, do the real repairs. But the nature of this boy's wounds made it harder to do a hit-and-run. He'd keep bleeding if they didn't get the damaged tissue out.

When Enzo had gotten the liver whittled down and in better shape, Kimberlyn pulled out the last round of cloths after they'd applied coagulants and frowned at the fluid on the pads. "Doctor...we're missing something."

Attention pulled from the cavity, Enzo tilted his head to get a better look at the pads and saw it—something there besides blood. "Is that bile? Damned tree limb," he muttered and immediately regretted it. Emotion. Ootaka. But he didn't dwell on it.

"I think it's from the stomach..." She didn't sound as sure as she had been sounding, but it was the time to sound uncertain if you were uncertain. They both gently moved tissues to the side to trace the leak.

Ootaka said nothing yet.

Enzo was about to ask his opinion, mentally sorting through the solid and hollow organs that could be leaking...

Wasn't the stomach.

Not the kidneys.

Not the intestines...

"Pancreas." He moved the stomach aside to visualize the pancreas.

Kimberlyn hurried to get irrigation and suction tools. "If the pancreas is leaking..."

"We can't close."

The only thing the pancreas leaked was digestive fluids. If they closed him up and waited for him to stabilize, everything in the vicinity would be damaged just like food broken down in digestion by those same fluids.

Sometimes what you didn't want to know could kill you. Or at least cause a lot of damage.

They found the damaged section and trimmed it in much

the same fashion as they had the liver. "Good eye, Dr. Davis."

They worked together, and that felt good, too.

When the pancreas had been drained and repaired, they put a mesh in place and stitched the skin closed as they'd likely have to open him up again later.

Ootaka said very little during the whole surgery. Enzo would have liked to pretend that was a good sign, but he would've probably only spoken up if they'd been going down the wrong path. Their performance could have been simply adequate and he'd respond the same.

She'd been the first to spot trouble with this shared patient, too. Seemed like the kind of thing that would usually bother him. But for some reason it didn't. He'd have to think about that sometime. Later.

CHAPTER ELEVEN

A KNOCKING ON her door crept into Kimberlyn's dream.

Then a voice calling.

A man.

Sam.

Behind his loud summons dragging her from sleep, she heard a smaller sound. Tiny, in fact. Had Sam gotten a kitten?

Kimberlyn dragged her still fully clothed self out of the bed and shuffled to the door.

Long shift. Long week. Long year... Or six. Or ten... Long surgery—or series of surgeries on the one patient. Gunshot. She'd call it a gut shot but the bullet had bounced around in there so much that the track hadn't been confined to the gut.

Enzo had assisted, and it had gone well... He hadn't made her look bad—not that she thought he would anymore. There had been a point where they had both been in need of instruction, and Ootaka had stepped in, but whatever the surgeon had been hoping his plan would evoke in them had failed to happen.

"I'm coming," she grumbled, hoping to stop the knocking before her head exploded.

One of her shoes was still on, but the other? Missing. Her lopsided stride made the soreness in her overworked and abused body that much more pronounced.

Too sleepy to try to manage her balance while kicking off the other shoe, she just went with it.

Tomorrow afternoon Ootaka had scheduled the announcement of his newly selected fellow for the following two years.

One of her eyes was also not working properly. Out of focus, no doubt from the makeup she'd failed to take off... however long ago she'd collapsed into bed.

Could you get a hangover from not sleeping?

Two misses of the lock and knob later, she managed to crack the door open and glare with her one good eye at Sam.

The Scot had a baby. Not a baby kitten. A baby human.

A baby human she knew!

Instantly much more awake, she swung the door open and reached out to take one of Maya's little hands. "You brought Maya to see me?"

Shy, the tiny almost-toddler buried her face in Sam's shoulder.

"Aww, she doesn't remember me."

"It's been a couple of months since that dinner," Sam reminded her, grinning.

Not that she could say anything about sparing adoring looks for the little princess. She hadn't even treated Maya and she already had a big squishy smile in place for her. "She remembers you, though."

"I see her at least every couple of weeks." Sam rubbed Maya's back and then coached her to say something.

Whatever she said, the only thing Kimberlyn thought she might have caught was a "Jo" in there somewhere. But she couldn't swear to it.

Sam placed a fancy cream-colored envelope in Maya's hand and told her to give it to Kimberlyn.

"The world's tiniest and most adorable mail carrier." Kimberlyn took it with extravagant thanks and praise, and then a somewhat less excited question directed at Sam. "What is this?"

"I believe it's called extortion," Sam explained, "Or blackmail. I can't keep them separate."

"Okay if I open my extortion envelope?"

"Yep." Sam rubbed Maya's back again, the little girl curling back against him. She stole everyone's heart. "We're going to go. Sophie is waiting downstairs to take the munchkin home."

She said her goodbyes, closed the door and opened the envelope.

Inside was an invitation on extremely nice stationery, written by someone with excellent penmanship. So not Enzo.

Invitation to Central Park that night. Suggestions about attire. Directions to which entrance to use into the park.

The right edge of the invitation had been embossed with tiny gold hoofprints running up the side, and the envelope had one sticky pink handprint on the corner.

Definitely extortion. Involving Maya and Sam? Pretty much meant she had to go.

But she pretended she didn't. Because she hadn't yet gotten over her willful stupidity when it came to that man, and she fell for the hit-and-run, guerrilla-style romance tactics every time.

Kimberlyn bypassed the subway in favor of a taxi to take her to the park. While technically not nighttime yet, it was close enough that she didn't want to ride the subway. She might never get used to that.

Her taxi stopped at the gate she'd been directed to, and Enzo stood waiting for her in something other than scrubs. She rarely saw him in anything else. His corduroy jacket was the color of old beaten leather, somehow straddling the same lines he straddled daily. Uptown tailoring on casual fabrics. Everything else selected to blend into the background.

"I'm glad you listened to my wardrobe suggestion," Enzo said when he got closer to her, hand outstretched. "I was afraid that you wouldn't even have winter clothing, being from the South."

"I grew up in the Smoky Mountains, I have winter clothes. It snows there and everything." She didn't take his hand. It was a step too far. Even with gloves on. She'd dragged herself to the park to meet him, but she couldn't hold hands with him.

Without missing a beat, he stepped to her side and put his arm around her waist. The man was either 100 percent focused on her or utterly ignoring her. There hadn't been any touching since the sex. Heck, there hadn't any anything outside work since the unfortunate decision to go home together had ended with his late-night scramble to get away.

"Why did you invite me here, Enzo?" She pretended his arm around her didn't feel good.

"You said you hadn't been to Central Park before."

"I haven't." This entrance of the park was actually fairly close to their hospital. She could have come straight there from work any number of days, but she never put sightseeing high on her list of things to do. There was always too much work to do, too many things she needed to read, too much to worry about and keep up with the chores of daily living—feeding herself, having clean clothes, sleep... "But that's not what I meant and you know it. No double-talk tonight, no answering without answers. Why now?"

"Why not?" he answered in that annoying way of his, then nodded to the horse-drawn carriage. The driver of the beautiful white carriage was watching them.

"I'm going to leave if you don't start— Is that carriage for us?" The tirade she was working up to died in her throat as she took in the white carriage with its red velvet lining, and the gorgeous white horse pulling it. "Did you rent us a carriage?"

"I've never been in one, but I heard they're nice."

His hand shifted to the small of her back, steering her toward the carriage. Rather than pushy and demanding, it felt like a hug. Caring. Protective. And she was still a woman... What woman could say no to a carriage ride through Central Park?

"You like to play dirty."

"Not always." He murmured the argument.

If he wasn't playing dirty, then this was him playing nice? Suddenly he'd decided to...

Her feet turned to lead, the tread catching on the sidewalk so she stumbled ever so slightly.

He was trying to soften the blow. Ootaka must have told him already.

The fellowship was his.

His hand shot up under her arm to stop her from falling. "Whoa, you all right?"

"Fine," she said quickly, waving a hand to him and calmly extracting her arm. "I just scuffed the bottom of my shoe. No big deal. But thank you." She forced a laugh and a smile she didn't feel. "I guess I'm having a clumsy day. Good thing we're going to ride through the park. Trusting my feet sounds like a bad idea."

A hop and a couple of quick steps pulled her ahead and she reached the carriage, climbed in and settled into the plush velvet seating without any assistance. All around the rim of the back of the carriage white twinkle lights had been installed. So cheerful and dazzling—something a good sport should be, too.

Whatever else had gone on between them, she'd still be happy for him as soon as it settled in. Giving the question voice right now sounded wrong. And completely out of line with the romantic aura these carriages always carried, especially on a crisp October evening that had finally started to feel like autumn.

Enzo climbed in beside her and then slid her over to tuck against his side.

He probably had to agree to some kind of nondisclosure until Ootaka could make the announcement tomorrow. Tomorrow, when all the things that they'd spent the past months denying would actually evaporate. The romantic carriage ride through the park was just an overture, and one she needed to get past rather than be swept up by. "So, tomorrow Ootaka is making his announcement."

Enzo looked out the side of the carriage as it started rolling and was soon off on the trails down into the park. "Yes, it is. I thought maybe this was the only chance I'd have to bring you to experience some quintessential New York. After tomorrow, one of us might not want to be around the other…probably even more so than the past couple of weeks."

"Maybe," she conceded. But, then, her chances with the fellowship had never been very high. She could let disappointment color the whole evening, or she could enjoy being there with him and not let her issues ruin this for him. "But, for the record, I didn't want to not be around you the past couple weeks, so I'm guessing you mean you didn't want to be around me."

He reached for a lap blanket and shook it out over their laps, uncharacteristically direct when he answered, "I just didn't know how."

"And now you do?

He gave a noncommittal shrug, tucking the blanket around her thigh and then laying his arm around her shoulders again. "Now it doesn't matter anymore. There's nothing either of us can do to change whatever Ootaka is going to decide. He will pick one of us. The other…"

"Will be left trying to pick up the pieces and figure out their new path." She finished that statement, going with the subterfuge. Sometimes it helped to pretend that neither of them knew what they were talking about.

He turned his head and brushed his lips across her temple. "If it's me who gets the fellowship, then I want to help you find another good program, to help somehow. And if it's you—" she didn't need to look at him to hear the strains of a rascally smile threatening "—I want you to baby me as I dramatically mope, brood and wallow in a manly fashion."

A grin tickled the corners of her mouth. Cute. A good time to play along. "Okay. I'll bring you cookies that someone else baked. So they can be edible."

She'd spent the majority of the past couple of weeks wanting to talk to him and wrestling her own willpower. Now that it seemed there was nothing left to do but wait for the official word, maybe they could finally talk. Maybe she could enjoy his company without feeling the ax over her head or that usual guilt eating at her.

"I've spent a lot of time making contingency plans the past month. It's not my usual custom. I don't like to give myself room for other plans, in case it jinxes me. But I had a list of other programs, and I cross-referenced it with the spreadsheet you sent. I thought knowing there were other options would make it easier to wait while feeling like I was being proactive or something. But I'm still antsy and irrevocably behind." And full of dread. Or she had been before she'd realized the race was over—some heady cocktail of excitement and dread.

"Behind?"

"I intended to already be in my fellowship by now. I really shouldn't have even been eligible for Ootaka's."

"You never told me what you wanted to study before your accident."

She'd never told him a lot of things. "I dithered between neuro and cardiothoracic."

"Wanted the exciting, hard ones, eh?"

"I guess." She let herself rest her head back on his shoulder and watched the trees overhead. "But all that changed. I'm not sorry it did. I like feeling like I have a calling... I just don't like how it all came about."

"Speaking with your surgeon?"

She tilted her head to look at him and then focused again on the canopy overhead. The sun was low enough now on the horizon that streaks of pink and purple sky showed through the patches of empty air among the brightly colored autumn leaves. "That's not really what did it. Dr. Anderson did help me, as much as he could, but I started those conversations when he came to see me every day on rounds..."

When Kimberlyn hesitated, Enzo looked at her face again. She wasn't looking at him. Her head was tilted back so that she could look at the trees overhead. Was the hesitation about him or the accident? She'd gotten the stiff-upper-lip thing down to an art. When the moment stretched on he prompted her, "But?"

She shrugged and finally looked at him. The sadness that always lurked in her eyes wasn't disguised at all now. "You ask me about my accident relatively frequently, but you never ask the one question everyone else asks."

There were a lot of questions about her accident that Enzo avoided asking. It was like a big bomb hanging over their heads, where all the wires were red so there was no way to know how to stop it from detonating. No way to fix things. That question—like all emotional questions—felt like adding another wire... But her pointing to that question announced its importance, and he couldn't ignore that. "What question is that?"

"You've never asked if I was alone in the car."

"No?" He thought about the things she'd said to him about the accident. She had snuck a couple of *"we's"* into the telling here and there, but usually it had sounded like a one-person story. And he'd gone with that idea because it was safe, and kept him from feeling that pain with her. "Who was in the car with you?"

"My best friend, Janie McIntyre."

The physical details were so much easier to deal with. He got information, but it was safer. The wreck was physically in the past. He knew what had caused the wreck— shredded tire on the road. He knew that the car had been upside down off a highway bridge but not in the water. He knew when it had happened. He knew the surgeries that it had taken to repair her body. He didn't know how long she'd waited for rescue, if she'd been conscious and scared at the time. He hadn't asked the questions that hurt him to contemplate. He hadn't asked if she had been alone because both answers were terrible in their own way, so he didn't think about it. "Who was driving?"

She looked back to the tree canopy and the sky beyond. "Me."

The finality in her voice pinged like the sudden sour taste in the back of his mouth.

If this conversation had been digging into his old wounds, he'd be looking for an escape hatch right about now. Hearing the pain in her voice, seeing the slight tremble of her lower lip as she looked skyward…hurt. That's why he didn't ask questions. Yes, it was selfish. It was the best way to keep from being eaten by the pain of loved ones.

Which, he suddenly realized, was a tactic he'd learned from his father.

Was that why Lyons…?

Not the time to think about Lyons. Everyone had reasons for the things they did, and right now he didn't care about those reasons. He cared about her. She wanted to tell him something, and she needed help getting it out. He asked the question burning a hole in his gut. "Where's Janie now?"

He watched the delicate column of her throat move as she swallowed and then she whispered the words. "She died."

Of course she had, and he should've known that weeks ago. He had to stop managing his responsibility and moderating his emotional response by minimizing his information about them.

He pulled her a little tighter against him. "At the scene? Were you aware...?"

His voice broke in a decidedly unsexy rasp over the second question. As much as she was forcing herself into other actions than she'd like, so was he. His instincts all told him to stop digging, but digging was precisely what he needed to do. If he didn't need to, he wouldn't have questions. He worried about her all the time anyway. Ignorance hadn't been helping. It had just let him pretend it helped.

"When the EMTs got the car peeled open, I was unconscious, skewered by a long piece of metal, but my vitals were fairly stable. They told me Janie was awake and able to talk and answer their questions. She asked them to take me first. They decided that I had the worst injuries, so they did as she asked. She died while another unit was working on getting her out."

Those feelings he could understand, without much more digging. She'd turned toward trauma because she was seeking balance. She'd been saved by one of Ootaka's fellows, and her friend had died because of her accident.

He pulled her more snugly against him and reached across her lap to catch her closest hand. What could he say? What was he supposed to say?

"That's awful. I'm sorry." The cold autumn air burned his eyes.

She nodded, the dampness in her eyes tearing at him.

With his new resolve Enzo kept her close and kept asking questions.

When it seemed as if she'd finally gotten it out, he pulled a bag from behind them, because doing something helped. "Hold this." Settling it on her lap, he pulled out a thermos and poured into the lid some of that gross mocha coffee she and Tessa were always drinking. Doing something helped. "We'll have to share the cup."

She accepted it with a couple of sips, then offered the cup back to him.

He'd planned to take her to the carousel—they weren't running it yet, that was still a couple weeks away, but when he'd thought to do this, he'd expected it would be a nice, romantic ride...

"What else is in your bag?"

"Stew, funnily. I conned Mom into making us something and she sent me off with two containers of soup and some good bread. There are usually a few vendors operating at this hour in the better lit areas of the park, but I thought something homemade..."

"Sounds wonderful." She smiled at him, sadness fading under the prospect of sustenance. "And I'm always hungry."

Because she was always running nonstop, and she usually forgot to eat.

But he could take care of her tonight.

He could even take care of her forever... If things were different.

The back of the taxi had that special smell, as if every contagion in the world had gotten together and had a kegger. But Enzo smelled nice. Kimberlyn let herself stay snuggled in the crook of his arm in silence as the world sped past her window.

One magical night—it was the stuff of every woman's fantasies. Carriage ride with a handsome prince, twinkle lights and chocolaty coffee. Best of all was that the revelation that should've been hard for her to take hadn't really been all that hard. At least once the initial shock of disappointment had passed.

As a perfectionist, Kimberlyn never viewed anything other than 100 percent as success. Knowing she had failed to be chosen by Ootaka for his fellowship should've put a damper on things. But somehow Enzo made it all right.

He didn't say anything about it—there was no way for

him to and maintain the silence he was no doubt sworn to—but he'd still made it all right. Because it was him. Because she wanted this for him as badly as she'd wanted it for herself. Her struggle to get through her residency wasn't the only struggle going on. Every single resident struggled to get through their training. It seemed never-ending when you were in the trenches.

While they still had several months left in the program before she'd have to head on to whatever fellowship she landed, it already seemed as if the hard part was over. The past couple of months had been so hard and stressful that it now seemed like a downhill coast. Regular duties. No killing herself to try to make an impression.

It surprised her how happy she honestly was for him. She wanted to be able to say it out loud. But this peaceful, warm bubble he'd built for them the whole evening would evaporate the instant she said anything. Congratulating him tomorrow would have to be soon enough. She'd have to hope for a front-row seat or a blow-by-blow of the action, if anyone decided to rub his father's nose in it.

The taxi stopped in front of the brownstone and Kimberlyn patted his hand where she held it, getting his attention. The ride in silence had been nice, but if she didn't say something soon, he'd continue home in the cab, and who knew what waited for them tomorrow? She wanted to hang on to this for a little while longer. "Do you want to come in?"

"Yes." He fished some money from his pocket and slipped it to the driver through the window, then opened the door and climbed out.

When he'd helped her from the back of the car it was a steady jog up the stairs to get into the house.

Neither of them made a move to stop or slow down until the door to her unit closed behind them.

As the latch caught, Kimberlyn cast off her coat, bag and boots, and then began helping him, too.

Though unspoken—like so much between them this evening and in the brief time they'd known one another—Enzo shed his outerwear as quickly as she did and reached for her at the same time.

The kiss she'd been waiting for all evening came hard and sweet. No matter the hours spent out in the chilly autumn night, they didn't carry any of the cold in with them. His mouth covered hers and want built in her so swiftly that all dexterity and grace fled. Her fingers fumbled over buttons and as he drove her toward the bed she staggered like a drunk.

In less than a minute all clothes were off and Enzo left her panting on her back, sinking into the plush satiny comforter.

Hungry kisses trailed down her throat and her shoulder, pausing over the scar left by the surgery to repair her shoulder. He looked at it, ran the tip of his finger over the puckered flesh and kissed it.

Her breath caught. What was he doing? Why was he kissing her scars? He hadn't done that before. He had on occasion touched them, but when they had been together before he hadn't even acknowledged them.

She couldn't speak. She could barely breathe. When he made his way to the still-angry scar on her chest, his touch became so reverent tears gathered in the corners of her eyes.

The way her breath caught must have registered as he slid back up over her to look into her eyes, capturing one of her hands and holding it to his chest. "I'm sorry your friend died, but I'm glad the paramedics took you first."

When she opened her eyes again, those remarkable golden-blue eyes were inches from hers. Truth. Acceptance. No blame, but a lot of regret. She couldn't bring herself to ask for answers. Maybe Enzo had the right way of thinking—don't ask the questions if you don't know whether you can handle the answers. Don't ask the questions if knowledge would ruin your peace.

She pushed against his chest until he rolled, and went with him. The first time they'd been together it had been frantic. Parched, cracked earth soaking up an unexpected storm.

And that had been before she'd known she loved him. Kimberlyn couldn't pinpoint when she'd crossed that line, all she knew was that she had. She loved him. That was probably the real clincher in why she wasn't so disappointed about how things had turned out. Confused still, feeling guilty—though not as much as she would've expected— but not so disappointed.

Sliding down his body, she paid back every kiss and lavished an especially long, wet kiss down the underside of his erection, along the length of him.

Deep shuddering breaths had her crawling back up him to pause, knees extended, holding herself just far enough away to share the heat rushing between them.

It was right there on the tip of her tongue to ask him not to wear a condom. Some primal part of her wanted every inch of him bare but knowing what was coming tomorrow and that in a few months they'd be apart... She fished one from the bedside table and worked it onto him with a slow, rolling stroke before taking him inside.

This time she'd make him the mindless one.

Tomorrow would take care of itself. It had to.

CHAPTER TWELVE

UNLIKE THE FIRST time Enzo had been with Kimberlyn, this time as she snuggled up to him and slept he lay awake, staring at the ceiling.

Last night had been thick with realizations, but right now one commanded his thoughts: the idea of similarities he had in common with his father… If Lyons's reasons were anything like his, it made it hard for his hate to burn as bright.

His plan at the outset had been critically flawed, he saw that now. Knowing him and his family—the reason that he'd fought for the fellowship day after day—wouldn't make her weak to him. But knowing her? Knowing what she'd overcome to be there made him weak to her. In reality, probably just knowing her made him soft to her.

He tilted his head to watch her sleeping. The rich chestnut tresses spread over his arm and the white pillow behind her. The fan of her eyelashes against the tan skin that would forever highlight her scars—even more so after they'd faded and lost their color.

The other scars, the ones he'd finally been ready to know, might never fade—the ghost of the friend that haunted her conscience. She hadn't said it, but the glassy look in her eyes had.

He loved her for it.

Making love to Kimberlyn again hadn't been part of

the plan for the evening, but only an idiot wouldn't have seen it coming. A romantic ride in the park, attraction that was eternally off the rails and consequences of the kind of knowledge he'd spent a lifetime avoiding.

Knowing all he knew about her now, he was supposed to find some way to let her go? Depending on who got the fellowship, one of them would have to leave. No new ground had been discovered last night...

Or it had, but it hadn't made things easier. Just more red wires, and he was still waiting for the yellow or the blue to show up. Anything but the steady stream of reds.

The biggest, reddest one was the realization that had come over the shared cup of coffee when she'd given him the last drink... She loved him, too.

His heart skipped and then began to beat really fast.

She loved him, and if he was feeling this weight, she was feeling it more. She'd been feeling it longer, no doubt.

Three weeks ago he still hadn't thought that the fellowship was going to anyone but him. But she'd done what she'd said she would—spent the past couple of weeks busting her butt to change opinions. The fact that Ootaka had used her so much in the past couple of weeks...he really had no idea which way the dominoes would fall.

What he did know was that he wanted Ootaka to pick Kimberlyn. What he didn't know was whether she'd even accept it if she was chosen over him. But she'd worked so hard to get there.

His chest constricted in a way he couldn't breathe through. If he left now, he could fix this. And if he did it right, she'd accept being selected. If she hated him, loyalty wouldn't stand in her way.

Enzo slid out from under her and hurried around the room, gathering up his clothing.

"You're leaving?"

He looked back at her, sitting sleepy and disheveled in her bed, the pink comforter pooled at her waist, breasts high and bare…no attempt made to hide her scars from him now. Streetlights illuminated the room enough to make looking at her hurt.

And he was about to cause another one. *Do it quickly.*

"I didn't intend to sleep with you." He tugged on his shorts and pants, then looked elsewhere. The more he looked at her, the harder it got. "I just wanted to end things on a good note with the carriage ride. Be a good guy before things change tomorrow."

In his peripheral vision he could see her sweet, bleary expression began to shift, sleep confusion replaced by shadows as her chin lowered. That absence of her face made it worse.

He sat in the chair across the room to get his shoes on. If she touched him, she'd feel his heart thundering in his chest. If he got too close, she'd hear the ragged sounds of his breathing. She'd know he was lying.

"That sounds like…" Her voice was soft, but there was a thready quality that made the words so much worse. "You're leaving me?"

"We haven't really been together, so it's not really a breakup."

Yes, it is.

He ignored the voice in his head. "I'm not going to lie, the sex with you is really good." True, in a watered-down version that felt like a lie.

"But that's all it is, Kim. Good sex is hard to resist." *Lies.*

No one called her Kim. Her friends called her Cricket sometimes, everyone at the hospital called her Davis and he frequently called her Mouse…but every real incarnation of her name felt too real for Enzo to say. "You know things would've had to change in a few hours anyway."

"You said that if it wasn't me, you wanted to help me find a new program."

He looked for his other shoe, and anywhere that wasn't

at her. If he had to do this, it would be in the dark, and he
would do it as fast as possible and get out.

"Yeah, well, that's the kind of thing you're supposed to
say, right? Social niceties that keep civilization running,
stuff you don't expect anyone to take you up on." He got
his other shoe and crammed his foot into it, stuffing the
socks into his pocket because they took too much time to
put on and he needed to get the hell out of there.

She pulled the comforter back and stood up, leaving him
an unobstructed view of her body in the golden glow of the
streetlights. The urge to touch her, to hold her as tight as
she always wanted... If he didn't go now, he'd fail. And,
more important, he'd fail her.

All the words he couldn't actually say lodged in his
throat, strangling him.

"Lock the door when you go, please. I need a shower...
I smell your scent all over me."

Her feet ate up the space between the bed and the en
suite and she slammed the door behind her.

He stood for what seemed like an eternity, staring at the
bathroom door. This was the end.

Or tomorrow would be, after he made sure she got the
fellowship.

The shower ran cold for an eternity. Turning on the water
before she knew that Enzo had gone had been a mistake.
Now she either had to turn it off and listen, which would
let him know she was waiting, or go look...and have him
catch her looking.

Unless he really was gone.

She opted to stand there with the water running, hoping
it would warm up and allow her to salvage some measure
of pride. It was better that he believe she had gotten into
the shower to get his scent off her as quickly as possible
than to think she was so pathetic that even after that display
she'd still be in here thinking pretty much only about him.

Even if that's what she was doing.

The water finally turned hot and she adjusted it as hot as she could stand and stepped under the spray. She didn't feel dirty. She felt raw. Exposed. Stupid?

She stayed in the shower, washing away his touch and scent, but all she wanted to do was crawl back into the bed and their sex sheets, and pretend that the date had ended differently.

If she'd understood what his plan had been last night, maybe she could feel a little better. Empathy was a thing she believed all good doctors should have—the ability to put themselves into someone else's shoes and understand them from the inside out. It made it easier to treat someone if you could guess what treatments they would and wouldn't stick with.

But she couldn't figure him out.

He'd gotten the fellowship, that much she felt certain of.

He'd wanted to give her a good night. Okay. Maybe as a way of saying goodbye? But it hadn't been like that. There had been a real connection, tenderness…right up until he'd suddenly sprang from the bed to leave.

Did he think she wouldn't be happy for him? Was this her fault? Had she made him feel guilty by finally feeling as if she could tell him about her accident without the fear that it would be factored into her performance?

Maybe it was pity. Maybe yesterday he'd found out that she was not getting the fellowship, then in the carriage he'd found out she was even more pathetic than he'd originally thought…and the sex had been pity sex.

Three different kinds of body wash to choose from… She put a little of all three distinctly different scents until it merged into one nightmare of fruity floral patchouli. The heady mix may have rid her of the smell of him she'd been wrapped up in before stepping under the water, but it couldn't clean her doubts away as quickly.

Once she'd showered clean, she stepped out, wrapped

a towel around herself and went to curl up on the chaise longue by the window, unable to face the bed.

Three in the morning, and she needed to talk to someone right now.

Sam was out, and he was Enzo's friend and didn't want to be in the middle.

Holly? Well, probably not.

Tessa would probably be asleep right now, or with her man, doing...

"Dang it." She got up long enough to get her phone, dialed Tessa and sank into the lounge again.

"What's wrong?" The man Tessa had moved out of the brownstone to cohabit with answered. No greeting. As doctors, they were all used to being called in the middle of the night for emergencies, and a twinge of guilt pinged her conscience. Did breaking up count as an emergency?

"Hi, Clay. Can I speak to Tessa?"

"Kimberlyn, what's wrong?" Clay repeated. She could hear the growl in his voice.

"Enzo broke up with me and I have to see Ootaka award him the fellowship tomorrow..." Blurting it out like that was even more pathetic.

"I'm sorry, but Tessa needs her sleep."

She tried again. "If you get dumped at three in the morning, you call your support system at three in the morning. And—"

"She's pregnant." His words bit her argument in half. "She needs rest."

"Oh." Not the right reaction. Her eyes burned and she swallowed. It took a second before her stomach settled and she managed, "Congratulations. Good night."

She disconnected and stared at the screen on her phone. The only other person who would listen at this hour and not turn her away even if she cried until she got the hiccups was in Africa with spotty cell service.

Right. She could take care of herself. She had a world-class stiff upper lip, and she had about ten hours to find it.

Grabbing a throw from the back of the chair, she curled into the lounge to try to sleep. Getting her sex sheets off the bed felt like entirely too much effort.

Although Ootaka had a penchant for formality in everything Kimberlyn had witnessed him doing, when he made plans to announce the recipient of his fellowship he simply had people gather in his office.

As soon as she entered, Kimberlyn was aware of exactly where Enzo stood. She tried not to look at him. Nothing good could come from it. His face was already burned into her memory, right along with his style of breakup.

Besides, she looked terrible today. There had been no nonstop crying last night, just a couple of—or a few—short spells and then the stiff upper lip she'd learned so well in her recovery had returned. Unfortunately, puffy eyes and dark circles didn't go away, no matter how stiff your lip was.

She slipped to the back with Tessa and Sam, who had been kind enough to come for emotional support. She'd stand behind the door if she could, but a back corner was as out of the way as she could get. All she needed was dry eyes and a big smile when Enzo's fellowship was announced. Show she was a good sport, and then quietly leave.

Sam had worked out that something was wrong—and as he'd played a part in her going on the carriage ride the night before, he probably knew it was something to do with Enzo. But, true to his word, he didn't ask. Didn't get in the middle. He just hung around by her and Tessa looking extra-brooding.

Enzo didn't look at her. No matter how she held her head, she could see him in her peripheral vision, all attention focused on Ootaka, who had begun his speech. Of course Enzo's attention should be there.

Hers should be, too.

She tried to pick up the thread of whatever the older surgeon was speaking about. Art in medicine, patience, nerves as steady as your hands.

Hah, if he happened to look her way, he'd be extra-glad of the choice he'd made. Her nerves were clearly not steady today.

Strength had been a matter of survival for her recovery, but at least this wasn't something that would require grief counseling. People broke up. It happened all the time. You played sad music, read lots of Emily Dickinson, possibly went to a bar and had questionable sex with someone inappropriate and then ate ice cream. After that, you moved on. There was a grieving process that your loved ones didn't need to shield you from because you had epic holes in your body, and maybe you couldn't handle the added stress...

Tessa grabbed her arm suddenly, focusing her attention on her friend.

As she opened her mouth to question the grab, she noticed that people were turning to look at her and clapping. Including Ootaka. And Enzo.

Tessa whispered, "Smile. Say thank you."

Kimberlyn whispered back, "Did he say my name?" The room swam in her gaze, and suddenly the other side of the room where Ootaka stood looked as if it was fifty feet away rather than ten.

"Yes," Tessa whispered and then slid her hand free of Kimberlyn's arm to flatten against her back and urge her forward.

Smile. Say thank you.

The instruction repeated in her head and she smiled, a big shaky thing, parroted the words she was to say and went to shake Ootaka's hand.

Did he want her to say other things?

People came forward to congratulate her. Other residents. Some with ribbing about the new kid being teacher's pet. She kept smiling and thanking…

Enzo waited until everyone had gone ahead of him, then stepped up to her.

As soon as she lifted her eyes to look at him, tears welled and made her vision swim.

She'd been so sure it was going to be him.

Now that she looked at him dead-on, he looked kind of bad.

Her mouth opened, and through her strangled voice, she whispered, "I'm sorry."

This was why he didn't want to be around her anymore? None of it had made sense before, and, looking at him now, it still didn't make sense.

"Don't be sorry." He held out his hand to shake hers. By rote, she put her hand in his.

Hand-shaking today, yesterday it had been hand-holding.

She knew her hand shook on its own, and when the brief up-down motion had passed, he let go. She looked down, a million miles of nothing to say filling her head.

His hand shook, too.

Most of the other students had trickled out now, only Tessa, Sam and Ootaka remaining.

Was she ever going to understand this man? The math that got her from last night to this morning didn't add up.

This was his home. He'd have to leave his home for one of the other excellent fellowships. And she'd come to a measure of peace at having the fellowship be his. He did deserve it. He'd done it all without his rotten father, he'd done it all for the pride of his family… And she could give that to him. Maybe that was the lesson she should've learned from Janie, how to sacrifice for others.

"Dr. Ootaka…" she said, turning away from Enzo to the surgeon whose admiration they all had been working for. "I can't accept the fellowship. I'm sorry. I don't want it."

"Mouse, no," Enzo barked out, grabbing her arm to spin her around. "You don't turn this down. You deserve it."

"I don't want it."

"Yes, you do. You're just...worried about me. You don't need to worry about me."

She looked closer. The dark circles and somewhat disheveled quality to his hair didn't speak of someone who'd gone home to have a good night's sleep.

If he'd slept poorly, it was his fault. "Shut up. You don't get to tell me what to do or who I get to worry about. You don't get to tell me what to feel. You made your decision to cut ties with me, and I've made my decision to cut ties with West Manhattan Saints." She gave a firm tug to free her elbow from his hand. "After the year is through, I want to move on somewhere else. Somewhere with more trees, somewhere I fit in better."

"You fit in here," he rasped.

Kimberlyn couldn't look at him. She turned to Ootaka and moderated her voice for his benefit. "I'm very sorry, Doctor. Please know I hold you in the highest esteem. I've made mistakes in the past, and people have sacrificed for me. I'm alive today and someone who should be isn't. She sacrificed for me because she loved me. It's my turn to sacrifice for someone...someone else."

She wouldn't say it was someone she loved, and she wouldn't say it was for Enzo. She couldn't make Ootaka choose him. She just believed he'd be the second choice if she dropped out. And his ego would learn to deal with it, since only the five of them had to ever know about it.

"You would not be sacrificing your position for Dr. DellaToro," Ootaka said finally, though he looked somewhat irritated by the whole thing. Indecision was not his favorite thing. Drama was also not his favorite thing.

When she frowned, he pointed to Enzo and ordered, "Tell her, DellaToro."

Enzo plowed a hand through his hair and paced away

then back. "I knew you wouldn't want to be chosen over me if we were together." His skin had gone pale, and he paced away again, this time sitting down.

Realization began to dawn as she watched his face. "You knew I would be chosen and you...you broke up with me because you thought I would be free of those pesky issues of honor and loyalty that way?"

Her words made him sigh, nose wrinkling in distaste as he did so.

"You're an idiot," she announced.

Ootaka made some kind of sound of affirmation but said nothing.

"It's not idiotic. I wanted it for you more than I wanted it for me. So I stepped out, and I thought I'd made sure that you would take the position and get what you deserved. You were supposed to think I was a rotten bastard and get on with your training."

"No. I was right. You're an idiot." She crossed her arms and with a sigh sat down across the room from him.

"Do you still wish to turn the position down, Kimberlyn?" Ootaka had used her first name, which he never did.

She didn't even need to think about it. "I do."

"Mouse..."

They were taking up his office when neither of them were taking the position... She could show all the emotion she wanted to right now. "Did you hear what I said about sacrifice? Do you really think I'd let you sacrifice for me after what I told you about Janie?"

"I did it because *I love you*!" Enzo yelled, standing up as if he was going to hit something—the wall, the furniture.

"Well, I love you too. Idiot!" Kimberlyn yelled back, because it seemed like the thing to do.

Enzo laughed, but the sound that came out was breathy and insubstantial, which fit his thoughts precisely. He knew she loved him, but there was something altogether different about hearing her say the words. Even when the ten-

der words were shouted and capped off by her calling him
an idiot.

He'd vowed to break the habit last night, but it was easier when he didn't have any plans to upset—like now. He
calmed, sat again and looked at her. "What do we do now?"

The exasperation that had colored her confession became tinged with amusement. "I suppose we'll have to
apply for a bunch of other fellowships and see where we
can go together. It's only rocket science if it involves having to go to an entirely different planet to a program that
will take us both when one of us is an idiot."

Ootaka's long-suffering expression reached out like a
tangible slap. They should be wrapping this up for him. He
had other things to do. But as chagrined as Ootaka's expression left him feeling, Tessa's and Sam's smiles countered
it. "Think we might be able to get a reference from...?"
He hooked a thumb in Ootaka's direction but kept his eyes
on Kimberlyn.

"Only if you leave my office right now," Ootaka said,
shaking his head and going back to his desk. "I have to consider the applications again, and I have a flight tomorrow. I
will write your recommendations and email them. Now go."

The tone in his voice said, *Don't stay a single second
longer.* As shaking his hand would have taken more than a
couple of seconds, Enzo stood, grabbed Kimberlyn's hand
and helped her out of the office in one go.

Last night had been hard on her. It'd been hard on him,
but it was his fault. She deserved some pampering. Or at
least some firm hugging. He needed it anyway.

Outside, pretty much everyone who had been in the
room—those who had applied—stood staring at Ootaka's
door.

A sea of questions came. They'd heard shouting from
the doctors' lounge—which was nearby—and had come
to investigate. Turning to Sam and Tessa, Enzo said, "Fill
them in?" and still holding Kimberlyn's hand hurried off

down the hallway. Her strides were shorter than his, but he couldn't slow down. With the pace he set they were soon out of the hospital and traversed the short distance between the hospital and Central Park, the site of his best-laid plans...

Just inside the park he turned and pressed her against the trunk of a tree where they'd have a little privacy.

He couldn't name what he saw in her eyes. Love, yes. A bit of fear, though, still. As sure as her words had been, he had to make her say it one more time. "Tell me one more time that you're sure."

"I'm sure that I love you." In the sunlight, he could see the hint of redness still clinging to her eyes. He'd definitely made her cry last night. And maybe this morning, too. After a long look into his eyes, she added, "And I'm sure that I want to be with you. I just have a few requirements."

Though pretty certain he knew what she was going to say, Enzo asked the question. "Lay them on me."

She cupped his cheeks and held his head where she could look into his eyes. "I want to know when you came up with that harebrained scheme?"

"While you were asleep."

"After the romantic carriage ride, picnic, conversation and sex?"

He nodded, though it was the last thing he wanted to admit to. "I panicked. Didn't know what else to do."

"Talk. For future reference, the solution is to talk." Her thumbs stroked his cheeks and she leaned up to kiss him. "About anything, everything. No forbidden topics. Got it?"

He nodded again, tilting his forehead against hers, his hands sliding up the back of her scrub top. "I also had another thought last night. When we were in the carriage. Before you told me about Janie... I never really put a reason to why I didn't want to know about the extent of your surgeries, but it was because I didn't want my thinking about you to be forced to change. I was comfortable with the facts that I knew."

He gave her a minute to absorb his words, but when she still looked confused he explained. "I learned it from Lyons. With all that I thought I'd learned from Ernst about how to love someone—family, friends—I never unlearned that first lesson. Lyons stopped asking about us. All communication with Mom stopped not long after he left. He didn't want to know anything. I don't really know his reasons for that, but I think I understand. I didn't want to know anything that would jeopardize my plans, and I think it would've worked if I could've just stopped asking questions. The more I knew you, the more I needed to know. If I were Lyons, if I felt like I needed out for some reason, I'm pretty sure it would've been with an all-or-nothing mindset. Not that I think I could do that with someone I loved, maybe he's just not as evolved as I am."

The smile that came went a long way to settling his nerves. "So, what if his offer was an olive branch? How does that idea change your plans?"

"I texted him this morning while I was waiting for Ootaka to show up."

For all that the morning had felt like running on shifting sand, that confession rocked Kimberlyn the hardest. Though his arms were around her, she wanted a hand to hold and slipped her arm around to grab one of his so she could link their fingers. "What did you text? Did he answer?"

"I told him that if something had changed, that if he wanted to get to know us, he should start with Maya. His granddaughter could be his clean slate, and we'd see where it went from there. Gave him information about her birthday coming up, sent a picture I had on my phone..."

"You had a busy morning," she whispered. It was like having a hope-filled prognosis for a terminal patient, that miracle she'd wanted for Mr. Elliot. "What did he say?"

"He said she has his mother's eyes."

Maya had Enzo's eyes. And Sophia's, and their father's… "Is he going to see her?"

"Sophia's going to let me take her to his house to visit. She's not ready to go there, and I think we should start small anyway… So, maybe you and I can take her there together?"

Kimberlyn nodded, not trusting herself to say anything right now. It wasn't a cure, but it was a treatment full of promise.

Enzo leaned his forehead against hers and added, "I'd really like to talk about going home now. Being alone with you. We have some other decisions to make, but I'm so tired…"

He'd still sacrificed for her, but she'd sacrificed for him right back. Everything was in the air, uncertain, at least when it came to where they'd be in six months. But at the center of all the uncertainty she could feel a rock rising. Wherever they ended up, they'd finish this together. They'd be together.

But that didn't mean she couldn't torture him a little bit first. "I don't know if I can invite you back after all these emotional displays." She found her smile, her damp eyes rapidly drying. "I might have to make you pay for all this drama."

"In orgasms?" The rascally smile returned, and the tenderness in his eyes made a perfect match for it.

"I haven't decided yet."

"Just so you know, it's a debt I intend to make good on." He pulled her away from the tree and steered her back toward the street for a cab, and home.

EPILOGUE

BRADFORD PEARS BLOOMED up and down the street in front of the Brooklyn brownstone. Kimberlyn paused after placing yet another box into the back of the moving truck, just to get a good look at the few white, puffy trees she could see.

"Are they talking to you?" Enzo asked, after loading what he carried of Caren's furniture into the back.

Kimberlyn looked over her shoulder as he came behind her, arms slipping around her waist. "The trees?"

"Is it going to rain or anything?" Enzo rested his chin against the bare skin on her shoulder. The scar there had faded enough for her to feel comfortable going sleeveless. First the shoulder, then maybe the thigh this summer when it became shorts weather. Every day they got a little lighter, and her guilt went along with it.

"Not that I can tell. You need green leaves for that." She leaned fully against him, linking her fingers with his—after a small pause to right the seat of the diamond ring on her finger. One day, after the fellowship was done and there was a matching wedding band to hold it steady, maybe it would stop turning like that. "I will teach you all about the weather-forecasting properties of trees once we get to Tennessee—where it's warmer and the trees will have green on them."

Caren had decided to extend her mission to Cameroon for another year, which left Kimberlyn and Enzo to pack the apartment and move her things back home. No one knew how long she intended to stay, or whether she'd return to New York when she came back to the United States.

Kimberlyn understood: Caren had found something worth fighting for, and she prayed every day that it turned out to be even half as good as what she'd found with Enzo. Grief healed more slowly than the body, and though every day Kimberlyn got a little bit better, there were certain promises she couldn't budge on.

She would become the best trauma surgeon she could be, even if that wasn't the world's best trauma surgeon. That detail wasn't within her control.

She would finish her training and establish her practice before she got married. Enzo had said he could live with a two-year engagement, and he'd stopped saying the wedding was just a formality anyway...because that jeopardized the letter of her promise. Because grief, and the heart, healed more slowly than the body.

"Okay. There's a couple more boxes, and my mom called—she packed up an unholy amount of food for the road. I think it's a ploy to make us swing by and say good-bye again."

"Did you tell her that we'll come back for the holidays and that anytime she wants to come stay we'd love to see her?"

"I told her." He kissed her neck and let go to dash back up the stairs into the house.

They'd given the same invitation to Marcus Lyons, though no one was at that point of comfort yet. He might visit, but he'd stay at a hotel if he came. It was progress.

Tennessee wasn't so far away. New York had just felt like another planet when she'd first got there. Enzo would get used to it there, and two years wasn't so long if he wanted to move back up north when they'd finished their fellowship at Vanderbilt.

Because being mentored by one of Ootaka's fellows

was the very next best thing to being mentored by Ootaka himself.

And there was nothing better than being where she was
right now, and there could never be anything better than
being loved by Enzo.

Though she might change her mind in two years, when
they could talk about a little cousin for Maya...

* * * * *

FALLING AT THE SURGEON'S FEET

LUCY RYDER

This book is dedicated to Kathryn Cheshire, whose encouragement and understanding got me through an incredibly difficult year. I simply could not have done this book without your support and guidance. You're awesome.

Also to my bestie, Marleine Dicks, thanks for all the reading you had to do of my earlier—and really bad—manuscripts. I eventually got it right, but I appreciate all the loving support and encouragement. Thanks too for all the laughter you bring into my life. I just wish we could spend more time laughing.

CHAPTER ONE

"HEY, LADY! WATCH IT."

Dr. Holly Buchanan grimaced and threw a breathless "Sorry!" over her shoulder at the guy she'd nearly trampled as she dashed through the automatic doors into the huge marble lobby of West Manhattan Saints.

She was late. Late, late, *late*, damn it. And it was the second time this month. She should have suspected the morning would go to hell when she'd slept through her alarm and then broken the heel of her favorite designer pumps—hopping on one foot while trying to find the other shoe.

But nothing could have prepared her for the absolute chaos that greeted her when she'd opened her front door and found furniture and boxes piled up against her door, littering the stairs and sidewalk.

It had taken a few shocked moments to work out that the avalanche was meant for the neighboring brownstone and not hers. *Thank God*. Unfortunately, it had taken a lot longer to convince the mover—a scary tattooed guy who'd towered over her by at least a foot and a half—that the address he was looking for was right next door. *Not hers*.

He'd folded his huge tattooed arms across an even huger chest and stared at her with a level don't-even-think-of-messing-with-me-lady look that had made her quail in her strappy heels. And because he'd startled her, she'd blurted out the first thing that had come into her head: "Did you know that prison inmates in Russia use melted boot heels mixed with blood and urine to make tattoo ink?"

His answer, when it had come, had been accompanied by raised eyebrows and a wry twist of his lips. "Marine corps," he'd drawled in a voice that had seemed to come from his large booted feet. "One tattoo for every skirmish survived." And Holly had sucked in a mortified breath.

"Oh, my g-gosh, I'm s-sorry," she'd stammered, wanting the earth to open up and swallow her. "Th-thank you for your service."

He'd quirked an eyebrow and replied with a dry "You're welcome. Now, where should I put all this stuff?"

It had taken her time she hadn't had to convince him to call the moving company, which he did while guarding her door like a bouncer at a shady nightclub. After what had seemed like an age—during which Holly had bounced from foot to foot in extreme impatience—he'd finally apologized for the mistake. Then he'd reached over a box almost as tall as she was and gallantly lifted her as easily as if she were a child. To her shock he'd carried her down the box-littered steps and gently deposited her on the sidewalk with a cheerful "Wouldn't want you to twist an ankle in those shoes."

She'd mumbled a breathless "Thank you" and had risked more than a twisted ankle running for the subway.

Setting off across the huge lobby toward the bank of elevators, Holly dodged people heading in the same direction and tried to tell herself that elevators were mostly safe and that the hospital had a rigorous maintenance schedule.

She growled and skirted a crowd of nurses gathered around a large board the hospital used to announce upcoming events, lectures by visiting experts, and new staff appointments. She usually took an interest in any new announcements as she hoped her name would soon be featured when the plastic and reconstruction surgical fellowship was announced.

This morning, however, she barely gave it, or the oohing

and aahing women, a cursory glance as she streaked past, heels clicking on the slick marble floor. She hated being late for meetings with the chief of surgery. He wasn't exactly the kind of man you wanted to annoy—especially if you were a surgical resident hoping for that fellowship.

The doors of one lone elevator slid open with a ding and she sent up a quick prayer and dashed into the car just as a group of noisy teens emerged. As they shoved past, one sneakered foot caught Holly's ankle and sent her flying. She valiantly tried to halt her forward momentum by grabbing for the aluminum frame and forgot that she was carrying her briefcase. It went flying one way and she went the other, landing awkwardly on her hands and knees. She heard a muffled grunt and the next thing she knew the contents of her handbag and briefcase were exploding all over the floor.

The doors swished closed and there was a moment of stunned silence during which Holly thought, *You have got to be freaking kidding me!*

She sucked in air and snarled a few choice words that would turn her mother's hair gray. But, jeez, it had brought back memories she didn't like to think about. Memories of a wildly tilting elevator and frightened screams as it plummeted and then exploded on impact.

For a couple of beats she struggled with control before remembering having heard a grunt. She lifted her head, hoping Monday madness was giving her auditory hallucinations on top of everything else. The last thing she needed was someone having witnessed her graceless flight.

Please, let me be alone. Please, let me be alone.

Holly blew a few escaped strands of hair out of her eyes and froze when her vision cleared. Bare inches from her nose was a pair of large scuffed sneakers attached to the bottom of faded, soft-as-butter jeans. She blinked and followed the long length of denim up endless muscular legs to something that made her eyes widen and her mouth drop open. And before she could register that she was checking out some guy's impressive package, the man dropped to his haunches and Holly found herself staring into a pair of concerned blue-green eyes surrounded by a heavy fringe of sun-tipped lashes—on her hands and knees.

Sucking in a shocked breath, she wondered if she was more embarrassed by her position or the direction she'd been looking then promptly forgot everything when she felt the sensation of falling. Right into a swirl of gold-flecked blue and green. It was only when he opened his mouth and "You okay?" emerged in a voice as deep and dark as sin that she realized she'd been staring into his eyes as though she was submerged in the waters of the Caribbean and had forgotten how to breathe.

Her skin prickled and heated in premonition—of what, she wasn't entirely sure. But it felt like something monumental had just happened. Then, realizing what she was thinking, Holly gave a silent snort. *Yeah, right.* More like *monumentally* embarrassing.

His light eyes were startling in a tanned face that was both brain-ambushingly handsome and rugged. Like one of those naturally hot guys they used for advertising extreme sportswear. The kind of man who got his tan in the great outdoors—like standing on the prow of a pirate ship—and not from a tanning salon.

"Just peachy," she squeaked, swallowing her mortification at having sprawled at the feet of the hottest guy in Manhattan—maybe even America—and being caught eyeing his package then staring into his eyes like she'd been hypnotized.

Her belly quivered and for a second she wondered if the disrespectful little twerps had done her a favor. At least she now wouldn't have to suffer the additional indignity of swooning at his feet.

"You sure?"

"I'm f-fine," Holly croaked, her eyes dropping momentarily to his mouth, where the sight of well-sculpted lips tipped up in an almost-smile had her tongue swelling in her mouth like she was fifteen and crushing on a hot lifeguard. Her face flamed and she pushed back to sit on her heels. "Just incredibly embarrassed," she mumbled, brushing her hands together. "So, *please*…just ignore me and let me die with my dignity intact."

Crinkles appeared beside his amazing eyes and the corner of his mouth curled up even more, revealing—horror of horrors—a dimple. She caught herself staring at the shallow dent in his tanned cheek and gulped. *Darn.* He just had to have a dimple, didn't he? It was the one thing that could turn her into an awkward ninth-grader.

"I…er…" He cleared his throat and Holly looked up sharply, catching his attempts to suppress amusement. "I think it's a bit late for that."

She squeezed her eyes closed and gave a low moan of embarrassment. "G-great. Now I'm…." She sucked in a shaky breath and waved her hand in a quick dismissive gesture. "You know what, never mind."

Abruptly turning away, she looked around for her purse and briefcase. And there—in freaking plain sight for *everyone* to see—was her emergency stash of tampons, littering the floor like white bullets. And for just an instant she wished they were so she could just lock, load and pull the trigger to end her misery.

They reached for the closest tampon at the exact same moment and Holly squeaked, "I'll get that," quickly snatching it up and stuffing it into the bottom of her purse. She then pounced on the remaining cartridges, hoping he hadn't seen—but when she sent him a quick glance out of the corner of her eye and saw his teeth flash, she realized he had.

Oh, boy.

Pushing out her bottom lip, she huffed out a breath and lifted a wrist to shove aside tendrils of hair obscuring her vision. *Could her day get any worse?* Then a hand reached for hers and she forgot all about her crappy day when a snap of electricity bolted up her arm the instant their skins touched.

He too must have felt that audible little zap because he grunted softly and his eyes narrowed speculatively before he gingerly turned her hand over to inspect her scraped palm. She barely heard him rasp, "You're hurt," over the blood rushing through her ears.

The hand engulfing hers was large and tanned with long, surprisingly elegant fingers that drew her fascinated gaze even as they sent tingles rolling over her skin. Then his thumb was brushing gently over her scraped palm and the tingles became a raging firestorm of sensation that shot directly to her breasts and…well…further south.

Her eyes widened. *Oh…oh, wow.* What the heck was that? "It's n-nothing," she managed to croak, both to herself and him, before sliding her hand from his when she realized her mouth had dropped open and she was on the verge of babbling. She scooted back a little and sucked in a shaky breath, averting her face in the hope that he couldn't read her turmoil. Because, well…*darn.* The last time she'd been this flustered had been in the seventh grade when Jimmy Richards had caught her drawing hearts and flowers around his name.

Absently rubbing her tingling palm against her thigh, she stared at the jumble of her belongings and wondered what the heck she was supposed to be doing. It was only when she saw a half-eaten candy bar that she snapped to attention and began stuffing everything she could lay her hands on into her purse.

Holy cow. Where had all this stuff come from? She couldn't even remember having seen half of it before. Certainly not the gold pen or the roll of mints. And how many hairbrushes did one person need, anyway?

She left him to gather up her textbooks, study notes and stethoscope, thinking there was nothing in her briefcase that could embarrass her—until she remembered the old before-and-after photographs of herself that she kept as a reminder of why she was doing P&R.

Whipping around, Holly was relieved to see that the photos were nowhere in sight, but the guy was holding aloft a small foil square she hadn't even known she had. And if it *was* hers, it had to be at least two years old. Maybe even older.

Holly tried to look innocent, but it seemed the guy had an evil streak because he lifted a brow over gleaming blue-green eyes and drawled, "Medium?"

Oh, God, really? He was going to comment on the size?

"Keep it," she croaked. "Most condoms have a shelf life of four years, anyway. As long as you keep them in a cool, dry place." And nothing could be cooler or drier than the bottom of her briefcase, especially the past couple of years when she'd been focusing on the P&R fellowship and not relationships.

His grin turned wicked, deepening that dimple in his cheek. "Way too small," he said innocently, as though they were discussing a pair of shoes and not a freaking condom. He tilted his head and squinted at the printing on the back. "Besides, I think this one's already a year and a half past that four-year shelf-life date you were talking about."

Her face heated and she mentally rolled her eyes. *Way to let a hot guy know your sex life is non-existent, Holly.* She groaned silently and reached out with a growled "Just give it here," before tossing the package in the wall-mounted trash bin. For a couple of beats he stared at the stainless-steel receptacle then turned to her with a level look.

"You know someone is going to find that and use it, don't you?" He shook his head at her. "How do you think you'll feel knowing you had a hand—even unwittingly—in an unplanned pregnancy?"

"Ohmigod," Holly burst out, wondering if the torture of this day would ever end and what she'd done to deserve it. *"Fine!"* She opened the lid and fished it out, shudder-

ing when her fingers encountered something sticky. She shoved the errant condom into her pocket and glared at him challengingly. The unspoken words *Are you happy now?* vibrated in the air between them.

Eyes crinkling at the corners, he rose to his feet and offered her a hand but Holly ignored it and scrambled up—all embarrassing items finally hidden, thank God—before accepting her briefcase from him with a strangled mutter of thanks.

She was careful not to let their hands touch. Her body was buzzing with enough electricity to light up Manhattan for a day—and she hadn't even had her coffee yet.

Fortunately, the elevator dinged its arrival at her floor and when the doors opened she escaped, hoping she never saw him again. Just before the doors slid closed he called out a friendly "Don't forget to replace that condom, it's the responsible thing to do."

A few people heard and sent her curious looks but Holly ignored them, stomping down the passageway and muttering about *not* being responsible for her actions when it came to hot smartasses. It was only when she passed a startled nurse pushing a bassinet that she realized she was on the twentieth floor and not the twenty-second.

Muttering to herself, she changed direction and headed for the stairs, resigned to the fact that she was nearly fifteen minutes late for her meeting.

The moment she slipped into the boardroom she felt the eyes of every person in the room turn to watch her entrance, including the laser-blue stare of the chief of surgical residents, Professor Gareth Langley. Flushing, she ducked her head and murmured an apology, and slipped into the only open chair around the huge oval table.

Fortunately, with the day she was having, she wasn't scheduled for any surgery. She'd probably slice and dice her fingers—or worse.

Without looking up, she drew the nearest folder closer

and opened it, knowing she would find the new surgical schedule. There were other pages inside but Holly ignored them and quickly scanned the list, sighing her relief when she saw that she was scheduled for a number of procedures with Dr. Lin Syu and two with the head of plastic surgery, Dr. Geoff Hunt.

She lifted her lashes and caught Lin Syu's quick smile before she transferred her attention to the head of P&R, who was—*oh, joy*—looking right at her. She flushed beneath his questioning look and bit her lip but after a brief nod in her direction and a dry "Now that Dr. Buchanan has finally joined us…" Geoff Hunt turned away, shoving his hands into the pockets of his perfectly creased pants as he rocked back on his heels. "Perhaps we can get to the real reason Professor Langley is here this morning."

Now that the heat was off her, Holly let out a silent breath and relaxed into her chair, only half listening as Langley rose and began talking about the proposed expansion of the P&R department and the upcoming charity ball. It was a subject that he'd brought up before and one that Holly's mother—as CEO of Chrysalis Foundation—was involved in.

The Chrysalis Foundation worked solely for children and young people who needed plastic or reconstruction surgery but had no way of paying for the expensive procedures. It was also an organization her mother had started after Holly's own traumatic experiences.

Half listening, she let her gaze slide around the table but it came to an abrupt halt the instant she locked on a pair of amused blue-green eyes that were shockingly familiar. For the second time that morning—and it wasn't even nine a.m.—Holly felt the breath leave her lungs.

Her head went light, her stomach cramped and she thanked God she was sitting down because there in the chair next to Langley's was none other than…elevator guy.

Oh, God.

Her tongue emerged to moisten suddenly dry lips, and she wished she could grab the nearby water jug and drown herself before anyone noticed.

One eyebrow rose up his forehead and all Holly could think was… *Who the heck is he?*

Realizing she was staring at him all wide-eyed and open-mouthed, Holly jerked her gaze away to stare unseeingly at the columns of numbers on the screen, her mind racing with a kaleidoscope of images from the last half-hour. And when she realized she was absently rubbing her tingling palm down the length of her thigh she clenched both hands in her lap and struggled to control her breathing.

Maybe she'd dreamed up the entire episode. Maybe she was still asleep and dreaming.

Or having a nightmare, she snorted silently, and sneaked a peek at him. He was still watching her, his expression a mix of amusement and confusion—as though he didn't quite know what to make of her.

He wasn't the only one.

Frowning, she returned her unseeing gaze to Langley, nearly missing the part about the generous donation the hospital had recently received to expand P&R and finance the expensive new procedures they would be developing over the next five years, courtesy of a prominent Beverly Hills plastic surgeon.

It was the "Beverly Hills plastic surgeon" that caught Holly's attention and her gaze jerked back to elevator guy as a bad feeling landed in the pit of her stomach.

She sucked in a sharp breath at the wicked gleam lighting his changeable eyes and barely heard Langley's words over the blood thundering in her head.

Oh, God, please let me be wrong.

"I'm sure you all saw the announcement in the foyer this morning," Langley was saying, and elevator guy must have caught her stunned look because he gave a tiny shrug as though to say, You should have seen that one coming. But she hadn't. Not even close.

How could she have thought—even if she hadn't blown through the foyer—that the guy in the battered sneakers and well-washed jeans molded to every inch of his muscular thighs and well...*everywhere* was some big Hollywood celebrity cosmetic surgeon?

It's not him, Holly. It can't be.

Besides, where was the thousand-dollar suit, the eight-hundred-dollar, hand-stitched loafers and hundred-dollar haircut? She sneaked another peek at him and ran her gaze over all that tanned skin, sun-streaked hair and languid grace and decided she could see him gracing the cover of an extreme sports magazine—or maybe *Surf's Up*—more readily than a fancy Beverly Hills fundraiser.

But then Langley said, "I'd like to formally introduce Dr. Gabriel Alexander and welcome him to the West Manhattan family," and Holly realized with an unpleasant shock that the hot guy who'd made her knees wobble and her breath hitch in her chest was the very same man who'd been linked to rumors of new procedures and extreme body-sculpting of many Hollywood A-listers and supermodels. Including her famous sister.

What the heck was he doing in Manhattan?

He even had a dimple, *darn it!*

CHAPTER TWO

Dr. Gabriel Alexander sighed and wedged himself into the movie-house-style chair, scooching down so he could tip his head back and finally close his eyes. It seemed like months instead of days since he'd shared a very interesting elevator ride with a certain surgical resident and he was exhausted—no thanks to said resident.

Crossing one ankle over the other on a backrest a few chairs down probably made him look like a long-legged spider squashed into a matchbox, but Gabe just needed some quiet time out from his hectic schedule. Besides, as a resident he'd slept anywhere; his favorite being observation rooms where it was usually quiet—especially after eight at night.

Popping his earphones in his ears, he sighed as rock music washed over him. It had only been four days since he'd been welcomed to West Manhattan Saints by a stunning briefcase-wielding assailant, but he kind of liked the vibe of being back in a large medical facility. Seems selling his partnership to some entitled young punk hungry for the Hollywood lifestyle had been the right decision after all.

For the past six years he'd been attached to a small private clinic that was so exclusive very few people even knew of its existence—except if you were famous, ultra-wealthy or both. Now, just thinking about what he'd left behind made Gabe shudder with an odd mix of pride, distaste and shame.

And if that didn't make him a candidate for the psych ward, nothing would. Not even his screwed-up childhood.

He'd had a mansion in Beverly Hills, a house in Santa Monica, a yacht and several luxury vehicles in his multiple-car garage and he'd been the most sought-after plastic surgeon on the West Coast. For a kid who'd spent his childhood believing he wasn't good enough, it had been a dream come true.

Looking back, he realized it had been a symbolic gesture to his rich and powerful grandfather. A man who'd used his connections to forcibly end the marriage of his son to a fellow student. A girl he'd deemed unworthy to carry the Alexander name—or the Alexander heir.

Only it had been too late for that. Third-year journalism student Rachel Parker had already been pregnant. When the old man had found out, he'd paid her a visit and along with thinly veiled threats told her to stay away from his family. Or else.

Afraid for her unborn child, Rachel had agreed. She'd moved across the country to ensure they never bumped into each other and Caspar Alexander had made sure that his son had been too busy—with his new wife and family—to be bothered with looking up his college flame. It hadn't stopped Rachel from telling her son all about his father and it hadn't stopped Gabe from dreaming—until he'd turned twelve—that his father would one day come to claim him. It had never happened. Both his father and his grandfather had conveniently gone back to their entitled lives as though nothing had happened.

Until about two years ago when the old man had decided he needed someone to take over the family business. It seemed Caspar's son and legitimate grandchildren were a huge disappointment and couldn't be trusted not to squander everything he'd spent a lifetime building.

The old man had told him how proud he was of Gabe's

achievements and that it was clear he was a chip off the old block.

Gabe had not so politely told him what he could do with his offer.

For a long time he'd been angry—at his mother and father—but especially the ruthless Caspar Alexander. And when he'd been invited to join the clinic he'd seen it as his ticket to the big league. *Look,* Gabe was saying to the old man. *I didn't need you or your family's money to become someone. I did it all by myself.*

Then his mom had been diagnosed with an aggressive form of leukemia and none of his money, contacts, fame or his skill with a scalpel had made a difference. By the time she'd slipped away, he'd realized his mother was right. He'd become the one thing he hated above all else. He'd become just like his grandfather. Ruthless, cold in his personal relationships and interested in only two things—money and status. It had been a rude awakening. One that had spurred him on to make some drastic changes in his life.

Someone bumped against the row of seats, jolting Gabe from the disturbing memories of his childhood and his non-existent relationship with a man who'd pretended most of Gabe's life that he didn't exist.

Grateful for the disruption, he cracked open one eye to see that a small crowd had gathered at the observation window overlooking operating room three.

A quick look at the overhead OR screen gave him a close-up of an open torso and disembodied gloved hands wielding stainless-steel instruments with skill and precision. And considering that WMS had some of the best trauma surgeons on the east coast, whoever was on the table was in good hands.

Tugging on one earphone, he tuned into the murmur of voices around him and discovered that someone called Dr. Chang was working on a young woman who had landed beneath a bus during rush hour traffic.

He replaced the earphone and watched the onscreen action for a few more minutes, admiring the dexterity of the leading surgeon's hands, before letting his eyes drift over the observers.

They were painfully young and even if they hadn't been dressed in light blue scrubs, he would have pegged them as residents. Their fresh, animated faces reminded him of his own resident days, which meant they were probably not discussing whatever was going on below. Most likely it was about a hot nurse, or complaints about their supervisors.

Hospitals were like small towns where everyone knew everyone else and no one's personal business remained private for long. People gathered during quiet times to gossip about patients; nurses liked to complain about doctors and doctors liked to complain about everyone, especially Administration.

And Administration? Well, they were the common enemy because they hoarded funds like Scrooge, cutting costs and fighting every requisition from floor wax to MRI maintenance.

And, Gabe thought with a dry laugh, he hadn't even realized until now just how much he'd missed it. Not so much the gossip but he'd missed the camaraderie of a large medical facility where the haves and have-nots were locked in a daily battle of survival. It wasn't just a place where the rich and bored came to buy the latest style of face or body— or have a steamy affair with their attending surgeon. This was real.

Sighing, Gabe slid his gaze over the rest of the observation-room occupants before letting his eyes drift shut. He knew he should get up and return to his temporary digs, where a ton of boxes waited to be unpacked, but he just needed to—

Abruptly something he'd seen registered and his eyes snapped open to zero in on a familiar figure standing off to one side.

Dr. Holly Buchanan.

Mouth curving in appreciation, Gabe watched her focus on the overhead screen, her small white teeth nibbling on lush pink lips. A little frown of concentration marred the smooth skin of her forehead. Every so often her slender hands and long, elegant fingers would move in what he recognized was a replica of whatever was happening below— as though she was practicing or maybe committing the action to memory.

He'd spent enough time among the wealthy to recognize that Dr. Buchanan came from money, and lots of it. She even had that cool elegance that seemed to come naturally to the very wealthy. A cool elegance that sometimes hid an ugly belief that people they perceived as inferior were to be exploited and that their money and social status gave them that right.

He didn't have far to look for examples either. His own gene pool, for one. An old ex, for another. A girl he'd honestly thought had loved him enough to overlook the fact that he had been a half-starving med student from a very modest background.

But instead of standing up to her powerful family, she'd laughed at his declarations of love and told him she'd been using him to get back at her father—and have one final hot fling before she married a man eminently more suitable to their social circle.

Okay, so he'd been a young, foolish hothead, out to prove himself worthy. Prove that his story, at least, would have a happy ending. It had just proved to him that people born into wealth weren't interested in anything more than a hot fling with someone from the wrong side of town—especially someone they perceived as illegitimate.

But even though he knew Holly Buchanan was from a world whose vanity he'd happily exploited, he couldn't help watching her. Her appearance was as coolly classy as it had been the last time he'd seen her, scowling across the boardroom table as though he was personally responsible for the national debt.

But that's where the similarities ended. There was nothing cool about those large heavily fringed blue eyes. And knocked to her hands and knees, she'd muttered curses like someone tugging impatiently at the constraints of her upbringing.

Then there were those paper-thin scars that had been expertly covered with a light brush of foundation. Someone had either done a hatchet job on the stunning young surgeon or…or some horrific injuries had been expertly repaired. He wondered which it had been then decided it didn't matter considering both would explain her interest in plastic surgery.

But it was her eyes—or rather the unguarded expression in them—that had caught his attention. Despite that outer sophistication, Holly Buchanan, it seemed, wasn't as poised as she would like the world to believe, and he wondered what her story was.

He slid a hand to the bruise on his thigh where her briefcase had whacked him and spared a moment to be thankful that it hadn't connected higher. Any higher and he would have been on the floor, having an up-close-and-personal view of her tampons.

He chuckled, recalling the way she'd snatched them up and shoved them to the bottom of her purse as though they had been contraband and she'd been afraid he was the secret police. But then he'd found the condom packet and despite the wild color blooming in her cheeks, the ruffled kitten had flexed her tiny claws by insinuating he used a medium.

Gabe closed his eyes to the sight of her nibbling on her thumbnail and frowning at the overhead screen while she ignored the little upstart twerp trying to chat her up. There was something about her that struck a chord of familiarity but he was sure he'd never met or seen her before.

He was just drifting off when something made him open

his eyes to see her edging up the stairs, giving him a wide berth as though he was a slumbering tiger she didn't want to disturb. Suddenly several pagers began beeping and she froze mid-tiptoe, her eyes snapping toward him, widening in alarm when she caught him watching her.

The residents crowded up the stairs, elbowing each other and muttering curses about slave-driver supervisors as they bolted for the door. In the ensuing scuffle, Dr. Buchanan was roughly jostled aside and Gabe had a brief glimpse of one sexy heel catching on the stair runner. Her arms wind-milled in a frantic attempt at regaining her balance…and the next moment she was toppling onto Gabe with a muf-fled shriek.

His hands shot out to catch her but she landed with a startled "Oomph" right in Gabe's lap—and hard enough to have him seeing stars. When his vision cleared he had an armful of curvy, fragrant female squirming around like she was giving him a lap dance to end all lap dances. And because he was a red-blooded guy who hadn't been any-where near a woman in way too long, his body instantly reacted, waking up to the fact that a beautiful, sexy woman was butt-planted over his groin. He gave a low groan and she whipped around to gape at him like he'd zapped her with his shock stick.

Hey, not his fault. *Innocently minding my own business here, lady.*

One look into her mortified blue eyes and he realized that she was trying to get away and not turn him on but, damn…sue him, it had been a long time since he'd had *sex*, let alone been close enough to a woman to catch the heady scent of her skin.

Their gazes connected and she froze; her eyes wide on his. As though realizing her mouth was barely an inch from his, she gave a distressed bleat and tried again to free her-self, shoving at him at the same time as she tried to get her feet on the floor.

But the angle was wrong and the more she struggled, the more his eyes crossed and the more mortified she looked until he finally took pity on them both and rose to his feet in one swift move. She gasped at the abrupt change of elevation and clutched at him as though she anticipated being dumped on her ass.

It was probably that unflattering assumption that prompted his next action.

Instead of releasing her and stepping away like a gentleman would have, he kept one arm wrapped tightly around her waist and let her slowly slide down the full length of his body until her feet touched the floor.

He knew by the flicker of her lashes and the wild flush in her cheeks that she could feel more than the hard planes of his chest and thighs. The instant she got her feet under her, she sucked in air and shoved away from him, stumbling back a couple of steps. She would have fallen into the row of seats across the aisle if he hadn't shot out a hand and yanked her back.

Their bodies collided hard enough to momentarily knock the breath from his lungs and he wrapped an arm around her to keep her from flying off down the stairs. Okay, and maybe because he liked having all those soft curves pressed up against him.

"Careful," he murmured. "You don't want any more bruises to add to the ones you already have."

She froze and stared into his eyes, alarmed to find herself in the exact position she'd tried to escape from a couple seconds earlier.

"Who...who told you I have bruises?" she demanded in a breathless rush that made him wonder about things that he had no business thinking about. Like how she'd sound in the throes of passion. And where else she had a bruise that he could kiss better.

It was an entirely inappropriate thought—not to mention stupid given that his body clearly liked the visuals that popped fully formed into his head—to have about a younger colleague working toward a fellowship in the same department.

Realizing they were still plastered together like glue on paper, she made a sound of distress and eased out of his arms, this time careful not to make any sudden moves that might result in him having to save her.

She cleared her throat. "I mean, how do you know about the bruises?"

Gabe arched a brow and folded his arms across his chest, letting his gaze roam over the delicate creaminess of her face and neck. "You winced when you sat down at Monday's meeting and I'm guessing that creamy skin bruises easily."

She continued staring at him warily for a moment longer before she said, "Oh," as though she'd suspected him of following her into the ladies bathroom and spying on her as she'd checked out her smarting bottom and knees.

Gabe felt his mouth curve. He'd never met a woman whose every thought flashed across her face louder than Dr. Buchanan's. That they were hardly complimentary was an added bonus to a man who'd spent the last eight years of his life being wooed by women all wanting something from him.

"I'm sorry I disturbed your sleep," she said in that low, husky voice that seemed to reach out and stroke his flesh in places that hadn't been stroked in way too long. And when he lifted a brow she hastened to add, "And for...well, nearly flattening you."

"You hardly flattened me," he drawled. "Besides, I wasn't asleep, just resting my eyes. You learn a lot about people when they think you're comatose. Take the guy trying to get your attention." He could see she knew exactly who he was talking about when she bit her lip and looked away. "I overheard him bragging about his performance and wondered if he was talking about the OR, ER or someplace more private." Heat bloomed beneath her skin. "He's the kind of guy that gives surgeons a bad name."

Her eyes snapped to his and her face settled into a remote coolness that surprised him but not as much as her words. "The only surgeons who give us a bad name," she observed coolly, "are those arrogant enough to think they know better than God how to improve beauty."

Gabe was smart enough to know she was referring to him. He opened his mouth to defend himself but the anger and accusation filling her huge blue eyes stunned him into silence.

What the hell?

He wasn't to blame for her scars. Was he? He would certainly have remembered if she'd been a patient and there was no way he would have forgotten if he'd ever dated her—even briefly. Firstly, she wasn't his type and, secondly...well, secondly, he didn't think any man would be able to forget those big blue eyes or that lush wide mouth. Not in ten lifetimes.

Then he thought about her accusation and his anger died. She was right. For a long time he'd aggressively participated in the Hollywood pursuit of perfection until he'd reveled in the challenge of improving on Mother Nature's handiwork. A nip here, a tuck there and maybe even a complete body-sculpt to anyone who could afford it.

Thinking about it brought back the shame and disgust at the knowledge that he'd been as culpable as any one of his patients in their futile pursuit of perfection. But that didn't mean he was going to let her get away with her accusation—or her attitude, which, now that he came to think about it, had changed right about the time Langley had introduced him.

He shoved his hands in his pockets and rocked back on his heels. "Want to know what I learned about you?"

"No," she said quickly, and took a step toward him, only to stop abruptly when he didn't move aside because for some idiotic reason he didn't want to let her go. "I'm sure your insights are simply fascinating," she continued, frowning at her watch as though she was very busy and couldn't spare the time. "But I'm not that interesting."

Gabe smiled, because in the few days—encounters— that he'd known her, Holly Buchanan had been anything but uninteresting. He lifted a hand to scratch his jaw and paused, his eyes narrowing thoughtfully when she sucked in a tiny breath as though the rasp of beard-roughened skin was somehow too intimate in the quiet room.

"You're intensely focused, keep to yourself and practice with your hands without realizing it. You bite your thumbnail when you're concentrating and hate being the center of attention. In fact, you mostly present only one side of your face to people you're talking to."

She bit her lip and looked away. Zeroing in on the move, he was suddenly tempted to lean forward and bite that plump lip too. But she was carrying her briefcase again and he didn't want to tempt her to use it as a weapon. This time her aim might just reach ground zero.

"How am I doing so far?"

He was rewarded when she rolled her eyes and pressed her lips together as though her silence would discourage him. He'd spent enough time strutting around California beaches during his adolescence to know when a woman was disinterested. He'd bet his entire surfboard collection that Holly Buchanan had been just as affected by their little skirmish as he had. Her dilated pupils, wild rosy flush and that soft gasp she'd given when she'd realized how close he was—and how hard—were as telling as the shiver that had gone through her.

She was attracted but determined to fight it. The question was why. What had he done to offend her?

"Okay," he mused, studying her through narrowed eyes. "My guess is you did all the girly-girl stuff, like ballet, piano and deportment. You probably feel like you have to excel at everything you do…maybe to make someone happy. Mother? Father? Boyfriend?" Her mouth dropped open and he grunted with displeasure at the notion. "Is it a boyfriend?"

"As if!" she practically squawked, and he smirked, strangely pleased by her reaction. Seeming embarrassed by her outburst, Holly pressed her lips together and tried to look bored.

He scratched his jaw again before sliding his gaze over her face, touching briefly on those silvery white scars. "I'd say your interest in plastic surgery stems from your own experiences or maybe some deep-seated need to fix other people's mistakes."

Her hand rose swiftly and then froze in mid-air, as though she was fighting an instinctive reaction to hide her face, and Gabe felt his gut clench as though he'd been carelessly insensitive.

Fighting the urge to wrap his arms around her and pull her into the safety of his arms—which was shocking enough—he let his gaze slide over her classically classy outfit, lingering overly long on her breasts, covered but not hidden by the expert fit of her jacket. He suddenly knew exactly how to put that spark of rebellion in her eyes and get the stubborn tilt back to that Irish chin.

"Or maybe I've got it completely wrong," he drawled smoothly, making no secret of the direction of his gaze. "Maybe I'm not the only one into cosmetic surgery?"

For a moment she stared at him like he'd uttered an obscenity before she huffed out a breath and crossed her arms beneath her breasts, making Gabe wonder if it was to hide from his gaze or keep from taking a swing at him.

"That's just insulting," she snapped, and Gabe grinned. He kind of liked the idea that she was struggling with some pretty intense feelings and he didn't mind the idea of getting into a tussle with her if she did take a swing at him.

In fact, he would enjoy it. Probably more than he should.

He expected a scathing response—or maybe a request

for him to get the hell out of her way. What he didn't expect was for her to open her mouth and say, "Did you know that women with breast implants are three times more likely to commit suicide or develop drug- and alcohol-related dependencies?"

Gabe tore his attention from her breasts with a "Huh?" and wondered if he'd heard correctly. She flushed and sucked in air before continuing and he struggled to connect the random facts with what they'd been discussing.

"Two-thirds are repeat clients."

"O-o-okay...." Well, he could certainly attest to that fact. But what the hell did that have to do with—?

"In fact," she continued peevishly, as though she held him personally responsible for women's dissatisfaction with their bodies, "more than five million Americans are addicted to plastic surgery, spending about thirteen billion dollars annually on a variety of procedures. That's enough to rival the national debt of a small country."

She stared at him as though waiting for his response but he wasn't sure what he would say if he did. Instead, he studied her silently for a couple of beats, his mouth slowly curling up at one corner. "Uh-huh. That's quite fascinating but doesn't really answer my question."

She rolled her eyes and muttered something that sounded like "Never mind," before taking a bold step toward him, no doubt hoping good manners would prompt him to move out of her way.

"I have mace," she announced when he remained blocking her escape.

"No, you don't," he disputed, his grin growing into a chuckle when she blew out a frustrated breath. Her eyes narrowed to dangerous slits and her hand tightened on her briefcase as though she contemplated whacking him with it. "I know exactly what you have in there, remember," he said, angling his shoulders just enough for her to slip past but not enough that she could avoid touching him.

But Holly Buchanan was obviously no pushover because just before she stomped from the room she sent him a level stare all women seemed to develop in the womb that said he was lower than slime for behaving like a jerk.

But, really, he didn't know of one guy who wouldn't have.

For a long moment he admired the straight spine, slender, curvy hips twitching with annoyance as she headed down the passage. The strappy heels that had caused at least one of her accidents this week tapped out an irritated beat on the tiled floor that for some odd reason he found damn sexy.

"By the way," he called out, "did you know that the world's largest condom is two hundred and sixty feet long with a base circumference of three hundred and sixty feet?" And when she paused in her stride and sent him a *what-the-heck?* look over her shoulder, he shrugged. "I'm just saying. Mediums are only good as water bombs."

CHAPTER THREE

HOLLY ROLLED HER eyes and set off down the passage at a fast clip, muttering to herself about men never growing up. While it was mostly true and not worth losing sleep over, it certainly beat thinking about her humiliating tumble into the lap of the one man she wanted to avoid. Or his physical reaction to her squirming around on his lap like a second-rate stripper hoping for a big tip.

Her face burned. *And, boy, had she been given the biggest tip of her life.* Before she could stop it, her skin prickled and heated and her heart set off like a vampire bat scenting warm blood. *Oh, God.* And to think that humiliating little incident had actually turned her on. Maybe this all-work-and-no-play plan of hers was making her a little crazy. Maybe all she needed was a few hours of hot, sweaty, heart-pumping exercise—at the gym, she added hastily—and she could get back to focusing on her plan to get the fellowship.

Besides, she was so close that she couldn't let herself get distracted. Not now and certainly not by a guy who either nipped and tucked women into physical perfection or made the backs of their knees sweat.

Groaning inwardly, Holly increased her pace, as though she could outrun the memory of hard thigh and belly muscles pressed firmly against her bottom and then from chest to knee—and *everything* between—as she'd slid down the front of his hard frame.

She got a full-body tingle just thinking about it. A gasp of horror burst out. Full-body tingle? *Oh, God.*

Absolutely no freaking way. And not with him.

Focus on the plan, Buchanan, and *not* on the way he makes your knees wobble or the fact that medium was too small. No. Not too small, she corrected a little hysterically. *Waa-aay* too small.

Oh, boy. And since she'd inadvertently stared at his package, she would probably agree. She got another full-body shiver and muttered a curse when it slid down her spine like a delicious thrill.

Stop that, Holly, she ordered sternly, *he's the guy that turned Paige's respectable B-cups into C pods.* And for what? So he could make a few thousand bucks? So her sister could flash a bigger cleavage to all her adoring "fans" when she appeared on the latest magazine cover? Or went topless on Bimini?

Big deal. Especially when there were people out there scarred by life-altering events who didn't have access to even basic medical care, let alone cutting-edge plastic surgery.

Weren't there enough butchers willing to slice and dice in the name of vanity that West Manhattan could focus on building the best P&R center in the world? Besides, everyone knew that most women would never be satisfied with their looks, no matter what.

She was trying so hard to convince herself that there were no redeeming qualities about Dr. Hotshot from Beverly Hills that she failed to realize the man himself had caught up with her until a flash of movement drew her attention.

Her stride wobbled for an instant but she sucked in a fortifying breath and marched on, determined to ignore him. Besides, she needed all her concentration to keep upright or she might end up breaking something the next time she took a tumble.

She grimaced. She'd seen him a total of three times and

managed to embarrass herself each time. Despite her klutzy childhood, it was probably a new record.

She clenched her jaw and sent him a narrow-eyed look out the corner of her eye but he appeared oblivious to her presence, loping along beside her with an easy, loose-limbed stride that was deceptively indolent, as though he was alone and liked it that way.

Holly rolled her eyes and ignored the pinch in her chest. *Yep, story of my life.* The hot guys always ignored her—especially when they discovered she wasn't perfect, like the rest of her family. That she wasn't as outgoing as her famous sister or as warm and beautiful as her mother.

Not that she *wanted* him to notice her, she amended quickly, especially if it meant she didn't have to make conversation.

"Are you following me?" she asked coolly, rolling her eyes at the faint huskiness in her voice.

So much for not wanting conversation.

He turned his head and their eyes met for a couple of beats until Holly felt the soles of her feet tingle. "I'm headed home," he said mildly. "Although...I could probably be talked into dinner somewhere dark and smoky."

She caught his harmlessly hopeful smile, which did absolutely nothing to reassure her—especially when his eyes gleamed all wickedly amused and challenging. But it was the smoldering heat in them that stole all her bones right along with her breath and common sense.

Gabriel Alexander was about as harmless as a tiger in a supermarket and had most likely perfected the art of seduction before he could walk.

"No? Coffee, then?" he suggested in that deep hypnotic voice that invited women to do things they wouldn't normally do. Things *she* wouldn't normally do, but was suddenly tempted to try. "Besides being starving, I thought I might be useful."

Useful? Holly licked her lips. Completely against her

wishes, her thoughts turned recklessly to just how useful he could be—to her exercise plan, of course—and then wondered if she was advertising her thoughts like a neon sign in the desert when his teeth flashed white in his handsome, tanned face. And because the notion flustered her, she blurted out, "Did you know that silicone is a better choice than rubber for medical purposes because it is more heat- and UV-resistant?"

Realizing what she'd said, she squeezed her eyes shut and prayed for death. *Ohmigod.* Wouldn't it be easier to just walk into the nearest wall? Or maybe step out into traffic? Because clearly the man just had to look at her and her mouth disconnected from her brain.

"It's also better at resisting chemical and fungal attacks, which makes it more durable," she finished miserably and when he made a noise that sounded suspiciously like a chuckle she glared at him, only to find him looking back at her with polite interest—as if blurting out random stuff was normal.

"Now, that I do know," he revealed, hitching a shoulder in a smooth, boneless move that she envied. "I spent most of the eighth grade water-bombing the girls' locker room. The fact that latex is so flexible means it's more prone to breaking when stretched beyond its limits." His teeth flashed. "But don't worry, you're safe. I've grown out of the urge to hear girls scream at the sight of latex."

Yeah, right, Holly thought a little hysterically. *Safe, my eye. He was probably* still *making women scream—before wreaking havoc with their hearts.*

And when she felt queasy at the thought of him making some faceless woman scream, she turned away from his appealing smile before she gave in to the urge to return it—or maybe smack him for making her forget her plan.

Just then the automatic doors opened to reveal a uniformed porter and Holly could have kissed the older man in sheer relief.

On seeing her, the porter's face broke into a wide, craggy smile. "Evening, Doc," he greeted her in his heavy Brooklyn accent. "No big date tonight?" Holly shook her head as she did every time he asked and he clicked his tongue, sending the man beside her a reproving look. "It's a sad day when a beautiful girl doesn't have someone to wine and dine her at one of those fancy downtown restaurants. What is the world coming to?"

Dr. Alexander sent her a silent look and shrugged as if to say, *I did offer.* Narrowing her eyes, Holly was seriously tempted to lie. Besides, she did have a date. Sort of. That it was probably takeout from the pizza place around the corner from the brownstone she shared with a couple of other surgical residents, along with a bottle of wine and a gallon of ice cream, was beside the point. A date was a date.

Conscious of blue-green eyes watching her, Holly flushed. "Dating isn't in my plan," she told the older man. "At least, not right now," she hastened to add when a soft snort reached her, and she wished she carried a stun gun in her purse because he now also knew that she didn't date. And found it amusing. *The jerk.*

"Plans change, Doc. Besides, you're not getting any younger," the porter advised, and Holly ground her back teeth together when Dr. Hollywood's snort turned into a cough. "Want me to call you a cab?"

"I'm fine, thank you."

She was tempted to add that she wasn't entirely opposed to dating. Just not right now, thank you very much. Besides, the last guy she'd been serious about had taken one look at her sister Paige and decided perfection was better for his image than scarred and brainy.

That Holly had thought to surprise Terrence Westfield one night and had found Paige already there—in his bed— was beside the point. The two of them had been discussing Holly like she was a freak and laughing about how naive she was to think a handsome guy like him could be inter-

ested in her. It had been even more devastating to discover
that Terrence had only dated her to get her father's attention in the hope that he could get an internship at her father's law firm.

She could have told him that Harris Buchanan only had
time for his son and couldn't care less whom she dated.

When—*if*—she found a man who was either blind or
could look beyond the surface flaws to the woman deep inside, she might risk it, but she first wanted to prove to herself
that she didn't need to be perfect or beautiful to succeed.

Sighing, she turned to see Dr. I-Can-Make-Women-
Scream watching her silently.

"What?"

His mouth turned up at the corners but his gaze was
unreadable.

"Wanna share a cab?"

Holly quickly shook her head. She was suddenly eager
to get away from him before she made a bigger fool of herself—which would be difficult after…well, everything that
had happened.

"No. Thank you."

He studied her silently for a couple of beats until headlights lit them up like they were on Broadway, signaling
the cue for them to launch into a heart-rending duet. But
this wasn't a Broadway musical and she couldn't carry a
tune to save her life.

He casually lifted his arm like a born-and-bred New
Yorker and like magic the empty cab slid to a stop. Holly
ground her teeth together. She usually had to step into traffic and risk serious injury before a cabbie deigned to stop.
And then it was mostly to yell abuse at her for being a "crazy
chick with a death wish."

"You sure?"

She swallowed an odd sensation that felt very much like
disappointment—but couldn't possibly be—at his immi-

nent departure, and nodded before she changed her mind. "I'm sure."

After a moment he shrugged. "Suit yourself." And leaning forward, he opened the cab door. Half expecting him to move aside so she could get in, Holly was momentarily distracted when he propped his arm on the top of the door and looked back at her, eyes dark and unreadable.

"See ya, Doc," he said, and slid into the cab, leaving Holly to gape at the departing vehicle.

Chivalry, it seemed, even California celebrity style, was well and truly dead.

The following week Holly had nearly double the number of scheduled procedures and didn't have a lot of time to brood. Her life was right on track with the plan and her goal was within sight. There wasn't time—or the inclination, she reminded herself—to be thinking about wicked blue-green eyes, let alone getting the opportunity to scream.

But that was easier said than done, especially when she happened to look up during a breast reduction plasty to see a familiar figure in the observation room. Only this time he wasn't sprawled bonelessly across the seats, head tipped back and eyes closed as his headphones pumped music into his ears.

With his long legs planted wide and his folded arms testing the seams of his black T-shirt, he looked like a modern-day pirate on the deck of his ship as he challenged the sea. And although his expression and his eyes were in shadow, Holly knew he was looking right at her.

She could feel the weight of that cool, assessing gaze and froze in familiar panic. It was only for an instant and scarcely noticeable by the people around her, but it sent her pulse racing and made her thighs tingle.

"Dr. Buchanan?" The calm voice of Lin Syu made her blink and suck in a fortifying breath. She dropped her gaze briefly to the attending surgeon, who was waiting for Holly's next move with a raised dark brow.

Altering her grip on the miniature scalpel, Holly prepared to make the inverted T incision that would both lift and reduce the size of the breast once the excess tissue had been removed.

She carefully followed the guidelines already drawn onto the skin. The patient, a thirty-four triple-D, with back, neck and shoulder problems, couldn't join her sports-crazy fiancé in outdoor pursuits because her heavy breasts caused discomfort, chronic pain and embarrassment. Kerry Gilmore had admitted that she'd spent her entire high-school years hiding her body and being unable to do things other girls did. Normal things like horseriding, swimming or joining the cheerleading squad. But it was the chronic pain that had finally made the decision for her.

She wanted her life back and Holly was preparing to do just that.

Exchanging the scalpel for surgical scissors, Holly carefully began separating the sectioned dermis from the breast tissue. The aim was to maintain a healthy blood supply to the nipple or it would turn necrotic. The drawback to any reduction was that large amounts of tissue were fed by a lot of blood vessels. Each time she nicked one of them, she waited while the OR nurse cauterized it and mopped up the blood.

Once the dermis had been properly detached from the breast tissue, Holly transferred it into the waiting hands of the attending nurse and went to work on excising the glandular and adipose tissue as per Lin Syu's murmured instructions.

By the time they'd removed five hundred grams of tissue from each breast, Holly was ready for the next stage. She and Dr. Syu made several complicated knots around the areola before gently lifting the nipple into its new position and nudging the remaining parenchyma into place.

She then temporarily closed and stapled the skin flaps so

she could assess the size, shape and position of each breast. The specialized operating table lifted the patient into a sitting position while Holly used the sizer to check the positioning before gently removing the staples and peeling back the skin flaps.

She attached strips of acellular mesh to the upper breast substance to strengthen the weakened muscles then patiently reconnected the mass to the dermal layers using a resorbable intradermal suture. This would reduce the pull of gravity and wound tension, speeding up recovery. It would also help keep scarring to a minimum.

She sutured the areola to the surrounding flaps before reaching for the staple gun for the final stage of the dermal resectioning procedure. When it was over she stepped back to allow the nurse to swab the wound sites with iodine in preparation for the daisy strips that would be applied around the areola in widening circles. They would serve a double function of protecting the wound from infection as well as provide additional support while the patient healed.

Five hours after the patient went under; Lin Syu supervised the insertion of the twin drains while Holly stripped off her mask, gloves and headgear.

"Excellent work, Dr. Buchanan," the older woman said, finally lifting twinkling black eyes to Holly. "We'll have you doing all our cosmetic procedures before long."

Holly grimaced, as Dr. Syu had known she would, and moved away from the table—her part of the procedure currently over. She sent a quick look up to the observation-room window and wasn't surprised to find it empty. Breast reductions weren't that interesting unless you were considering specializing in plastic surgery. And since Dr. Hot Celebrity was rumored to have done hundreds if not thousands of boob jobs, he had probably only wanted to rattle her.

And succeeded. *Darn it.*

"As long as the patient is satisfied with her new size," she said, stretching out cramped back and shoulder muscles as she moved toward the doors. She knew that she would have to perform cosmetic procedures but in this case it helped knowing she could restore someone's self-confidence while alleviating their pain.

Dr. Syu followed, stripping off her gloves. "You just saved her from a lifetime of pain and discomfort, Holly. That she wants to wear a bikini on her honeymoon doesn't make cosmetic procedures wrong."

Holly stifled a yawn. "I know," she mumbled, feeling somewhat chastened. "Besides being the object of curiosity and ridicule, Kerry Gilmore said she was tired of men making lewd comments about her breasts."

"Well, that's just juvenile and typical," Lin said in disgust. "Anyway, as long as she follows medical advice and wears the support garment, she'll be wearing her string bikini on her honeymoon come summer."

She untied Holly's surgical gown and waited while Holly returned the favor before saying over her shoulder, "You don't have to like them but you also shouldn't forget that cosmetics procedures—especially the big-bucks ones—help fund the reconstructions."

Holly sighed. Dr. Syu was right. Besides, she had firsthand experience of the emotional trauma caused by others' perceptions to be reminded of why she'd chosen to specialize in plastic and reconstruction surgery.

She'd spent her entire childhood struggling against the stereotype of beauty-versus-brains and was tired of people judging her by her looks or her family's accomplishments.

As a child she'd often thought she'd been adopted, switched at birth or maybe dumped on their doorstep by a wicked witch. It was only much later that she had accepted she was dark like her father and brother. At the time, though, she'd felt like an alien—a thin, scrawny, ugly duckling that her father couldn't possibly love.

She'd been clumsy, awkward and—she'd be the first to admit—cripplingly shy, geeky and snotty as hell. She'd hated being compared to her incredibly beautiful, blonde outgoing mother and her famous photographic model sister. And because she couldn't compete with her brother or sister for their father's attention, she'd tried to be the smartest so he could be proud of her too. And just when she'd begun filling out and growing into her large eyes, big mouth and long legs, she'd fallen a couple of stories when the cable on a glass elevator had snapped.

She'd been forced to undergo countless surgeries to repair the damage caused by flying glass, once again becoming the object of ridicule and pity. Boys who hadn't known about her accident had even called her The Scar, like she was some kind of comic-book villain or something.

"So," Lin Syu said casually, jolting Holly out of disturbing memories of her past. "What do you think of the new guy?"

Holly froze. "The new guy?"

"Yep." Dr. Syu dropped her soiled surgical gown into the hamper. "Our new celebrity hunk. I hear the nurses are all fighting to get on the surgical roster with him."

Holly rolled her eyes as heat crept up her neck. "I really hadn't noticed." Lin eyed her levelly, expression wry as though she could see right through Holly's lie. "What?" Holly asked, trying to look innocent. "I've been busy."

"So the looks that day at the meeting were my imagination?"

"What looks?"

"Everyone paying attention saw the looks, Dr. Buchanan." She grinned and waggled her eyebrows. "I just wondered if you two already knew each other or if it was lust at first sight."

Holly's head shot up, eyes wide with shock. "*Wha-at? I don't... Ohmigod!*" she spluttered, feeling her face burn with mortification as she thought back to those oddly intimate moments in the elevator and then again when their eyes had met across the boardroom. She hadn't thought anyone had seen. Clearly she hadn't been as discreet as she'd thought.

Her body instantly reacted to the memory of that weird sensation of the earth wobbling off its axis and she shivered and huffed out a breath.

"That's…um…" She gulped and cast around for something intelligent to say but all that emerged from her mouth was a strangled gurgling sound that Dr. Syu seemed to find hilarious.

Struggling to get her emotions under control and stall for time, Holly busied herself by carefully folding her soiled surgical gown and placing it neatly in the hamper.

"It's n-not what you think," she finally murmured, huffing out a couple of breaths like she was about to give birth. "But we…um, did meet in the elevator on the way up."

The surgeon pulled off her mask and cap and waited patiently for Holly to elaborate. When she didn't, Lin's brows rose up her forehead. "That must have been some meeting," she drawled, snorting out a laugh when Holly uttered a sound of distress. "I think he likes you."

Holly averted her head and wished she could sink through the floor. "That's…that's ridiculous," she denied a little too hastily. "Guys like him aren't…well…interested in people like um…" She gestured vaguely to her face. "Like me."

"You're a beautiful—yes, Holly," Lin insisted when Holly opened her mouth to argue, "beautiful and graceful woman. Not to mention a skilled and talented surgeon. Why wouldn't he be interested? He's a man, isn't he?"

"I wasn't always graceful," Holly admitted dryly, recalling how elegant she must have looked on her hands and knees. "It took a lot of hard work on my mother's part. Even now when I'm flustered…I, um…" She broke off, flushing when she realized what she was about to reveal.

"You what?

Holly sighed. "My…inner klutz emerges," she mumbled,

then grimaced when Lin snorted. "It's like I'm fifteen again and have no control over my feet or my mouth."

"And he flusters you? Hmm." Lin's mouth curved and her eyes twinkled with wicked humor. "I sense a story there," she said, just as her pager went off. "Which will unfortunately have to wait. Damn. Just when I thought I could finally get to know my kids again. They probably think I'm just the woman that comes in at night to sleep with their father before disappearing again in the morning." She sighed and threw "Great job in there, by the way," over her shoulder as she hurried off.

Holly took a moment to savor the senior surgeon's praise and went off in the direction of the locker rooms to change before heading home. She knew she should go to her office and catch up on paperwork but she'd promised her housemates that she'd be home for dinner.

It had been kind of weird since Kimberlyn Davis had moved in after her cousin Caren had left and then Tessa Camara, another surgical resident at WMS, had moved out, leaving Holly in a house of strangers. Okay, Sam Napier wasn't exactly a stranger but, then, the hot brooding Scot wasn't all that easy to get to know.

He mostly kept to himself but in a house filled with women she couldn't really blame him. She'd kind of had a little crush on him when he'd first moved in but he was a bit intimidating and didn't share himself with others. Thanks to her scars and her incredibly geeky adolescence, she still felt shy and awkward around him.

Tessa, who'd basically moved in with her fiancé, Clay, since she'd dropped the baby bombshell a couple months ago, had promised to join them for dinner. After the week Holly had had she was ready to talk about babies and forget about big bad celebrity doctors who could make women scream.

CHAPTER FOUR

GABE SLID INTO the back of a cab and gave the cabbie his Brooklyn address as he sank back against the seat. He'd been invited to join a few colleagues at a nearby bar but he'd been on call for over two weeks straight and he was exhausted. Besides, he still hadn't finished unpacking his boxes and he was sick of living out of suitcases and eating out of cardboard cartons.

He wanted real food that he'd cooked himself and he hadn't even had time to unpack his kitchen stuff.

When he couldn't swim or surf, cooking relaxed him. He didn't know if it was growing up in California, where everyone was a health nut or alternative lifestyle guru, but he liked eating freshly prepared food.

What he hated was eating alone. But that was something that couldn't be helped, especially after the telephone conversation he'd had earlier that day with his grandfather. Talking—if the cold, stilted exchange could be termed talking—with the old man always left him restless and angry.

He wondered how the old man had found out he was in New York then decided he didn't want to know. The less he knew about Caspar Alexander's business, the better. Besides, the only thing he had in common with his grandfather—or with his father, for that matter—was their last name and a few bad genes. Everything else he'd got was from his mom. *Thank God.*

The cabbie turned a corner and hooted at some poor pedestrian who'd had the bad judgment to cross at a green light, jolting Gabe out of his disturbing thoughts. This was a new chapter in his life and he didn't intend to ruin it by thinking about the sharks in his paternal gene pool. That was about as productive as standing in an observation room, watching a woman do a breast reduction plasty when he had rounds and a ton of paperwork waiting.

He may have been watching the skilled movements of Holly Buchanan's hands but he'd been thinking about those long, slender fingers on his skin. And when he'd realized that he'd been getting turned on, he'd left before someone in the OR had looked up and noticed his jeans had been a tight fit.

The cabbie pulled up in front of a neatly refurbished brownstone and Gabe got out, bending to glare at the guy through the open passenger window when he called out an outrageous fare.

The cabbie shrugged. "I have a wife and three daughters," he explained, accepting the notes shoved at him.

"My condolences," Gabe drawled, slapping a hand on the yellow roof as the cab roared off. He swore he heard the guy laugh and call him a crazy dumbass before the taillights disappeared around the corner.

Turning to survey the building he was temporarily calling home, he wondered if he'd made the biggest mistake of his life to have replaced his Santa Monica home with its sunny view of the ocean for this.

Sighing wearily, he shoved a hand through his rumpled hair and headed across the sidewalk. All those boxes waiting to ambush him weren't going to unpack themselves and he was tired of dodging obstacles and stubbing his toes.

Even before he'd received the phone call from West Manhattan, inviting him to join the P&R department, he'd been questioning the direction his life had taken. And thinking about that direction made him think about his mother, and his heart squeezed.

"Apparently you raised a crazy dumbass, Mom," he muttered, rubbing the heel of his hand over the pinch of grief in his chest. And then in the next instant he gave a rueful smile as he imagined how she'd react. She'd level her green gaze at him and say that it was better to be a crazy dumbass than a capitalist warlord—which was what she'd called his grandfather. His father, on the other hand, had the dubious honor of being the warlord's sidekick.

His mouth twisted in a bitter-sweet smile. *Damn* but he missed her. He missed her oddball sense of humor and the absolute joy she'd found in simple things; like growing herbs and making her own dandelion wine or chamomile tea, or scavenging wild herbs for her colorful salads. As a kid he'd been embarrassed by the weird stuff she'd made him eat and recalled how the other kids had used to torment him for being too poor to afford real food.

They hadn't been that poor and she hadn't tolerated any rudeness—from him or his friends. Her narrow-eyed stare had often been used to make him question some of his decisions. Like getting caught on camera, tp'ing the principal's car or being forced to clean the girls' bathroom after bombing it with paint-filled balloons.

He wondered what she'd have said about Holly Buchanan, blurting out random facts one minute, falling at his feet or into his lap the next, only to have her duck through the closest doorway to avoid him the rest of the time.

She'd probably laugh, say it served him right for being so pretty and then she'd tell him to hold onto the girl because she was obviously smart and he needed someone who wouldn't be taken in by his I'm-up-to-no-good smile.

But Gabe didn't need to hold onto anyone, especially a woman like Holly Buchanan. He'd fallen hard for a girl from her world once and had learned the hard way that they didn't consider guys like him suitable for anything but a good time. He'd been happy to comply ever since, keeping his relationships superficial and short-lived.

He'd never told anyone about his father out of respect for his mother. She was gone now but he no longer had any interest in people knowing that the owner and CEO of the company holding the largest US government defense contract was his grandfather, a man who'd told Gabe's pregnant mother to "get rid of it" because "it" wasn't good enough for the Alexander name.

Holly Buchanan might look at him like he was a decadent dessert and she was looking to fall off the diet wagon, but she'd made it perfectly clear that he wasn't part of her plan. No doubt she also had some eligible socially acceptable fiancé tucked away somewhere until she could fit marriage into her plan.

Besides not wanting to go down that path again, Holly was a colleague and Gabe didn't date colleagues—especially the young vulnerable ones depending on his professionalism for their career advancement.

He was heading for the stairs to his front door when he heard the sound of an approaching vehicle and turned just as a bright yellow cab pulled up beneath the streetlight. Even before the vehicle came to a stop, the passenger door opened and a strappy black sandal emerged.

Curious, he angled his head to get a better view and caught sight of a pale slender foot attached to the strappy feminine contraption. And when the sight set his heart pounding and his grip tightening on his house keys, he froze, because…because it was suddenly the most erotic sight in the world.

What the—?

Where the hell had that thought come from? Especially as he'd never had a fetish for women's footwear before. It either meant he needed sleep or had lost what was left of his mind. Considering he'd sold a hugely lucrative practice back in LA to join the staff of a Manhattan teaching hospital, it was most likely the latter.

His fascinated gaze took in the endless length of perfectly creased trousers and the slender curvy form that followed. He let out a soundless whistle when he recognized it as one he'd had plenty of opportunity to study over the past couple of weeks—usually disappearing through the nearest doorway to avoid him.

Oblivious to his scrutiny, she tugged briefly at the neat little black jacket and bumped the door closed with her hip while rummaging around in her shoulder bag.

She bent at the waist—giving Gabe an eyeful of her long slender legs and perfectly rounded bottom—and thrust her arm through the open passenger window. She said something to the cabbie that had him gesticulating wildly and Gabe decided she was probably cursing the hefty fare.

She turned with a muttered "Darn highway robbery," and stumbled back a step when Gabe chuckled in sympathy. Her sharply indrawn breath was clearly audible on the quiet street.

"Hey, careful," he called out before he could help himself, and breathed a sigh of relief when she didn't go ass over head into the street.

"*Ohmigosh*, D-Dr. Alexander, you scared me," she squeaked, and cast a nervous glance at the departing cabbie as though she was considering running after it. "Um… are you…are you coming to dinner?"

She cast a surreptitious look between him and the neighboring front door as though she was considering making a mad dash for it and suddenly all Gabe's moodiness and grief vanished and he found himself smiling.

Propping his shoulder casually against a huge earthenware pot halfway up the stairs, he studied her in the pool of light cast by the old-fashioned streetlamp.

Was the lady surgeon a neighbor or visiting? he mused. Or living with her husband or l—?

For some reason the idea of her with a lover annoyed him and then he wondered why the hell he cared. He didn't. Besides, she was exactly the kind of woman he'd promised he would never get involved with—the kind that fitted perfectly into his grandfather's world. Rich, classy and uptight.

He arched a brow. "Are you inviting me to dinner, Dr. Buchanan?"

A hunted look came into her eyes. "What? No…I mean… I thought that's why you're here." She sucked in an audible breath. "Aren't you?"

Gabe watched the conflicting emotions flash across her mobile features. After a couple of beats he took pity on her and held up his keys.

"Relax, Doc," he drawled, wondering why the idea of her going to dinner with some faceless man made his teeth ache. "These are my new digs."

She looked stunned and more than a little disturbed by the news as she edged up the neighboring stairs. "Your new, um…digs?"

"Uh-huh." He looked at her sideways and tried not to laugh at the sight of her nibbling on her thumbnail. It was something he'd noticed she did when she was disturbed. "Why, did you think I was stalking you again?"

"Wha—? No!" She gave an embarrassed laugh that ended on a cough. "Why would I think that?"

"I don't know," he said mildly. "Maybe because you're usually using escape-and-evade tactics that would do a marine proud."

"That's…that's just ridiculous," she spluttered, and even in the ambient light Gabe saw the guilty flush rise up her neck into her face. "We work on the same floor and…" She shrugged helplessly. "It's been hectic."

"Uh-huh." He folded his arms across his chest. "Would it help if I told you that you're not really my type?" He knew he'd thought it before but he'd been wrong. *She was so his type.* He shook his head and laughed again. This time at himself. Because, really, despite the uptight attitude, she was *everyone's* type.

Especially with those big blue eyes and soft mouth that made him think of deep, wet kisses in the dark. Maybe with a big fat harvest moon hanging in a midnight sky and bathing the street in a romantic glow. He could easily picture her beautiful features bathed in moonlight as she turned up her face for a kiss. His kiss.

Snorting softly at his uncharacteristically fertile imagination, Gabe decided he'd been in California too long if he was creating romantic movie scenes in his head.

She looked annoyed and maybe a little insulted, which dispelled his imaginary romantic scene. "What is your type?" she asked curiously, then, as though realizing what she'd said, grimaced. "No, don't tell me." She stomped up the stairs to her front door. "Blonde, stacked and vapid, right? And most likely a surgically enhanced beach bunny. *Yeesh.* Big surprise." She turned and glared at him. "Did you know that in ancient Greece, blonde hair was associated with prostitution?"

"Is that a fact?" Gabe grinned and realized with a jolt of surprise that he kind of liked the way she scowled at him—like a ruffled kitten ready to spit and scratch at the slightest move from the neighborhood mongrel. It made him want to reach out and stroke her until she arched into his caress and purred.

And as he'd never had any similar urges before, he decided that he'd slipped over the edge for real and should probably have himself committed.

"I thought the saying was blondes have more fun," he taunted, and chuckled when she snorted her opinion of his questionable taste in women...and in hair color.

"You're such a...a man," she growled in that oddly husky voice that did strange things to his gut. Shoving the key into the lock, she pushed open the door before throwing "Incapable of looking past bleached hair, a pair of large breasts and long tanned legs" over her shoulder. Then, without another glance in his direction, she disappeared into the building and slammed the door behind her.

For a long moment Gabe stared at the empty spot, gradually becoming aware of the growing lightness that had replaced his previous black mood. And when he realized he was grinning like a loon, he shoved a hand through his rumpled hair. He was vaguely surprised by his new neighbor's ability to make him smile when he hadn't felt like smiling in what seemed like forever.

Yet despite her prickly, less-than-friendly attitude, he kind of couldn't wait to see her again so he could tease an irritated scowl—or an adorable blush—to her face. Or maybe he just wanted to find out what other weird and wonderful facts she had tucked away inside that dark head.

He had a feeling she had one for every occasion.

With a cheerful whistle, Gabe turned and shoved his key in the lock and pushed open the door. "G'night, blue eyes," he murmured, before slipping inside. "Sweet dreams."

His day—and maybe the future—had just got a whole lot more interesting.

Holly's breath whooshed out noisily as she sagged back against the door. *Oh, boy,* she thought, feeling strangely buzzed and exhausted. And then, because she didn't know what else to think, she rolled her eyes, and said it out loud. "Oh, boy."

The sound of someone clearing their throat made her jump and squeak for the second time in as many minutes. Her gaze flew to where her friend and sometime housemate Tessa stood in the open doorway to the sitting room, watching her curiously. "You're late," Tessa accused lightly. "And you didn't answer your cell."

Dr. Enzo DellaToro, fiancé to a new housemate, Kimberlyn Davis, popped his handsome Italian head round the door. "She was getting ready to call the police."

"The police?" Holly squeaked, still feeling a little tongue-tied in his presence. "What for?"

He shrugged. "Maybe it's hormones."

Tessa waved that aside and folded her arms beneath her breasts. "Who were you talking to? I know for a fact that it's too early for Mr. Steiner to walk his dog."

Holly ducked her head. There was no way she could tell them about...well, him. Tessa would ask a million questions and try to set her up again and Holly was honest enough with herself to know that Gabriel Alexander was *way* out of her league. She'd learned a long time ago that guys who wore that casual confidence like a pair of soft well-fitting jeans mostly didn't even notice she existed. She was too serious, too quiet, too nerdy and...and boring.

Not to mention scarred.

"I'm sorry," she said with an apologetic grimace, "but did you know that the actual statistics for people going missing is lower than the reports?"

Enzo and Tessa exchanged silent looks and Holly hid a wince because she knew what they were thinking. Hoping she could head them off before succumbing to the guilty need to explain herself, she pushed away from the door and walked toward them, avoiding their searching gazes by focusing on the three large buttons on her jacket.

Ignoring the questions she could see Tessa was dying to ask, Holly led the way into the living room, where dinner was clearly under way.

"What happened?" Kimberlyn asked in her sexy Southern drawl before Holly could apologize for being late.

She felt her cheeks go hot and bit back a curse. Damn it. What was this, focus-on-Holly night? She tried for a casual "I don't know what you mean" only it emerged sounding defensive instead.

"You're flustered," Tessa, who'd known her the longest, said. "And you always come up with random facts when you're nervous."

"Nothing happened," Holly hastened to reassure them. "Not really. I…er…I just got home and there was a guy on the street."

"Is he still there?" Sam asked, wandering into the sitting room from the kitchen.

"Why didn't you use your mace?" Tessa demanded, and Holly laughed.

"Relax," she said, feeling her cheeks heat. "I, um…I didn't need to. It was the new neighbor."

"Ooh," Tessa said, eyes alight with curiosity. "Is he hot?"

Sam tapped the neck of the beer bottle thoughtfully against his lip. "Next door, huh?" he drawled, distracting Holly from asking Tessa what an almost married pregnant woman was doing checking out hot guys. "Isn't he the new cosmetic surgeon? The Hollywood guy?"

Holly blushed and gaped at him a little because it was the most she'd ever heard him say. She turned to throw her shoulder bag onto the nearest surface and shrug out of her jacket, hoping they hadn't seen that annoying tell-tale re-action that had haunted her adolescence.

"Yes…and it's, um…he's from…um, Beverly Hills." She rolled her eyes at herself. She'd gone for casual and ended up sounding like she had something to hide.

"Ooh." Tessa grinned, her eyes alight with glee. "She thinks he's hot."

She totally did.

"I do not!" Holly said defensively as she kicked her san-dals off a little viciously. Her mother would have a fit to see the elegantly appointed sitting room littered with ap-parel. "Besides, sixty-five percent of men prefer surgically enhanced blondes with fake…tans, not pale brunettes who um…never…get…any…sun."

"Hey," Enzo and Sam objected simultaneously, both looking a little affronted by the "surgically enhanced blondes" quip. Holly rolled her eyes and huffed out a breath. Damn it, she was embarrassed enough, without getting into a discussion about blondes being more fun. Especially with Tessa—who knew a little about Holly's family—looking empathetic.

Better just to pretend it was no big deal. Because it hadn't been. *Really*. No big deal at all.

"Sorry, Enzo." She shrugged and sent Sam a look beneath her lashes because she'd seen a surgically enhanced blonde chatting him up at the hospital festival a few months earlier. She blinked innocently and added, "I was going to say he's okay if you like the tanned beach type. Which I don't."

"Oh, honey," Kimberlyn snorted. "Everyone does."

"Let's invite him to dinner," Tessa teased.

"No!" she practically squeaked, and Tessa laughed and threw herself into the nearest chair. She picked up a glass filled with what looked like mojitos from the sweating jug on the coffee table. "So-o-o," she said, sucking down a mouthful and licking her lips. "What's he like?"

Holly shrugged. "Okay, I guess," she lied blithely, and dropped onto the sofa, quickly releasing her hair from its high ponytail so it fell around her shoulders in a dark silky mass…hopefully hiding her expression. "And why are you drinking?"

"Oh, I'm not. Sam made me a virgin." There was a short pause as everyone absorbed that statement before Holly snorted.

"Won't Clay have something to say about that?"

Tessa's mouth curled and her eyes got that dreamy look Holly associated with people in love. The sappy one that made other women sigh with envy. "Of course he would." She waved aside Holly's attempts to change the subject. "Don't change the subject, Dr. Buchanan. Is he the tall, dark and handsome guy with blue eyes and a wicked smile?"

"That's your fiancé, Tessa," Kimberlyn pointed out, and Tessa blinked in surprise. Surprise that slid into a secret little smile, making her resemble a sleek cat that had recently swallowed a fat, juicy pigeon. "Oh, yeah, so it is. Lucky me."

Enzo snorted but Holly just felt relieved that their attention had finally shifted away from her. She exhaled with a soundless whoosh and reached for what was obviously the non-virgin jug of mojitos. She was in the process of pouring herself a hefty drink when she realized everyone had gone silent and was staring at her like she'd announced she was an alien from a distant galaxy who liked to suck guys' hearts out with a kiss.

"What?" She carefully replaced the jug, her gaze warily bouncing from one face to the other. "What's wrong?"

Behind Tessa's curiosity was concern. "Are you sure you're okay?"

Holly's brows wrinkled and she looked down at herself, half expecting to see her buttons open, that she was wearing a black bra under a white shirt or that she'd spilled something unmentionable on her blouse. Seeing nothing unusual, she looked up in confusion. "What?"

They all looked pointedly at the glass in her hand. "You're drinking cocktails now?" Tessa demanded, and Holly flushed, cursing Tessa's eagle eye and the realization that the encounter with their new neighbor had rattled her.

It had been bad enough that she had to see him at work, now she was probably going to fall over him every time she left her house too.

Instead of admitting that she was rattled, she shrugged casually, like she drank cocktails all the time, and sank back against the cushions with a sigh of relief.

Look at her, all sophisticated and casual.

"Well, since I'm not pregnant, I thought I'd stop being so predictable. Maybe I need to loosen up a little. Or…something. Anyway," she added quickly, as heat rose in her face, "it's been an exhausting day."

"You're acting weird," Tessa said, with a little frown. "What aren't you telling us?"

"Nothing. Really." Holly shrugged casually then exhaled a little shakily when she realized she hadn't sounded convincing even to her own ears. Maybe if she stuck with a half-truth they'd be satisfied and drop the subject. "Okay, it wasn't nothing," she confessed a little guiltily, and took a sip of mojito, grimacing at the strong taste of alcohol. *Yeesh, someone here had a heavy hand.* "I heard the code blue and full house call for OR three and went in to watch for a while."

A "full house" was the med students' term for a full trauma team consisting of all the main disciplines. It only rarely happened that a case needed so many specialists on urgent standby.

Suddenly ravenous, Holly snagged a large slice of pizza and between mouthfuls of crispy base, gooey cheese and spicy pepperoni she told them about the guy who'd fallen from construction scaffolding, thinking how amazingly clever she'd been to distract them.

Besides, she thought with a quiet huff of relief, they'd knocked back a couple of mojitos before she'd arrived and were already buzzing along quite nicely. Even Tessa, despite drinking the non-alcoholic version.

Although Holly rarely drank anything more lethal than white wine, she slugged down her first drink like it was medicine and found she kind of liked the tangy minty lime flavor and the way it made her lips tingle.

By the time her lips turned numb, so had her brain— which was great because it meant she could stop obsessing about her humiliating behavior and forget about the new neighbor.

So-o-o-o forgetting about the hot new neighbor.

Especially, she mused, surreptitiously fanning her hot cheeks, those embarrassing facts about blondes. Besides, if she wasn't his type, *he* most definitely wasn't *hers*.

Not by a long shot.

She tended to go for the serious business type. *He* was

too…um…the word *laid-back* came to mind and…and carelessly put together with an indolent, unconscious grace that made her feel like that clumsy awkward kid again.

Another thing that really annoyed her was his natural self-assurance. She would like to call it arrogance but it wasn't…not really. It was like he'd popped out of his mother's womb knowing his place in the world and didn't care if anyone disagreed. She had a feeling that air of casual affability hid a razor-sharp intellect. She'd seen ample evidence of a wicked sense of humor too and, *jeez*, she wished she didn't find that so attractive. Especially as it had being aimed at her most of the time.

Her cheeks grew hot when she recalled falling into his lap, only to find him huge and hard beneath her bottom.

She wasn't interested in him, she assured herself. He wasn't part of her plan—especially someone used to physical perfection. She was just annoyed to discover that after all the hard work she still hadn't outgrown the nerdy, clumsy adolescent that blushed and stuttered in the presence of a hot guy.

But later, when she slid between crisp, clean sheets and snuggled down into her pillow, along with a gently spinning room, Holly had a sudden and vivid image of a naked surf god sprawled across a sea of white on the other side of her bedroom wall. For the first time in her life she experienced a full-body flush that she promptly blamed on all those darn mojitos!

CHAPTER FIVE

WHEN SHE WAS stressed Holly sometimes had nightmares about the accident that had changed her life. She didn't often think about it but the following week she assisted a senior surgeon in repairing the face and torso of a maintenance worker who'd been caught in a gas explosion.

It had brought back memories of waking to a world of eerie silence filled with dust; the realization that she'd been unable to move and blinding pain when she'd tried.

She'd later learned that her face and right arm had been lacerated by flying glass as she'd been flung twenty feet from the exploding elevator car. The worst had been when she'd turned her head and seen the lifeless stare of a kid about her own age lying nearby. The sight of that empty eye socket where his merry brown eye had once been still haunted her dreams. One minute he'd been laughing and chatting with his friends, the next he'd been an unrecognizable bloodied mess.

Other than laceration injuries, she'd broken both arms and a collar bone and the ragged edges of her tibia had torn through the flesh of her right leg.

What she remembered most about the incident was the moaning and screaming.

Spooked by memories she hadn't thought of in years, Holly left the hospital and headed for the gym not far from West Manhattan.

Where other people enjoyed sweating and grunting through their workouts, Holly preferred the cool solitude of the pool. Besides, there was plenty of scientific evidence proving that submersion in water lowered blood pressure as well as stress levels. Besides relaxation, Holly liked the full-body workout swimming gave her. After the accident, it had been one of the physical therapy sessions she'd looked forward to and she'd eventually become a good swimmer.

And, boy, after the day she'd just had, she needed relaxation as much as she needed some alone time. Although she wouldn't have minded a little screaming to go with it, that wasn't on the cards. And until she landed the fellowship, the plan took precedence. Over everything.

She needed to do research for a paper she was writing on micro-surgical techniques but she was too wired to concentrate on anything and knew sleep would remain elusive if she went home. And recalling that what little sleep she'd managed lately had been filled with dreams of sun-warmed beaches, cool seas and…and hot surfers, Holly rolled her eyes because she was thinking of a certain hot celebrity surgeon. Again.

She dodged a couple necking on the stairs and entered the gym. Smiling a greeting at the girl manning Reception, she headed for the women's change room.

Within minutes she'd changed out of her street clothes and into her swimsuit. Scooping up her towel, she headed for the pool, hoping she would be alone. Alone meant she could get into her zone faster without having to dodge other swimmers. Alone meant she could get her workout done in record time and head home to food and her bed.

Okay, so she was also a little self-conscious about her scars, which were a lot more noticeable when she wore a swimsuit. Granted, they'd mostly faded but *she* knew they were there and in her mind's eye they were still livid and ugly.

Her heart sank a little when she saw the pool was already

occupied but after a few indecisive moments the need for the soothing feel of water closing over her head drove her onto the pool deck.

After a quick glance around, she realized that since the lone occupant appeared oblivious that he was about to have company, she could slip unnoticed into the water and pretend she was alone.

Dropping her towel over a nearby rail, she turned to face the clear blue water and wrestle with her hair. She twisted the heavy mass into a tight bun at the top of her head and secured it with a couple of holders as she approached the edge of the pool, taking a moment to admire the man's efficient, deceptively lazy style. He moved with the kind of fluid effortless grace only found in professional swimmers.

Pausing to stretch her tight muscles, she watched his long, tanned body power easily through the water toward her. Nearing the wall, he executed a languid racing turn as though it was as natural to him as walking. Fascinated, Holly followed the path his body made underwater until he surfaced some ten meters away, turning his head just enough to take advantage of his body's streamlining to breathe.

Darn, she thought with admiration as water glistened off his wide tanned shoulders and long powerful arms, she wished she could look half as good breathing, let alone swimming laps.

She spent another minute practically hypnotized by the dip and rise of wide shoulders and the shifting of muscles in a long tanned back until he abruptly disappeared in yet another turn at the opposite wall. Realizing she was standing transfixed by the sight of some guy doing nothing more interesting than swim up and down, Holly blinked as heat rose into her face.

What the heck are you doing, Holly? You came here to de-stress and get some exercise, not get all hot and bothered by some hunk out for his evening swim.

Feeling guilty for her somewhat racy thoughts, Holly took a deep breath and dived. Her foot slipped at the exact instant she realized she'd forgotten her goggles and instead of her usual graceful dive, she belly-flopped with a strangled shriek and sank like a stone.

The water was colder than she'd expected, closing over her head and rushing in on the heels of her startled gasp. For a few ragged heartbeats she panicked and flailed around like she'd forgotten how to swim, confused about which way was up. Just when she thought she'd run out of air, large hands clamped around her arms and hauled her upward.

Instinctively fighting the firm grip, Holly nearly lost what was left of the breath in her lungs when she was yanked roughly against a big hard body. They broke the surface in a tangle of limbs, gasping breath and gushing water.

"Jeez, lady," a deep familiar voice growled near her ear, and Holly's belly clenched before sinking as gracelessly as she had. "Are you trying to drown yourself?"

Gabe held the woman and waited while she spluttered and coughed, wondering if she'd pretended to drown, hoping to attract his attention. He'd had women do that and more, trying to get him to notice them.

It was only when she lifted her head and blinked huge dark blue eyes that he realized he was holding Holly Buchanan and she was staring at him like she'd suddenly found herself in the jaws of…well, Jaws.

"You?" she gasped.

He felt his mouth curl up at one corner and made no effort to release her. In fact, he drew her closer. "Well, well," he drawled softly, enjoying the feel of her body, still warm and incredibly smooth and soft, against his. The skin across his belly tightened in reaction. "What a…surprise. Are you by any chance stalking me?"

"Me?" she squeaked, her mouth round with outrage. "I was about to ask you the same thing."

"I was here first. Unless..." His eyes narrowed on her in mock suspicion. "Unless that was you hiding behind the pillar when I arrived earlier," he drawled, referring to the way he'd caught her ducking around corners or through the closest doorway when she'd seen him coming at the hospital.

Heat rushed into her face but she ignored his comment, her lips parting on a stuttered "I—I... Th-that was you? In the water, I mean?"

A frown tugged at Gabe's mouth at her incredulous tone. He wasn't sure she'd meant it as a compliment, which also meant she hadn't followed hoping to run into him. He ignored the odd feeling in his gut that couldn't possibly be disappointment.

"You sound surprised."

For a couple of beats she blinked myopically at him. It was fascinating to watch the conflicting expressions race over her features as if she couldn't decide if she was annoyed, impressed or embarrassed. It made him wonder what the heck was going through her mind to make her frown and blush.

"Not at all. It's just..." She suddenly blew out a breath and rolled her eyes. The idea that she'd been watching him was oddly satisfying, considering how much time he'd spent either thinking about her lately or watching her run for cover every time she saw him coming. Especially today, when evaluating her technique hadn't been the sole purpose of his presence in observation room six.

She licked her lips and he instantly forgot what he was thinking. "I...um...I didn't know you swam... At this gym, I mean."

His gaze dropped to her mouth and his skin tightened as heat gathered low in his gut. "And a good thing too or you might have drowned yourself."

"Don't be silly," she wheezed, lifting a hand to wipe moisture off her face. "I slipped, that's all. I'm an excellent swimmer."

He felt a chuckle rise in his throat. "Yeah? Then what was that incredibly graceful dive called? Because I can tell you I've seen preschoolers with more style than that."

She rolled her eyes. "The tiles are slippery," she muttered, dropping her gaze to his mouth. She sucked in a shuddery breath that pressed her breasts against his chest and made his eyes cross. It also made her realize she was plastered up against him like wet silk—okay, and maybe she'd discovered what the feel of her smooth warm skin was doing to him. She squeaked and tried to shove away but they were both slick and her hands kept slipping until she finally growled something that sounded like "Damn it, this is a nightmare" and managed to knee him in the thigh. He wasn't so sure that was an accident.

He muttered, "Wet dream is more like it."

She gasped and gaped at him. Her furious *"Ohmigod, I can't believe you just said that"* ended on a hacking cough, and Gabe shook his head as he slid his hands from her waist to lift her arms above her head even as she tried to take a swing at him.

"Come on, who didn't see that one coming?"

She choked and spluttered a bit more and he got kicked in the shin this time. He chuckled. "Breathe, Doc, before you hack up another lung or maybe knee me in the nuts."

"You...you deserve it," she croaked, when she could talk without spluttering.

He pulled back and dipped his head to peer into her face. "Is that any way to talk to the guy who just saved your life? For the fourth time, I might add."

"What are you doing here, *Dr.* Alexander?" she demanded in a husky voice that heated him up on the inside and gave him a few indecent thoughts. Thoughts he shouldn't be having about someone he was going to be working with. Thoughts about pushing her up against the side of the pool and practicing mouth-to-mouth.

"You mean, other than saving your sexy ass?"

Wild color rose beneath her creamy skin and Gabe was seriously tempted to lean forward and lick her pink mouth—see if she tasted as delicious as she looked.

"I'm perfectly capable of saving myself," she snapped, and shoved at hands that had ended up very close to her breasts—which were full and firm and incredibly enticing in that skin-tight black sheath. Did she know their hard points were practically begging for attention that he was all too willing to give? "And let me go, damn it."

His blood heated in his veins at the thought of getting his hands on her bounty and his grin turned mocking, as much at himself than anything. He was mostly a leg and butt man, probably because of all the boob jobs he'd performed. But despite the number of breasts he had his hands on, none of them had made a fraction of an impact on him compared to Holly Buchanan's shrink-wrapped curves.

And he'd just this instant become a breast man too.

"Aww," he drawled, his voice a rough rasp filling the inch separating them. "Do I have to?"

"No… Yes…I mean… *Damn it*." Confusion chased annoyance and desire across her face as Holly put a couple of inches between them. Despite the move making him chuckle, the distance gave him an even better view. She saw the direction of his gaze, looked down and with an outraged squeak slapped her arms across her chest, glaring at him like he was a pervert for enjoying the view. "They're… they're all me," she snapped. "In case you were wondering."

He chuckled. "Yeah, I can tell."

His gaze drifted up her throat, past her stubborn little chin to her mouth, where he got stuck for a few heart-stopping beats. He finally locked eyes with her…and got caught up in the incredible dark blue depths surrounded by a heavy fringe of dark spiky lashes. For an instant his world tilted and then his heart rate spiked like he'd been zapped with a cattle prod.

The hair on the back of his neck prickled and a shudder of pure panic stomped up his spine with size thirteen army boots. Blinking, he shoved shaking fingers through his hair. *What the hell?* Next thing he'd be spouting poetry or something equally cheesy—not to mention freaking embarrassing.

When just the thought of it made his nuts shrink, Gabe didn't know whether to be relieved or freaked out. *Jeez.* This was exactly what happened when a guy went without for more than six months, he told himself. He got caught up in sexy blue bedroom eyes and starved his brain of oxygen when his blood drained south of the border.

"Stop…stop looking at me," she rasped, turning away from his gaze. He blinked her face into focus, finally realizing his scrutiny was upsetting her and that she was a little hunched over as though to protect herself. From him? What the hell?

"What are you talking about?"

"I feel like a…a bug under a microscope."

"A very attractive *wet* bug," he interjected, and dropped his gaze in time to see her bite her lip. And because he hadn't eaten since noon, he was tempted to take a nibble too but she turned wounded eyes up to his and he froze. "What? What's wrong?"

"I'm d-damaged."

He laughed but when her expression turned fierce, like she wanted to slug him, he frowned, confused as hell because the woman was damn beautiful. The last thing he'd call her was damaged.

Stunning, sexy and hot? Yes. Snotty as hell? Definitely. Damaged? No way. Scars and all. There was too much elegant bone structure, stubborn chin and lush mouth for that.

Frustrated, he shoved a hand through his hair. "What the hell are you talking about?" He felt like one wrong move from him and she'd… Hell, he didn't know, just that he'd go crashing through the ice any second and be plunged into deep frigid waters. She glared at him and he felt like an insensitive jerk. He didn't have a clue why.

"I'm damaged, flawed, broken," she muttered fiercely. "Take your pick. I've heard it all before, and more. Including ugly."

"Ugly?" He made a sound of irritation. "Did someone tell you that?" he rapped out.

She lifted a hand to cover the pale thin scars and blinked at him warily. "I've got eyes. I know what I look like."

He reached out and wrapped his fingers around her wrist, gently pulling her hand away so he could study the thin silvery scars marring her creamy skin with professional interest and clinical detachment. He had a feeling anything else would offend her.

Through the delicate skin on the inside of her wrist her pulse beat a rapid tattoo. Even if he hadn't felt the racing heartbeat, he couldn't ignore the anxiety leaking from every pore.

She made a sound of distress in the back of her throat and tried to tug free but he held her easily, lifting his free hand to gently turn the scarred side toward him.

He wanted to lean forward and kiss each imperfection, run his tongue along the pale lines. "I don't think you do," he said mildly. "Have you heard of body dysmorphic disorder?"

She jerked her chin away and flashed him a scowl of outrage. "Of course I have. Are you suggesting I have BDD or that I'm vain?"

Gabe shook his head and sent her a faint smile. "Neither. I merely wondered if you knew about it. I'm not going to lie and say your scars are invisible, Holly, but I think they're more noticeable to you because you know they're there."

She rolled her eyes and tried to twist free but he ignored her, his large, warm hand holding her captive. "I know they're there," she said in a low, fierce voice, "because I had to live through the stares as well as the endless procedures to get rid of them."

"And…" he guessed, lightly tracing one thin line across the top of her cheekbone to where it disappeared into her hairline. She sucked in a breath and after a moment a tiny shudder went through her. Gabe had to steel himself against the urge to wrap his arms around her, offer his strength. "You remember what they were like when they were new," he pointed out gently. "But unless you deliberately did this to yourself, it's not your fault."

"Of course I didn't do it to myself,' she snapped, then sucked in a huge breath that was probably an attempt to calm her but which nearly gave Gabe a heart attack when the round globes of her breasts swelled above the neckline of her swimsuit. "It was…an accident."

He had to clear his throat twice and fight the overwhelming urge to drop his gaze to her plump curves and drool like a guy. "Well, from a cosmetic point of view, even *I* couldn't have done better."

She snorted. "Modest much, Dr. Alexander?"

He chuckled. "No. In Beverly Hills you have to be good or word gets around and the next thing you know you're in Tijuana, doing budget nip-and-tuck tourist deals. Switzerland or Germany?"

She tugged again on her wrist and because he was somewhat distracted he let her go. She immediately wrapped her arms around herself. He could have told her it was too late. *Waa-aay* too late. Now that he'd seen—and felt them pressed against his chest—he was sure the image was burned into his brain for all time. And why he found that sexier than if she'd been naked, he didn't know. Clearly he'd lost brain cells along with his testosterone leakage.

"Switzerland. How did you know?"

At the question his gaze rose from watching her mouth form words. He blinked in confusion and got lost in the smoky blue depths surrounding enlarged pupils.

"I, uh…" What the hell were they discussing? Oh, yeah,

he thought with a rush of relief—her scars. "I recognized the technique from a study I did in med school."

She looked back at him and her expression was as dazed as his had been a few seconds ago. Clearly she was also having difficulty keeping up with their verbal exchange when their bodies insisted on conversing on a whole different level. A level that left his skin tight, his blood pounding through his veins and his body in pleasurable pain like he was an addict suffering withdrawal.

Holly licked her lips and Gabe's blood went instantly hot. She must have recognized the look in his eyes because hers widened and she edged away, watching him warily.

"Stop that!"

"Huh? Stop what?"

"Stop looking and…and talking about my flaws."

"Everyone has flaws," he murmured distractedly, his body following hers like he was a divining rod and she was a hidden source of water. He caged her against the wall with his arms, his voice a rough, low sound between them that heightened the feeling of isolation and intimacy.

Slick, naked skin brushed, sending goose-bumps marching across his skin like an invading army, and the water separating them heated until he thought he saw steam but maybe that was just his brain smoking. "My one ear is higher than the other and I have big feet."

She gaped at him like he was a lunatic for equating big feet with trauma scars. "You're kidding, right?"

"No, I'm serious. I bet if you looked you'd probably find a lot more. Like I broke my nose when my surfboard smacked me in the face."

She grimaced sympathetically. "What happened?"

"I was sixteen and showing off," he sighed. "Instead of being impressed, the girl fainted when she saw blood and the rest of my summer was ruined."

Her eyes lightened, as Gabe had intended, and he wanted to close the distance between them and kiss her, tease a

smile to her lush mouth. He wanted to make her laugh—
really laugh. Not the polite little smile he'd seen her aim
at people she wanted to keep at a distance. Hell. He'd like
any kind of smile, considering all she ever did with him
was scowl.

"That's really tragic."

Yeah, about as tragic as a grown man behaving like a
sixteen-year-old.

He gave a wounded look. "It was a traumatic adolescent
experience that scarred me for life," he accused, when she
smothered a snicker. "Anyway, in addition to a broken nose,
my one eyebrow arches more than the other and an old girlfriend told me I look permanently mocking."

"The one who fainted?"

"No." *Smartass.* "That one was history before I could
impress her with my manliness. It was another…girl."

"Well, you are mocking," she pointed out, and when his
lips curved up at one corner, her eyes dropped to stare at his
mouth and he knew she was as affected by their proximity
as he was. After a moment her gaze slid away a little guiltily
and when her tongue emerged to flick over her lips he felt
it all the way to his big feet—and every inch along the way.

"Maybe a little," he rasped, struggling to follow the conversation. "What I'm trying to say is that people are not
perfect."

"You haven't met my family."

"Why?"

The movement of the water bobbed them together and
their bodies bumped, skin brushing skin, soft curves against
hard. Her breasts brushed his chest, sending sensation zing-
ing through him until his back teeth ached with the effort
not to yank her against him and taste her soft mouth.

"My mother was a beauty queen," she was saying in a
husky tone, as though the accidental touch had affected her
too. *Damn.* Maybe he should move away. Maybe he should
get out of the pool and take a really cold shower until he

could breathe without inhaling the scent of her, move without the memory of her soft skin brushing against his.

But instead of getting the hell out of Dodge, he pressed a thigh between hers and shifted closer, until the plump curves of her breasts were pillowed against his chest and her thighs quivered and clenched around his. She made a little sound in the back of her throat that emerged as a gasping squeak and he nearly came out of his skin. It was so hot he was surprised the water didn't evaporate. It was so hot he felt the back of his skull tighten and his skin buzz.

She gulped and pressed herself against the wall before continuing. "She was…um…runner-up for Miss America and w-won Miss World that same year." She sucked in a breath. "She's beautiful and perfect. Like my sister Paige. Like my father and my brother Bryant."

Something tugged at his memory but when her tongue peeked out between her pink lips it vanished and all he could think about was tasting the moist pink pillows of flesh just beneath his mouth.

Maybe it was the hour or the fact that her eyes were heavy and smoky with the kind of need thundering through his own veins. But with her lips just below his and the smooth skin of her inner thighs making his gut clench with an almost violent need, he was powerless to do anything but slide his hand to the back of her neck and lower his head.

She gasped. "What are you…doing?"

Just before their lips touched, he murmured, "Proving how perfect you are."

Bare skin and thin elastane pressed into his belly and thighs. It flooded him with a need so powerful that he felt momentarily dizzy.

Oh, yeah, she was perfect all right. Perfect for him… perfect for his hands. Perfect for his mouth and he'd bet his grandfather's entire fortune she'd be perfect for his body too.

He reined himself in with difficulty but her breath hitched audibly in her throat and shot all his intentions—

to keep it light and teasing—straight to the bottomless pits of hell.

With a growl he covered her mouth with his in a kiss that instantly turned greedy and hot. He was thirty-five. A man who loved women; loved their bodies and the way their bodies felt against his. He loved the way they tasted and smelled and he loved the feel of their soft, firm flesh beneath his hands. He loved everything about them and he especially loved taking his time. But everything he'd ever learned about women went right out of his head the instant her mouth opened beneath his.

It was like he'd been sucked into a vortex created by her soft, wet mouth and soft, warm body and he couldn't think beyond getting more. More of her mouth, more of her silky curves pressed to the front of his jammer swimming trunks. More of her.

He pressed closer and when she uttered a breathy moan Gabe instantly took advantage and slid his tongue into her hot mouth. Without realizing he was doing it, he groaned low and deep in his throat and adjusted the fit of his mouth over hers, creating a light suction that made her whimper and arch into him, her hands clutching at his shoulders.

Blood roared through his head and he felt himself go under—submerged in liquid heat and drowning pleasure where his only lifeline was the feel of her soft mouth beneath his. And if he heard the alarm warning in the back of his mind, he ignored it in favor of murmured sighs that filled his ears and the slick, warm feel of her mouth beneath his.

Holly was aware of only two things. The big, hard body pressed to hers…the tangle of their limbs and the way his hand cradled her head as he devoured her resistance along with her breath. Okay, and she was also aware of the hard thigh between hers and the evidence of his arousal pressed almost painfully against her belly.

Her mind spun even as her eyes drifted shut and her

body softened, cradling that huge, hard shaft. He groaned. It came from so deep in his chest—like it'd been dragged up from the depths of his soul—that the responding vibrations swept through her like a subwoofer turned on high. And before she could remember her plan or think that maybe this was a very bad idea, she surrendered to the taste of him, greedily eating at his mouth and the hot, hungry kisses he fed her. Kisses that were deep and drugging and told her he was ravenous and that she was his next meal.

She'd never known kisses could be so hot or…hungry. Or that a man's mouth was capable of making her head spin, her belly dip and her body feel like one move and she'd go off like a bottle rocket.

And then there were no more thoughts as need and greed sucked her under, stole her breath along with any thoughts she might have to resist.

But there was no resisting the unstoppable force that was Gabriel Alexander and if she was honest with herself she didn't want to. Didn't want to push him away or stop the onslaught on her senses. Didn't want to resist his hot hardness sliding up to press against the apex of her thighs where she was hot and damp and aching with emptiness.

It was also wildly exciting to discover that someone like him could want her…with such rough urgency.

Then it didn't matter because all her thoughts drained away along with her breath, sucked out by his greedy mouth. But she found she didn't need breath as much as she needed this. This wild out-of-control feeling that sucked her under and sent her mind into a tailspin. And if she'd been in any condition to do anything but groan, slide her hands up the heavy muscles of his arms to his shoulders and press her body closer, she might have freaked at the ease with which he'd unraveled her defenses.

He fed her more deep, wet, hungry kisses that made her gasp and return them, just as hungrily, as if they were alone instead of in a public swimming pool where anyone might see them.

She didn't care. All she wanted was the hot, wet slide of his body filling the deep, empty ache within her. An ache she'd only discovered this very minute. An ache that she'd never thought existed, let alone experienced—especially in a brightly lit pool in central Manhattan.

He broke off the kiss to croak *"Damn,"* against her mouth and drag air into his heaving chest like he'd just sprinted three lengths of the pool without breathing. For several long beats they shared air until Holly lifted heavy lashes to see if he'd been as affected by the kiss as she had.

He looked a little shell-shocked. Kind of like she'd kneed him in the groin and he didn't know whether to throw up or pass out. Heck, she felt a little like passing out herself, and if she'd been in any state to do more than gulp air and cling to him, she might have panicked. Because…because, *damn*. Who'd have thought that Holly Buchanan would end up making out with Dr. Beverly Hills in a public swimming pool like a couple of randy teens? And want more? A whole lot more?

But her shock was about as little as the heavy evidence of his arousal, clearly outlined by his jammer suit practically shrink-wrapped to his lower body and visible beneath the water.

Okay, so she'd looked. It was better than seeing the hot blue-green eyes staring into hers until her thighs went up in flames. Her vision grayed at the edges and she thought she was having a panic attack until she realized she was holding her breath. She had to exhale or pass out.

And then he'd be forced to save her by performing mouth-to-mouth. *Oh, yes. Please.*

She must have swayed because his hands shot out to steady her. "You okay?" he rasped, and Holly stared up into his eyes and wondered why she'd never noticed how stormy they could get. Like the waters of the Caribbean stirred by hurricane winds.

"I…um…" And when nothing else emerged, he gave her a quick, hard shake to snap her out of her trance. But Holly was well and truly speechless. Who wouldn't be after that… that feeding frenzy?

"You going to pass out?" emerged rough and hoarse, as though he had as little control over his vocal cords as he had over his breathing. She inhaled and exhaled a couple more times until the urge to lose consciousness eased.

"Wh-a-at?"

A ragged chuckle scraped up from the depths of his chest and after a couple beats he shoved shaking fingers through his hair. "Damn it. I have to go." He sounded frustrated and a little like he was about to lose it. And, *oh, boy*, she could identify. "Are you going to be all right?"

"Oh…um…yes." She sucked in a couple more breaths and blinked up at him in confusion until she finally recognized the beeping noise she'd thought was the little warning sound in her head.

He was being paged and she hadn't even heard it over the pounding in her ears. Her head cleared a little more and she blew out a ragged "Go."

CHAPTER SIX

HOLLY WASN'T ABOUT to tell him that she felt like someone had smacked her against the head and left her ears ringing. She wasn't about to admit that every muscle in her body trembled—either with unfulfilled need or shock at her own behavior.

She white-knuckled the side of the pool with one hand and lifted unsteady fingers to her tingling lips, watching with dazed eyes as he hauled himself onto the pool deck. She felt shaken to her core. Kind of like finding out that aliens existed and that the government was helping them experiment on humans in return for their technology. Only... more.

Holy cow. Who knew anyone could kiss like that? Kiss *her* like that? As though he'd wanted to swallow her whole.

Water gushed down his body as he rose to his full height and she finally got a good look at what he'd been hiding beneath his jeans and sweatshirts—everything his jammer suit was supposed to cover, but didn't. *Gulp.*

She didn't realize her mouth had dropped open until he turned and caught her ogling his tight butt. His brow—the one that was usually arched in subtle mockery—rose up his forehead and a little lopsided grin sent that dimple creasing the lean planes of his cheek.

Oh, God. He'd caught her in the act of ogling him like he was a delicious pastry.

"Are you going to be okay? I hate leaving you alone when you're not such a great swimmer."

Holly's blush turned to a grimace at the reminder of her graceless dive. She didn't know what was worse—being caught leering at the goodies or…or having him witness her clumsiness. Again.

"I'm fine, Dr. Alexander. I…uh, slipped, that's all." She rolled her eyes as he wound a huge towel around his waist, his arched brow probably questioning her sudden attack of professionalism. But it was either that or drown herself at the memory of the way she'd whimpered and clutched at him like she'd been starving and he'd been a chocolate fudge sundae. "Maybe I'm not in your league, but I can hold my own."

"Uh-huh," he said, like he didn't believe her, and shoved fingers through his wet hair. Droplets showered around his head and shoulders and Holly felt equal amounts of glee and astonishment when she noticed his hands were shaking.

"I'm a great swimmer."

"If you say so." His phone started ringing and he grunted, looking for a moment like he'd love to toss the thing in the pool. But surgeons on call didn't have that luxury. "Look, I've gotta go. Promise me you'll be okay."

She rolled her eyes again, secretly pleased by his obvious reluctance to leave—although that might have something to do with his inability to walk in his…uh, condition. She bit her lip and watched his eyes go dark.

"I promise I'll be okay," she said hastily, and he finally sighed and gathered up his stuff.

He paused to send her one last look from beneath heavy, aroused lids. "A rain-check on the…other thing."

Holly shivered and dropped lower into the water to hide her body's reaction and stop her suit from melting beneath that laser-bright gaze. "The…thing?" One corner of his mouth curved and her breath caught in her chest. "Oh."

She swallowed hard and clenched her thighs together. "You mean…the, um…kiss?"

His grin turned wicked and his eyes burned a molten blue-green as they slid over her exposed skin, setting fire to her hair and her thighs. Jeez. It was a good thing she was submerged in water or her swimsuit—along with her thighs—would be history. "Oh, yeah," he rasped, his voice a dark slide of sin against her sensitized nerve endings as he turned and headed for the exit. "The kiss."

And just before he disappeared through the door she heard him say, "Definitely going to be another kiss."

And because he sounded so sure of himself—so arrogantly sure of *her*—she called out, "Don't hold your breath, Dr. Alexander. That was simply a thank-you for saving me." His response was deep laughter that floated across the pool and went straight to all her happy places that were feeling decidedly unhappy…and frustrated, *darn it*.

"Keep telling yourself that, Dr. Buchanan," rang in her ears, and Holly stared at the door for a few moments more before shaking her head as though to dispel the images lodged there. Sucking in a shuddery breath, she looked down to check that she was still clothed and wasn't sporting singe marks on her skin.

She was surprised to find that her suit hadn't vaporized and that the water hadn't boiled her like a lobster. Puffing out her cheeks, she blew out air in the hope that she could dispel the bubbles lodged in her brain. Because it was the only reason that would explain her wanton behavior. Especially with a man like Gabriel Alexander. A man who'd dedicated himself to the pursuit of perfection. A man who wasn't blind enough to ignore just how imperfect she was.

After a few moments getting her breathing under control, Holly squared her shoulders and sank beneath the water, ignoring the muscles trembling in her limbs like she'd just stepped off a carnival ride.

It was time to douse the fire and get into her zone, she

told herself firmly. A zone that didn't include sexy Hollywood surgeons with hot eyes, hard bodies and big warm… hands.

She had barely found her rhythm and was approaching the wall to turn when movement caught her attention. Stopping abruptly, she reared out of the water, her gaze automatically taking in a pair of battered sneakers at the edge of the pool.

She followed the long line of jeans-clad legs, over the bulge of a button fly and up a wide expanse of black T-shirt-covered chest to a tanned neck and square jaw gleaming with gold-tinted stubble. Stubble, she recalled with a shudder; that had scraped against her skin with rough eroticism.

She was surprised to see him. Dropping her head back, she quickly submerged then rose, lifting both hands to smooth her hair off her face. When she opened her eyes she found he'd dropped to his haunches and was looking hot and cool all at once. Their eyes met and a wild flush raced over her flesh at the memory of what he could do with his mouth.

"I thought you left?"

He shook his head. "I need you," he said, and the flush became a shudder, along with tightening breasts and clenching belly. Momentarily stunned, she gaped up at him as though he'd suggested something hot and forbidden…and incredibly tempting.

"I… You… What?"

He must have correctly interpreted her confusion because his mouth curved and that darned dimple made an appearance in his tanned cheek. "That'll have to wait for another time, Dr. Buchanan." He laughed and held out a hand as though he expected her to take it. Holly looked at his big brown hand and got a little dizzy just thinking about how it made her feel.

"Wha-at?"

He chuckled. "Pay attention, Doctor. I need you to get

out of the pool and get dressed. The hospital can't reach Dr. Frankel and we urgently need another surgeon. You're it."

"I'm not a maxillofacial surgeon."

"Close enough," he said a little impatiently, and waggled his fingers.

Without questioning him further, Holly took his hand and the next instant she was standing beside the pool, swaying a little on wobbly legs as water gushed down her body. He wrapped her towel around her shoulders and nudged her toward the exit.

"You have five minutes to change while I call a cab."

Holly walked into the gym lobby with a minute to spare to find Gabriel propped casually against the wall, laughing and chatting up a couple of women dressed in gym wear that looked three sizes too small. Both women looked taut and toned enough to bounce a coin on their tight butts and abs. And because she would never be able to do that, Holly was grateful her designer trousers and jacket covered her from the neck down.

The instant he saw her Gabe pushed away from the wall and wrapped his fingers around her elbow. The smile he aimed her way was warmly intimate as he called a quick "Night" over his shoulder. It also left her a little confused.

"Thank you," he murmured, steering her toward the automatic doors.

"For what?"

"For saving me from the barracudas." Oh, well, that certainly explained that, she decided with a pang that wasn't really disappointment. That smile hadn't been for her at all. Curious, she looked back over her shoulder and decided they did kind of resemble a couple of barracudas trawling the reef for a quick snack.

And to a woman who hadn't eaten all day, Gabriel Alexander was kind of snack-worthy.

"You looked like you were having a great time."

"Seriously?" He scowled at her as the doors swished

closed behind them. "Did you see how ripped they were? I was worried the blonde would wrestle me to the floor and put me in a headlock." *Or a something lock.* Holly hid a smirk. "It's humiliating," he muttered. "Besides, I don't like women who are so obsessed with the way they look they can't relax and have a good time."

The look he sent her made her hair smolder and her belly dip and quiver. "Women are supposed to be…soft," he murmured wickedly, his hot gaze dropping to her breasts. "Not have muscles in places they shouldn't. It makes a guy feel inferior."

He opened the cab door and stepped aside for Holly to get in. She couldn't see him feeling intimidated by anyone, let alone a couple of hot, sculpted gym bunnies. He'd have to care what people thought about him and he didn't strike her as a guy who worried overly much about that.

He got in behind her and she sneaked a peek out the corner of her eye when his thigh pressed against hers and their shoulders bumped. It sent warm little tingles of awareness pricking her skin.

She shifted over a little.

God, he was big, his wide shoulders taking up space she wasn't used to sharing with anyone and dominating it with a kind of smoldering masculine aggression that made her feel small and fragile when she looked most men in the eye.

By the time they arrived at the hospital Holly was wondering if she'd made a mistake by agreeing to accompany him after that kiss. She needed at least a week—okay, maybe a month…or three—to recover her equilibrium and stop wanting to either run for cover or…or jump his bones. Jumping his bones would be bad. Bad for the plan and bad for her heart.

"Get suited up and meet me in room two," he said briskly, with none of the misgivings or embarrassment she was experiencing. But, then, he was a guy. Kissing women and then going on to remodel a few breasts and thighs was all in a day's work. For her…? She sucked in air and let it out slowly. Well, not so much.

That kiss had been—

"You okay?"

Startled, she looked up into Gabriel's handsome face. "Of course." But instead of sounding coolly professional, she just sounded stunned and unsure. He must have thought so too because his eyebrow arched toward his hairline. "I'm fine, Dr. Alexander," she said, this time managing cool and confident, although it cost her. "But you might want to order me a glass of fresh orange juice. I can't remember the last time I ate."

One corner of his mouth curled. "I'll see what I can do. I'd hate for you to fall at my feet."

Holly rolled her eyes and hurried into the women's locker room. Falling at his feet was a habit she was determined to break.

She grabbed a pair of light blue scrubs, wondering how soon she would be permitted to wear the dark blue scrubs worn by all senior surgeons. It would be the final sign that she had reached the goal she'd work for years to achieve.

But there wasn't time to think about that now.

She quickly changed and headed for OR two, where the team would already be assembled. A ripple of anticipation tripped up her spine when she wondered what was waiting for her because she was fairly certain it would not be anything remotely cosmetic. Plastic surgeons didn't get called out for boob jobs or tummy tucks. Not at eight o'clock at night.

Maybe this would be her chance to show her real skills.

Already scrubbed, Gabe stood patiently while an OR nurse tugged the surgical gown over his shoulders and fastened the rear ties. Holly drank from the bottle of orange juice he'd ordered for her and waited for her turn to scrub up. When she'd finished she dropped the empty bottle into the trash and moved toward the basins.

He slid his gaze from the top of her dark head over the curvy body hidden beneath her scrubs, down her long legs to her surgical booties. Despite the outfit, she looked elegant and composed.

His gaze returned to her face and he frowned at the sight of her swollen lips. Lips he'd practically eaten off her face in his eagerness to taste that wide, lush mouth. Heat crawled up the back of his neck at the memory of the way he'd kissed her—like a green untried adolescent with his first crush. *Jeez*. It was no wonder she'd been stunned speechless. He'd been about as smooth as the Sawtooth Mountains.

"Is something wrong, Dr. Alexander?"

Realizing the nurse was addressing him, Gabe said, "Huh?" and tore his gaze from Holly. *Damn it*. He was standing here staring at her like a lovesick teen stunned stupid by big blue eyes and kiss-swollen lips.

"Is something wrong?" the nurse repeated, and Gabe dropped his gaze to her brown eyes for a moment before shaking off his odd mood. *Yep. Something is wrong. I'm wondering if I've lost my mind.*

"Just mentally preparing myself," he told her crisply, sliding one last hooded look at Holly and backing up to the swing doors. "Ready, Dr. Buchanan?"

Holly turned toward him, her face composed and serene as though that searing kiss hadn't happened. Then he caught a quick glimpse of her eyes before her lashes swept down and he realized she was fighting embarrassment and maybe apprehension. Whether for the upcoming procedure or the fact that he'd recently had his tongue in her mouth... he wasn't certain. Only that she avoided any eye contact as she brushed passed him and stepped into the sterile environment.

"Where do you want me?"

* * *

Three hours later Gabe lifted his eyes from where Holly's deft hands skillfully carried out his brisk instructions and recalled her last words.

Where do you want me? He could have told her that he'd have her anywhere he could get her but everyone was listening with big ears and he didn't want to provide fodder for gossip. He had a feeling Holly would do anything to avoid attention.

Over the last couple of hours he'd watched her carefully and couldn't suppress his admiration for her surgical skills. Watching from the observation room hadn't quite given him a sense of her abilities despite the video footage of other procedures he'd watched. He preferred the up-close-and-personal approach...of observation, he hastily amended. Working side by side with surgical residents gave him a better idea of their knowledge, skill and their surgical temperament. Despite what people thought, Gabe believed the difference between a good surgeon and an excellent one lay in their ability to stay calm and motivate people without resorting to temper tantrums or abuse. And he was pleased to discover that Holly's surgical temperament complemented his.

She was also a quick study. Calm and steady in a crisis, she didn't hesitate to follow his murmured instructions. In fact, she instinctively seemed to know what he would do next and was poised waiting for his cue or quickly moving in to assist when he'd appreciate another pair of hands attached to his brain.

The patient had been through massive facial trauma and ended up in reconstruction to stabilize his facial bones before something shifted and ended up in his brain.

Gabe had used a new technique he'd been developing to keep shattered bones stable while the swelling subsided enough for further reconstruction.

By inserting an ultra-thin malleable mesh beneath the

bones and over a specially made saline bag that would mold the cheekbone, he'd re-sculpted the facial bones to approximate the uninjured side. He'd explained that he was attempting to reduce the need for unnecessary additional reconstruction, especially in heart patients. He'd only used the procedure once before, on a teenager who'd fallen off his snowboard and shattered his nose and both cheekbones. He'd had to resort to pins and wires to reconstruct the lower jaw, but the cheekbones had healed nicely with the new procedure, which included experimental bone-generating injections.

Once he was satisfied with the position and shape of the mesh-encased bone, he and Holly began the complex task of reattaching and re-forming the tendons in the jaw. It was tedious, painstaking work, requiring each connective bundle to be stretched and sewn onto its counterpart.

When he finally ordered the area closed with acelluar mesh, he could see Holly was exhausted but wildly buzzed. She'd just assisted in a ground-breaking procedure that was a first at WMS and had done remarkably well with the unfamiliar procedure. The patient would still need ear, nose and lip reconstruction but that was for some time in the future when he'd healed from his other injuries and they could harvest skin and adipose cells.

They were finally wrapping up when Gabe noticed a tiny tremor move through her hands. She'd been on her feet since early morning and this had been her third lengthy procedure for the day. His gaze snagged hers, recalling how she'd gulped down the orange juice. But that had been hours ago and even he was ravenous.

"You okay there, Dr. Buchanan?"

Startled by the personal question after hours of impersonal orders and directions, she blinked a few times before nodding and dropping her gaze to where she was completing the wound closure.

"Any special instructions?" Her voice was low and con-

fident and Gabe relaxed, stepping back from the action.
Rolling the two sets of latex gloves off his hands, he smiled
behind his face mask.

"You're doing fine," he murmured, dropping the latex
into the medical waste bin. "I'll leave you to finish things
while I write up a report and send instructions to ICU." And
with a quick word of thanks and congratulations to each
member of the surgical team, he left the room, stripping off
his gown, mask and bandana.

Leaving her to supervise the final stages was an unspoken vote of confidence that everyone in the room understood. It was well deserved. She might be an adorable klutz
in her personal life but there was nothing clumsy about the
way she handled herself in surgery. She just needed to believe in herself—go with her gut instinct. She knew what
she was doing and she was good. He felt confident that with
practice, expert guidance and encouragement she would
become a highly skilled professional.

A half-hour later he spotted her heading across the hospital lobby toward the huge glass entrance. It was almost two
in the morning and he was tired but knew from experience
that he wouldn't sleep. He was still buzzing with adrenaline
and though he usually preferred to be alone after a challenging procedure, he suddenly yearned for company.

Holly Buchanan's.

The realization that he was actively seeking out the company of a woman who usually went out of her way to avoid
him was a little disturbing. He shook off the unwelcomed
thoughts. This was just a post-operative conversation between colleagues.

That's all.

He quietly came up behind her, ignoring the fact that he
didn't quite believe it himself. "Wanna share a cab?"

Startled, she jolted and flashed a look across her shoulder
that could only be interpreted as guilty—especially when

her gaze slid away from his and color seeped beneath her creamy skin.

Gabe wondered what she'd been thinking and if it had been about him. It wasn't ego that prompted the thought, he told himself, because he rarely obsessed about women or wondered if they obsessed about him. In Holly's case it was only fair considering the number of times he'd been distracted by the scent of her, teasing his senses over the antiseptic smells of the OR.

"I don't know. Are you going to leave me on the sidewalk if I say no?"

He chuckled and steered her through the automatic doors with a hand to the small of her back. "Not this time." Her sideways look was loaded with suspicion despite the shiver he felt go through her at his casual touch. "Promise. Scout's honor."

"I don't believe for a minute that you were a Scout."

"Hey, I'm a helpful kind of guy," he cut in, stepping off the curb and lifting his arm when he spotted a lighted cab half a block away. "Just ask my mom. And I'm always prepared."

"For what?" Holly asked beside him.

He shrugged. "For anything. Everything."

"Like what?"

He paused for a couple of beats like he was seriously considering her question then a wicked glance across his shoulder prompted a raised eyebrow. "Like paying close attention to expiration dates."

She huffed out a startled laugh as the cab pulled up, her look filled with censure for bringing up the condom incident. "With all your surgically enhanced beach bunnies, I would hope so," she said primly as he stepped forward to open the rear door. "They probably don't last long enough *to* expire."

"That's not entirely true," he drawled as she slid across the seat and gave the cabbie her address. He wondered what she would say to the news that his most recent stash had been dangerously close to expiration or that he hadn't thought about replacing them. Which was about as pathetic as his need for her company. Besides, he'd been in a relationship when his mother had been diagnosed. A relationship that had tanked faster than the *Titanic* the second the woman had found out he was thinking of giving up his lucrative practice to move east.

He'd been somewhat preoccupied and had completely missed the signs that she'd already transferred her affections to one of the other partners. When she'd thrown it in his face in a fit of pique, it had just reinforced the notion that he wasn't relationship material. And when all he'd felt had been relief, he'd known then it was time for him to move on. Besides, with his mother gone, there was nothing keeping him in California.

Holly's eyebrows rose up her smooth forehead. "Planning to live dangerously?"

Recalling that they were talking about his stash, Gabe chuckled and slid in behind her. "Hell, no. I have no intention of being caught in that particular web of lies and deceit."

Her eyebrows rose in surprise. "Lies and deceit?"

"Do you know the lengths some women are prepared to go to snag themselves a rich doctor husband?"

"As a matter of fact, I do. It's a common enough problem in med school, even though most med students have huge study loans to pay off and won't make any money for years."

"Yeah." He shuddered. "I had a brief moment of terror in my fourth year that turned out to be a false alarm but a couple of buddies weren't so lucky. One is already divorced and the other heading that way fast." He watched the purity of her profile in the lights off Broadway and wondered at her belief that she was imperfect. Everyone was imperfect. It was what made people interesting.

He recalled something she'd said about her family and

wondered if it had anything to do with her scars. But that was probably just speculation from his dysfunctional perspective.

"What about you?"

She turned toward him and his eyes slid over the elegant lines of her face gilded in warm gold from the streetlights. He'd like to say his examination was purely professional but he'd be lying.

"What about me?"

At this angle her scars were in shadow and he caught his breath at the stark beauty of her bone structure. He knew a lot of women who would kill to look like Holly Buchanan, scars or no scars. In fact, they just made her more interesting and...alluring, especially with emotion simmering in her eyes or when they darkened to a deep smoky blue when she was aroused.

He tried to stretch out his legs and ended up pressing his thigh firmly against hers. Heat gathered where they touched and the slight tremor he felt zip through her sent arrows of hunger and need into his belly until his jaw ached and his skin felt tight.

"Did you have to fight off party animals eager to marry a beautiful rich doctor and live a life of leisure?"

Her mouth dropped open and he could see he'd shocked her. Whether by the beautiful and rich statement or fighting off men, Gabe couldn't tell.

"You're kidding right?"

"Actually, no. I've lost count of the number of guys I've seen checking you out."

She laughed, her genuine amusement filling the interior with warmth.

The sound settled into his gut alongside the clawing lust and made him stare. *Damn.* She should laugh more. It transformed her from merely quietly beautiful to breathtaking, and filled her eyes with warmth and light. She seemed suddenly *alive*. As if she'd forgotten her plan, forgotten to be serious and was simply living in the moment.

He wondered if she'd always been so serious or if her "perfect" family had somehow squashed the life and joy out of her. And the sudden impulse to bring her joy made the hair rise on the back of his neck.

Whoa. A trickle of unease slid down his spine like a drop of icy water. Since when did he fall over himself to make women happy? Maybe he was just tired and hungry. Maybe he just needed a shower, food and about twelve hours of sleep.

She sent him a sideways look filled with mischief and he swallowed. Hard. *Holy crap.* The back of his neck tightened and his chest clenched. *This is bad. Very bad.*

"You're a funny man," she said, her eyes sparkling like deep sapphires.

His eyes dropped to her lips, curved in merriment, and he thought, *Oh, yeah. I'm hungry, all right.* But it wasn't for food. "Maybe you should do stand-up comedy." He opened his mouth, although he had no idea what he was going to say.

"Huh?" was about the sum total of his brainpower.

"People stare at scars, Dr. Alexander," she pointed out gently. "You, of all people, should know that. It's what keeps plastic surgeons in business."

What he did know was that when she spoke, all he could concentrate on was her mouth…and her eyes. The rest just faded away, retreated to the edges of his mind. Okay, maybe not faded because he was always aware of her soft, curvy body, but he didn't see scars. He was too busy fighting the urge to yank her into his lap and study the shape of her with his hands and mouth.

"And maybe you should be more observant."

"What's that supposed to mean? I'm very observant."

"Uh-huh." The cab turned and headed into Brooklyn. Gabe shifted in the seat to relieve the growing tightness behind his button fly but he knew he was fighting a losing battle. With every breath he took, her subtle feminine fragrance filled the cab and flooded his senses. It made him feel a little drunk.

Maybe it was just exhaustion.

He *hoped* it was just exhaustion.

The cab finally pulled up in front of her brownstone and he let out a relieved breath that he could escape before he did something he'd regret.

Like pull her into his lap and suck on that lip. Or run his hands under her snug little jacket to her soft, silky skin and lush curves.

"I'll get that," he said when Holly reached into her purse for the fare. He pushed open the door and slid from the cab. "Consider it payment for leaving you stranded the other night."

CHAPTER SEVEN

HOLLY SCRAMBLED FROM the cab, bumping the door closed with her hip. Gabriel straightened and stepped back from paying the cabbie and she had a flash of him as he'd looked earlier in Theatre. Tall, steady and *hot*—despite the laid-back charm he'd dispensed with equal measure to everyone on his team.

Although she'd deliberately avoided any opportunity to observe him in action, she could readily understand why the surgical nursing staff fought to be on his team. Other than the obvious hotness factor, he was patient and quick to break any tension with supportive praise or a few wise-cracks. He controlled the proceedings and the people around him with such skillful ease that everyone practically fell over themselves to please him.

Even her, she admitted with a frown. She could scarcely believe how they'd worked together—perfectly in sync—like they'd been doing it together for years instead of just a few hours.

It had been a little unnerving to discover that the man she'd been ready to dislike simply on principle wasn't the spoiled Hollywood celebrity she'd been expecting. And he was good, damn it. Good at kissing and making the breath catch in her throat. Good at making her forget the plan, and really good at saving a man's shattered face. So good that she couldn't help the little niggle of jealousy at the way he made things look so easy when she had to work so darned hard.

Sighing, she watched the cab disappear around the corner. A chilly wind had kicked up a few fall leaves and she shivered, hunching into her thin jacket as she looked up into a clear night sky. The moon was large and fat and seemed closer to the earth than usual and the halo around it promised a cold winter ahead.

She usually hated winter but for some reason it made her think of half-empty bottles of wine, a roaring fire and the flash of naked limbs and satisfied sighs. Her pulse leapt and heat rose from deep in her belly until it surrounded her in a shimmering glow—like a banked fire smoldering in her core, just waiting to burst into flame.

Puffing out her cheeks, she rolled her eyes because… because the tangle of limbs in her vision belonged to her and…and…

Another shiver moved through Holly.

She was in trouble.

Big trouble.

Spooked by her realization as much as the wildly erotic visions in her head, she turned and caught him watching silently from a few feet away. And in that instant her perception of him underwent yet another metamorphosis.

With only one side of his face starkly lit by moonlight and the rest in deep shadow, he looked big and bad and a little dangerous. Like a fierce golden angel banished from the heavens for inspiring illicit thoughts and needs in mortal women.

Gone was the laid-back flirt as well as the brilliant innovative surgeon with a knack for getting the best out of everyone. In his place was a man seemingly shrouded in mystery and…and aching loneliness.

The image made her heart squeeze in her chest and she had to resist the urge to go to him, press close to his big body and chase away the shadows she sometimes saw in his eyes.

But Gabriel Alexander was big and bad and beautiful and he certainly didn't need her. He didn't need anyone—especially someone scarred and focused on reaching her goals.

Shrugging off the uncomfortable realization that he was more than the hot, sexy Hollywood celebrity that made her tingle in hidden places, Holly became aware of the intensity of his gaze. His utter stillness unnerved her. She opened her mouth and said, "Did you know that Neil Armstrong was a Boy Scout?" before she could stop herself. "In fact, seventy one percent of astronauts," she continued determinedly, "are believed to have been Scouts."

His mouth curved, dispelling the image of a remote celestial being, and for once Holly didn't care if she sounded like a crazy person. She'd hated seeing that remoteness surrounding him like a thick, impenetrable cloud.

She bit her lip at the memory of the way his mouth had felt closing over hers. Of the way it had created a light suction that had made her breath hitch and her bones melt. She shivered again and this time it had nothing to do with the chill wind blowing from the north, announcing that winter was on its way.

Exactly what her shiver *was* announcing, Holly couldn't tell. Only that it made her heart pound, her skin tingle and her knees wobble like she'd tossed back one too many mojitos on an empty stomach.

"How did we get from being stranded in New York City to Neil Armstrong?"

"The moon, Boy Scouts…" she said a little breathlessly. "It seemed…I don't know…logical." She was helplessly caught in his eyes and the web of heat and tension that surrounded them. A tension that grew thicker by the minute, stealing her oxygen and her bones.

Her stomach chose that instant to growl loudly and she pressed a hand against the rumble, hoping he hadn't heard. But then it dawned on her that her weird dizziness—and possibly the hallucinations of lonely celestial beings—was simply a matter of low blood sugar. Her breath rushed out in a noisy whoosh of relief. *Oh, thank God,* she thought dizzily. All she needed was a quick meal, about ten hours of sleep and she'd be back to normal.

Whew. She gave a husky laugh that sounded a little too hysterical for comfort and headed for the steps leading to her house. *What a relief.*

She opened her mouth to call out goodnight and gave a surprised yelp when Gabriel took her elbow and steered her away from her brownstone.

Toward his.

"What…what are you doing?"

"Hmm?"

"That's your house, Dr. Alexander, not mine."

"I know, and don't you think we're past the stage of calling each other doctor?"

She wasn't going to talk about the kiss and calling him Dr. Alexander helped remind her that he was a colleague. She tugged on her elbow and growled when he ignored her attempts and continued to steer her calmly across the sidewalk, up the stairs past the late-blooming flowers in pots to the heavy wooden door. "Gabriel…why are you taking me to your house?"

The overhead light illuminated his features, revealing a wicked grin and gleaming eyes. She gave a mental eye roll. *Yeesh, so much for the lonely celestial being image.* He looked more like a fallen angel hell-bent on mischief and mayhem.

"Well," he said, fishing his keys from his pocket one-handed and jiggling them till he found the one he wanted. "I'm going to cook." He shoved the key in the lock.

She couldn't have been more surprised. "But…it's after one in the morning."

He arched that mocking brow at her and pushed open the door, drawing her closer despite her obvious reluctance. "You have a meal waiting for you?"

Hovering uncertainly on the threshold, she tugged on her arm and sent him a look filled with feminine exasperation when he tugged her closer instead. "Well, no, but…"

He drew her all the way in and shut the door, instantly surrounding them in deep silence that only emphasized her unsteady breathing and fraying nerves. "You haven't lived till you've sampled my…er…omelets." His grin flashed in response to her squeak as though he knew her mind had descended into the gutter. "Relax. I'll feed you and send you home. Scout's honor."

"I thought we'd established that you were never a Scout."

"No." He chuckled. "You established that."

Holly chewed nervously on her bottom lip as she looked around at the boxes still littering the floor. Not knowing what to do with her hands, she smoothed them over her thighs to disguise their trembling. "Maybe I should—"

He lifted a long tanned finger and placed it gently on her lips. "Food first." His touch made them tingle and she had to fight an overwhelming urge to open her mouth and lick him. Or maybe nibble on that long tanned digit.

She sucked in a sharp breath. *Holy cow.* She'd never had that kind of impulse before, which either meant low blood sugar was making her hallucinate or…or she was headed down a one-way street to disaster. She knew exactly which one *she'd* put her money on but hoped like hell she was just hallucinating.

His eyes gleamed as though he knew what he was doing to her, and in addition to her growing sense of looming disaster was an impulse to bite.

Huh.

Maybe she was just hungry after all.

"It's the least I can do after hijacking you at the gym."

At the mention of the gym, her face went hot and a little voice in the back of her head told her to run and keep running until the memory of those few minutes faded.

But he was taking her shoulder bag and briefcase hostage and to cover her tripping pulse she turned her attention to the furniture dotting the space not taken up by boxes.

It looked like one-tattoo-for-every-skirmish guy had simply dumped everything in Gabriel's sitting room and left.

"Interesting décor," she murmured, thinking there weren't even drapes at the windows and he'd been living here, what…three weeks already? But she'd seen his schedule and he'd probably only had time to come home, shower and sleep before returning to the hospital.

A glance over her shoulder caught Gabriel's grimace as he dropped her bags onto the nearest box. He pulled his black hoodie over his head, briefly exposing his flat, tanned belly before dropping the garment over her briefcase. The stark white T-shirt tested the seams of his shoulders and stretched across his chest, emphasizing the depth of his tan and the width of his biceps. She dropped her gaze to where she'd seen that flash of taut, tanned flesh and wondered why the brief sight of his belly button had seemed so…intimate. More intimate somehow than his earlier kiss. The one that had sucked the breath from her lungs along with her mind and any thoughts about her future.

"I haven't had much time to unpack or find someone to do it for me," he was saying, and Holly had to tear her gaze away from where her eyes had dropped to his button fly before he caught her ogling his package again.

Crap. Maybe she was losing her mind. Maybe this…this feeling of impending disaster was just the first sign of her unraveling mind.

Sucking in breath in an effort to calm her skittering nerves, she said, "My mother has a concierge service that could probably help." *There*, she silently congratulated herself. *That didn't sound crazy, did it?*

"Yeah? That'd be great." He thrust a hand through his hair, tousling the overlong strands even further, and she had to curl her hands into fists to stop from reaching out and smoothing the thick sun-streaked locks. "I hate unpacking," he admitted sheepishly, seemingly oblivious to her chaotic thoughts. "Even if I'd had the time, I wouldn't know where to put all this stuff. I just want my couch and TV set up so I can watch the games."

It was such a guy thing to say that she hid a smile and tried not to imagine his big body sprawled on his huge leather sofa, watching a ball game.

His body radiated clean masculine heat and where his hand touched the small of her back, as he ushered her toward the back of the house, an insidious heat spread across her flesh. She wanted to sink back into him and maybe rub against all that heat and hardness. Just as she'd done earlier.

Get a grip, woman, she ordered herself silently. *Since when did you have urges to lean on a guy for support?*

"I'll...um...call my mother in the morning." Her voice emerged low and slightly husky and she ignored the little smile teasing the corner of his mouth that she was tempted to bite right off.

She rolled her eyes. Clearly she needed food fast or she'd start nibbling on the closest patch of masculine skin.

Looking around his sparkling, modern kitchen, Holly discovered a mild case of kitchen envy but then he started pulling things out of his refrigerator with quick efficiency and she discovered another kind of envy too. The kind where she could wield a corkscrew or maybe a spatula with the same skill she handled a scalpel.

Gabriel Alexander—*the jerk*—didn't seem to suffer from the same challenges. He drew a bottle of white wine out of the cooler and efficiently uncorked it while he directed her to an overhead cabinet for wine glasses.

"I usually prefer beer," he said. "But good food demands a good wine."

She handed him the glasses. "You're a foodie?"

His eyes crinkled at the corners at her disgruntled tone. "You sound surprised."

She sighed, propped her hip against the nearest cabinet

and folded her arms beneath her breasts. "Not so much surprised as envious," she admitted. "I'm a kitchen klutz." His lips twitched and she narrowed her eyes to dangerous slits because she knew what he was thinking. He was thinking the kitchen wasn't the only place she suffered from klutziness.

He clearly valued his life because he just chuckled and handed her a glass of chilled white wine. "You're a cute klutz, though." Then he stunned her speechless by tracing a line of fire across her lips with his finger before turning away to reach for a bowl and a carton of eggs.

It took her a few moments—okay, minutes—to recover her breath and gulp down a mouthful of crisp Riesling. It jolted her back to reality before warming up her belly and clearing her head.

She offered to chop something but he shook his head and said he was off duty. She didn't know whether to be relieved or offended since he'd probably meant that he'd seen enough blood for one day. *Smartass.*

So Holly sipped her wine and watched him work, which, God knew, wasn't a hardship. It was also kind of hot to see a man so at home in a kitchen.

When she was stressed she liked to bake but her efforts were mostly inedible, which sucked because she loved chocolate-fudge brownies and chocolate-chip cookies. Granted, she made an excellent salad but she was ashamed to say she often just nuked one of the casseroles her mother kept stocked in the freezer for her. It was easier than cleaning up after her disasters.

She licked a drop of wine off the back of her hand, impressed by his one-handed method of cracking eggs into a bowl without adding a ton of shells. *Show-off.* He then went on to chop and sprinkle with quick efficiency until delicious smells filled the kitchen and her stomach set up an almost continuous growl.

Over another glass of wine and light, fluffy harvest omelets that he'd teamed with herbed bruschetta, Gabriel entertained her with stories of his youthful exploits. Holly found herself laughing more than she had in years and soon a warm glow radiated out from the center of her chest. She was flushed and light-headed—like she'd drunk too much champagne or maybe sucked on a little too much helium—and she could scarcely believe that she was sitting in a kitchen with the Hollywood Hatchet Man, actually enjoying herself.

Before she could remind herself that he'd seen countless beautiful and famous women—including her sister—naked or that he'd worked in an industry that was mostly to blame for the low self-esteem of ordinary women like herself, Holly swirled the wine in her glass and looked up, only to become snared by the sleepy heat in his eyes. *Yikes.*

"So what about you?" he asked.

Her laughter died and a palpable tension replaced the friendly mood—a tension that had absolutely nothing to do with her opinions of his former career. She blinked.

It didn't take a genius to know what he was thinking. It was there in the glowing heat of his gaze that set her pulse skittering even as a heavy ache settled between her thighs.

It might have been the wine, knocked back on an empty stomach, but her tongue felt suddenly too thick to form words. And like the night she'd slugged back mojitos, her lips went numb.

For long moments she stared into his eyes, hypnotized, until the thickening tension made it difficult to breathe. She blinked. "I…uh…"

Her voice came to her through a long tunnel and the breathless huskiness of it might have shocked her if she'd been thinking clearly…okay, thinking, period. But for the same reason her mouth couldn't form words, her brain couldn't form thoughts.

In slow motion she licked her dry lips and his gaze dropped to catch the path of her tongue. His eyes darkened and he said her name. "Holly." Just her name, but his voice, rough and deep as sin, scraped her already ragged nerves and she had to gulp in air or pass out.

Her skin gave a warning prickle an instant before her brain melted along with the muscles in her thighs.

"Hmm?" She was in big trouble and for some reason she couldn't seem to drum up the energy to care.

His eyes dipped to half-mast and she could practically feel the enormous control he was exercising over himself. It was there in the tight lines of his face and the sudden stillness of his body, which practically vibrated with tension.

And there was absolutely no mistaking the sensuality in his gaze.

"If you're going to leave," he rasped in a voice she scarcely recognized, "I suggest you do it now."

Feeling dazed and strangely lethargic, Holly sucked in a shuddery breath. "Um…now?" Frankly, she didn't know how he expected her to move. She was frozen to the spot by the laser-bright gaze, the gold flecks swirling in the blue-green depths having stolen her ability to move.

"I'm giving you ten seconds." The warning came as a low deep growl that sent a dark excitement skittering through her blood until her body was practically humming with anticipation.

His gaze darkened—"Nine"—and her pulse gave an excited little blip. Instead of scrambling to her feet and escaping, she continued staring into his eyes, wondering at this odd dark need to ride the edge of danger.

A voice in her head ordered her to move, but her body refused to obey. "And then what?"

He leaned forward until there was barely an inch separating his lips from hers. Fascinated, she stared into the swirling depths of his eyes and was stunned by the intensity burning in their centers. He appeared seconds away from pouncing and a thrill of alarm zinged across her skin.

Dropping her gaze, she found his finely sculpted mouth

almost touching hers. *Oh, God.* He was so close she could already feel the searing imprint of his mouth. She eagerly awaited a kiss she knew was just a heartbeat away.

And when he didn't so much as lean in her direction she was the one to make the move that closed the gap between their mouths. Through the roaring in her head she thought she heard him say, "And then I'm going to drag you over the counter and there'll be no escaping until—"

She froze. "Until?"

She felt him smile against her lips and the sensation of it sent a firestorm of sparks exploding in her brain like fireworks. "Until your eyes roll back in your head and…" Her breath escaped in a shuddery whoosh. "And you forget your plan."

She wondered why he was still talking when all she wanted was for him to grab her and make her eyes roll back in her head. Oh, wait. They'd already rolled back in her head to check out the state of her brain and "My plan? What plan?" popped out of her mouth in a breathless rush. It took a few seconds for her words to finally register. And when they did, her head cleared.

"Oh." She abruptly shoved back from the counter, nearly toppling the stool in her haste. For a breathless moment she stood, swaying, and stared at him with wide, panicked eyes. "I…um, I have to go."

Gabriel made a growling sound deep in his chest that had the hair on her arms lifting like she'd got too close to an electrostatic generator. Spooked by the sensations and the thoughts racing through her head, Holly backed away, turned on her heel and walked blindly into the wall.

"Careful," he murmured, and even without looking she knew he was fighting a smile. She rolled her eyes and altered her course, heading down the passage to the front of the house, suddenly eager to escape. Before she did something she regretted.

Like turn and grab him. Like lose herself in his hungry

caresses or forget that she had a plan that had no room for hot, sexy surgeons.

"I have to go," she repeated, feeling a little dazed and more than a little freaked out. Her ears buzzed and her knees shook so badly it was a miracle they didn't buckle and dump her on her ass.

"I'll see you home." His voice came from right behind her and a wide-eyed look over her shoulder revealed him fighting amusement. *Oh, God, how embarrassing.* She increased her pace until the urgent tap-tap of her heels on the wooden floorboards nearly drowned out her panicked thoughts.

"There's no need," she babbled, as she finally reached the door and tried to tug it open, only to find it locked. "Besides, I'm right next…door and—" emerged on a breathless squeak when she swung around to find him only inches away.

Gabriel regarded her silently for an endless moment before he scooped up her shoulder bag and briefcase. She held out a shaking hand. "I'll see you home," he repeated in a gravelly voice, and reached around her to open the door.

She might have escaped unscathed if she hadn't made the mistake of lifting her gaze off his white T-shirt-covered chest, up past his tanned throat, the hard square jaw and sculpted mouth to his gaze.

She froze.

His pupils were huge and very black, his eyes hot and steamy in his tanned face. More blue than green, they blazed with an emotion that was unmistakable even to a social klutz like her.

For long charged moments their gazes locked until with a savage growl Gabriel kicked the door closed and hauled Holly up against him. And before she could squeak out a protest at the rough treatment, he'd backed her against the door and closed his mouth over hers in a kiss so hot it singed her skin and set her hair on fire.

Ohmigod.

Incredible heat poured off him in waves that engulfed

her, threatening to drag her under and drown her in a flood of heat and urgency. *Help,* she thought an instant before his tongue breached the barrier of her lips, surging into her mouth and stealing her breath. *I'm in trouble.*

His tongue slid against hers and the next instant the kiss turned greedy, his mouth eating hungrily at hers. She moaned and desperation rose along with the heat in his kisses. Any thought of escaping faded.

In fact, if this was trouble she welcomed it, along with the slick slide of his tongue against hers and the warm press of his big hard body.

Fever rose in her blood and her skin prickled with an almost embarrassing need to be touched, a need for his big warm hands to slide over her naked flesh.

He broke off the kiss to feather his lips across her jaw to the delicate skin beneath her ear, leaving Holly fighting for breath and the urge to beg him to hurry. Heat exploded along her nerve endings and she shuddered, her breasts tightening until they ached.

She flattened her palms against his belly; the bunching muscles making her hands itch with the need to explore every hard inch of him, including the long thick evidence of his arousal against her belly.

Unable to resist arching closer, Holly angled her head and "Gabriel…I…um…" emerged on a low moan. She wasn't sure what she'd meant to say, only that a voice, somewhere in the far reaches of her mind, was urging her to get the hell away before it was too late. "I have to…I need to I think I should…"

"Don't," he murmured against her throat, and she murmured in dazed agreement. "Don't think." Nipping at the slender column, he drew her skin into his mouth, soothing the small hurt when she uttered a tiny shocked gasp. "Feel, Holly. Just…feel."

Okay, so that was doable. Besides, thinking took too much effort, especially with his mouth, hot and wet as it dragged across her skin, making secret hidden flesh respond with tiny spasmodic clenches.

She stiffened. *Oh, God.* He'd yanked her right to the edge so fast she was fighting to keep from exploding right out of her skin.

Then he was taking her mouth again in a hungry kiss, thrusting a hard thigh between hers and pressing his erection into the notch at the top of her thighs. His big hands slid to her hips, his fingers sinking into her soft flesh as he ground against her, groaning like he was in pain. And before she could give voice to the fiery need clawing at her belly, his muscles bunched and she found herself lifted off her feet.

Instinctively wrapping her legs around his hips, Holly clutched at his shoulders. Muscles shifted beneath her hands, a solid anchor in a world suddenly whirling with chaotic hunger, ragged breathing and wild exhilaration.

Her hair, a dark silky nimbus, floated around their heads. Somehow he'd unraveled her hair with the same ease that he'd unraveled her defenses.

"Hold on," he said, pushing away from the door to stand swaying for a couple of beats, breath sawing from his heaving lungs like he'd crossed the Brooklyn Bridge at a dead run.

"Wha-at?" Holly's lashes fluttered up and she stared at him uncomprehendingly. Without replying, he turned toward the sitting room, cursing when his foot caught on something and he staggered. She squeaked and tightened her grip and his muttered curse of "Damn boxes" became a soothing growl. "Don't worry," he murmured against her mouth between kisses. "I won't let you fall."

CHAPTER EIGHT

HOLLY HAD A brief thought that it was too late for that. Way too late to prevent her heart from getting bruised by a man as handsome and flawless as his celestial namesake.

Then a couple feet beyond the door his knees connected with something solid and the next instant she found herself literally falling. She sucked in a startled breath, tightened her grip, and before she could squeak out a protest she was on her back with Gabe's big body sprawled over the top of hers.

"Oomph."

"Sorry," he breathed beside her ear. "You're heavier than I expected."

"Or maybe," she retorted, unable to prevent the pleased grin from forming when she turned her head to give his earlobe a punishing nip and a groan accompanied the shudder moving through him, "you're not as manly as you think."

His response was an explosive snort that questioned her sanity.

"Oh, yeah?" he breathed, his teeth flashing white in the near darkness as he levered himself onto his elbows. The move pressed his hips closer, setting off an explosion of starbursts behind her eyes. "I'll show you manly."

She groaned, as much at the typically macho statement as the feel of him, long and thick and incredibly hard as he pressed tightly against her crotch. Suspended in sensation and every nerve ending firing simultaneously, it was more than she could handle. More than she could ever remember feeling. And just as a glimmer of panic threatened to break free of the haze of need and greed clouding her brain, Gabriel smoothed a hand from her bottom down the long length of her femur to her knee and back again.

"God, you have no idea how much I want you," he murmured, leaning forward to run his tongue from the corner of her mouth to the sweet spot beneath her ear.

But Holly did, and in response her core melted and clenched in anticipation.

He rose up onto his knees with a low, thrilling growl and reached for the back of his T-shirt, yanking it over his head in one smooth move that left Holly speechless. And not just from the speed of his actions.

His torso was a marvel of masculine perfection that she couldn't help but reach out and touch. She wanted to see him. Wanted to explore his physical perfection with her hands and her mouth.

Unable to stop herself, she slid her hands over his skin, reveling in the tanned skin, taut and smooth across his hard, ridged flesh. His skin was slightly damp beneath her questing fingers as muscles bunched and rippled at her touch.

Light spilled from the foyer, surrounding his darkened form like a full-body halo, and the image of a golden angel, fallen to earth to tempt mortal women to sin, returned. And, *darn it*, she was more than ready to become one of the fallen right alongside.

He was a beautiful man and for a blinding moment of panic she wondered what he was doing with her—what he would say when he saw the rest of her scars, especially the ugly one marring the length of her thigh. But then he fumbled, his hands shaking in his haste to undress, and she realized that she'd made him tremble. Her touch had made him shake like a boy.

It was a little overwhelming.

Then he was unbuttoning his fly. Her eyes widened along with every inch that became exposed and suddenly overwhelming was nothing compared to the sight of him.

"Wha-what are you doing?"

He looked up, his teeth gleaming in the near darkness. He took in her wide-eyed expression and rasped out an incredulous laugh. "Well, Doc," he managed roughly. "This is what's called getting naked. It's what happens before a man pulls out—"

Holly squeaked and slapped her hands over her ears in a move that belied her professional status. Gabriel's eyebrows almost disappeared into his hairline and he leaned forward to pull one of her hands free. "I was going to say protection, Dr. Buchanan," he finished dryly.

She gulped and fought the blush heating her face. "But… but we're in the sitting room."

He sent an indifferent glance across his shoulder at the huge bay window before turning back to renew his button attack. "I can't wait," he growled, lifting her up so he could strip off her jacket.

Her breath hitched at the impatience in his voice, his every jerky movement, and felt her core quiver in anticipation of the big event. "But…the curtains."

"No one can see you." He shoved the jeans down his legs and kicked them aside, settling back to study the lacy shell molded to her curves. "Besides, it's dark."

Not that dark, Holly thought. *You'll see me.* And, oh, boy, she could see him too.

"That's the point," he murmured in a voice as rough and deep as sin, telling her she'd spoken her thoughts out loud. "I can't wait to get you all the way naked so I can see you."

That's exactly what she didn't want.

"All of you, Holly." He dropped his hands to the hem of her shell, his fingers brushing the bare flesh of her belly. It quivered. "And then," he promised in a wicked whisper,

"I'm going to take you upstairs and I'm going to start all... over...again."

Her splutter of surprise ended on a gasp when he whipped her shell over her head and dropped it on the floor beside the sofa. She tried to shield herself from his gaze but he grabbed her wrists to prevent her from hiding.

Finally his eyes lifted and locked on hers. Holly sucked in a sharp breath as heat rose up her neck into her face along with the heat heading for her core. "Gabriel," she whispered beseechingly, but he leaned forward to trace a shaking finger across the tops of her breasts, interrupting her with a growl of appreciation when her nipples peaked.

"Don't hide, Holly."

She turned her face away. "You're...um...staring."

His chuckle was a deep velvet slide across her senses that made her quiver. "God, yes," he drawled. "You're so damn beautiful." And then quietly, as though he was talking to himself, he murmured, "More beautiful than I remember."

Her mouth dropped open and for a moment she wondered if he was hallucinating or drunk. Her words rushed out on a rising squeak of outrage. "You saw me naked? Wh-when?"

His hands soothed a fiery path up her arms to her shoulders where he slid his fingers beneath the lacy straps of her bra. "That black swimsuit doesn't hide a damn thing." He grinned, tugging them down over her shoulders.

Her mouth open and closed a couple times and he shook his head, although Holly wasn't sure what it meant.

"My plan..." she began breathlessly, but he leaned down and gave her a hard kiss.

"Will still be there tomorrow."

"Well, okay, then..." she murmured against his mouth. "I guess just this once...won't...um...hurt. Will it?"

"No." His voice shook with laughter. "I promise it won't hurt." Then his hands slid back over her shoulders. His knuckles brushed her collarbone as he moved to the tops of her breasts. It was difficult to read his expression.

Heck. It was difficult to think.

Then she stopped caring because his sensual mouth slid to her throat and his hand slid beneath the layer of stretchy lace to cup her bare breast. Her shocked breath was loud in the heavy silence and shudders of pleasure leapt and grew at the feel of his warm calloused hand cupping and squeezing her gently, his thumb scraping a line of fire across her flesh.

Her nipples tightened into hard points and she couldn't prevent a moan from escaping at the exquisite pain. Her back arched, the move pushing her breast into his warm, rough palm. Her hands moved across his shoulders, up his neck to fist his warm silky hair, pulling him closer…closer to where his mouth could close over her nipple and soothe the terrible ache he'd created.

If she'd been thinking she might have been horrified by her wanton behavior, but she wasn't…couldn't…because within seconds Gabriel had stripped her naked and the sound he uttered, a mix of pain and strangled laughter that came from deep in his chest, made her ache. And thrill. *God, what a thrill!*

Before she could get self-conscious or beg him to press his naked body to hers, he leaned down and placed a soft kiss on each breast. She trembled at the tenderness of the gesture and when he drew one peak into his mouth, his tongue sliding across her nipple, hot and wet and relentless, a ragged moan tore loose from deep in her throat.

He lifted his head. "Your heart is pounding." She blinked up into his face but his expression was hidden in shadow and she couldn't tell what he was thinking.

"What?"

His eyes were dark and fathomless. "Tell me you want me."

Oh, God. "Wha-a-at?"

"Say it and I'll give you what you need."

Holly sucked in a breath. "I…I…" For some reason she couldn't get the words past the hot lump of need in her throat. He lowered his head and gave her nipple a tiny punishing nip and the words finally escaped on a rush of air. "Ohmigodiwantyou."

And then, tired of waiting, Holly reached up and with hands fisted in his soft hair brought his mouth down to hers so she could kiss him, reveling in the ragged groan wrenched from deep within his chest. She loved the way he kissed; like he was starving for the taste of her. She was starving for the taste of him too and the kiss became an avaricious frenzy of mouths and tongues and grasping hands. And when Gabe shifted and thrust into her, Holly arched her back and begged for more.

Holly begged for more and Gabriel gave her more. More kisses, more climaxes and more...everything. He'd given her more than he'd given any woman in a long time. Maybe ever. And when it was over and she lay in a boneless heap across his chest, Gabe wondered what the hell had happened.

What had started out as simply satisfying a physical need had taken on a life of its own until he'd felt a desperation to take her someplace she'd never been. The only thing was—he'd been taken there too. And he wasn't entirely comfortable with the discovery.

They were both damp with exertion and his thundering pulse almost drowned out the sound of her ragged breathing.

Or was that his ragged breathing?

He felt completely wrung out and too lethargic to move them somewhere more comfortable. Like his bed.

He had plans for Holly and his bed.

After a few minutes, he groaned and lifted a large hand to soothe a line from her shoulder, down her back to her bottom. She was soft and silky and so touchable he couldn't resist repeating the move until she murmured in the back of her throat and shifted against him, so slowly and sinuously that he went instantly hard.

"Someone stole my bones while we were busy," he murmured sleepily, smiling when she grunted softly against his skin.

"Are you sure? I think I feel at least one they left behind," she murmured, her breath tickling his chest and sending arrows of heat into his groin, hardening his erection and fueling his hunger. "If they hadn't also stolen mine I'd help you find it."

She sighed sleepily and nuzzled closer. He slid his arms around her and nudged her closer, burying his face in her wild hair and breathing in her unique scent. It was warm and fresh with a hint of something elusive. Kind of like the woman herself.

Realizing he was breathing in a woman like she was his air, Gabe stilled. He'd never been a nuzzler. Or a cuddler, for that matter. He was usually looking for his clothes by now, ready to make his escape. But he didn't want to escape. In fact, he wanted to find the source of that scent and was prepared to spend the rest of the night searching for it.

He'd thought once would be enough. He'd rock her world, walk her home and go back to getting his life on track. *Hell.* Hadn't she been the one to put a limit on this?

And he'd been okay with that. Surprisingly, only a few minutes had passed since he'd climaxed but he was already gearing up for round two.

Clearly he wasn't done with her yet.

"Damn New York thieves."

Her mouth curved against his skin. "What makes you certain they were from New York? Maybe they followed you from California."

"Yeah, and maybe you need to move your knee before you cut off my blood supply."

She snickered and gently shifted her knee until he swore he saw stars. He grunted and grabbed her thigh to halt her movement. She said, "Oops, sorry," in a voice that didn't sound very sincere. "Guess I found that bone." Then she yawned and stretched all those silky curves against him and the stars became firebursts of renewed lust.

"I guess it's also time to go," she murmured sleepily. "Make me go, Gabriel."

He didn't like the idea of her leaving. "Not yet," he said, wrapping his arms around her and heaving up off the couch where he stood swaying for a few beats while he waited for blood to reach his brain. "Later."

Much later.

Holly didn't know how she'd ended up in Gabe's bed. He'd hauled her into the shower, soaped every inch of her and then ensured she'd been completely soap-free with his hands and mouth. And when she'd been a boneless lump he'd wrapped her up in a huge towel and lifted her in his arms.

"And now," he growled in a voice as deep and rough as if he'd just awakened from a night of sin, "I'm taking you to bed."

The thought of getting to explore his big body sent tingles of anticipation racing over Holly's flesh. They'd been too desperate earlier to do more than race for the finish and Holly wanted to explore his big, brawny body with more than her hands. She wanted to use her mouth and tongue and eyes to explore every last inch of him. Her mouth watered.

Oh, and she wanted to discover the rest of him too.

He tossed her roughly on the bed, following her down to nip her shoulder lightly, chuckling when goose-bumps raced over her damp skin. Instead of ravishing her, like she'd thought—okay, hoped—he stretched across her body to pull out an unopened box of condoms from the bedside table.

"I thought you said you didn't have any," she said a little breathlessly, and reached out to untie the towel hiding his goodies from her.

Gabriel snorted out a laugh. "I lied."

"Some Boy Scout you are."

"I lied about that too," he admitted, straddling her body

and unwrapping her like she was an unexpected gift he'd found on his pillow. "I was too busy impressing the girls with my awesome skills." He chuckled at her expression and leaned forward to plant a lightning fast kiss on her mouth. "I meant in surfing." He fumbled with the box. "Damn it," he snarled, "I can't open this thing."

By this time he was panting and swearing and when Holly tried to help, the box popped open and silver squares flew everywhere. Gabe simply snatched one, planted a big hand in the middle of her chest and shoved her backwards. Holly gave a breathless laugh and before she could tell him to hurry, he'd covered himself and was sliding between her legs.

"Now, Dr. Buchanan," he growled, "I'm going to rock your world. Again."

Holly's skeptical snort ended on a long, low moan as he thrust into her, her body stretching deliciously as it accommodated his size.

Oh, God, he totally had, was her last conscious thought. *He'd totally rocked her world.*

Holly jerked awake with no idea of the time or where she was. One thing she did know was that something heavy pinned her to the bed. Something heavy, slightly hairy and toasty warm.

She frowned sleepily and stretched, wondering at the slight ache in her muscles. Like she'd spent the night in… rigorous…exercise… *Oh…my…God*, she thought, sucking in a sharp breath as recollection returned in a rush of heat and embarrassment and…and… *What the heck have I done?*

For several long seconds she lay there, not breathing, until a firm voice in the back of her head told her to get her butt into gear.

Exhaling shakily, she took stock of the situation and tried not to panic. But despite the overwhelming urge to jump up and run screaming from Gabriel's house, she couldn't help noticing the large body surrounding her like a living blanket.

Fine. So one would think that she'd noticed enough of that big, muscular body in the hours they'd spent… Yes, well, she wasn't going to think about that now. If she did she might lose it or…or jump his bones…again.

Kind of like she'd done in the deep, dark hours of the night.

Her face flamed. And when something else flamed deep in her belly, it galvanized her into action.

Holding her breath, she carefully slid out from beneath his sprawling body and felt cool air brush her exposed skin. She shivered. It was touch and go there for a while when every strand of DNA urged her to slide back against the heated furnace while instinct told her to get the heck out of Dodge.

Besides, they'd agreed. One time only. So maybe it had stretched to two and then three…*gulp*…but it was still one night.

Right? Her breath escaped in long whoosh. Right.

She made the mistake of looking over her shoulder at him and got stuck on the stark beauty of his long swim-mer's body, sprawled face-down across the huge bed and il-luminated by the light spilling from the bathroom. His back was a marvel of masculine perfection, the wide, powerful shoulders tapering to narrow hips, a tight butt—with those sexy little scoops at the sides—and long muscular legs end-ing in large brawny feet.

For one yearning moment she fought against the desire to reach out and touch but then he grunted and shifted as though he missed her already—boy, she could identify—and the instinct to flee returned.

Stifling a little squeak of panic, Holly slid off the bed and headed for the door. Her clothes were still downstairs—scattered all over his sitting room. *Yikes*.

She paused at the bedroom door, wondering if she should

wake him, but the thought of facing him after everything they'd done was just too disturbing. And considering where he'd had his mouth not too long ago—okay, and where she'd had hers—the last thing she needed was looking into his blue-green gaze and seeing knowledge and…awareness.

She'd rather run through the streets naked. Something she might have to do if she couldn't find her damn clothes.

Turning, she hobbled down the stairs in the dark, wondering where the heck all these aching muscles had come from. She stubbed her toe on her way into the sitting room and hopped on one foot as she hunted around for her clothes, pulling on items as she found them.

After a fruitless search for her underwear, she huffed out an impatient breath and swiftly buttoned her jacket over her unbound breasts. *Damn it*. She felt like everyone would know it too but the longer she lingered, the more chance there was of Gabriel waking and— And that was the absolute last thing she wanted.

So she'd have to ditch her underwear. Darn. And it was new too.

She knew she'd have to face Gabriel sometime but as for right this minute? No way in hell was she sticking around to find her panties and bra. Besides, glossing over someone's scars while in the grip of a desperate hunger was one thing, looking into his eyes in the cold aftermath of a hot night was something else entirely.

No. Not gonna happen. She'd rather lose her underwear and hope they'd disappeared altogether. Poof. Into thin air.

Grabbing her strappy heels, she headed into the foyer, where he'd dropped her briefcase and shoulder bag what seemed like days ago rather than a few short hours. Then with a quick guilty glance over her shoulder she quietly let herself out of the house.

Her one night of screaming exercise was over.

Time to get back on track.

It took her less than a minute to hightail it to her own

front door, all the while looking around guiltily and wishing she didn't feel like an errant adolescent sneaking in after curfew.

She let herself in and quietly thunked her forehead against the door a couple times, her breath escaping in a whoosh of relief and for some reason fighting the urge to cry. Damn it, what the heck was wrong with—?

"Long night?"

Holly gave a startled squeak and whirled so fast she nearly fell over. She backed against the door to give her shaky knees much-needed support and stared wide-eyed at Sam, slouched casually in the sitting-room doorway, watching her over the top of his mug.

He was dressed in a pair of unbuttoned jeans...and nothing else. Just a few months ago the sight of his sculpted chest would have sent her heart racing and her tongue swelling in her throat. But now all she wanted to do was run and hide and maybe freak out, because she'd seen Gabriel Alexander's awesome body and no one else could compare.

Sam's dark eyes took in her rumpled appearance and his expression turned wry. "Ah," he drawled, and lifted his mug in a silent toast.

Holly didn't need any interpretation of the brief flash of amusement but she opened her mouth and "What?" popped out before she could stop it.

"Really?" he murmured, his eyes going unerringly to her mouth then dropping to her neck before lifting to lock gazes with her. Beneath the humor was understanding. "You want to go there?"

Holly assumed an innocent expression. "I don't know what you're talking about."

"You bailed, Buchanan."

Guilt flashed like a neon light behind her eyes.

"I...uh...pfft... No."

"It's okay, Holly," he interrupted quietly, his eyes going oddly flat. "We've all done it." And then without another word he turned and disappeared, leaving Holly battling curiosity, embarrassment and a desire to go pull the covers over her head and hope that when she woke she'd find it had all been a horrible dream.

An image flashed into her head of Gabriel's expression as he rose over her and she got a full-body flush and shiver all at once.

Okay. Maybe not so horrible.

CHAPTER NINE

LIGHT STREAMED IN through the cracks in the curtain and fell across Gabe's face. He groaned and tried to lift his head but he felt like someone had run over him with a compacting roller—the ones they used on golfing greens—leaving him flattened.

Almost immediately he realized what had woken him. Firstly, his pager and his cellphone were both buzzing angrily in his ear, and secondly…his bed was cool and empty.

The buzzing was an annoying reminder that he needed to get to the hospital, but the latter…hell, he didn't know what to think. Only that he wasn't happy that she'd left without waking him—especially with the smell of her still clinging to his pillow and sheets.

He turned and sniffed his shoulder.

And his skin, damn it.

Rolling over, he grabbed his phone and told himself it was a good thing because now he wouldn't have to deal with any morning-after expectations. He just hadn't pegged Holly for the hit-and-run type. But what did he really know about her other than she wore class and refinement like a shield, and that she hated being stared at?

She was just another woman, he reminded himself, and he'd learned a long time ago that he wasn't cut out for more than a good time. It was coded into his genes.

Besides, she'd been the one to say this was a one-time thing and one-time things were his specialty.

He growled, "Yeah?" into the phone and listened to the nurse on the other end then ended the call. Then he rolled off the bed and headed for the bathroom. His day promised to be a whirlwind of surgeries and meetings, and with the information the nurse had just given him, he might just have to alter his schedule.

He arrived in ICU just as Holly was leaving. Her stride faltered when she saw him but even though she greeted him, she avoided his gaze. If he hadn't seen the wild tide of color surging beneath her creamy skin he might have thought she'd forgotten his existence the instant she'd walked out his front door.

But it was the sight of her, once again coolly elegant, that made him want to push her up against the wall and mess her up a little. Starting with her hair, which was pulled into a neat French twist.

She hadn't seemed to mind so much last night, he told himself, recalling with perfect clarity the dark, silky curtain framing her face and brushing against his skin as she'd memorized every inch of his body with her mouth.

Just that fast he was hard—harder than he'd been last night. Harder than he'd ever been, because now he knew that beneath the prim little suits and cool, professional mask was an incredibly enthusiastic woman eager to give as much as she received.

"Holly—" he began.

But she interrupted him with a hasty "Excuse me, Dr. Alexander, but I'm needed in surgery," leaving him gaping at her straight spine and swaying hips as she disappeared down the passage with an urgent tap, tap, tap of those sexy slingbacks.

What the—?

"Dr. Alexander?"

Gabe turned to see the head of ICU pop her head out the door. "Yeah?"

"We need you."

Yeah, well. Looks like you're the only one.

He sighed and shoved a hand through his hair, wondering if he'd lost his mind. Here he was, standing staring after a woman who'd made it abundantly clear that he was a one-time deal and... *Hell*. He shoved a hand through his hair again and blew out a frustrated breath. What the heck did he think he was going to do when...*if*...he caught up with her? Grab her? Push her up against the wall and kiss her until she moaned and looked at him through dazed, smoky eyes?

Jeez.

"I'm all yours," he sighed.

And chuckled when the older woman pretended to swoon and muttered a heartfelt "If only," before disappearing back into ICU.

Yeah, he thought dryly. If only. If only his one-night stand hadn't managed to rock his world. Three times.

Realizing he was standing around, obsessing about a woman who wasn't interested in a repeat, Gabe scowled and shoved through the doors, wondering when the hell he'd turned into such a damn girl.

Holly practically ran from ICU as if the paparazzi were in pursuit after an anonymous tip-off. Her skin burned with the mortification of having to face him so soon after...well, so soon. Because, frankly? She'd like to forget last night had ever happened.

Good luck with that.

"Oh, be quiet," she snarled to the annoying snicker in her head, startling a couple of nurses passing her in the hallway. They gave her strange looks but Holly was accustomed to people staring so she ignored them and headed for the nearest bathroom.

Once she made sure she was alone, she headed for the

basins and flipped on the cold water. Breathing like she'd stepped out and found herself at five thousand feet, she splashed her face until her ears stopped ringing and she didn't feel like her head was about to pop off her shoulders.

She made the mistake of looking into the mirror and nearly gave herself a stroke when she encountered her smoky, heavy-lidded gaze. *Ohmigod, I look like I just got lucky.*

A low sound emerged from her throat that sounded too much like a whimper for Holly's peace of mind. Her gaze dropped unerringly to her bruised, swollen lips and she recalled with absolute clarity the way Gabriel kissed. He'd consumed her like she was a rare delicacy he was determined to savor…as if his very life depended on it. A shiver of remembered delight skated up her spine. As if that light suction was an invitation to surrender, her soul along with her body.

Realizing she was hyperventilating, Holly splashed herself again. She didn't think she could walk out of this bathroom and not have people look at her without them knowing exactly what she'd been up to.

Groaning, she grabbed a wad of paper towels from the dispenser just as the door opened. Hoping it wasn't anyone she knew, Holly began patting her face dry.

"Holly?"

She froze. Oh, God. It had to be Tess, didn't it? Tess would see at a glance that she was a total mess.

"Are you okay?"

Sucking in a steadying breath, Holly met her gaze in the mirror, casually patting her skin dry. "Sure," she croaked. "Why?"

Tess moved closer. "Kimberlyn said she saw you tear out of the house this morning as though your underwear was on fire. Did something happen?"

At the mention of her underwear, Holly gave a strangled gurgle that she tried to cover up by coughing. Had something happened? Where to start? Forget that her underwear had practically caught fire—which was why it was currently gracing Gabriel's sitting room. Somewhere.

"No." Not going there.

The next instant Tessa was whipping her around, her eyes concerned as she took in Holly's expression.

"Oh, honey, what's wrong?" she urged. "It is your mother? Father?" Her concern abruptly turned to a gasp when she caught sight of Holly's neck. *"Ohmigod."* Her eyes widened with shock. "You've got a…*hickey*?"

"No! Jeez." Holly slapped a hand over the offending mark she'd discovered this morning—along with at least three others in embarrassing places—when she'd stripped in the bathroom, intending to wash away every trace of the night.

"It is." Tessa looked absolutely delighted by the sight. "It so is a hickey." She grabbed Holly's hand. "Let me see."

Holly squeaked and slapped her free hand over the mark. "Damn it, Tess." She covered her flaming face with her free hand and groaned. "What are we, in high school?"

"Oh, come on." Tessa spluttered with laughter. "Let the pregnant woman have her way or she'll get all hormonal on your ass." Then seeing the embarrassed misery on Holly's face she froze, her eyes going soft and concerned again.

"Oh, honey, why the long face? It's supposed to relax you, not make you tense enough to shatter."

Holly ignored her statement because she felt as though one wrong move and she'd— "I didn't mean for it to happen," she wailed helplessly as she pulled at her collar and turned to study the mark on her neck. There was another high on the inside of her thigh, one in the crease separating her hip and thigh and one—fine, two—on her breasts.

She blushed.

"Did the bastard say something about your scars?" Tessa demanded. "I hope you punched his—"

"N-no-o." Holly spluttered out a strangled laugh. "He didn't. He really didn't," she repeated, recalling exactly what he done to every single one of the blemishes marring her skin. With his lips and tongue.

Tessa's gaze turned sympathetic. "Oh, God, it was awful. Is that it?"

"Will you just stop?" Holly spluttered out on a mortified laugh. "No, it wasn't awful, it was…um…fine." By this time she wanted to climb into the basin and drown herself. Instead, she opened the faucet again, this time burying her burning face in her water-filled cupped hands, hoping Tess would just go away.

So, okay, it had been more than fine. Try spectacular. Amazing. Incredible.

And it was over.

Tessa was still there to hand over a wad of paper towels. Holly muttered her thanks and sent her friend a narrow-eyed sideways glance when her mouth twitched. Tessa quickly lifted a hand to hide her smile.

"Okay, so it was…*fine*," her friend said agreeably, but her voice wobbled as though she was fighting laughter. "Then why are you so…um…upset?"

Holly sucked in a breath and—*thank God*—was saved from replying by a sudden beeping. Whipping out her pager, she glanced at the screen. "I've got to go," she said apologetically, hugely relieved because she had absolutely no idea why she was freaking out and even less idea of how to explain it.

She dropped the wadded paper towels into the trash and headed for the door, yanking it open so fast she nearly bopped herself on the nose.

"I want details, Dr. Buchanan," Tessa called out, and a horrified Holly sent her a you-have-got-to-be-kidding-me glance over her shoulder. She left Tessa standing in the doorway of the bathroom with a secret smile.

Holly managed to avoid Gabriel for a whole week. And it wasn't easy. First, by being so busy she barely had time to think, and, second, by peeping out the bay window to see if the coast was clear before bolting from the house.

The nights? Well, she hadn't been so lucky there. Now that she knew where Gabriel's bedroom was located she realized they shared a wall. A wall that gave her endless nightmares—okay, sleepless nights—and really, *really* hot dreams that made her blush when she thought about them.

It was like her mind had...well, a mind of its own, emerging at night to torment her with images she was able to control during the day. Fine. Mostly control.

Besides, she'd known him, what...six weeks? And for most of that time she'd gone out of her way to avoid him. For most of that time she'd considered him the Hollywood Hatchet Man.

"I won't let you fall," he'd said. But he'd lied. Because Holly was in danger of doing just that and there would be no one to catch her. Fortunately for her, now that she knew the danger she could protect herself by continuing to avoid him like a tax audit.

Good idea.

No problem.

No problem at all.

"How's that working out?"

Holly's head shot up. "What?" She blinked at Dr. Syu over the final stages of the tissue expansion procedure they were performing on a snakebite patient.

"You said 'No problem at all,' and attacked that scar tissue like it's a blight on the butt of humanity."

"Just thinking out loud," she lied, returning her attention to what her hands were doing. Good idea to focus on what your hands are doing, Holly, instead of thinking about "it"...*oh, God*...and him.

Holly finally completed the task of reattaching the expanded skin over the wound and was stripping off her surgical gown.

"Great job as usual, everyone," Lin Syu called as she hurried for the exit. "Holly, go home, get some rest and work out those issues you're having with yourself. The noises in your head are starting to show."

An hour later, she was heading out, exhausted and seriously considering sleeping for the next few days—which she had off.

Her mother had called that morning, inviting her home for the weekend, ostensibly to talk about the charity ball, but Holly knew Delia had other motives. Like casually introducing some unattached guy she just happened to invite—along with a bunch of other people—to her father's birthday dinner.

She planned on showing up for dinner but there was no way—no way in hell—she was getting sucked into her mother's machinations, no matter how well intentioned.

Scrolling through messages and emails that had backed up over the past few days, Holly strode through the automatic doors and barely escaped colliding with a brick wall. Her gasp turned into a muffled shriek when the wall spun around and she caught a glimpse of surprised green-blue eyes.

He must have anticipated another graceful Holly moment—which was ridiculous considering both her feet were once again firmly planted on the ground—because warm fingers wrapped around her wrist and he yanked her against him, hard enough to knock a startled "Omph" from her.

For long moments she stared at the small white button an inch from the tip of her nose and tried not to notice that she was pressed up against the very chest, belly and hard thighs—*oh, boy*—that she'd spent the past week trying not to think about.

And failing spectacularly.

After a couple of beats she lifted her gaze up his throat and square jaw, shadowed with a day's growth of stubble, to his sculpted lips, where she got caught. Her mouth watered. One corner curled with what she knew was amusement at her clumsiness and she had to seriously tear her gaze away or end up drooling like an idiot.

"Good evening, Dr. Buchanan. Fancy bumping into you," he drawled, his deep, intimate voice sending shards of longing arrowing into places that should have gone back into hibernation. Should have, darn it. But hadn't.

Lifting her gaze almost reluctantly, her breath caught at the heat burning in the blue-green depths. Heat, irony and... and an odd emotion she would have sworn was loneliness. It flashed for an instant and then was gone and she was left wondering if she'd imagined it.

Lonely? Dr. Celebrity? *Phfft!* Yeah, right. There were probably a hundred women waiting this very minute for him to turn that sexy, sleepy look their way.

Wrestling with the shocking notion, she managed a strangled "Oh" and stared up at him, wondering why it felt like her chest was being squeezed by a giant fist. Finally realizing she was holding her breath and fisting his pristine dress shirt like she was afraid she would fall at his feet if she let go, Holly unclenched her fingers one by one and slowly exhaled.

She dropped her gaze to where her hands were flattened against his chest and tried unsuccessfully to smooth the wrinkled cotton. The muscles beneath her hand hardened and the raw sound he made, low and deep in his chest, had her gaze flying upwards. His eyes turned black and he sucked in a sharp breath as if he was struggling to control some pretty powerful inclinations. Inclinations she was fighting as well.

Realizing she was stroking his chest, she gave a bleat of distress and used her flattened palms to shove away from him. Okay, so she tried to shove away, but Gabriel's arms tightened and every part of her pressed against him did a happy celebratory dance—especially the parts that could feel *his* very substantial parts...part.

She made a helpless sound that she wanted to bite back

the instant it emerged. He growled out a ragged "Holly" and her head went light and her belly clenched at the rough, raw sound.

It scraped against her jangled nerves, making her shiver. A full-body shiver he couldn't help but notice. He cleared his throat and slid a fiery visual path across her features. "You've been avoiding me." There was accusation in his tone if not in his eyes—which were soaking her up like a sponge.

Guilt sneaked up on her and she blurted out, "Wha—? No…I—" His permanently arched brow rose up his forehead, the very move chiding her blatant lie. "It's just that… I…um." She broke off on a ragged breath and cast around in panic for a believable excuse. But she'd never been particularly good at lying. "It was a one-time thing," she reminded him weakly. "I just thought it would be easier if we didn't…I mean… Oh, God…help me out here."

"Have dinner with me."

The quiet request—that seemed not so much a request as a command—startled her. She cautiously eased herself out of his arms and drew in a lungful of air that smelled only faintly of him. *Thank God.* Plastered up against him, all she'd been able to smell had been something dark and masculine. Something that had hit her brain like a blast of pheromones and had made her sway dizzily, and when he reached out to steady her, she backed up like a startled deer.

She lifted a hand to her spinning head. "Dinner?"

Looking somewhat baffled by her behavior, he shoved his hands into his trouser pockets and stared at her, his normally wicked gaze solemn and a little brooding.

After a couple of beats, his mouth twisted into a wry smile that reminded her of that momentary flash of loneliness she sometimes saw.

"Yeah. You know. Dinner. Where two people walk into a restaurant, sit down, order wine and a meal and then…."

He paused for a moment and just looked at her. Before

Holly could stop herself, an image of what would happen "then" popped into her head and she actually blushed. And because he wasn't blind or stupid, his eyes lit with amusement and those darn dimples made their appearance, stealing her bones and her breath.

"And then we talk."

A frisson of panic skittered up her spine. Oh, God, that was almost worse than what she'd been thinking. Almost but not quite. Because she had no intention of going "there" with him again. She was back to focusing on the fellowship and her future, neither of which had room for hunky surgeons with sexy dimples.

She nervously licked her lips and sent him a wary look. "About what?"

"About why you bailed without at least thanking me."

She blinked. "Wh-a-at?"

"And letting me thank you."

"Uh…thank you?"

He inclined his head and studied her through narrowed eyes that gleamed with a host of emotions she couldn't read. "Yep. And then we're going to talk about you."

"We are?"

"We're going to be working closely together," he pointed out quietly. "And the tension between us is bound to cause gossip I'm sure you'd rather avoid."

She sighed and swallowed the instinctive urge to say she had other plans. Which might have been the truth but if she told him she had a date with her bed, he might offer to join her there. Maybe. Or maybe he was happy with the whole "This is just a one-off thing" and just needed some friendly company.

"Fine," she said a little impatiently, but it was mostly at herself for feeling a bit insulted by his "Then we talk" comment.

Abruptly realizing that she'd dropped her cellphone, Holly sighed and turned. She really had to stop doing this.

Suspiciously quiet, Gabriel bent to retrieve it.

"What?" she demanded, when hooded eyes continued to watch as she shoved it into her purse. He shook his head, a small smile teasing the corners of his mouth as he lifted a hand and tucked a dark, errant strand of hair behind her ear.

The move, the feel of his fingertips brushing her skin, sent a shiver of longing through her. A longing so powerful that even as her nipples peaked and her breath hitched in her throat, she experienced a moment of panic. Damn it. This was precisely what she'd wanted to avoid. Being reminded of what she was missing by the "this-is-a-one-off-thing" promise she'd made.

"Any preferences?"

"For?"

An image popped into her head about preferences and she had to bite back the urge to tell him she'd liked…loved… everything he'd done. So much so that she couldn't stop thinking about him…it.

Realizing she was having hot, racy thoughts while he'd been talking about food, Holly ducked her head to hide the heat crawling up her neck into her face.

Gabriel's warm hand curled around her neck and his thumb slid beneath her chin. Very gently he lifted her face. His expression was filled with simmering heat and gentle humor. "Dinner, Holly. Just dinner. Tonight I need a friend."

After the day from hell, Gabriel had honestly planned for *just* dinner. But that had been before he'd sat across a candlelit table from her and watched her expressive face go through a host of emotions he got dizzy trying to identify. She gradually relaxed enough to smile and laugh at his stories while sharing a little of her childhood—of herself.

"Tell me about the accident," he said, when it was clear that she wasn't going to go there without some prompting from him.

Her laughter faded and he tried not to feel bad. He had

a feeling her plan to avoid everything but her career had
something to do with whatever had happened to her.

She dropped her gaze to the tablecloth and fiddled with
first the silverware and then her wineglass until he reached
out and took her hand in his. Her fingers jerked and a fine
tremor went through them.

For long moments she stared at their hands, hers delicate
and pale against the tanned bulk of his. Finally she slid her
hand away and reached for her wineglass again, downing
the contents.

Face pale, she cleared her throat and, still not looking at
him, she said, so quietly that he had to strain to hear her,
"I was with a few friends at a mall and the company contracted to service the elevators had a reputation for cutting
corners. Their maintenance schedule was forged and the
elevators hadn't been checked in nearly a year."

She drew in a deep breath. "Well, apparently there was
some malfunction that had been reported but ignored. Anyway, I…um, left my friends in the music store to go up a
couple of levels to the book store and took the glass elevator
because the escalators were out. On the way down I had the
misfortune of picking an elevator that a noisy group of boys
followed me into. The instant the doors closed they started
jumping up and down, trying to frighten me."

Recalling her terror and claustrophobia, Holly paused to
suck in a couple of breaths. She hated talking about it and
only had nightmares when she was stressed.

"Little bastards," Gabriel muttered, and when Holly lifted
her head she caught the hard light in his eyes. Strangely,
that angry glitter on her behalf steadied her as sympathy
could not.

"They were just kids," she excused, recalling that one of
the boys had paid for that stupidity with his life. She lifted
her hand in a vague gesture at her scars. "The wheel casing
on the elevator car that held the cable wheel snapped and

we plunged nearly three stories. There was a lot of glass
and twisted steel and…and I was in the way."

After a long moment he said quietly, "It's not your fault."

Holly sighed. "I feel like I should have done something."

His eyebrow rose up his forehead. "Like?"

"Like stop them from jumping up and down."

Gabriel grimaced. "A bunch of teenage boys? Not likely."

Holly gave a small laugh of agreement and shook her
head. There was nothing she could have done and she knew
it.

"I guess that explains a lot."

"About?"

"Your nervousness in lifts."

Holly groaned. "That was just clumsiness on my part."

His expression was unfathomable as he slid his gaze
over her face. "It could have been worse." Yes, it could.
She could have died along with that other boy. "You want
dessert or coffee?"

Holly let out a shuddery breath of relief. He was giving
her the space she needed to get her emotions under control
again without spouting off a lot of platitudes. "Coffee would
be great, thank you."

Although Gabe hadn't had more than a couple glasses of
wine with his meal, by the time they stood on the street outside her house he felt a little drunk. And staring into her
upturned face, he discovered he couldn't keep his promise.

He couldn't let her go. Not tonight.

Yanking her against him, he closed his mouth over hers
in a kiss filled with heat and a wild desperation that might
have scared him if he hadn't finally had his mouth and
hands on her after what felt like a lifetime of frustration.

After her initial surprise, she wrapped her arms around
his neck and clung, returning his kisses with as much hunger
and heat as he felt. *God.* He'd never experienced anything
like it. Like she was as eager to get as close as she possibly

could, maybe permanently imprint the feel, the taste and the smell of her on his senses.

Unable to resist, he drew her closer and then closer still, sliding his tongue against hers even as he molded her against him until there was nothing between them but a few too many layers of fabric.

And before he knew it they were in his house and he was pushing her roughly against his front door to ravage her mouth and slake his raging thirst.

With shaking hands they tore at each other's clothing until he could thrust a hair-roughened thigh between her silky-smooth ones and take her breast in his mouth.

Clutching at him, Holly arched her back and emitted a long low moan that grabbed his gut and gave it a vicious twist. He didn't know how they ended up on the floor in a tangle of limbs and discarded clothing. He was too busy whipping her up again and again until she was moaning and begging him to take her.

And then he did. With one hard thrust that drew a ragged moan from her throat even as she arched her back, her inner muscles clamping down on him so hard he saw stars.

He froze, eyes locked on her face.

"Did I hurt you?" he gasped, his sides heaving like he'd run the length of Manhattan Island in three minutes flat.

Looking flushed and dazed and so incredibly beautiful that Gabe had to keep a tight rein on his inclination to pound his way to completion, Holly blinked her eyes open. Damn, he thought, feeling a little dazed himself, she took his breath away.

Or maybe that was just because she was wrapped around him like a ball of twine, arching her long, curvy body and making those breathy little sounds that had the top of his head threatening to explode.

"Whydidyoustop?" she demanded in a breathless rush, sinking her nails into his back, sending shudders of pure heat streaking down his spine to his groin.

"You…" He swallowed the groan building in his chest and felt his eyes cross when she slid her inner thighs up his flanks and clenched her inner muscles around him. "Damn it… Holly…stop a minute, will you?"

Her response was to lift her head to give his lip a punishing nip. He shuddered and the last slender thread of his fraying control snapped. Grabbing her hands, he tethered them beside her head and pressed her writhing body into the floor. "Look at me," he commanded, waiting until her eyes fluttered open and locked with his.

"I want to see your eyes when you come," he growled fiercely. "I want to look at you and know I'm all you see… all you feel."

"Gabriel…"

"Just," he murmured, dropping a hard kiss on her mouth, "just as I see only you." And then with a groan that seemed to originate from somewhere near his knees Gabe withdrew only to slam back into her body as though to fuse them together for all time.

Light burst behind his eyes and Holly cried out, trying to wrench her hands free, but Gabe knew if she touched him he'd lose it big time. He was that close.

He wanted this to last. Needed it to last.

Slowly, savoring the incredible sensations of being inside her again, Gabriel withdrew and with his eyes locked on hers entered her more slowly. She gave a soft mewl and her eyes darkened to midnight. Dropping his lips to the soft spot at the base of her throat, he smiled at the feel of her pulse fluttering wildly beneath the delicate skin.

Her hands tightened into fists. "Gabriel," she pleaded softly, her breath catching when he softly kissed the outward sign of her rioting emotions. Hell, his emotions were all over the place too and when he lifted his head and stared down into her flushed face the world tilted wildly on its axis. Some inexplicably painful emotion gripped him then and before he knew what was happening he'd lost the last fragile grip on his control.

All too soon Holly was arching in his arms, her smoky gaze locked on his as he pounded into her like he couldn't get enough—would never get enough. Then her eyes went dark, blind, and with a low ragged sound she went hurling off the edge, leaving him helpless against the violent storm crashing through him.

CHAPTER TEN

HE DIDN'T KNOW how long they lay there in a tangle of limbs, damp skins clinging as their thundering hearts slowed and their ragged breathing eased.

Tiny aftershocks spasmed through her, keeping him hard until she finally drew in a shuddering breath. "Oh, God," she rasped. "Wha—?" He felt her swallow convulsively and draw in another wheezing breath. "What the hell was that?"

He grunted. Besides being the only response he could manage, he didn't have a clue either. He hadn't had nearly the number of relationships that people liked to believe but he was thirty-five years old, for God's sake. Granted, he was more experienced than he cared to admit but not even when he'd been a randy fifteen-year-old had he lost it so completely.

With a groan he got his elbows beneath him and levered the bulk of his weight off her. He was about to roll off her but he caught sight of her face and he froze. She looked dazed.

His chest squeezed and he lost his breath all over again. This time with dread. "What?" She stared at him for a couple of seconds then blinked as though coming out of a trance.

"Sorry, what?" she rasped.

He frowned, beginning to think something was seriously wrong. "Are you okay?"

Her cheeks reddened. "Define…um…okay."

"Oh, God, I hurt you, didn't I?"

"What?" Her eyes widened. "No! Why would you think that?"

"You're acting weird."

Her eyes slid away. "Oh. Well…I…um…" She paused and licked her lips, another blush working its way up her throat. Her pulse beat a rapid tattoo in her throat. "You're… heavy, is all."

"Uh-huh." He didn't buy it for a minute. Especially not now when he'd shifted most of his weight off her. "Try again."

Her gaze slide to him and then away. She licked her lips, looking adorably flustered.

"You're saying I didn't hurt you?" he pressed. She gave quick headshake and tried to wriggle away but he was still buried deep, tearing a distressed squeak from her throat when he hardened even more.

"Holly."

Her breath escaped in a loud whoosh along with an eye-roll. "You're…um…you're still hard."

A smile of pure deviltry curved his mouth. "Oh, yeah. And I'm going to take care of it. Right now."

"Now?" she asked a little breathlessly, her eyes going wide. "So soon after…well, that?"

"Oh, yeah," he repeated, his voice emerging on a low growl when her inner muscles fluttered around him. "As soon as I can move without my blood pressure shooting out the top of my head, I'm going to try and repeat that."

She giggled and smoothed her hands down over his abs to where they were locked together like two puzzle pieces. Drawing in a ragged breath, Gabe gritted his teeth and slipped out of her body. He froze when she made a tiny sound of protest then surged to his feet in one determined move.

"But I'm not doing it here," he said, reaching down to

wrap long fingers around her wrist. With a tug he hauled her to her feet, wrapping his arm around her waist when her knees threatened to buckle and dump her on her very delectable ass. She clutched at him. Okay, they clutched at each other, because if he was being perfectly honest here his knees were a little shaky too. Especially when her incredibly good parts bumped his.

"Bedroom," he croaked.

"Can't move," she managed sleepily, smoothing her hands over his flanks to his back. And in the wake of that languid caress, his skin tightened and he was suddenly impatient for her all over again.

"That's okay," he murmured against her temple. "I've got this." *I've got you.*

Unlike the last time when she'd awakened to find something heavy and deliciously warm pinning her to the bed, Holly knew exactly where she was and how she'd got there.

And like the last time Holly blamed the wine. Okay, maybe it was also because she couldn't resist dimples and wicked blue-green eyes.

She was weak.

And it was all his fault.

For two years she'd managed to concentrate on her surgical career without once forgetting her plan or losing sight of her goal. Okay, and maybe there'd been no one who had tempted her, but then Dr. Hot Stuff had flashed his package and his dimples her way.

Her breath hitched.

Darn dimples.

And darn the hard warm body currently pressed against her back—heavy arm pinning her to the bed and a large hand cupping her breast—tempting her to repeat her mistakes.

Holly didn't normally repeat mistakes but it seemed all

he had to do was ply her with food and wine and she was a goner. No more, she told herself, she was going to be strong.

Slowly, carefully, she lifted each finger and then the rest of his hand from where it cupped her breast. Just as she was about to inch out from underneath his arm he moved, pulling her back against his body. His very aroused body.

She slammed her eyes closed with a muffled little squeak, hoping he'd think she was just moving and making noises in her sleep.

"Where are you going?" His voice, a sleep-roughened rasp in her ear, had her body tingling in unmentionable places. Holly held her breath, conscious of her heart trying to punch its way through her ribcage. She wondered if he could feel it too since the panicked *boom, boom, boom* shook the bed like a five on the Richter Scale.

He moved a hair-roughened leg between hers, his huge sigh disturbing the long tangle of hair obscuring her vision. Her breath escaped in a silent hiss when she felt something hard poke into her bottom. She rolled her eyes and stifled a snicker. *Damn.* Who'd have thought the sexy surfer would be a snuggler? Or that he'd awaken with his surfboard between them.

She waited until he was breathing evenly again before easing out of his hold. Once she was clear she edged her way carefully across the huge bed and was just congratulating herself on having made a clean getaway when he said, "Do I have to tie you down?"

Slapping a hand over the shriek that emerged, Holly cast a wide-eyed look over her shoulder and caught sight of Gabriel lying sprawled across the bed in nothing but gloriously tanned skin, looking at once satiated and exasperated.

Looking better than he had any right to look after being up half the night.

Finally realizing he was studying her nudity with open interest, she gave a strangled squeak and grabbed for the sheets. Unfortunately, she had to stretch about a mile for them and because he was closer he simply snagged the soft cotton and yanked it out of reach.

Her mouth dropped open and she glared at him for a couple of beats until she realized she was caught out in the open in nothing but her Wildman from Borneo hair.

Slapping both hands over her naked breasts, Holly blew hair out of her face and narrowed her eyes as she considered her options. It was either sit there like an embarrassed virgin or get up and saunter from the room.

Buck naked, of course. Because her clothes were littered all over Gabriel's entrance floor. Again.

He must have read her mind because he simply arched his eyebrow and waited. She finally sucked in air and made a dive off the bed, but he moved like lightning and before she could clear the edge of the bed he caught her, fingers wrapped around her ankle, holding her as effectively as if she'd been shackled.

Holly gasped at discovering she was face down and hanging over the edge of the bed—*oh, boy*—her position giving Gabriel a view that made her blush.

She gave a squeak of distress because he tightened his grip and began to reel her in until she was all the way back on the bed. There was a moment of silence. She sucked in air and waited—anticipation buzzing through her blood like a swarm of excited bees.

His hand smoothed a path of fire up the back of her leg to her knee. There he paused and something brushed the soft skin. Fiery heat that she'd thought extinguished in the dark early hours of the morning arrowed right up the insides of her legs to ground zero and Holly had to bite back a whimper of need. A quick glance over her naked shoulder told her he'd kissed that tiny erogenous spot and was looking up the long length of her thigh. Right where his touch had sent an erotic message.

Squirming with embarrassment, she gasped out a horrified "What are you doing?" drawing his hooded gaze.

"You planning on bailing again?"

Darn it. She'd wondered when he'd bring that up again. "No," she squeaked, feeling her entire body blush. "I, um… I need the bathroom. Really, really badly."

Holding her gaze, he bent his head and nipped the curve of her butt. Her muscles quivered. "If you're not out in three minutes I'm coming to get you."

"What? But…but I've got to…um…go. I've got an… um, thing."

"You've got the day off," he pointed out. "Heck, you've got the next three days off and so do I." He let that news sink in before saying, "I want to you spend them with me," in a voice that washed a heady eroticism over her. But it was his expression that had Holly stilling. He was preparing for her to say no.

"You…do?"

His gaze locked with hers, his thumb brushing the curve where her bottom joined her thigh. "Yes," he said seriously. "I do."

Over the long line of her naked back Holly searched his expression then nodded. She had to swallow the huge lump lodged in her throat before she said breathlessly, "Okay, but I have to attend my father's birthday dinner tonight and I still haven't got him a gift."

"We'll go together."

Surprise had her blinking. "Shopping? Or dinner?"

"Both," he said, before abruptly stilling. After a few beats he lifted his gaze from where he'd been watching his hand rub her bottom, his expression carefully neutral. Her pulse fluttered. "Unless you don't want me to meet your family." His hand slid away and he sat up, looking all hot and naked and pissy. "Unless you already have a date."

"No!" She turned, wondering what that was all about. But she had other things to consider. Like how she would introduce him to her family. Her mother would be over the moon that Holly had a date and would start reading all sorts of things into it, but Paige…? Unless…

Her belly quivered and she racked her brains, trying to remember if her mother had said anything about Paige being off displaying her expensive body for the camera somewhere.

The last she'd heard, her sister was in Fiji with her current lover. Holly hoped she stayed there.

In fact, taking Gabe to dinner would solve a lot of problems, the most urgent one being her mother. Delia kept throwing men at Holly like confetti, hoping she would find one acceptable, marry and give her more grandkids to dote on.

"No," she said again, this time more calmly as she mulled the idea over in her head. Not only would it keep her mother off her back but she wouldn't feel like a permanent fifth wheel. Or that awkward nerdy kid dragged to every social engagement against her will.

A smile grew. "I think that's a great idea." She paused and frowned as she thought about what it would be like for him. "Are you sure you want to be bored…? I mean, it's just family."

Gabriel's expression darkened. "You don't think I'll fit in?"

She rolled her eyes and huffed out a laugh. "God, no." Then, seeing his face, she hurried to explain. "That's a good thing, believe me."

"It is?"

"Heck, most of the time I don't fit in. Especially if my sister's there and if mother's invited all their friends." She made a face. "Believe me, boredom is nothing to what you're likely to experience with a bunch of dry attorneys and judges discussing the law." She shuddered. "If it wasn't my father's birthday, I'd invent something serious and cry off."

After a long moment during which his blue-green eyes

searched hers Gabriel nodded, a small smile lifting one corner of his mouth. "Okay, then," he murmured softly, reaching out to snag her hand. He yanked her down and rolled
her beneath him, his eyes hot and heavy. "What should we
do in the meantime?"

If Gabe had forgotten exactly where Holly had come from,
her childhood home reminded him. Set in the town of Stony
Brook, Long Island, it screamed old money. Surrounded by
expansive lawns and trees heavy with autumn foliage it was
everything he would have had if not for Caspar Alexander.

Pulling the rental to stop in the sweeping drive, he shook
off his odd mood and ignored the fact that he might be nervous. He wasn't. He had nothing to be nervous about. He
might enjoy spending time with Holly Buchanan—in and
out of bed—but he knew from experience that he wasn't in
any danger of falling for her. At least, not the forever kind.
Beside him she drew in a deep breath before flashing him
a brave smile. "You ready?"

She's nervous, he thought, exiting the luxury vehicle and
rounding the hood to open the passenger door. She nibbled
on her bottom lip, looking uncertain, which prompted him
to ask, "The question is, are you?"

"Me?" She shrugged, looking stunning in a dark blue
silky sheath the color of her eyes. "They're my family."
She drew in a deep breath, expelling it in a long whoosh
when he grabbed her hand and drew her from the vehicle.
"They can just be a little overwhelming…and protective,"
she warned. "My mother especially. She'll probably hug
you and maybe flirt a little."

"That's okay, Holly." He smiled, giving her hand a reassuring squeeze. "I'm good with that, especially if she's as
beautiful as you."

"Oh, I'm nothing like my mother," she said with a laugh,
and turned to gather up her purse and her father's expertly
wrapped gift. "She's beautiful and loves people—really

loves having them around. She doesn't look a day over forty and people often mistake her for Paige's older sister. My mother loves it but Paige?" She gave a short laugh. "Well, Paige's another matter altogether."

Before they'd taken a dozen steps a tall, slender blonde burst out of the house and swept down the stairs to gather Holly into a fierce hug. "Oh, my darling, I'm so glad you're here."

With such evident emotion shining in her beautiful face, there was no doubt that Delia Buchanan loved her daughter. Gabe felt his chest tighten and lifted a hand to rub the ache that settled next to his heart. He hadn't realized until this moment just how much he missed his mother and wondered if Holly knew how lucky she was.

Delia moved back to plant a kiss on each of Holly's cheeks. "Your father's going to be thrilled. It's been an age since you were home," she said chidingly.

"Hi, Mom," Holly said, kissing her mother's cheek. "Missed you too."

"Oh, let me look at you," she murmured, drawing back to study Holly's face. Her eyes, so much like Holly's, widened. "Oh, darling, you're…glowing. And since you left word with Rosa that you're bringing someone I guess I owe him for that."

She turned toward Gabriel and he got his first good look at the ex-beauty queen. She was indeed stunning and so much like Holly that he could understand people mistaking the two of *them* for sisters, as they had very similar bone structure and the same eyes.

She squirmed. "We just spent the day on Staten Island and the ferry…and, well, stuff. Gabriel's a…a surgeon."

He arched his brow at her a little challengingly but she sent him a desperate look that begged him to back her up.

"Don't be silly, darling. If anyone can get you out of that hospital and into the glorious fall air then I'm over the moon with gratitude." Still clutching her daughter's hand, she smiled at Gabe. It lit her entire face from within, exactly the way Holly's did. "And he's so handsome too, darling. Where did you find him?"

Holly blushed and elbowed her mother. "Mom, jeez. He's standing right there."

"I know," Delia said, sounding thrilled. "Isn't it wonderful? Oh, don't mind me." She laughed, taking Gabe's face in her hands and reaching up to kiss his cheek. "It's simply been an age since Holly was home, let alone brought a date."

"It's a pleasure to meet you, Mrs. Buchanan. I hope I'm not intruding on your family occasion."

"It's Delia, and don't be silly." She tucked her hand into the crook of his elbow and led him up the stairs to the front door, leaving Holly to follow. "It's just family and a few close friends. Bryant and Richard are here so you won't feel like you're the only young man among all the stodgy old men."

"It's been a long time since a beautiful woman called me a young man," Gabe said, smiling over his shoulder at Holly, who rolled her eyes and bumped the front door closed with her hip. "I can see where Holly gets her sweet nature."

There was a short silence and then both Holly and her mother burst out laughing. Delia grinned at him, gave him a fierce hug. "Oh, you're sweet. I think we'll keep you." She turned to Holly. "Darling, why don't you two go on into the salon? I'm just seeing to some last-minute food emergencies and your father's sitting around like a king waiting for his adoring subjects. And if he's smoking those awful cigars, remind him about what the doctor said."

Once Delia disappeared, Gabe drew in a deep breath and turned to Holly with a look of confusion. "I did warn you."

"No, I'm confused by the laughter."

"Oh, that." She shrugged. "No one's ever called me sweet before. Believe me," she added, when he arched his brow, "I was a really difficult kid. I was skinny as a pole, wore glasses and braces and I was forever walking into things and tripping over my feet. I used to hide when it was time to attend social functions."

Gabe's mouth curled up at one side and he let his gaze slide over her, from the intricate twist she'd managed to coax her long dark hair into, over her face and breasts to the slender, curvy body and dark blue strappy heels that made her legs look incredibly long.

"Well…maybe you're still a little accident-prone but no one could call you a pole and…" he leaned forward to add into her ear "…I know exactly how sweet you are. *All* over. Especially that spot…"

"Now, this," a coolly amused voice came from somewhere over Holly's shoulder, "is the true meaning of sweet." Feeling Holly stiffen, he flicked a curious look over her shoulder. In the middle of the stairs leading to the upper floors—and illuminated as though she stood in a spotlight for maximum effect—was a woman Gabe couldn't help but recognize. He'd have to be living in Outer Mongolia not to recognize supermodel Paige. And suddenly those weird flashes of familiarity made sense. Not to mention he'd also done a host of cosmetic procedures on the woman a couple of years ago.

Conscious of the odd tension pulsing off Holly, he straightened, watching as Paige Buchanan swept down the stairs in something long and floaty, trailing her hand on the banister as she descended. "Ms. Buchanan."

"Oh, Gabriel," she sighed with a pout as she floated closer, reaching up to pat his cheek. "There's really no need for all the formality. Besides, you've seen me naked and had your hands on my breasts…and…well, everywhere else." She blushed prettily and fluttered her lashes, before looking up at him in a move he remembered as being a tad overdone. It was as if she was constantly playing to an invisible camera. Her hand touched his arm. "And now here you are, with…Holly? That is surprising." She finally turned to her sister and did the air-kiss thing as Holly stood looking suddenly remote and cool. "Oh, sis," Paige crooned. "I'd love to hear how you two met. I'll bet it's an…interesting story."

"Not so interesting," Holly said smoothly, sending Gabe a hooded glance that he found difficult to read when before she'd been an open book. He narrowed his eyes on her, wondering at the undercurrents suddenly swirling around him like a thick fog, as well as the white-knuckled grip she had on the gift she clutched. "Gabriel's taken the opening in Plastic and Reconstruction."

Paige's smile widened. "Well, now, that's an amazing coincidence as I'm thinking about having a few things done."

Out the corner of his eye Gabe caught Holly's eye-roll. "I don't do cosmetics anymore," he told the model. "Dr. Syu at West Manhattan is an excellent cosmetic surgeon. Besides, you're beautiful enough without resorting to surgery. I told you that before."

"I don't want Lin Syu," she said, gazing up at him imploringly. "I want the best." She sent Holly a quick look under her lashes. "I want you." And for some odd reason Gabe got the impression she was talking about something else entirely. "Besides, it's just a few minor tweaks. Anyway…" She suddenly tugged playfully at his arm and drew him toward the double wooden doors to Gabe's left. "Do you have a drink? I can't believe Holly hasn't offered you a drink yet."

"We only just arrived," he said coolly, casting a look over his shoulder in time to see Holly's expression go carefully blank as if all the vitality had been sucked out of her. "In fact, we were on our way to see your father."

"Oh, don't worry about that. Holly will handle it and you can meet Daddy later. Besides, I'm parched and I'll just bet you are too."

Gabe was startled by the barely concealed hostility. "No. I—"

"It's fine," Holly said without expression. "You go ahead.

I'll just…" She gestured to her right before turning and hurrying down a short passage.

Gabe resisted Paige's attempts to pull him through the doors. Carefully removing her hand from his arm, he turned and narrowed his eyes at her.

"What was that all about, Ms. Buchanan?"

She looked startled. "I…I don't know what you mean."

"That little show you put on for Holly."

A secret little smile tugged at her famous mouth and she snuggled close, pressing her equally famous breasts—that he'd provided—against his arm. "Oh, relax. It's just a little game we play. We bring dates home and the other tries to lure them away. She does it all the time."

Gabe sincerely doubted that. His skepticism must have shown because Paige laughed, looking incredibly beautiful but to his discerning eye there was something off with her. A hardness in her eyes, a brittleness to her laugh.

"Oh, come on," she wheedled. "Let's have a drink. I'm in a party mood. Besides, Holly will be presenting Daddy with her incredibly thoughtful gift and hoping for a little paternal attention." She rolled her eyes. "You don't want to see that, believe me. It's nauseating in its desperation. And," she drawled lightly, "I've resolved never to gag before dinner."

CHAPTER ELEVEN

HOLLY FOUND HER father in his den with a couple of his closest friends, puffing on cigars and talking shop. Her breath caught in her throat, just as it used to when she was little and couldn't believe that such a handsome man was her father. Just as it did whenever she approached his den, wondering if he would even remember her name.

He was laughing as he turned and caught sight of her hovering in the doorway. "Holly," he said, discarding the cigar and dropping a brief kiss on her cheek when she stepped into the room.

"Happy birthday, Dad," she murmured, handing him his gift.

"I bet old Bergen wishes he was half as beautiful as you," her father's oldest friend said when he hugged Holly. "It might sweeten his disposition." He turned to the room. "Isn't she just like her mother?"

"The spitting image."

Holly rolled her eyes. It was a ritual everyone in the room had played since she'd been a shy, withdrawn teenager.

"When can I make an appointment?" her father's senior partner said, rising to greet her. "My foot is bothering me again. I need a second opinion."

Laughing, she hugged the old man. "If you're thinking about a facial reconstruction, Uncle Franklin, I'm your girl. But if you want to improve your fasciitis, you'll have to stop drinking red wine and smoking those cigars. Oh, and you might want to cut back on the red meat."

"You're as bad as Dr. Bergen," Franklin said in disgust, but his eyes twinkled, making Holly laugh.

"The girl's right, Frank," another partner added cheerfully. "Maybe a facial reconstruction will help. God knows, Sophie would probably approve. She might even agree to that second honeymoon you've been talking about."

With laughter filling the room, Holly left them to shoptalk. She headed for the salon and found Gabriel with her brother, Bryant, while Holly's sister-in-law chatted to the other guests. He looked perfectly content with Paige cleaved to his side like a surgical skin graft. But, then, why wouldn't he? Paige drew men like flies to a cadaver. She was beautiful, fun and exciting. According to a top men's magazine she'd also been voted as one of the ten sexiest women in the world. What man would want to look at—be with—*her* when Paige was around?

He looked up and smiled when he saw her but Paige pulled on his arm to get his attention. With her eyes on Holly, she leaned into him and reached up to brush some non-existent lint from his lapel before smoothing her palm down his abdomen to the waistband of his pants.

It was a game her sister had played since they'd been teenagers and suddenly her head was pounding like she'd spent the day drinking mojitos. She knew exactly how hard and touchable Gabriel's abs were and hated…really, *really* hated seeing her sister slide her hands over him as if she had the right, all the while silently challenging Holly with her eyes.

"Go over there and get your man," Delia murmured, slipping her arm around Holly's waist.

"He's not my man, Mom," she said wearily, and lifted shaking fingers to rub at the pain blossoming behind her eyes. "We're just colleagues."

"Oh, honey, I saw the way he looked at you and—"

"Yeah," she interrupted, turning away from the concern in her mother's gaze. "He's wondering how to ditch me so he can have Paige."

"Oh, my sweet girl. No, don't you look at me like that, Holly Noël Buchanan," Delia snapped. "You are sweet. I know we joke about it but you are, even when you're being an idiot."

Holly sent her mother a half-smile. "You have to say that, Mom, you're my mother. But I can't compete with Paige. I never could, and you know it. No, Mom, don't," she said wearily, when her mother looked like she was about to object, vehemently. "Let's be honest here, not many women can compete with someone on the top ten sexiest women list."

"You're not just any woman, Holly," Delia snapped. "And being sexy is more than flashing your body and pouting for a camera."

"It made her famous."

"It also made her spoiled," Delia said firmly. "For which I blame myself."

"It's not your fault, Mom. Paige always craved attention. She got it."

"And you shunned it."

"I liked books more. Anyway," she sighed, waving her hand dismissively, "I was just wondering what happened to Darian. I thought she was over the moon in love and planning to become Mrs. Darian Something…and now here she is." *All over my date.*

"It was Andreas," Delia corrected quietly, and Holly could see her mother's concern for Paige in her worried expression. "Darian was the one before." She sighed. "And like Darian, Andreas apparently forgot to mention that he was already married."

Holly rolled her eyes and nearly yelped when her brain threatened to explode inside her skull. She didn't say what was obvious to them both: Paige liked taking other women's men. It made her feel powerful and…desirable. And now it looked like she wanted Holly's. Again.

If only to prove she could.

Not that Gabriel was hers, she amended quickly. Two incredible nights didn't make him hers any more than it made her his. He was free to do anything he wanted and she…well, she'd had her exercise and now it was back to her plan. A plan that didn't include getting worked up over a man who could make women scream one minute and cozy up to another the next.

Holly pretended, for her mother's sake, to have a wonderful time but she couldn't wait for the evening to end. Her sister had somehow switched the name settings so she could sit next to Gabriel, whom she proceeded to manipulate with soft touches, coy looks and, Holly was certain, feeling him up beneath the tablecloth. Heck, she'd seen it all before. A hundred times.

Holly sat between Franklin and Richard Westchester, the son of a family friend that Delia had invited before Holly had called to say she was bringing a date. And if she smiled a little too brightly at Rick and leaned toward him a little too closely, Holly told herself it was simply because she was being a gracious dinner companion. It certainly wasn't because Gabriel was being attentive to Paige or watching *her* with a brooding expression.

The instant dinner was over she shoved back from the table and quietly excused herself. Her head throbbed like an open head wound and she headed upstairs to her parents' bathroom.

After downing pain meds and splashing her face with cool water, she made for the French doors that led to the balcony. Maybe a little fresh air and alone time would help soothe her aching head before she put on her game face and returned downstairs.

She let herself out and shivered in the cool night air but it was dark and quiet. Wrapping her arms around herself to ward off the chill, she leaned her hot forehead against the old stone pillar, staring out across the lawn toward the water.

She'd been out there a minute only when she became aware of murmured voices. One deep and achingly familiar, the other…well, it wasn't a surprise to hear her sister's smoothly amused tones.

She didn't mean to eavesdrop and wasn't in the least bit interested in Paige's plans to have some imaginary defect fixed, but when she heard her name she couldn't help peering over the balustrade and holding her breath so she could listen.

Paige was draped artfully in a pose she often used to display her amazing body to maximum effect. She took a sip of champagne from the flute she'd brought from the dinner table and Holly had to wonder how many times it had been refilled. She wondered too if her mother had noticed that as dinner had progressed, Paige had become more and more flushed and animated.

Watching now, she saw Paige tip back her head, luxurious waves of silvery blonde hair cascading over her naked shoulders. For a moment she thought Paige looked right at her and although she was in deep shadow, Holly drew further into the darkness.

"I came with Holly," she heard Gabriel say. "What do you want, Paige?"

"I just needed some fresh air and as I'm not feeling well…" her breath hitched dramatically "…I thought having a doctor around would help."

"You don't need a doctor to tell you that laying off the champagne would help."

Paige gave a dramatic sigh and set her glass aside before pushing away from the balustrade. "You're right," she purred, sliding her hands over Gabriel's chest and linking her arms behind his neck to smile up into his face. "You've got me. I know you came with Holly, but it's clear she's otherwise occupied and…well, I just didn't want you to feel left out, that's all."

Holly wondered if she was the only one who'd noticed that Paige had been the one feeling left out, which was why she'd attached herself to the best-looking man in the group.

"I saw you change the seating arrangements," he observed, putting his hands on her waist, whether to push her away or an excuse to touch her Holly couldn't tell. "I wondered about your motive."

"Oh, Richard's such a bore. I can't understand why Mother insists on inviting him but, then, I suppose it's because Holly always had a thing for him. Besides…" she pouted charmingly "…I just wanted you to myself without her watching every move I make. She's incredibly…possessive for someone who claims you're just colleagues."

"She said that?"

She shrugged. "Anyway, I thought I might convince you to change your mind about doing me that teensy favor."

"I've already told you I don't do cosmetic surgery anymore, Paige. Besides, I'm booked solid for the next six months. Probably longer."

Annoyance flashed across her features and she spun away to say sulkily, "Fine, then maybe you can use your incredible sex appeal to persuade Holly to have a little work done."

"Work?"

Light spilling from the salon illuminated Paige's face, giving Holly a clear view of the flirtatious look she sent over her shoulder. She gave a little laugh and turned back to slide her palm over his heart. "Don't pretend they're invisible, Gabriel." She shuddered delicately. "Those scars are awful and people don't realize how hurtful pitying stares are. In fact, I used to feel so bad when boys called her Scarface that I wondered if you could persuade her to have them…fixed?"

Like hell she'd felt bad, Holly thought darkly. She'd

laughed, telling Holly she should have an infamous comic book badass named after her.

"Hmm…" Gabriel rocked back on his heels as though he was considering her words.

Holly sucked in a sharp breath, the betrayal like a blow to her heart. She couldn't believe that after kissing every one of those scars, moving his lips against her skin and murmuring that she was beautiful, he— She bit her lip. Clearly, after seeing Paige's flawless beauty, he was reconsidering.

She pressed the heel of her hand to the spot between her brows as pain lanced through her head. Oh, God, she needed to get out of here. Away from…them. Away somewhere where she could fall apart in private.

She was about to turn away when she heard him say, "So what else would you suggest she have…done?"

Feeling the backs of her eyes burn, she waited with a huge hot lump of devastation in her chest for her sister's reply. When it came, it sliced at the self-confidence she'd spent so many years trying to build. And even though she understood that Paige's opinions reflected her own insecurities and jealousy, it made Holly feel like the ugly adopted sister Paige had always called her.

"Well," Paige said demurely, "I was thinking a breast lift and maybe since her hips and thighs are getting chunky, a little lipo? And she could certainly do with a nose job. What do you think?"

And when Gabriel laughed and said, "Chunky? You really think so?" she couldn't listen anymore because Paige reached up and twined her fingers in his hair.

His hands came up to her shoulders and the sight of them plastered together like a seal-a-meal ripped at the tender new feelings that had been blossoming inside her chest. But she couldn't…*couldn't* bear to listen to every one of her flaws discussed like a grocery list. She'd survived it once before when Paige had slept with and then dumped Holly's last boyfriend and she would survive it again.

Right now she couldn't bear to stick around and watch it happening again.

The last twenty-four hours had been fun but it was over and time to return to the real world. Time to return to planning for her future and time she forgot about a hunky surfer from California. No matter how hot he was or how good he was with his hands. And his lips.

Oh, God.

Turning, she walked blindly into the safety of her parents' bedroom, her mind spinning as she wondered how she was going to make a clean getaway. There wasn't time to fall apart however, as Delia entered as she was closing the French doors.

"There you are, darling," she said, catching sight of her. "We're getting ready to serve coffee so your father can blow out his candles." Holly turned and her mother stopped abruptly, her eyes widening when she caught sight of her expression. "I'm going to slap that girl," Delia said fiercely. "She's not too old for it."

"Mom…it's fine. Really," she insisted, when her mother opened her mouth to object. "Besides, I'm not feeling well and I wondered if you'd please tell Dad I'm sorry and make my apologies to everyone else?"

She searched Holly's face and then sighed, her eyes filled with so much compassionate concern that Holly was tempted to walk into Delia's arms and bawl. But that would only upset her mother more.

"All right, darling," Delia agreed softly, "but I think you're making a terrible mistake. I like him and…well, I guess I shouldn't interfere." She rolled her eyes before turning with a muttered "I promised myself I wouldn't interfere." Then over her shoulder she asked gently, "Do you want me to ask Gabriel to take you home?"

"No!" she yelped, and when her mother's eyebrow rose, she said more quietly. "Please, Mom…don't. I just…I…" She

heaved out a heavy breath and tried to wrestle her spinning emotions into submission. "I'll call a cab. You can tell Gabriel the hospital called."

For a long moment her mother silently studied her until Holly thought she might break down beneath that blue gaze. Finally she stepped closer and gave Holly a warm hug. "All right," she murmured softly, "but you're not calling a cab. I'll ask Richard to drive you back to the city."

Holly's eyes abruptly filled but she drew in a deep breath and willed away the tears. "Thanks, Mom."

Gabe was furious—with Holly for leaving without a word and with Paige for her machinations. But mostly he was furious with himself for thinking Holly was different. He also felt very bad for Delia Buchanan, who'd seemed genuinely upset when she gave him Holly's message.

"I'm so sorry, Gabriel," she said, taking his hands in hers.

"You have nothing to be sorry about, Mrs. Buchanan," he said. "This is not on you."

"No," she agreed quietly. "It's on both my daughters and I'm very sorry you got caught in the middle. Paige…well, Paige was always incredibly jealous of Holly even as a child, and after a while it was just easier for Holly to withdraw and let Paige have her way."

"That's insane."

"Yes, well," she said with a sad smile. "Paige is beautiful but there's just something a little fragile in her make-up. Holly was always the strong one, even when she was so adorably skinny and clumsy. She was smart and funny but couldn't get the hang of all those coltish arms and legs. I tried to help with ballet lessons, deportment and acting classes but I fear I just made things worse."

"You did what any mother would do," Gabe said, recalling the sacrifices his own mother had made for him. "But she's made her feelings perfectly clear."

"Yes, she has," Delia said sympathetically, laying her hand on his tense arm. "And you've misinterpreted her actions."

"How can I misinterpret the way she acted with Westchester during dinner or that she left with him the minute it was over?" he demanded, feeling once again like that poor med student invited to the mansion and humiliated by Lauren's family's condescending attitude.

"You appeared engrossed with Paige," she reminded him gently. "And for Holly at least, it seemed like history repeating itself all over again. So she did what she's always done when it comes to Paige. She withdrew. But I know she cares for you, Gabriel. She wouldn't have invited you or gone off like that if she didn't."

Sighing, Gabe thrust a hand through his hair. He didn't know what to think.

"Don't give up on her," Delia begged softly. "Get her to talk to you, please. And for God's sake don't get sucked into Paige's dramas. She has a bad habit of wanting what Holly has and destroying everything good in her own life."

But Holly didn't have him, Gabe thought furiously as he drove back to the city. She'd made it perfectly clear that she preferred someone from her own social circle. Someone from old money and an ancestry that could probably be traced back to Ellis Island. Maybe the Buchanan sisters were letting their history repeat itself but there was no way he was going to make the same mistake.

Not again, he vowed fiercely as Holly's phone again went to voicemail. He ground his back teeth together until his jaw popped.

Great. Now he was grinding his teeth into powder.

Disconnecting with a short jab, he ignored the angry honking around him and whipped across three lanes to take the Brooklyn exit. He was done with women, and he was especially done with Holly Buchanan.

So why, when he got home and smelled her on his pillow, did he get a hollow feeling in his chest that felt very much like grief? It wasn't, he told himself, lurching off the bed to strip the sheets and pillowcases.

It was humiliation and disgust with himself that he never seemed to learn his lesson. He was still hankering after women from the world his grandfather had denied him. Well, he was done with it, with her, he told himself as he threw himself across the freshly made bed that he'd shared with her. Twice. Which didn't explain why it suddenly felt so damn cold and...empty. Or why he couldn't stop thinking about her with another man.

He really hated thinking about her with—

Damn it!

He grabbed his phone and after a couple of indecisive beats hit redial. She'd done him a favor, he told himself, growling with frustration when the call again went to voicemail. Done him a favor by reminding him that he couldn't rely on anyone but himself and the professional reputation he'd earned through his own hard work and skill.

It had landed him the job of his dreams and he wasn't going to screw it up, especially not over some woman with big blue eyes that exposed her every thought and emotion. A woman who was soft and sweet even when she thought she wasn't. A woman who had a habit of falling at his feet and quoting random facts when she was flustered. A woman who— He stopped breathing and stared into the darkened room as the truth finally dawned.

Oh, man, he thought when he realized his mouth was curved into a sappy grin, he was in trouble. The kind of trouble that started with *L*.

His breath expelled in a hard, dry laugh.

He might as well go out and shoot himself.

CHAPTER TWELVE

INSTEAD OF GOING back to Brooklyn, Holly had Richard drop her off at her grandmother's summer house in Bay Shore. He offered to keep her company but she declined. She needed to be alone to work on her shaky defenses before facing Gabriel on Monday.

But when Monday rolled around, all Holly had to show for her days off were dark circles under her eyes and a bone-deep certainty that there was no way she could accept a fellowship in the same hospital—*oh, God, the same department*—as Gabriel. And as much as she hated the idea, she needed to review her options. And fast.

She spent the next week researching P&R programs in other cities while avoiding everyone, including her mother. She just happened to quite successfully avoid Gabriel too. Not that he'd come looking for her, she admitted with a pang. But, then, she hadn't returned his calls, even when he'd left a dozen *"Call me"* messages. And if she'd listened to his voice over and over again as she'd lain in bed at night, it hadn't been because she'd been yearning for the sound of his voice or the smell and feel of his body against hers.

He finally stopped calling and when she caught herself scouring the papers for pictures of Paige, or holding her breath every time her phone rang, she realized she'd been secretly hoping he'd... Well, she didn't know exactly, only that she'd hoped he wouldn't quit.

But he had. So…that was that, then.

The week was frantically busy. She stood in for another cosmetic surgeon whose wife went into early labor and ended up with more than enough to keep her busy and too tired at the end of each day to stay awake and brood.

The week leading up to the Chrysalis Foundation's annual charity ball she wasn't so lucky. On Tuesday she was called to Theatre for two late-night procedures when Gabriel's scheduled assistant called in with stomach flu. And because everyone was way behind schedule, Dr. Hunt assigned Holly to pick up the slack.

Fortunately there wasn't time for him to do more than study her with a penetrating blue-green gaze that made her heart flop around in her chest like a landed catfish and make quiet suggestions or give orders that everyone—including Holly—snapped to obey.

During the last stages of the second procedure, on a guy who had gynecomastia and wanted his man boobs removed, he was called away, leaving Holly to finish up the routine procedure.

She didn't see him again until late Friday afternoon as she left the surgical ward.

Scrolling through the dozen messages Delia had left about her dress and shoes for the ball, as well as her tickets, Holly rolled her eyes at her mother's OCD and…walked into a wall of living muscle and bone.

Startled, she lurched backwards—okay, shrieked and jumped about a foot in the air—and bumped into a nearby medicine trolley that hadn't been wheel-locked. A hand shot out to grab her but she yanked her arm away, the abrupt move sending the trolley skidding out from under her. She fell hard against the sluice trolley and went down in a tangle of limbs, another shriek and—yay—a half-dozen bedpans that crashed around her like the sounding of the Apocalypse.

For a couple of beats she lay there stunned until she became aware of two things. One: her notes were fluttering to the floor like confetti and, two—*oh, God*—Gabriel was dropping to his haunches beside her. Through the roaring in her ears she thought she heard him ask repeatedly if she was all right.

Realizing he was feeling her up, she jolted like she'd been shot. "What...what the heck are you doing?" she gasped on a rising inflection, shoving at his hands.

But he brushed her aside and growled, "Damn it, Holly. Stay still until I'm satisfied you're—"

The door burst open and three nurses spilled out, coming to an abrupt halt when they saw Holly flat on her bottom, bedpans and folio paper scattered all over the floor—and Gabriel Alexander's hands high up on her inner thigh.

Their eyes bugged.

"Dr. Buchanan?"

"Dr. Alexander?"

"Omigosh, are you all right?"

Sucking in a breath, she did a lightning-quick assessment and decided that other than her bruised bottom and her battered pride she was fine. "I'm...fine," she said, shoving Gabriel away and scrambling to her feet to hide her hot face.

Gabriel shot out a hand to steady her when she swayed and though she stiffened she didn't pull away. She did a mental eye-roll. Not after what had just happened—all because she hadn't wanted him to touch her.

"What happened?" the head nurse demanded, popping her head out the door and frowning at the debris scattered across the floor.

"The brake was off the meds trolley," Gabriel said, his voice more steely than she'd ever heard it.

"No," Holly hastened to say. "It was my fault. I wasn't looking where I was going and Dr. Alexander had to save me from—"

"It's not all right," he interrupted tersely. "Dr. Buchanan could have been seriously injured because someone didn't follow safety procedures." He frowned at the head nurse as the others scurried to pick up the scattered bedpans.

"Dr. Alexander—"

"Leave the papers," he ordered tersely, ignoring Holly's attempts to smooth over the situation. "I'll help Dr. Buchanan collect them."

Once the bedpans had been returned to their place and the trolleys locked, he waited until the frosted door closed on the cowed nurses before releasing his grip on Holly.

Without speaking, she dropped to her haunches and silently began gathering up her notes. She was shaking inside and had to bite her lip against the pain radiating from her elbow. She tried to hurry, wanting to escape without making even more of a fool of herself.

Unfortunately it was *waa-aay* too late for that.

She was on her knees when they both reached for the last page. Holly froze. With her heart in her throat, she was compelled to lift her gaze to his—and felt herself fall all over again. This time into a pair of blue-green eyes. *Déjà vu.* Blue-green eyes that swept over her face as though they'd been starved of the sight of her.

"Holly," he said coolly, his face expressionless. But there was a wealth of emotion in his eyes—anger, frustration, accusation, even concern, and something so dark and hot it sent hurt slicing through her.

Swallowing the sob that rose into her throat, she shook her head, snatching at the pages in his hand before surging to her feet in one smooth move. She abruptly swung on her heel and surprised herself by not falling flat on her face. Before she could stomp off with her head held high, he grabbed her arm.

Instantly pain ricocheted from her elbow to her shoulder and she flinched, unable to prevent a gasp from escaping.

He immediately released her. "What? What's wrong?"

Tears—that had little to do with the pain in her elbow—blinded her and she shook her head again and turned her face away. "Nothing. It's nothing. I just bruised my elbow, that's all."

"Let me see."

"No." She sucked in a steadying breath and said it again, this time quietly. "No. It's nothing, really. I'll be fine." She wasn't talking about her elbow. At least, not just.

"Fine, but we need to talk."

She gulped and thought, *Go away, Gabriel, can't you see I'm having a mini-freak-out here?* "There's nothing to say, Dr. Alexander."

His eyebrows flattened across the bridge of his nose and his lips firmed. "What's that supposed to mean?"

"It means you've already said everything I need to hear."

"What?" He looked so confused Holly almost relented but then she recalled the sight of her sister clinging to Gabe and her resolve hardened.

Folding her arms beneath her breasts, she thrust out her chin in silent challenge. "To Paige."

He rubbed the lines of exhaustion between his eyes and Holly was tempted to reach out and smooth them away. "Paige?" he demanded testily. "What the hell does Paige have to do with anything?"

Holly's mouth dropped open. "You're kidding, right?" Her hands curled into tight fists to keep her from taking a swing at his thick head. Maybe jolt his memory? Knock him out?

"I honestly have no idea—" He abruptly shook his head as though to clear it. "What about Westchester?"

She tried to look innocent. "What about Richard?"

"Yeah, right. It's fine to find fault with me when you ran off with him, leaving me to face your mother. Do you have any idea how humiliating that was? For both of us?"

"No more humiliating," she snapped, "than you discussing me…my scars." *Not to mention devastating.* She sucked in a steadying breath when she realized she was starting to hyperventilate. "Not to mention my sagging breasts and my huge ass and thighs!" She lowered her voice to a fierce whisper when a couple of nurses passed, eyeing them with avid curiosity. "With my sister?" She jabbed a finger at him and hissed, "My sister!"

He had the grace to wince. "You heard that?"

Suddenly Holly was exhausted. She'd been functioning on pure adrenaline since that night and she wanted to curl up in a ball and sleep for a month.

"Of course I heard it," she said wearily. "Paige made certain I heard it. Like she made certain I saw how she touched you and plastered herself…" She sucked in a steadying breath. "And how you did nothing…*nothing*…to stop her."

Her phone rang and she checked the caller ID, viciously punching the disconnect button when she saw who it was.

"Now, just a minute," he said incredulously. "*That's* what this is all about?"

Holly glared at him.

"*Damn it!* I can't believe—!" He broke off with a muttered oath and shoved his hands through his hair, looking agitated and…and hot, damn him. "Did you…did you hear everything I said to Paige out on the terrace?"

"I…I heard enough," she snapped. "Enough to know you agreed with her. But that's okay since it's nothing I haven't heard before," she said coolly. "A million times. But I can't believe you agreed with her. Not after—"

Fortunately Gabriel's furious "I did nothing of the sort" interrupted what she was going to say. Then her phone rang again and she was just about to throw the thing against the wall when she realized it wasn't Paige this time but her mother. "You know what, never mind. I have to go."

"We need to talk."

"I hardly think—"

His hand closed over her shoulder and whipped her around. "We're going to have that talk," he said firmly, his eyes glittering with determination and something else that Holly couldn't identify. It made her stomach drop then bounce back up like she'd fallen from the top of the Empire State building.

"I have to go. My mother's sent a car to take me to the hotel. I'm helping with the last minute details of the charity auction for the ball tonight," she explained when he looked like he wanted to throttle her.

"Fine," he said shortly. "I'll see you there. Save all your dances for me."

"You have an invitation?" she asked, mouth dropping open. She shook her head. Of course he had an invitation. "I mean, I might not have time—"

"I'll see you there," he ground out an instant before he yanked her against him and slammed his mouth down on hers in a hard, punishing kiss. It stunned her with its heated ferocity and even after he'd shoved back and disappeared into the surgical ward she stood open-mouthed, wide-eyed and more than a little dazed.

He'd tasted of anger and frustration, she thought dizzily. And a wild, wild lust that had just a hint of what she thought was desperation. But that was ridiculous. Wasn't it?

It took a passing med student asking, "You gonna answer that, Dr. Buchanan?" to realize she was staring at her buzzing phone as though she'd never seen it before.

A look at caller ID galvanized her into action. Once Delia Buchanan was on a roll, it took a force of nature to stop her.

Gabriel paid the cab driver and turned to look up at the blazingly bright façade of Manhattan's finest hotel. It figured that the charity foundation, which he now knew was run by Delia Buchanan, would host it here. Its five-star rating, as well as the richly appointed furnishings, would draw New York's social and moneyed elite.

It was clear by the number of glittery ballgowns and designer tuxes that the elite had converged on Manhattan for the prestigious occasion. Gabriel entered the hotel and was immediately struck by the intricate laylight high overhead, brilliantly illuminated and casting a rich warm glow over the huge lobby.

He'd stayed at the hotel only once before, when he'd flown out to see the chief of surgery, P&R head and the hospital CEO about heading up their special cases team. He hadn't seen it filled with so many bejeweled women in long glittery dresses or starched stiffs then, and despite the reek of money and breeding all but choking the atmosphere he had to admit he was impressed as hell.

Delia Buchanan must be very pleased with the turnout, he thought. He just hoped she was even more pleased when the contributions came pouring in.

He nodded to a couple of hospital board members gathered near the entrance and paused on the threshold. The enormous neoclassical ballroom had recently been renovated to its original opulence, a perfect setting for dining in splendor and emptying out fat wallets.

Gabe wondered what little Lacey Carmichael, his latest patient, would say about all this. She'd probably think she'd stepped into a fairytale with music and dancing... and gorgeous princes and princesses. She, as well as a lot of other children, was in dire need of the care the money raised would provide.

His lips curved as he thought about that morning when he'd carried the tiny four-year-old into the OR. Bright, sweet and with an adorable lisp, she'd wrapped her arms around his neck and planted a kiss on his cheek.

Lifting a hand, he was surprised not to feel the damp spot her lips had left and his heart ached for the brave little girl who'd cheerfully told everyone who'd listened that Mr. Doctor was going to make her beautiful again.

Fortunately she was still very young and the trauma of being savaged by a friend's pet would fade, along with her scars.

When Holly's mother had called him last week to urge him to attend the ball, he'd told himself that he'd accepted for Lacey. He'd lied to himself. It was also a chance for him to get Holly alone and...

And what?

Apologize? Bare his soul? Force another kiss on her? He didn't know. Only this afternoon he'd looked into huge blue eyes full of hurt and pride and had known one irrefutable fact: he loved Holly Buchanan more than he'd thought it possible to love another person.

It had left him reeling, totally off balance, like the world had spun off its axis. Like he'd been head-punched by a linebacker. Hell, he was still reeling. Or maybe he'd always been a little off center and Holly just...righted his world. Made everything better. Brighter, sweeter... Hell...it had sounded sappy and a little goofy even thinking about it.

But this bizarre feeling growing inside his chest had had his emotions seesawing between elation and pure terror. It had left him feeling shaky and sick. And then he'd heard that Holly had talked to Dr. Hunt about taking up a fellowship in another city and the sick feeling had morphed into outright panic.

She was planning to leave—because she thought he preferred Paige. As if anyone, especially that spoiled shallow supermodel, could ever make him feel the way Holly did.

Suddenly the thought of being without her had filled him with a determination born of fear. A fear he'd shoved aside with the knowledge that if she didn't care about him—even a little—she wouldn't be thinking of ditching her plan. Or him.

He was going to make her listen and he was going to do it tonight. And then he was going to take her home and tie her to his bed.

Fingering the invitation Delia had delivered to the hospital, he recalled the neatly penned instructions on the back.

Gabriel. Table 1 to the right of the dais. 7:30. Don't be late or I'll send out a search party. Delia.

He checked the seating plan on the easel at the entrance and headed across the dance floor. The live orchestra, all students from the Manhattan Music College, filled the ballroom with lively music, proving that Delia Buchanan supported young talent as well as raised funds for the disfigured.

She was a remarkable woman, he thought. Just like her daughter.

He skirted a group of people sipping champagne and debating the safety of air travel when a familiar voice purred behind him, "You all alone tonight, Gabriel?"

He didn't have to turn around to know that Paige Buchanan was on the prowl.

"No, actually," he said, turning to find a stunningly made-up Paige clinging to the arm of the man she'd not two weeks ago said was a dead bore.

"Ms. Buchanan, Westchester." He greeted the other man blandly but he guessed his feelings were pretty clear because Richard Westchester's brown eyes twinkled as he thrust out his hand in greeting.

"Alexander." His handshake was firm. "If you're looking for Holly, I saw her talking to the senator and Mrs. James over at the auction table."

A senator? "Thank you." He was just about to head off when Rick tilted his head, studying Gabe with narrowed eyes.

"You know, you remind me of someone. I thought so the other night but I just couldn't think who it was. Seeing you again has reminded me. Are you by any chance related to the Long Island Alexanders? Mark Alexander's son, Steven, is about your age, maybe a little younger, and you look a lot like him."

Gabe had known this moment would eventually come. Had prepared for it. But it still gave him a jolt. "No," he said casually. "I'm from California."

"Oh, that's right," Rick mused. "Funny how life is. I

guess it's true what they say about having a twin some-where in the world."

Gabe was saved from replying by Paige. Clearly tired of being ignored, she tugged impatiently on Rick's arm. "Come on, Ricky." She pouted. "I want to show you the dresses I donated to my mother's little pet project."

"The auction," Rick said, by way of explanation to Gabe, who couldn't have cared less unless they brought in a lot of money.

"I'm sure the foundation is grateful for your loss," Gabe said politely. Paige sent him a cat smile.

"And you, Gabriel?" she purred. "How grateful are you? Considering most of the funds will be going to pay for your salary?"

"God, Paige," Rick groaned. "Give it a rest, will you? You know very well that Chrysalis can't afford to pay Dr. Alexander's fees. Anything made here tonight only goes to the medical costs for the miracles he performs."

Furious with Rick for daring to contradict her in front of Gabriel, she rounded on him. "I'm only saying—"

"Yeah, yeah," Rick interrupted wearily. "We get it. The great Paige Buchanan threw a couple of her old rags at the foundation and now everyone must be overcome with grati-tude. You're thirty-one years old, for God's sake. Don't you think it's time you stopped behaving like a spoiled brat?"

"I am not that old," she whispered furiously, two spots of color appearing high on her famous cheekbones.

Rick sighed. "We're the same age, Paige, and I'm thirty-one. Almost thirty-two, in fact, which means—"

"I know what it means, Rick. It means you're an insen-sitive jerk and I never should have agreed to come with you tonight."

"No one else would bring you," he said brutally, to which she replied by sending him a look that should have sliced him to shreds before spinning on her heel and flouncing off.

After a short silence Rick shoved a hand through his

hair. "Sorry about that. The thing is…" He let his breath out in a long hiss. "I've been in love with Paige since I was six." He gave a hard laugh. "And you can see just how that worked out for me."

Gabe was confused. "If you're in love with Paige," he asked, "then what the hell was that display with Holly the other night?"

A dull flush rose up Rick's neck. "My pathetic attempt to make Paige jealous." He gave an embarrassed laugh. "I thought you'd arrived with Paige and…and ended up embarrassing myself. Look, Holly's the best, but Paige? Well, it's always been Paige for me."

Gabe understood because he had a feeling it would always be Holly for him. "My condolences."

Rick's laugh burst out and he grimaced. "Thanks. And now I think I'll just go drown my sorrows. Coming?"

He shook his head. "I need to speak to Holly."

"Hope you have better luck," Rick muttered.

After he left, Gabe spotted Holly across the ballroom and sucked in a hard breath at the picture she made; slender and stunning in a long column of ice blue that complemented her dark hair…and deepened the blue of her eyes.

She looked both touchable and as distant as a star, and she literally took his breath away. The one-sleeved dress was a feat of engineering that hugged and draped her curves before falling to the floor in a luxurious cascade of soft folds from an artfully draped row of fabric blossoms at her hip. It was at once modest and incredibly revealing, and while it cleverly covered her scarred right arm it exposed her flawless shoulder and arm entirely.

He didn't realize he'd been standing there staring at her like a lovesick schoolboy until someone bumped into him, jolting him out of his trance. With his eyes on her, he murmured an apology and started forward.

She must have sensed his stare because she looked up and their gazes locked. It was like one of those sappy movie moments when two people locked eyes across a crowded room. Everything faded—the people, the noise, the opulence—until there was only the two of them.

After a few heated beats a tentative smile trembled on her lips and warmth filled him, rising in his chest like bubbles in a champagne glass. Her gaze dropped to the dimple in his cheek and he realized he was smiling too.

Oh, yeah, he thought, she couldn't resist his dimples. Or his kisses. He just hoped she listened to what he had to say.

"Oh, Gabriel," a low feminine voice came from behind him. "I'm so glad you made it."

CHAPTER THIRTEEN

GABRIEL TURNED TO find Delia Buchanan at his elbow and wasn't the least bit surprised when she cupped his face in her hands studied him for a few beats before reaching up to kiss his cheek.

"Good evening, Mrs. Buchanan. *Wow.* You look amazing." She wore a simple off-the-shoulder black jersey dress only a true blonde could pull off.

"Oh, darn." She laughed up at him. "I was hoping the best-looking man in the room would call me by my name and make all the other women jealous."

Gabe smiled and kissed her cheek. "You're the most beautiful woman here, Delia," he murmured, his gaze sliding to Holly, who was watching them with an odd expression on her face. A kind of hopeful yearning that grabbed him by the throat and tugged him toward her. "After your daughter, of course."

She squeezed his arm. "And you're incredibly sweet, Gabriel. I only hope she knows how lucky she is."

"I'm the lucky one," he said, watching as color blossomed beneath Holly's skin. "Or I will be when I finally corner her and—"

She gasped softly, looking stunned and desperately hopeful. "Oh…oh, my…you're in love with her."

Gabe felt the back of his neck grow hot and grimaced. "It's that obvious?"

A lovely smile transformed her features and he caught his breath at how very much alike Holly and her mother were. "Only to a mother who's been waiting for this moment for a long, long time," she said on a rush of emotion. "For someone to love her enough to overlook the scars."

"She's beautiful," he murmured, taking in Holly's creamy skin, heavily lashed eyes and the tendrils of dark hair framing her oval face. "Inside and out." He turned to Delia. "Like her mother."

Tears filled her eyes and her breath hitched audibly. "Oh, you." She pressed her hand into the center of her chest and blinked a few times. She gave a soft sniff. "Look what you've done now. You've made me all weepy."

Gabriel felt his skull tighten. The last thing he'd wanted was to upset Holly's mother. Not tonight. Not ever. He shoved unsteady fingers through his hair and looked around for an escape route but there wasn't one.

Maybe he should have taken Westchester up on that drink after all. "Oh, man, I'm…sorry. Can I get you anything? Water, champagne? *Anything?*"

Delia laughed tearfully as she nudged his shoulder and he realized he'd started to sound desperate there for a second. "Look at you, getting all panicky over a few tears," she hiccupped. "Besides, what's a little smudged mascara when someone loves my baby?"

Embarrassed, Gabe rubbed the back of his neck and shifted his feet, feeling fifteen again. "Yeah, well," he said, clearing his throat. "Maybe I should see if she'll forgive me for being a colossal ass first."

"Oh, before you do," Delia said, as though she'd suddenly remembered. "There's someone I want you to meet first. He's a huge contributor to both the hospital and the foundation." She slipped her hand into the crook of his elbow and urged him forward. "In fact, he's responsible for the planned expansion of the P&R wing. And if I'm not mistaken, he was also instrumental in getting you here."

Gabe reluctantly allowed her to pull him forward.

"Me?"

"Oh, yes," she said with a lovely smile. "We only wanted the best for the program. In fact, the endowment depended on you heading up the team."

Gabriel frowned and wondered at the sudden bad feeling in his stomach. "That's a bit harsh. I'm sure there are other surgeons who could have filled the position."

"They wanted the best and apparently that's you." She squeezed his arm and sent him a proud smile. "Here we are," she said brightly, reaching out to touch the shoulder of a much older man who had his back to them.

When he turned, Gabe's blood froze.

Through the dull roaring in his ears he heard Delia Buchanan say, "Mr. Alexander, I'd like to introduce you to the hospital's newest acquisition. He's already made a huge difference to some of our recipients." As though she'd felt the instant Gabe's muscles turn to stone, she flicked him a concerned look before including the other members of the group.

"This is Dr. Al…ex…an…der?" Her eyes widened as enlightenment slowly dawned. She gave a shocked gasp, her gaze whipping up to his—looking suddenly shaken and distressed. "Oh." She lifted a trembling hand to her chest. "Oh, Gabriel, I'm so sorry."

As though Gabe's worlds weren't suddenly colliding, Caspar Alexander took Delia's hand and pressed a kiss to her cheek. "You're looking more radiant than ever, my dear. And the ballroom's never looked better." Then he straightened and turned his cold blue eyes on Gabriel.

He didn't offer his hand—probably because Gabe looked ready to take a bite of anything that moved. "Gabriel," he said smoothly. "You're looking well."

Gabe's reply, "Sir," as frigid as the north wind, slid like an icy blade into the sudden silence. He ignored the shocked expressions around him as he zeroed in on Mark Alexander, looking as stunned as Delia Buchanan. She tightened her fingers on his arm and pressed closer to his side as though she instinctively knew what was happening and was offering her silent support.

And Gabriel, grateful for her warm maternal presence, fell in love for the second time that day. He covered the hand gripping his arm and gave it a reassuring squeeze.

"Hello, Dad," he said with a blade-sharp smile. "Long time no see." And had the satisfaction of seeing Mark Alexander turn white. As though Mark had seen a ghost—or maybe his past coming up to bite him in the ass. And though Gabe wanted to hate him, he realized Mark was as stunned as the rest of the Alexander clan. A quick glance at Caspar showed the old man looking pleased, as though he'd orchestrated the events for maximum shock value.

Clearly Caspar wasn't done controlling his family. But Gabriel wasn't family and he had no intention of being manipulated by anyone. Especially the old bastard.

Oh, wait, he thought savagely. *He* was the unwanted son. *He* was the long "lost" grandson Caspar wanted to pull into his web of lies, deceit and tight-fisted control. He hadn't managed to bribe Gabe with riches and power three years ago so he'd gone for the jugular. He'd bought Gabe the one thing he'd needed after his mother's death—to do something worthwhile. To help people who really needed it, not just because they could afford to pay for their vanity.

The expression on her mother's face sent Holly's pulse ratcheting up a couple of thousand notches. Something was wrong, she thought, murmuring an excuse to Senator James and his wife. Seriously wrong.

Gabriel, looking coldly furious, appeared to have been

turned to stone but it was the distress on her mother's face
and the way she clutched at his arm that had Holly moving
quickly toward them.

She recognized the old man facing her and if she wondered what Caspar Alexander had said to make Gabriel so
mad, she arrived just as he turned to his son with a coldly
satisfied smile.

"Mark," he said airily. "Meet your son. Steven, Jade
and Courtney, meet your brother. *Dr.* Gabriel Alexander."
Holly's gasp was drowned out by other shocked gasps
around them. Gleefully enjoying the drama, Caspar turned
to Gabriel and with a gesture of disgust he said, "Son, meet
your family."

Holly froze, her eyes locked on the frozen tableau before her. Gabriel had stiffened even more until the air vibrated with tension.

"You don't get to call me son," he said quietly, lethally.
"You don't get to call me anything. You gave up that right
the night you tried to force my mother to have an abortion."

Holly's horrified gasp covered her mother's soft moan
and she grabbed Delia's hand and squeezed. The ballroom
had gone ominously quiet and people were beginning to
stare.

And to Holly's shock, instead of denying the claim, Caspar just snorted derisively. "I did you a favor, boy," he said.
"Look at you. You're a self-made man. If I hadn't, you might
have ended up just like them." He waved a whiskey-filled
glass.

"Father?" Mark Alexander asked faintly, looking alarm-
ingly pale. "Is that true? You threatened Rachel? You told
me she'd lost the baby. You told me she'd moved west to
get over the loss. How could you do this? I did everything
you asked of me."

"Yes, you did." The old man nodded, casually lifting the
whiskey tumbler to his lips. "Maybe I would have respected

you more if you'd defied me. Maybe these blood-sucking offspring of yours would have grown up to be more like Gabriel. More like me."

"I'm nothing like you," Gabriel snarled.

"Oh, yes, you are," Caspar interrupted. "You wouldn't have dragged yourself up from the gutter if you weren't."

Gabriel looked like he was contemplating murder. "I did it for my mother, not for you."

"I was wrong," Caspar said, but Holly's gaze was locked on Mark's face and knew the instant he was in trouble. "Rachel Parker was a fine woman, and a good mother. Look how well you—"

"Gabriel, your father—" Holly began, stepping toward the older man, who was clutching his chest and starting to buckle. Gabriel, quickly assessing the situation, leapt forward, catching Mark before he fell.

"Mom," Holly murmured. "Call 911." She dropped to her knees beside the gray and gasping man. "Gabriel, I'll do it," she began, placing her hands on Mark's chest to begin CPR, but Gabriel brushed her aside.

He pulled his father into a sitting position and thumped him hard on the back. "Cough," he said sharply. "And hard, like you've got something in your throat."

Holly's gaze snapped up. "What—?" Of course. "He's right, Mr. Alexander, cough really hard." Mark looked at them like they were crazy. "Please," Holly said, her eyes filling with tears. "It'll get your heart beating properly again."

Her encouragement worked and with Gabriel's help Mark started coughing, a little feebly at first, then harder until his color gradually returned.

Holly sat back, her eyes locked on Gabriel's face. He'd had every right to turn and walk away—had had every opportunity—yet he hadn't. And here he was, saving the man who hadn't been there for his mother. Hadn't been there for him.

As though sensing her gaze, Gabriel suddenly looked up

and their eyes locked. The stark fear and desperate hope in them nearly crushed Holly and it was in that moment she realized the naked truth.

She was in love with him and she would do anything—anything—to help him through this.

"I'll get some brandy," she said, and rose to her feet.

CHAPTER FOURTEEN

HOLLY PAUSED OUTSIDE the hospital room, her gaze riveted on Gabriel's broad back and the rumpled sun-streaked hair that appeared even more rumpled than usual.

She wanted more than anything to go to him and smooth the unruly locks that tended to flop onto his forehead but her heart was hammering against her ribs and she was still struggling to catch her breath after dashing halfway across the island.

Okay, she'd only dashed a few blocks, but in four-inch glittery heels and a long snug evening gown it was a miracle she hadn't broken her neck.

Her heart now, well, that was another matter altogether, especially when it gave a sharp wrench at the picture he made, silhouetted against the darkened sky. Her breath caught in her throat.

Oh, God. He looked so lonely and solitary…as if the weight of the universe rested on his broad shoulders. And suddenly she wanted to go to him, rest her head against his broad back and give him what he needed.

With his back to the room, and hands buried deep in the pockets of his tux pants, he faced the darkened window overlooking the lights of Manhattan. At any other time the view might have distracted Holly, but her attention was riveted on his tense back and the I-want-to-be-alone aura he'd wrapped around himself like an invisible cloak.

She'd returned to find Mark recovering nicely but planning to return to their room. There'd been no sign of Gabriel but she'd known instinctively where to find him.

"You shouldn't be here, Holly," he said quietly.

"Why not?" she asked, just as quietly, her heart suddenly aching with the realization she'd made a short while ago. She'd suspected she was in love after her father's birthday but she'd hoped it was just a little crush. Hoped it would fade with time. It hadn't. Wouldn't…ever.

"You said we needed to talk."

He gave a ragged laugh. "Really? You want to talk now?"

She stepped into the room. "It's quiet, we're alone. What better time?"

"I made a mistake." His voice was so low and ragged in the quiet room that she strained to hear the words that seemed to be wrenched from a place of deep pain. The suppressed emotion in it drew her across the room.

"With what?" she asked, joining him at the window.

He sighed heavily. "Coming here. You."

Oh. Her breath caught at the unexpected shaft of pain his words sent lancing through her heart. And she knew in that instant how it would feel—as though her heart was being ripped from her chest and crushed. "You…" She gulped. "You can't mean that?"

"Yes," he asserted, sounding unbearably weary. "I do. I knew I should stay away from you but now…" He sent her a brief glance.

"Now…what?"

He shook his head. "I can't imagine that you would want to have anything to do with me. Not now."

Her eyes widened and she licked her lips. "What do you mean?"

"You heard me, Holly." He gave a short laugh. "Hell, the entire ballroom heard me."

Holly was confused. Yes, she'd heard him but couldn't remember him saying anything to be ashamed of. "You mean when you called your grandfather a ruthless war-lord who didn't deserve to breathe the same air as the rest of humanity?"

He snorted out a laugh. "Yeah, that would be it."

She was silent for a couple of beats. "Is that the truth? Did he pay your mother to have an abortion?"

"Yeah. Pretty much. Although it apparently went more along the lines of 'If you don't take care of it the next person I send will make sure that thing doesn't survive another week' kind of thing."

"Well, then, the shame's on him, isn't it?" She bumped his shoulder with hers. "I'm glad your mother didn't take his money." She sent him a warm smile. "It showed guts. She must be awesome. I can see where you get it from."

His somber expression lightened. "She was. A real fighter. She lost the fight to cancer a few months ago."

She faced him now. "Oh, Gabriel, I'm so sorry. Is that… when you decided to move east?"

He frowned and Holly could see the subject change upset him. A muscle in his jaw flexed. "I got a letter from West Manhattan offering me my own team of top surgeons, promises of unlimited funds and the most up-to-date technology in the best teaching hospital in the world." He barked out a hard laugh. "I was flattered. I couldn't believe they'd chosen me to—"

He broke off with a muttered oath and turned away, fisting both hands as though he was controlling himself with effort. But she'd seen the fury and humiliation burning in his blue-green gaze and her heart broke for him. She could understand what it would do to such a proud, determined man.

"Do you have any idea how humiliating it is to find out that I was forced onto Langley, onto Hunt?" he demanded.

"Oh, Gabriel. My mother's devastated that she said anything. She didn't know. She would never do anything like that knowingly."

"It's not Delia's fault I handled it so badly." He shifted

his shoulders as though to loosen some of the tension there. "I can't think what she must think of me."

"My mother said if she was twenty years younger, she'd divorce my father and marry you herself."

He laughed and Holly's heart lifted at the sound, even though it was ragged and a bit rusty. "Yeah." His dimple emerged, distracting her from his next words. "I think I love your mother." And when they finally penetrated the jumble of emotion swamping her, she blinked.

"You…do?"

"How could I not?" he demanded. "When she's so much like her daughter."

Her heart stuttered and the fragile hope that had been slowly blooming in her chest shriveled. "What…what are you saying? Paige?"

"No, Holly," he said gently, taking her by the shoulders and turning her so she faced him. "*Not* Paige. You."

Her world tilted and swam, forcing her to blink up at him or pass out from shock. "M-me?" she stuttered, breaking off to swallow the rusty squeak emerging from her tight throat.

A half-smile teased his lips but his eyes were intense, watchful. "Yeah," he said firmly. "You."

"But I'm…you're—"

"I'm what? You're what?" he asked, when she continued to splutter and stare at him as though he'd suggested she jump from the window.

"Look at me, Gabriel. I'm…and you're…" She stopped because she was beginning to stutter and hyperventilate like she used to as a child.

"You're not making sense, Holly. Take a deep breath and try again."

Holly breathed in and then out a few times till the urge to pass out faded, staring at him silently for a few moments before gesturing to the window.

"Tell me what you see," she said quietly, her pulse hammering in her throat.

He searched her expression before turning to stare at their reflection in the window. "I see a beautiful woman with a soft heart and a quick mind. A woman who isn't afraid to face the world, even with her scars." He turned to stare down into her face. "I see a woman who's a little clumsy at times but only when she's flustered. And I kind of like that I'm the only one who makes her nervous." He drew in a deep breath and turned away. His next words were low and hoarse. "I see a woman who's too good for a man like me."

She blinked. "Wha—?"

"I'm the dirty little secret, Holly. Isn't that what this mess is all about? Caspar Alexander's unwanted grandson causing a scandal on your mother's big night?"

"*No!* How can you say that?"

"It doesn't matter, because I've decided to go back to California."

"You…you have?"

He sighed. "Yeah. It's best."

"For whom?"

He looked startled. "For you, of course. I would never humiliate you or your mother. My staying does that."

"Don't be an ass," Holly snapped, suddenly so furious she wanted to punch Caspar Alexander for what he'd done to Gabriel. And she wanted to punch Gabriel too; for letting the old man control his life. "That's just your pride talking."

"What are you talking about? I have no pride left. I accepted the position at West Manhattan because I thought they wanted *me*…not the Alexander money."

Frustrated, Holly grabbed his shirt and yanked him close until they were nose to nose. "I've seen you work, Gabriel. I've heard people talk about what you've done. The amazing techniques you've pioneered and not with vain, shallow women looking for bigger boobs or thinner thighs. But there…" She gestured wildly to the small bed holding a sleeping child. "Where a little girl disfigured by a dog attack is telling everyone that you're going to make her beautiful again. Or…or a man looking to rebuild his shattered face and self-esteem."

She drew in a shuddery breath. "That," she said fervently, smoothing her hands over the creases she'd made in his shirt front. "That's why you're here. Not because of the Alexander money." She looked into his stunned face. "Don't you see? We need you here. They need you here."

After a long pause, Gabriel asked softly, "And you, Holly? What do you need?"

"I…" She felt a shaft of panic go through her when he continued to stare at her, waiting. She sucked in air and took the plunge. "I…" She gulped. "I need you too."

"Oh, boy," he said, looking stunned and relieved and terrified all at once. His reaction confused her and she stumbled back a step but he gave a ragged laugh and yanked her close, wrapping his arms around her so she couldn't escape.

"Say it," he ordered, the expression in his eyes making her knees weak. Her eyes dropped to his mouth.

"Wha-at?"

"Say it."

She licked her lips nervously. "You…first."

His mouth curled up at one corner and his eyes shimmered with tenderness. "God, is it any wonder I love you as much as I do?"

Holly gasped as shock and happiness burst inside her head like a meteor shower. "I…uh, what did you say?"

He laughed and pressed a quick kiss to her mouth. "You heard me. I said—"

"I thought you were in love with my mother," she said breathlessly.

"No," he said with a chuckle. "I said I love your mother." He gazed at her for a long moment, his eyes touching on every inch of her face as though he was committing her face to memory. "It's you I'm in love with. Only you."

"Oh," Holly said, tears filling her eyes at the emotion blazing in his. "You're sure?"

He chuckled. "How could I not be?" He tucked her closer and bent to kiss her mouth tenderly. "You threw yourself at my feet; gave me a lap dance I'll never forget and tried to drown yourself to get my attention." He dropped a smiling kiss on her intricate hairdo when she gave an embarrassed groan and hid her face against his throat. After a few beats he cupped her neck and drew her back so he could look into her eyes.

"Every time you fell at my feet I was the one falling until there was no getting up from what you make me feel."

Her breath hitched. "I…I… *Oh!*"

"Say you love me, Holly. Say you'll stay in Manhattan and build a future with me."

She grimaced at the reminder that she'd discussed her plans to apply for a fellowship in another city. "You heard that?"

"Yes, and it sent me into a panic." He gave her a quick shake. "Now. Your turn."

For long moments she studied the face of the hottest man in Manhattan and decided that she'd never curse her clumsiness again. It had, after all, landed her at Gabriel's feet and she knew without asking that he'd always be there to catch her.

She lifted her hands to cup his cheeks. "I love you," she said, rising onto her toes and sealing the words with a kiss. "Always."

* * * * *

LET'S TALK

Romance

For exclusive extracts, competitions and special offers, find us online:

- facebook.com/millsandboon
- @MillsandBoon
- @MillsandBoonUK

Get in touch on 01413 063232

For all the latest titles coming soon, visit

millsandboon.co.uk/nextmonth